A COIN FOR THE FERRYMAN

Also by Rosemary Rowe and available from Headline

The Germanicus Mosaic
A Pattern of Blood
Murder in the Forum
The Chariots of Calyx
The Legatus Mystery
The Ghosts of Glevum
Enemies of the Empire
A Roman Ransom

A COIN FOR THE FERRYMAN

ROSEMARY ROWE

headline

First published in 2007 by
HEADLINE PUBLISHING GROUP

1

Cataloguing in Publication Data is available from the British Library

ISBN 978 0 7553 2743 0

Typeset in Plantin by Avon DataSet Ltd,
Bidford-on-Avon, Warwickshire

Printed and bound in Great Britain by
Mackays of Chatham plc, Chatham, Kent

Headline's policy is to use papers that are natural, renewable and recyclable
products and made from wood grown in sustainable forests. The logging and
manufacturing processes are expected to conform to the environmental
regulations of the country of origin.

HEADLINE PUBLISHING GROUP
A division of Hachette Livre UK Ltd
338 Euston Road
London NW1 3BH

www.headline.co.uk
www.hodderheadline.com

Foreword

The book is set in the early part of AD 189. Most of Britain had been for nearly 200 years the most northerly outpost of the hugely successful Roman Empire: occupied by Roman legions, criss-crossed by Roman roads, subject to Roman laws and administered by a provincial governor answerable directly to Rome, where the increasingly unbalanced Emperor Commodus still wore the imperial purple – though his unpopular reign was soon to be brought abruptly to an end.

The Rome to which Marcus, in the story, is planning to return was not at this time a comfortable place. The Emperor's excesses, capricious cruelties and lascivious lifestyle had become a legend throughout the Empire. The stories in the text concerning his taste for freaks and novelties (including the incident of serving up the dwarf) are derived from near-contemporary sources, and while this is of course no guarantee that these accounts are true, it does suggest that they were at least widely believed and circulated at the time.

Also attested is his fear of plots: an assassination attempt early in his career had made him suspicious of everyone surrounding him (with justification as it was later to appear) and a series of the most powerful men in Rome, including his chief advisers, had found themselves the victims of sudden paranoid distrust, stripped of power and executed (usually after a token trial, at which the Emperor himself officiated, of course). This had been the fate of successive holders of the prefecture of Rome – probably the most influential post in the Empire apart from the emperorship itself – leading to the promotion of others in their place. At the period when this book is set, the holder of the office was none other than a previous governor of Britannia, Pertinax, who in the story is a friend of Marcus's.

Against this background of intrigue, Julia's reluctance to travel to the imperial capital – one of the elements in the story – would have been quite justified. (I say 'the imperial capital' since Rome was not at this period legally called 'Rome'. It had been restyled 'Commodiana' in honour of the Emperor, just as the names of the months had all been changed, so that each designation now derived from one of the numerous titles that he had given to himself, instead of from the pantheon of gods. This was not disrespect, he once explained, since he himself was a divinity: the living reincarnation of immortal Hercules.)

Of course for most of the inhabitants of Britain such political considerations were remote, and they were content to live their lives in the relative obscurity of provincial towns and villages. Celtic traditions, settlements and languages remained, especially in country areas, and one such Celtic farming household features in this tale.

Most towns, however, had adopted Roman ways. Latin was the language of the educated, and was widely used for trade (rather as English is in many places today), and Roman citizenship – with its legal, economic and social benefits – was the ambition of all. Citizenship was not at this time automatic, even for freeborn men, but a privilege to be earned – by those not fortunate enough to be born to it – usually by service to the army or to the Emperor, though it was possible for the slave of an important man to be bequeathed the coveted status, together with his freedom, on his master's death. The son of a citizen was a citizen by right, as were those born free within the walls of a few specific towns (*coloniae* like Glevum, in particular) thanks to a recent imperial decree, but the huge majority of people did not qualify. To impersonate a citizen, when one was not, was still at this time a capital offence,

So, most ordinary people in Britannia were not citizens at all. Some were freemen, or freedmen, scratching a precarious living from trade or farm; thousands more were slaves, mere chattels of their masters with no more rights or status than any other domestic animal. Some slaves led pitiable lives, but others were highly regarded by their masters and might be treated well. Indeed, a slave in a kindly household, certain of food and clothing in a comfortable home, might have a more enviable lot than many a poor freeman struggling to eke out an existence in a squalid hut.

None the less, freedom was the dream of every slave, and there were various methods of achieving it – a process generally known as manumission. The most common way was through the master's will – as in Libertus's own case – but there were other methods too, several of which are mentioned in the text.

The most formal of these, *vindicta* – so called after the wand that was used in the ceremony, and from which our word 'vindicated' derives – was a complicated procedure: a fictitious lawsuit before the magistrates, claiming essentially that the slave was really free. The plea had to be brought by someone who did not own the slave, and not contested by the man who did. (There is some evidence that slaves were notionally sold on, so that the master could bring the case on their behalf – as here – but there are differing opinions on this point.) Generally such cases were brought before the Praetor, but more senior magistrates – such as a governor (or Marcus, here) – might officiate. If a slave was under twenty, as Junio clearly is, he could only be manumitted by this method, and even then only for 'sufficient cause', such as outstanding service.

More informal – and less expensive – methods were available, and might be used where the manumission was not likely to be challenged under law, or where the slave had little value in the marketplace (as, for example, when she was a girl). These methods included a signed written statement that the slave was free; a spoken declaration of this in front of five witnesses – who must all be citizens; or by inviting the slave to join a formal dinner as one's guest – as in the second manumission in the book.

Legally a slave had no possessions of his own, of course – although some servants were permitted to keep their tips and perks and even given a small *peculium* which they might save up to buy their freedom with. For a citizen, however, there was the question of estate.

The Romans set a great deal of importance on family lineage; it was almost a civic duty to produce an heir, and ensure a line of citizens to carry on the state. Many eminent Romans married several times, in the pursuit of sons, since 'barrenness' was generally presumed to be the female's fault, and might be the grounds for a divorce, which was not in any case difficult under Roman law – although a woman, if she had not committed an offence, might carry her dowry away with her when she was divorced. That estate, though hers to use until she wed again, was not in general hers to bequeath, since she was not considered capable in law. Her possessions would revert to her nearest male relative if she died without a spouse.

Even for a male, bequeathing an estate was not always simple. In the absence of an obvious heir, it was not uncommon for a man's will to be contested on his death, often resulting in expensive lawsuits. Unexpected claimants might arise from anywhere – including, in some cases, the imperial purse, which would seize everything automatically if the whole will failed. If a man could not produce an heir naturally, therefore, the law allowed him various methods of obtaining one. He might achieve one by *adoptio*, in which case he would fictitiously buy a male child three times from its natural father – thus ending the father's jurisdiction over the boy – and then, in a collusive court case, claim before the magistrates that the child was his own and obtain a binding judgement to that effect; or he might 'abrogate' an heir – as in the story – where the young man, had no known father living and entered into a contract on his own account. This meant that the candidate for abrogation must be free – a slave could not contract in this way – hence the double court case mentioned in the book.

Abrogation was only permitted where it would prevent the extinction of a family line, and the rules concerning it were very strict, although they seem to have varied somewhat at different times. No female could be abrogated, since that did not ensure the lineage. Originally, abrogation could only be approved by a special body based in Rome: but increasingly a system of imperial rescript came about (as in the book) thus allowing abrogation in the provinces.

The importance of lineage was also evident when a death occurred in a Roman family. Not only was the heir expected to perform the first crucial services for the dead – closing the eyes, calling three times upon the name of the deceased (thereby giving the spirit every chance to return), placing a coin in the mouth 'to pay the ferryman' for the journey across the Styx – but, once the body was prepared for burial, usually by paid undertakers, it was also the heir's task to begin the lament, the wailing ululation which might last for several days, with different people taking turns at it. The body was then taken on a bier – often with accompanying musicians and paid mourners and dancers – to a funeral pyre, which had by law to be outside the town. It was traditionally accompanied on its final journey by the *imago*, the death mask, not only of the corpse, but of his most important ancestors – another demonstration of the significance of family line – while the relatives wore torn, dark clothes to show respect, and sometimes ashes from the altar rubbed on to their head and hair.

A part of the deceased, most usually a finger, was cut off and ceremonially buried in the earth, even when the corpse was to be burned; a pig was sacrificed, the gods were called upon and the body was consigned to the flames. Some authorities suggest that the old tradition of providing grave goods extended to the pyre, and that valued possessions were offered in the flames to serve the dead man in the nether world. When cooled the ashes were collected and buried in an urn, or the container was placed reverently in a special niche, where it could be visited on the anniversary of the death.

Afterwards a ritual cleansing was required, including the sacrifice of a young ram without a blemish on his coat, to 'close' a family death. There would be a funeral feast where tributes were read out, and sometimes solemn dancing and music was performed. On the anniversary of the death the relatives offered tributes at the grave, pouring food and wine to keep the soul alive.

Poor men, of course, could not afford such luxuries, but a proper funeral was an important thing and even slaves were often members of a funeral guild which would see that their bodies were decently disposed of with at least the minimum ritual required, to ensure that the ghost could rest in peace and was not required to walk the earth without a home.

Such superstition still played a major part in Roman life: every Roman householder began his day with due oblations to the household gods, every serious problem demanded a sacrifice, and proper care was taken to observe the rituals. On 'inauspicious' days – when the omens were not good – even the law courts did not operate.

Few days were less auspicious than 9 May, since that marked the beginning of the Lemuria, the second and more dangerous Festival of the Dead. In contrast to the first Festival, or Paternalia, (where the family brought gifts and homage to their departed loved ones every year) this was the time when the homeless, vengeful spirits of those who had died unloved – and had therefore not received a proper funeral – were thought to walk the earth. These ghosts were called the Lemures, and their festival was so ill-omened that the temples closed, marriages were forbidden, lawsuits ceased, and curious midnight rituals (as in the book) had to be performed in every house to keep the ghosts at bay. The ceremony outlined in the story is mentioned in a contemporary account.

The Romano-British background in this book has been derived from a wide variety of (sometimes contradictory) written and pictorial sources. However, although I have done my best to create an accurate picture, this remains a work of fiction and there is no claim to total academic authenticity.

Relata refero. Ne Jupiter quidem omnibus placet. (I only tell you what I heard. Jove himself can't please everybody.)

Chapter One

I stood at the entrance to the huge basilica and sighed. In a moment I was going to have to walk the length of that impressive central aisle, with its massive pillars towering up on either side. I knew that all eyes would be upon me as I went. There are few things more impressive than a Roman ritual, and this occasion was as formal as they come.

Not that I usually have much to do with ceremonial, apart from the public sacrifices which all citizens are expected to attend; and even then – as a humble ex-slave and mosaic-maker – I am generally watching from behind a pillar, or some other inconspicuous position at the back.

Today, however, I was centre stage, dressed in my best toga, which was still giving off a whiff of the sulphur fumes in which it had been whitened specially for the occasion. (Fortunately the other cleaning agent – the urine collected in great pots from the households and businesses around – had been largely rinsed out of it by the fuller's slaves who trampled the garment afterwards in clean water and fullers' earth.) My wife had insisted on my having new sandals for the day, and also at her behest I had submitted to a painful hour at the barber's shop – having my nose- and ear-hairs plucked, my cheeks rasped and my thin grey hair rubbed with bats' blood and grease to stimulate its growth.

I felt as scrubbed and polished as a turnip ready for the pot.

My appearance was as nothing, though, compared to the resplendent glory of the presiding magistrate. His Excellence Marcus Aurelius Septimus sat enthroned at the dais end of the great basilica, flanked by a dozen other eminent officials and councillors – including an ambassador from Rome – and accompanied by a bevy of attendant slaves. His toga was woven of the finest wool, white as milk and boasting a purple border so wide that it put the lesser magistrates to shame. He had his favourite golden torc round his neck – a present from some Celtic vassal chief – an imperial seal ring on his hand and a wreath of fresh bay leaves anchored in his boyish curling hair, to signify his great authority.

And certainly he had authority. As the local representative and personal friend of Pertinax, the previous governor of the province, he had always been a person to be reckoned with; and now – since Pertinax was promoted to the prefecture of Rome, second only in importance to the Emperor himself – Marcus Septimus had become overnight one of the most powerful men in the entire Empire. This ceremony was the last over which he would preside before he journeyed to the imperial city to congratulate his friend, and it seemed the whole of Glevum had come out to stare.

People were jostling behind the pillars, elbowing and craning to get a better view. Even the official copy-scribes and account-clerks for the town, who usually worked in the little rooms which flanked the area, had given up all pretence of writing anything today and had come out of their offices to watch.

A trumpeter came forward and blew a long, high note. The crowd stopped fidgeting and there was a sudden hush.

'In the name of the Divine Emperor Commodus Antoninus Pius Felix Exsuperatorius, ruler of Commodiana and all the provinces overseas . . .'

There was a little snigger from the assembled company at this, and a muffled jeer or two as well. People had become accustomed to the titles Commodus gave himself – the Dutiful, the Fortunate, the Excellent – and even when he declared himself to be a god, the reincarnation of Hercules (instead of decently waiting until he died for deification, like other emperors), few of his subjects really minded very much. Renaming all the months in honour of himself had not had much effect; unless there was imperial business to be done, most people conveniently forgot and went on using the familiar names. But this latest whim, of changing the name of mighty Rome itself to 'Commodiana', was a step too far. Somebody was bold enough to hiss 'For shame!' and was carried off struggling between a pair of guards. The fellow would pay dearly for his impudence, no doubt.

The herald looked discomfited at the interruption, but went on manfully, 'This special court is now in session. Let the first supplicants approach the magistrates.'

It was my cue. Slowly I walked up between the crowds towards the central group. I was carrying a ceremonial wand, and my sandals were ringing on the patterned floor. The air was still full of the sacrificial smoke from the official offering on the imperial shrine, and the light struck slantways from the high windows overhead. It illuminated the official inscriptions carved in stone, the vivid red and ochre of the semicircular 'tribunal' alcoves at each end – with their wall paintings of simulated drapes – and the life-size statue of the frowning Emperor. It was intended to be awesome, and I was duly awed.

However, I made my way to stand before my patron, in the place which the chief petitioner always occupied. 'I bring a petition against Lucius Julianus Catilius in the matter of a slave he claims to own,' I muttered. A little frisson ran around the room. Lucius Julianus Catilius was the visitor from Rome.

The man in question looked at me impassively but rose with dignity, and came down to stand beside me in front of the dais on which he had so recently occupied a chair. The fashionable magnificence of his cloak and shoes, and the width of his aristocratic stripe, which rivalled Marcus's own, brought a gasp of admiration from the onlookers. Lucius Julianus was a patrician through and through: smooth, tall, silver-haired, with a hooked nose and an air of permanent disdain.

I had met him only once before, and that was this morning on the forum steps, when he had used an age-old formula to buy my slave from me for the minimum possible amount. He acknowledged me now with a distant nod, and an arch of his aristocratic eyebrow.

His Excellence Marcus Septimus looked unsmilingly at me. 'You are Longinus Flavius Libertus?' he enquired, as though I were a stranger, and not a trusted confidant who had been under his personal protection for years.

I made the expected obeisance, cleared my throat and agreed that this was indeed my name. I even remembered not to look behind me as I spoke. I knew what I would see if I did so: the slave in question, my servant-cum-assistant Junio, standing behind me like a sacrificial lamb between two self-important officials of the court.

He was dressed in a humiliating fashion now, I was aware – no tunic, only a loincloth wrapped round his waist, his feet bare and a sort of conical slave cap on his head. It was the sort of thing I'd never asked of him in all the years since I acquired him. I had him from the slave market when he was very young – how old, exactly, he did not know himself. He might have been six or seven at the most, but he was so small and underfed and terrified that I'd taken pity on his plight and parted with some coins. Not many, even so. I think the slave-trader was grateful to be rid of the pathetic little wretch. I wonder what he would have thought to see the strapping, tousle-haired young man walking dutifully behind me in the basilica today.

It had proved the best bargain that I had ever made, I thought. Junio had been the most faithful of attendants and he was intelligent besides: quick to learn and adept at helping me with my designs in my mosaic workshop in the town. He had slept on a mat beside my bed and served my every need. And now it was all over. He was my slave no more.

Lucius Julianus identified himself and then said in his well-bred Roman tones, 'It concerns the matter of the slave named Junio, here present. Let Marcus be the judge.'

Junio came forward between the two of us and prostrated himself at Marcus's feet, as if to kiss his sandals. He did not rise but stayed there on hands and knees.

I looked at Marcus and I swallowed hard. He was my patron but I was still in awe of him. 'I assert that this man is not a slave, but free according to the law of the Quirites.' It was an ambiguous formula, of course: what I was really claiming was that he was a slave no more, but my throat tightened as I struck the boy lightly on the shoulder with the rod. Junio was legally the possession of the Roman visitor now, and it was still possible that he would play us false and simply decide to keep the boy.

Marcus looked at Lucius. 'Do you deny this claim?'

The man from Rome said nothing, but looked at us with all the condescension of a senator forced to join a children's game. Marcus asked again. Again there was no answer. Then – as I held my breath – Marcus challenged for the third and final time, and still the senator made no reply at all.

The law was satisfied and it all seemed to happen very quickly after that. Marcus took the rod and touched Junio on the back. 'Then, by the power invested in me by the Emperor, I rule that all impediments to manumission are in this case void, and before all witnesses I adjudge him free.' He touched the rod on Junio's shoulders one by one. 'You may arise.'

Junio rose slowly to his feet, a free man for the first time in his life. Vindicated, literally – by the staff or *vindicta*. One of Marcus's red-haired slaves appeared, bearing a tunic and a pair of shoes, and Junio followed him into a vacant writing room to put them on. There was a little smattering of applause, but not a lot. The crowd had come to see the visitor from Rome and hear Marcus's farewell speech. This little household drama had bewildered them.

However, it wasn't over yet. I stepped up once again to the petitioner's place and presently my ex-slave came to join me there, now dressed like any other freeman in the town.

'Libertus, you have a further petition to bring before this court?' Marcus was obliged to ask the question, although the whole form of these proceedings had been his idea.

'I have, Excellence.' In fact, the most important part was yet to come. I cleared my throat and started on my plea. I had practised the speech so many times that I could say it in my sleep. I was childless, I argued, and thus legally entitled to abrogate an heir. (I could not acquire the one I wanted by *adoptio* – buying a child from his father fictitiously three times – since Junio didn't have a father I could buy him from.)

I advanced the proofs that I met the requirements of the law – one of which, these days, was that he should not be my slave. As a freeman, however, he could give his own consent. 'I am clearly more than eighteen years his senior,' I said, not dwelling on the matter, since I had no formal proof of Junio's age, 'and I am demonstrably capable of marriage since I have a wife. Furthermore,' I added wickedly, 'by permitting me to abrogate the boy, the court would also save itself expense, since it would otherwise have to appoint a legal curator for him until he's twenty-five.' Again I did not raise the issue of how one might determine when that age was reached.

It was all an elaborate, but necessary, charade. The laws were fashioned to protect the young (unscrupulous men had adopted wealthy orphans in the past and, having thus legally acquired the estate, promptly disinherited the child) but Junio had no possessions of his own in any case.

My patron listened carefully to what I had to say, though he had coached me in every word of it. 'Normally such abrogations should be heard in Rome,' he said 'but the Emperor has granted a rescript in this case, and has written in answer to my formal preliminary request to say that the petition is approved, provided that the Praetor and magistrates are satisfied?'

It was another fiction, naturally. Once the agreement of the Emperor had been obtained, the opinion of the council hardly mattered. It was unlikely that Commodus had really taken any personal interest in the case, I knew, but Marcus had powerful friends in Rome these days. The consenting seal on the letter had probably been granted at Pertinax's behest.

It did the trick. A spokesman for the council rose and agreed that they approved. Clearly – given the circumstances – they hadn't needed to consult.

Marcus turned to Junio. 'Do you consent to this arrangement?'

Junio could hardly speak for grinning, but he managed, 'I consent.'

Marcus turned to the assembled company. 'Then I pronounce that Longinus Flavius Junio should be henceforth the legal son and heir of Libertus the pavement-maker, with full rights as a Roman citizen.'

So it was done. I was a *paterfamilias* at last. Another little red-haired slave appeared, this time with a toga for my adopted son. It was a present from Marcus, or more probably the lady Julia – she was far more generous than her husband and understood how much this gesture meant to me. Junio was clearly absolutely thrilled. From the moment that he put it on, assisted by the slave, he looked more like a proper citizen than I had ever done and I realised for the first time that he probably did have Roman blood in him. After all, he was born into slavery – no doubt the product of his owner and some female serving girl.

There was only one thing remaining to be done, and Lucius was looking expectantly at me. I reached into my toga folds and produced the purse of money which my fictional opponent would expect for his part in the proceedings. It was a considerable sum – to me in any case – arranged a day or two ago with Lucius's chief slave: a sandy-headed fellow with calculating eyes, whose expensive olive tunic could not disguise his air of general menace, and whose steely courtesy – combined with the flexing of his enormous hands – had somehow induced me to agree to rather more than I could comfortably afford.

Lucius weighed the purse a moment in his hand, rather disdainfully I thought, before he slipped it into a belt-pouch underneath his robes. Then he turned and with conscious dignity went back to occupy his former seat, while I bowed myself backwards by a pace or two. Junio did the same. Then, having completed the formalities, we made our way out of the basilica into the brightness of the forum, leaving Marcus and his fellow councillors to deal with the other official business of the day.

The forum was full of business, as it always was. Colourful stalls and fortune-tellers huddled round the walls, scribes and money-changers plied their trade in booths, and self-important citizens went striding up the colonnaded path, or stood on the steps of the basilica to be seen.

Gwellia, my wife, was waiting for us there. She had been watching the proceedings inside the hall, though of course, as a woman she'd played no part in them – a female is not legally entitled to adopt, being technically only a child herself in law. She smiled, but gave Junio only a very brief embrace – not because she was not delighted to greet him as her son, but because public displays of emotion are not expected of Roman citizens.

Besides, there was a little sadness in the greeting too. We had hoped – Gwellia and I – to adopt another child, an infant orphan girl, whose remaining family had fled into exile and left her behind. It would have been a much simpler matter than adopting Junio, since she was both female and freeborn – merely a question of fictitiously buying her, just once, from someone representing her missing family.

But events had not transpired as Gwellia had hoped. We had taken the child into the household for a moon or so and she had not thrived. She refused to eat and grew quite pale and sick – used, I suppose, to childish company, though perhaps also partly because she was not fully weaned. She proved to be a constant worry in the house, attempting to climb into the fire and eating Gwellia's dyes. In the end we were forced to place her with a family in the woods, a woman with several children of her own who had looked after the infant sometimes when her mother was alive. The joyful reunion was almost unbearably touching to see, and the decision was clearly for the best, especially since the few *denarii* we paid towards Longina's keep were an enormous bonus for the family. We'd declared ourselves her sponsors (simply a matter of a statement to the court) so she was still officially our ward, but it had been a painful decision for my wife. Gwellia had always longed for children but we two had been wrenched apart when we were young and sold to slavery, and by the time we were reunited we were too old to have any natural offspring of our own.

Nevertheless, she now had a strapping son. He'd called her 'Mother' and it pleased her, I could see. 'Perhaps I should find a litter for you,' he went on. 'There is to be a banquet for us all at Marcus's villa tonight, and you will want to get home and prepare.'

I shook my head. 'Junio, you are not a slave,' I said. 'If we want transport, we will find a hiring carriage that will take all three of us. And Cilla too, if she is still about.'

'Here, master!' Cilla was at my elbow, flourishing a fish. 'I was only over at the fish market buying this, but they had so many good fish in the pool that it took me a little moment to decide. I'm sorry, master. The mistress sent me, but I did not mean to leave her unattended for so long.'

I nodded. Cilla was my wife's attendant slave, given to me some little time ago by Marcus Septimus in return for a favour I had done for him. She was a plump, resourceful little thing, and Gwellia was very fond of her. And so, I knew, was my adopted son, who was looking at her with approval now.

It was mutual. She looked him up and down. 'My word, Master Junio, you look so elegant,' she said. 'You are so Roman in that toga, I hardly dare to speak.' It was nonsense, though. Cilla would have chattered cheerfully to Jupiter himself, if he had happened to appear in Glevum.

'There will be time enough for compliments a little later on,' I said. 'After the banquet, when we get back to it. In the meantime we should go and find that cart.'

Cilla had turned a charming shade of pink. She knew exactly what I was referring to. The banquet had been arranged by Marcus for his Roman guest, and my little family had been invited too. It was a kind of triple compliment to us – a token of respect and thanks for me, a celebration for Junio, and an opportunity for me to informally emancipate the girl, by announcing before the assembled company of Roman citizens that Cilla was now free and inviting her to join us for the final course. It was all the ceremony needed to free a female slave.

'I can't believe it, master. Me, at such a feast! With Lucius Julianus there as well. And the mistress has given me such a pretty gown.'

I grinned. No doubt Lucius Julianus would look disdainfully at us, but Marcus was such a power now that an invitation to his table was an honour to be sought, however lowly the other guests might be. 'Then, when you and Junio are wed, I hope you remember who made it possible and are duly grateful to His Excellence. I don't have the wealth and contacts to host such a feast myself – nor the servants either, especially after this!'

Gwellia nodded. 'There is only little Kurso to run the household now.' She said it ruefully. Poor Kurso'd had a dreadful master when he was young, and could still move faster backwards than forwards. He had come to us as a kitchen slave but he was so nervous and clumsy that he was not much use at all, except outdoors. He was happy enough caring for the animals and plants, but in the house he was a liability – likely to drop what he was carrying if you spoke to him. He had already cost me a great many bowls.

Junio must have read my thoughts. 'Don't worry, master – Father, I should say – Cilla and I will be living very close to you. The lady Julia has arranged for us to have that piece of land so we can build a roundhouse just next to yours. And it won't be long before we can begin. She's already had the standing timber removed, and she's sending a group of land slaves to clear the site today.'

I nodded. 'She mentioned it to me. Cilla was her personal

servant once, she said, and this is to be a sort of dowry, I suppose. It's very generous of her.'

'She has never forgotten that you saved her life. And Marcus would be fairly easy to persuade. The land is only forest – he won't miss that small piece,' my wife said wryly, adding with a smile. 'It's just the kind of gift your patron would approve. Something generous which didn't cost him anything at all.'

I knew what she meant. I have received a number of such gifts before, including my own roundhouse and young Cilla herself. My patron has made a habit of asking for my help in matters which might otherwise be politically embarrassing, but refuses to 'insult' me, as he says, by offering me money for my services. As his business always takes me from my own, it was an insult I could easily have borne.

I laughed. 'Well, I am grateful that Junio and Cilla will be next door to us. Though we shall have to think about another slave, I suppose. We can't expect these two to go on serving us – though I suppose that Cilla might go on ahead right now, and try to find a carriage for us at the gates.' It would have to be outside the walls, of course. Wheeled traffic is not permitted in the city during the hours of daylight, except for military purposes.

Cilla dimpled. 'That won't be necessary, master. It's already done. And here are your messengers to tell you so.'

I glanced up. Threading their way through the assorted throng, dodging round the leather merchant and the live eel stall, were the two red-headed slaves who had presented Junio with his garments earlier. I knew the lads: one of Marcus's carefully selected 'pairs' – servants matched for colouring and height; a piece of conspicuous extravagance with which he dazzled visitors to his country house. Except that these two, being rather young, were no longer properly a pair at all: the younger of them, Minimus, was quickly outstretching his older counterpart.

It was Minimus now who came panting up to me. 'We have found you a carriage, master . . .' he began.

'Waiting for you at the southern gate,' Maximus chimed in, out of breath after catching up: they often talked like this, one of them completing what the other had begun, as if they'd worked together for so long that they shared a single thought.

'Thank you.' I reached into my toga for my purse, and remembered, too late, that I had given it away. It didn't matter for the carriage, I had money at the house, but I had nothing with me now with which to tip the slaves. 'I'll see you at the villa later on,' I said. 'I'll give you something then.'

Maximus looked sideways at his fellow slave, who shrugged expressively, and turned back to me. 'Didn't His Excellence tell you, citizen? We are to serve you, while he's overseas . . .'

'He says you are losing a couple of your slaves and will be glad of someone . . .'

'And since he's closing up the house, he would only have had to sell us otherwise . . .'

'So we found your carriage for you, and now here we are!' Minimus finished, with a triumphant air.

I looked at Gwellia, and she looked at me. It seemed that we'd acquired a pair of household slaves, though not perhaps the ones we would have chosen for ourselves. These lads would not be skilled in cookery, or used to cutting wood and the general rough and tumble of a roundhouse life. They were accustomed to the villa with its exquisite ways, and a whole hierarchy of slaves to do the menial tasks. But Marcus had arranged this, and I could not refuse.

'Very well then, my temporary slaves. You may lead the way,' I said, and we trooped across the forum and out into the street.

'There is your carriage, master,' Maximus began, indicating a hiring coach with leather curtains and a roof, and one of those devices on the wheels which counts the miles.

I hesitated. I prefer to make a bargain for the trip before we start – I am not convinced that these devices, clever as they are, don't sometimes calculate more miles than they should. Perhaps it was as well that I demurred. A moment later and I would have missed the arrival of a flustered Kurso, perched on Marcus's land cart by the look of it.

'M-m-master,' Kurso stammered, before he had even properly climbed down. 'I am g-g-glad to see you. Your p-p-patron's wife sent us. You must come at once.' He flung himself before me. 'They have f-f-found something in the g-g-ground that they were clearing for J-Junio and Cilla's house.'

Chapter Two

I went in the land cart with him and Junio, leaving the women and the red-haired boys to follow in the hired coach. We took the short way – not the military road, but a twisting and sometimes vertiginous route down narrow rutted lanes – plunging through mud and overhanging branches at a pace which threatened to shake the axles off the cart and forced us to grip on with all our might.

'So what exactly is it that the land slaves found?' I managed, although it was hard to say anything at all when one's teeth were being jarred together hard at every bounce.

Kurso shook his head. If it was difficult for me, it was almost impossible for him. 'B-b-bad,' was all I could make out.

'What is it, Kurso? Money?' That was possible. There had been a lot of trouble with Silurian rebels recently, setting on travellers and robbing them. They operated chiefly over to the west, but they were rumoured to have secret hideouts in the woods where they concealed their loot. This might be one of those. If so, it would certainly be 'bad'. At the very least it would infallibly interrupt our plans and mean that Junio's house could not be built.

Marcus was a magistrate and honest to a fault. He would demand that the place was closely searched and watched, and that would require a dozen burly guards trampling about our roundhouse day and night. Almost certainly there would be a court case too before he handed the find over to the imperial purse, and since the site was on my doorstep, so to speak, I could expect to be questioned repeatedly myself. In fact I should be grateful that – if there was a cache – it had come to light before Marcus and his family went abroad: it might have been difficult to persuade an unknown magistrate that I had no connection with the stolen goods. I did not want to think about what might have happened then. 'A hoard of stolen coins?' I said again.

But Kurso was shaking a determined head. 'B-b-body,' he finally got out.

A body. That was different. Curious, of course, but more explicable. There were often corpses in the forest, when the snows withdrew. Wolves, perhaps. Or bears, though they were not so common as they used to be. Perhaps some aged forest dweller had simply starved to death, or a benighted traveller met a frozen end in one of the winter's more ferocious storms. There were a hundred possibilities. It was unlikely to be anything very sinister, since there had been no news of any local disappearances, but it was still a problem and I could understand why Julia had sent for me at once.

It was appalling luck to come across a corpse in a place where you intend to build a dwelling house. Of course an unknown person of no particular account found dead in the forest in the normal way would not cause much concern. It might either be left exactly where it was, or be taken to the common pit and flung in with the beggars and the criminals. But a body discovered on a house site was quite a different thing. The spirit of the unquiet dead would haunt your doors for ever, if the body was not somehow laid decently to rest.

A different explanation had occurred to Junio. 'I hope they haven't disturbed a grave of any sort?' he said. 'That would be dreadful at this time of year.'

I understood his fears. We were approaching the second Roman Festival of the Dead, the Lemuria, when kinless, hungry, homeless ghosts of those who had not received a proper funeral were said to prowl. These Lemures are known to be malevolent spirits anyway, ravenous and dangerous if the proper ceremonies are not observed – so much so that the temples close, and marriage is forbidden during the festival. But their worst spite is said to be reserved for those who unearth their buried bones.

It was such a bad portent that even I could feel a shiver of alarm, and I was not raised in a Roman household, as Junio had been. To him the threat was very real. I could see that he was looking shaken and alarmed.

'Was it a grave?' I echoed.

Kurso shook his head. We had slowed to let a donkey squeeze past us on the road – narrowly, since it was laden with wicker panniers full of quacking ducks – so he managed to answer more coherently. 'N-n-not a proper one. J-just a shallow ditch. J-Julia says we'll have to f-f-find out who it is, and get the f-f-family to bury it. Otherwise it will c-c-curse the h-h-house for ever afterwards.' Then we went lurching on again, and we abandoned speech in favour of clinging to the wagon-sides and praying that the bone-juddering torment would soon be over.

After what seemed like a lifetime, but was probably closer to an hour, we joined up with a proper highway once again – a paved spur from the military road which led towards the villa. My roundhouse was near the junction and I expected we would stop, but the cart-driver did not draw up outside my gate. Through the palisade of woven stakes which formed my outer fence, I could see the new area which the villa slaves had cleared: one or two land-slaves were still working with an adze, grubbing out some bushes which were growing near the road. Clearly, however, the project had been largely abandoned, for the moment anyhow.

I was about to call to the cart-driver to stop, but Kurso saw what I intended and said hastily, 'They'll have t-t-taken the body to the v-v-villa now. If no one c-c-claims it in a day or two, the s-s-slaves will make it ready for the f-f-funeral pyre. J-Julia said you w-w-wouldn't w-w-want it in your house.'

I nodded. I was sincerely grateful. The presence of a dead body in my roundhouse, just when I was bringing home my son, would have been an omen that even I could not ignore, though I am not very superstitious about these things as a rule. At Marcus's spacious villa, on the other hand, there were a dozen places where it might decently be put, without impinging on the family's living space and bringing evil luck. There was even a special room out in the stable block where dead slaves could be taken and laid out, and a cremation site out on the villa farm. Most of the servants were members of the Guild of Slaves, of course, which would arrange to give them a decent funeral – Marcus, like all good masters, paid their dues himself – but there were always one or two who had not yet enrolled, or poor freemen labourers who died on villa land, and Marcus always saw that they got at least the basic rites.

Clearly Julia intended to deal with this corpse in the same way, if we couldn't find its family to perform the rituals. That would do a great deal to appease the vengeful Lemures, I told myself, hoping that the body had not been hidden for so long that we were already past the half-moon after death which – tradition said – was the maximum permitted before a funeral, if one wished to keep the ghost from haunting afterwards.

I was still thinking about this when we reached the villa gates and the cart did stop at last: I scrambled down, with Junio and my slave, and was immediately accosted by the gatekeeper. I knew the man, a swarthy rogue called Aulus, who always carried a faint scent of onions and bad breath.

He greeted me as though I were a friend. 'Well, pavement-maker, here you are at last. We've been expecting you. The mistress will see you in the atrium – I'm to find a slave to take you to her straight away, she says.'

I was about to protest that I knew my way around the villa very well and did not need a slave, but a young pageboy was already hurrying out to us. Obviously they had been watching for my arrival from the house.

The page was not a servant I'd seen before. Marcus's usual pageboy was a more flamboyant lad. I looked at Aulus. He knew everything.

He gave me another of his leering grins. 'Pulchrus was sent to Londinium a day or two ago – the morning of that last important feast it must have been – to make arrangements for the master and his wife to start their trip to Rome. You must remember, citizen. I'm sure you've heard about that.'

I nodded. Julia, like me, did not enjoy the sea, and had refused to contemplate the long ocean voyage from Glevum, so Marcus had decided to send the boy ahead with messages and imperial travel permits, requisitioning their passage on a naval ship from Londinium to Dubris, and from there on the shortest possible sea crossing to Gaul.

This substitute was a good deal younger, seven or eight years old perhaps, but he was fair-haired and pretty and desperate to please. He spoke in a piping, eager voice. 'If the two citizens would follow me,' he said.

Junio looked at me and grinned. It was the first time anyone had called him 'citizen'. He followed me (walking with some difficulty, true – togas are not easy to manage if you are not used to them, and his was showing a tendency to unhitch itself) and we were shown into the atrium. We had hardly reached it before Julia arrived. That was an indication of how distressed she was. There was none of the usual fashionable delay, intended to make lesser mortals like myself appreciate the honour of an interview with her.

She was attended, as usual, by a pair of maidservants, and was looking as lovely as she always does. Her *stola* and overtunic were of the softest pink, and she had woven ornaments into her hair. But her face was strained and tense. She managed a smile for Junio, and then turned to me. 'Libertus, I am very glad to see you. This is an unhappy business, I'm afraid. I've had my land slaves take the body to the stable block – the room where we prepare dead slaves for burial – and I have sent some servants out to make enquiries, to see if anyone is missing in the area.'

'Recently dead then?' That was a surprise.

'It seems so. But my slavemaster thinks that you should come and take a look at her yourself.'

'It is a female?' I was quite surprised. No reason why it

should not be, of course, but most people travelling the forest – off the paths – are men.

'A girl. Quite young, from what I understand, and dressed in peasant clothes, though obviously I haven't been to see.' She swallowed. 'They tell me that she is not a pleasant sight. I understand the face is battered in, and there are other injuries. When they reported that they'd found her, I just instructed them to bring her here.'

I nodded. Nobody would expect a lady of her rank to concern herself with an unlucky corpse at all, let alone a bruised and battered peasant one. 'So you sent for me?'

'And now I'm doubly glad I did. The chief of the land slaves came to ask for me, not half an hour ago. He seems to think there's something slightly odd about the look of it.'

'Odd? Apart from having a battered face, you mean?' All kinds of pictures were flitting through my brain. 'In what way odd?'

She shook her head. 'She's dressed like a poor peasant, as I said, but when they came to put her on a board, and carry her over to the stable block, it seems he noticed that her hands were very soft. The nails are clean, he said, and nicely shaped as if they'd been rubbed with a pumice stone or something of the kind – not black and broken as a peasant girl's would be. And, he tells me, the feet are much the same. It made me wonder . . .'

I whistled. 'Perhaps she is not the pauper she appears to be?'

She smiled. 'Exactly. Libertus, I knew you'd understand. Supposing this is a wealthy girl, found on what is still officially our land? It makes it rather awkward for Marcus and myself, when we are due to go to Rome in less than half a moon. What was she doing in the forest, on private property?'

I found that I was nodding once again. 'Some wealthy citizen's daughter, perhaps, attempting to escape a marriage that she didn't want? It has been known for such things to occur. If she disguised herself as a peasant to meet someone in the woods, it is possible that she was attacked and robbed.'

Julia met my eyes. 'I thought of that myself. But I have not heard of any young lady missing in the town. And surely, you'd think, we would have known of it? A wealthy father would have called on Marcus for a search, and got the town guard looking for the girl. It's not as though there's not been time for that. The body had not been dead for very long, but clearly it has been there for at least a day or two.'

Junio, emboldened by his new rank of citizen perhaps, dared to join the conversation. 'Pardon me, madam – Father – but there is another thing – if I might speak.' We signalled our assent, and he went on, 'If it was a failed elopement, why smash in the face? It can't be to prevent the family from identifying it. Surely they would lay claim to an uncovered corpse at once, if they were looking for a missing daughter anyway? And they would recognise the fingers, if your land slave did.'

I nodded. 'And having made the corpse unrecognisable, why bury it at all – especially in such a shallow ditch as I understand this was? Yet clearly it did not get there by itself. Someone put it there. The body of a wealthy girl, dressed in peasant clothes. Your slave is right, it does seem very odd.'

Julia gave that tight-lipped smile. 'Exactly so. That's why I called for you. I very much fear, Libertus, that we may have an inconvenient murder on our hands – probably of someone of good family. And what with the Festival of the Dead and our impending trip – to say nothing of our important visitor from Rome – it has come at a very awkward time indeed.'

I sighed. I knew I'd have had to work out who the body was, if possible, and arrange to give the corpse a decent funeral – for Junio's sake if nothing else – but the matter was already becoming more complicated than I would have wished. 'Well,' I said, 'you'd better get a slave to show me where she is, and Junio and I will take a look at her.'

Chapter Three

I was not really hopeful of discovering very much as my new son and I followed the blond pageboy from the house and through the inner court. If this girl was dressed in someone else's clothes, I thought, they could have been obtained from anywhere, so there was probably little to be deduced from them. As for establishing exactly who she was, we would probably have to wait until someone came forward to claim the corpse as some missing member of their family, since the face was said to be unrecognisable. However, I was interested to see those hands and feet.

'There, citizens.' The pageboy indicated the outbuilding where the body had been put. He was clearly unwilling to go near the place himself, so I took pity on his youthful sensibility and Junio and I walked forward on our own.

The door was already ajar as we approached, and the swarthy figure of Marcus's chief land slave could be seen inside, standing guard beside a sheeted bundle on a plank. I knew the fellow slightly. His name was Stygius: a big man, strong and powerful from long years in the field, with muscles and sinews that stood out like knotted ropes, and speech as slow and deliberate as his walk.

He came out to greet me with a worried frown. 'Citizen Libertus, I am glad you're here. The mistress told me you were on your way. And you too, citizen, of course.' He nodded in Junio's direction with a vague, respectful air, twisting his fingers together in front of his leather apron and bowing to us both. 'The mistress told you what I noticed about the skin and nails?' He avoided looking us directly in the face. Life had taught him to be subservient.

'She did indeed, Stygius,' I said. 'And I was impressed. It was very intelligent of you to notice it. Many people would not have spotted the significance of that.'

His face was browned with sun and wind, but I would almost swear he blushed. 'It's kind of you to say so, citizen,' he said and stared down at his hands.

I realised that it was probably not often that anyone commended Stygius for his intelligence – it is not something expected of a land slave on the whole. Strong arms, a strong back and an unwavering application to the task in hand, however dreary and repetitive, were the important attributes, even for a chief man like Stygius. I felt a sudden surge of sympathy for him, labouring in the fields from dawn to dusk, at the mercy of all extremes of sun and rain: he was slow of speech and movement, but it was clear his mind was sharp. 'You did very well,' I added, and he flashed me a shy smile.

My praise had given him more self-assurance, it appeared. 'If it was just a peasant I would have left her lying here,' he said, raising his head to look at me, and lumbering into confidential mode. 'But I thought that, with it being a wealthy girl perhaps, there should be someone with her in case the parents came. Give her a bit of dignity, at least, by standing guard over her instead of abandoning the body like an empty sack. The mistress did not send a household slave to keep vigil here, so I thought I had better do the job myself. I've left my deputy in charge out in the fields.'

He was half apologetic, and I understood. Had I been Stygius, I too would have found it more attractive to be here – keeping guard over a quiet body in a warm dry shed – than bending over the spade and hoe till darkness fell and urging labour out of other weary men. 'I'm sure your intentions were sincere,' I said, and followed, with Junio, as he led the way inside.

'There you are!' He pulled the door half closed behind us as he spoke, as if to exclude other prying eyes and afford the corpse a little privacy. The room was heavy with the smell of death.

The lack of window-spaces made the place quite dark, even though it was scarcely past midday, and it took me a moment to become accustomed to the gloom. When I did, I knew what I should see – I had been there once or twice before. It was a longish, narrow room, with stone walls and a floor of trodden earth. Sometimes there were boxes of funeral herbs about, but today it was empty except for the makeshift bier on which the body lay, covered with a piece of unbleached linen cloth. A pair of candles burned at head and foot, each supported by an iron spike, and these threw eerie shadows on the shrouded form.

'You have prepared the body for burial?' I asked. I imagined that the body had been washed and oiled, and sprinkled with the herbs.

Stygius shook his head. 'The mistress thought that we should leave her for the family to do that – supposing that we find out who they are. My only instructions were to bring the body over here and make it look as decent as I could, so that's what I've tried to do. The face was so awful that I couldn't look at it, so after I'd got rid of all the ants and things I just brushed the leaves and dust off the clothing to clean it up a bit, and covered her all up with a piece of cloth I found.'

Junio had been standing patiently at my side through this exchange, but now he stepped forward and asked quietly, 'You cleaned the clothing up a bit, you say? But weren't there bloodstains on it, Stygius? Surely, compared to that a bit of dust would hardly signify?'

Stygius peered at him a moment, and then burst out with a laugh. 'Why – it's Master Junio, by all the gods! I knew that they were going to set you free today, but I'd never have known you in that fancy garb – saving your presence, citizen, of course.'

'Junio is wearing garments which befit his rank,' I said, and then – feeling that the rebuke had been severe – 'More than this dead girl is doing, it appears. You have sharp eyes, Stygius. Answer his question: were there bloodstains on the clothes?'

Stygius thought a minute, puzzled, and at last he shook his head. 'It's a strange thing, Master Junio, now you come to mention it,' he said, 'but I don't believe there were. A smear or two round the neck, no more. And you would have expected, with her poor face in that appalling state . . . But, here, you'd better see for yourselves.' He approached the bed, and with a single gesture stripped the cloth back from the shrouded form.

It was indeed a most appalling sight. The face was nothing but a bloody pulp, battered into formlessness. Nose, chin and cheekbones were all in fragments now and there was so little undamaged skin that the whole face looked as though it had been flayed – though doubtless rats and beetles had played their part in that. If the girl's parents did arrive to claim her, I thought, the poor souls would find few features that they could recognise. But one thing was quite certain: this was no accident.

I had still been toying with that possibility, wondering if the girl had really run away – as I had suggested to Julia earlier – and somehow managed to lose her way and plunge down from a height, killing herself and leaving her stricken lover to hide her corpse somehow. But seeing the evidence, I knew there was no chance of that. Someone had wielded a heavy item, with enormous force.

I drew a little nearer to the corpse and looked more closely. Slight, with a boyish figure and of less than average height, the pathetic victim had clearly not been very old, and the garment she was wearing was too generous for her. Made of coarse woollen fabric in the Celtic style, it was very far from new, heavy and shining in places with years of unwashed grime. The broad plaid was roughly fashioned into a sort of gown, the hems ragged with use and the long sleeves patched and mended at the ends. It was tied in at the waist with a piece of battered rag, and a frayed shawl in a different plaid was tied round the head, so that no hair emerged, making a grotesque frame for that poor damaged face.

But as Stygius said, there was very little blood. Even in this dim light it was possible to see that. No spreading telltale stain of darkness on the dirt-encrusted chest, no brittleness of dried blood even on the scarf. A tiny smear upon the shoulder, when I looked carefully, and another on the shawl. Almost as if . . .

'She wasn't wearing those clothes at the time she was attacked.' That was Junio, echoing my thoughts as usual. 'Someone must have dressed her in them after she was dead.'

I nodded. 'I'm almost sure of it.' I picked up one of the candles – forgetting the vengeful spirits for a moment – and brought it close to get a better light. 'And what's even more peculiar, the smears – such as they are – seem to be on the outside of the dress.' I lifted back the tattered material to show him as I spoke. The neckline was grimed to grey with mingled dirt and sweat, in contrast to the smooth and flawless skin it circled, but there was no evidence of bloodstains anywhere.

My action had exposed the shawl-ends which were tied about the throat, and it occurred to me that we should remove it and see what was beneath. Even without the features, we could learn something from the hair – if it was sculpted in a Roman style, it might be helpful in identifying the girl by and by. Rather gingerly I undid the knots and let the plaid cloth fall back on the bier.

The effect was startling. 'Great Minerva!' Junio stared at me. 'Someone has hacked her hair off at the roots.'

It was true. The hair had been cut off in savage, random clumps close to the scalp, so that only a few haphazard strands remained. 'And look, there is no blood across the scalp, and nothing on the inside of the shawl. You see what that implies?' I glanced at Junio and he raised his brows at me. I knew we understood each other perfectly.

He gave a whistle of amazement, then turned to Stygius. 'Have you examined her at all? Is there any indication how she died?'

The land slave goggled at us. 'But . . . surely, citizen? The face . . . ? Nobody could survive that sort of attack.'

'We think it's possible that the damage was inflicted after death,' I said. 'That would explain why there's so little blood. If she had been alive there would be bloodstains everywhere.'

Junio nodded eagerly. 'And you would expect the smears to be on the *inside* of the clothes if somebody had killed her, smashed her face, and then put her in these garments afterwards.'

'And there's your proof.' I pointed to the neck. There was a thin purple-red line around it – not where the shawl had been, though that had left a white mark in the flesh, but higher up – as if a cord had been passed round and then drawn tight. 'It looks like a strangulation. Almost a garrotte.' We might have seen evidence, if the face was there – the change of colour and the protruding tongue – but all trace of that had vanished, together with the features. 'So it looks as if he killed her first, then dressed her up like this – and then inflicted the damage afterwards.' It was a dreadful image, and I shuddered at the thought.

'But . . . ?' Junio began.

I answered the question before he'd uttered it. 'To disguise her identity, I suppose. Perhaps the simple change of clothes did not prove to be enough. It must be something of the kind. Why else would anyone do a thing like that?'

'Great Ceres! I suppose it's possible.' Stygius furrowed his tanned face in a frown. He paused a minute and then spat thoughtfully. 'Somebody was really anxious to do that, wasn't he? Putting her in clothes that weren't her own, chopping off her hair and mashing up her face as if it was a turnip – then going to the trouble of putting her in a ditch and piling leaves on her. And in part of the forest that was off the beaten track – on private property. He can't have imagined that she'd be found so soon. Even we land slaves never usually go there.'

It was my turn to frown. This was an aspect of the affair which had not occurred to me.

Stygius saw that he had made a point, and went on in his slow unhurried way, 'Well, it stands to reason, doesn't it, citizen? If the mistress hadn't told us to clear that piece of ground, to make way for a roundhouse for this young gentleman, that body would have been there years and years. Nobody would ever have had cause to go in there – it's not even a place where poor people go to pick up kindling. There were a few old trees – which we've cut down now, of course – but it was mostly dense undergrowth and nasty prickly things.'

I held the candle higher and looked hard at him. 'But someone must have forced a way in, mustn't they, to hide the body there?'

He seemed to take a moment to acknowledge this. 'I suppose they must have, when you think of it. Unless they used the tracks that we had made ourselves. We took the taller timber down a half a moon ago, and carted it out on sledges, so we made a sort of path.'

'And didn't you say the body was hidden in a ditch?' That was Junio. He was looking at the body with horror, but was taking a lively interest in all this, as well he might. It was his roundhouse that was threatened by the Lemures, after all.

Stygius gave his slow nod. 'The body had been pushed down into it, and covered with a great pile of fallen branches and dead leaves. It would have been nothing but a bag of bones, you'd think, before anybody found it in the normal way – and it couldn't have been identified by that time anyway.'

Junio turned to me. 'What do you think, mast— Father? It does sound as if whoever put this body there was very anxious not to risk its being found. Yet it can't have been entirely safe hiding a body in the forest anyway. The area is right next to your roundhouse and the lane, so somebody could easily have seen them doing it. Kurso, for instance, when he was dealing with the animals; or anybody passing on the road. The ditch was hidden, but the access can't have been – they could hardly have come through from the villa side. They would have had to be on Marcus's private land for that.'

I shook my head. It was a mystery to me. Why take such trouble to obliterate the face and chop off all the hair when the body was to be hidden in a place where no one was likely to find it – as Stygius said – for years and years? When it was covered with large branches in that way, not even wild animals could dig it up – until all chance of identifying it was long gone, anyway. There must be something that I was missing here.

'Take this, Junio.' He was standing next to me, and almost without thinking I handed him the light, and bent to look more closely at the corpse. A quick inspection of the hands persuaded me that Stygius was right. They were far too clean and pumiced for a peasant girl and they showed no signs of heavy work at all – though they were by no means dainty. In fact, they were rather large and angular, and there was a bruise-mark on one finger where a ring might once have been – a tight one, pulled off forcibly, by the look of it.

It was rather a similar matter with the feet and ankles too. It was clear that the owner of that soft, clean, supple skin did not go barefoot as a general rule. The toes and soles were virtually unmarked by calluses, which suggested that they were usually encased in proper shoes or sandals (and probably expensive ones at that) rather than the makeshift boots of rags, or fresh hide bound around the feet and left to cure, which peasant women usually wear.

Yet these were not the dainty, aristocratic feet of which ladies like Julia were so justly proud – they were not as big as Junio's or mine, but even my slave Cilla had smaller ones, and her ankles were less raw-boned and prominent. These legs were pale and muscular, and smooth as kidskin – as if they had been painfully pumiced, shaved or plucked.

'Is there any other damage?' Junio was bending to get a closer look.

'We shall soon see,' I said. I untied the waistband, and to Stygius's obvious dismay, motioned him to help me to take off the garment so that I could see the body underneath. As I lifted up the hem-front, my fingers felt something hard hidden in the cloth. Something round and solid, like a largish coin.

'Bring that light a little closer, Junio,' I said, running my fingers further round the hem. And indeed, right by the clumsy side seam of the skirt, there was a spot where the stitching was undone, leaving a small opening to the space beneath and allowing the owner to use it as a kind of makeshift purse. I slipped my fingers down into the hole and with the other hand I worked the object round till I could take it out.

'What is it, Father?' Junio was watching me.

'A coin!' I produced it with a flourish.

He laughed. 'For the ferryman, perhaps?'

This was only half intended as a jest. It is the custom, at

Roman funerals, to slip a coin into the mouth of the deceased as payment for Charon, the boatman who is supposed to take the spirit across the Lethean stream – the River Styx, the Greeks would call it. If this girl was high-born, some such coin must be found, though a Celtic peasant woman would not have needed such a thing.

But this was no copper coin. Not even a silver *denarius* – a large coin for a pauper – as I'd expected it would be, hidden in the hemming as a precaution against thieves. This was a piece of solid gold. An *aureus* – so rare I had seen only a handful in my whole career. And, as my fingers worked along the hem, I found another coin, and a third and a fourth.

I pulled them out and held them up one by one in the candlelight. They were all different – provincial, foreign or tribal coins perhaps – and though they were all quite clearly made of gold, only the *aureus* was a standard Roman coin, and bore the image of a proper emperor. And that – perhaps – was the strangest thing of all, for the head was unmistakably that of 'Little Boots', or 'Caligula' as the Romans say.

I found myself staring in amazement at the coin. All coinage that bore the head of Little Boots had been officially withdrawn after his assassination and reminted with the face of his successor, Claudius. It was illegal coinage, rare and potentially quite dangerous to own – though still, quite literally, worth its weight in gold. I explained the circumstances to the other two.

Stygius frowned and Junio commented, 'That's very peculiar, master, isn't it? Why bury her in a garment which had a fortune in the hem?'

I shook my head. 'I don't understand it. Perhaps the killer

didn't know. There is something very peculiar about this crime. Let's take the garment off her, Stygius.'

It was no easy matter, but we half sat the body up and gently eased the gown away from it.

'She cannot have been very old,' I said. 'Her chest is as smooth and formless as a child's. And the mystery isn't over.' I had glimpsed the back. 'Have a look at this!'

There was what looked like a stab wound on the shoulder area, as if a whole lump of flesh had been removed. Yet there was no sign of the copious bleeding which such treatment would be expected to produce: only a tiny runnel of dried blood on either side. Another injury inflicted after death? And if so, to what purpose? I laid the body down.

There was a modesty-binding wrapped around between the legs, and almost without thinking I released the piece of cloth to see if there were more wounds in the lower area.

Junio whistled for a second time, and even Stygius let out a startled cry.

'Great Ceres! You were right about this being peculiar, citizen!' What we were looking at was unquestionably male.

Chapter Four

For a moment we all stood quite dumbfounded, and then – as if at some unseen signal – we all three moved at once. I tucked the loincloth back in its proper place, but it seemed indecent to dress this unfortunate young man in some peasant woman's filthy clothes again, so I simply pulled the shroud-sheet over his half-naked form and covered him from sight, leaving the cast-off garments underneath the bier. Junio, meanwhile, was stuffing the candle back on to its spike while Stygius hurried to the door and flung it wide. None of us uttered a single word throughout: we were all too shaken by the discovery.

It was a relief to come out into the stable court, to fresh air and sunshine and the normal world. The blond pageboy was still waiting patiently for us. He had been perching on the corner of a transport sledge on which a load of chopped wood was piled – destined for the bath-house furnace, probably – and he leapt guiltily to his feet when we appeared.

'You have seen what you required, citizens?' he asked, and then – observing that Stygius had accompanied us – 'My orders were to show you two gentlemen into the atrium again, and fetch you some refreshment. The mistress is anxious to hear what you report.' He was looking with disdain at our companion as he spoke. There is almost as wide a gulf between a pampered page and a grubby land-worker as there is between a master and his favourite household slave.

Stygius shuffled and would have gone back to his post, but I intervened. 'I will take responsibility for Stygius,' I said. 'There are some developments I think your mistress ought to know.'

The pageboy gave me a disarming smile. 'Then you have solved the mystery? Some of the servants were taking bets on it. They say the master always calls on you when there is a problem that he needs to solve.'

'Then I hope they have not staked more than an *as* or two,' I said. 'I've not solved anything. The mystery, if anything, is grimmer than before.' I stood back and gestured that he should go ahead, so that – although he was brimming with curiosity – there was nothing he could do but lead us in. We followed him, into the inner courtyard garden and round the colonnaded path which links the individual bedrooms and storerooms to the central block. When we came to the door that gave into the atrium from the rear, he opened it, stood back to let us in, and then disappeared in the direction of the kitchen block – to fetch the promised refreshments, I assumed.

I led the way into the atrium to wait. As soon as I crossed the threshold, however, I stopped, embarrassed. The room was not empty after all.

Julia was kneeling at the *lararium*, the shrine dedicated to the household gods, which was set into a niche on one side of the room. She was not making an offering, of course – since she is a woman, it is not her place – but she had pulled her mantle up across her head and seemed to be talking to the statues of the gods, watched by two maidservants who stood by on either side. They looked at one another when they saw us coming in, and if they had been close enough to nudge each other, I'm sure they would have done.

I was surprised and a little astonished to find Julia doing this. Of course there were several altars in the house and grounds, each consecrated to a different god, and necessary rituals were dutifully observed – especially when people were visiting the house. Marcus, like many other Romans of his rank, would not dream of lying down to dine without making a libation to the goddess of the hearth, and the leftovers remaining after any feast were always offered to the storehouse guardians – though, as usual, whatever the Lares themselves did not consume was left to be shared between the servants afterwards. (I well remember, when I was a slave myself, being grateful that the household gods had so little appetite.)

Yet these observances were symbolic ones: rituals expected of a wealthy magistrate. As a senior official of imperial Rome, Marcus was required to set a good example in such things – just as he attended public sacrifice and made a show of consulting the auguries on affairs of state. But – again like most of his fellow countrymen – he did not genuinely expect the gods to take an active interest in his day to day affairs. Women are sometimes different, of course – it is known that some pious Roman matrons engage in private prayer, or at least have expensive prayer tablets engraved and nailed up on temple doors – but Julia had never exhibited such idiosyncratic tendencies. She attended household rituals as propriety required and always looked suitably demure, but I don't believe she generally communed with deities.

Indeed, she seemed embarrassed when she realised we were there. She hesitated for a minute; then – with a final mutter in the direction of the shrine – she rose and smiled at me.

'Ah, Libertus!' She had turned faintly pink. She made no mention of my two companions, who were still waiting behind me at the door.

There was an awkward silence. I took a step towards her. 'Your pardon, Julia. We should have announced our presence, but the slave boy indicated that we should come in . . .'

She made a tutting sound. 'It's Niveus, that new page of ours. He should have knocked, of course. We only bought him a few days ago: Pulchrus has gone to Londinium, as you know, and Marcus decided – the minute he had gone – that he simply couldn't manage without someone in the role. This boy came recommended – from a wealthy household, too – but I think they only really kept him as a pet. He does not seem to have the least idea of what to do and when. I said to Marcus when he bought him that the boy was far too young, but of course my husband was enchanted with his looks and wouldn't be dissuaded. You know what Marcus is.'

I did. Marcus had had a succession of pages, all of them chosen for their looks. Not that my patron had an interest in such boys – not since he was married anyway – but he liked to be attended by an eye-catching young man. He dressed them strikingly as well, in a scarlet cloak and tunic with gold edging round the hem, to show that their owner was a man of wealth; Pulchrus had looked magnificent, though the uniform made Niveus seem very young and pale.

'I'm sure the boy will learn. I'm sorry we disturbed you. I

see you have been petitioning the household deities,' I said.

She flushed. She was always beautiful, but the colour in her cheeks made her even lovelier. 'I felt I should do something. It is the feast of the Lemures in only three days' time. And here we are with an unburied body on our hands. It was one thing when we thought it was just a peasant girl, but if she is from a wealthy family, even if we give her a sort of funeral, we may still offend the ghosts. So I thought . . .' She made a little helpless gesture with her hands. 'This family is about to make a perilous journey overseas. You see what I mean, Libertus. One cannot be too careful. Especially when Marcellinus is so young.'

And then I understood. Julia would have prayed to any god on earth – in sackcloth and with ashes in her hair – if she thought it might protect her precious son. She was taking no chances with the Lemures. I only wished that I had better news.

She seemed to read my face. 'I assume that Stygius was right? This is not a peasant girl?'

'I can promise that, at least,' I said gently. And then, seeing that the page had reappeared, at the head of a little army of servants bearing folding stools, a table and a tray of food and drink, I added, 'Why don't we sit down?'

It was not my place to issue an invitation of this kind, but Julia realised that I was preparing her for a shock. She gestured to the slaves, and we watched in silence as they arranged the seats and began to set out goblets, fruit and wine.

She took a chair and gestured me to sit. She proffered another stool to Junio, and indicated that Stygius should take up a position at my back. But it was to me that she addressed herself. 'Well, go on. You have discovered who this mysterious young lady is – or was?'

I shook my head. 'We have discovered that she is not a young lady after all,' I said.

She gestured to the goblets, signalling the slaves to pour the watered wine for Junio and me. Ladies did not generally drink, except at dinner time, and Stygius clearly did not merit such hospitality. She took a sugared fig, and nibbled daintily at one side of it. 'But I understood . . . the hands?' she said.

'Not a young lady,' I said again. 'A young gentleman, perhaps. Stygius and Junio will explain to you.'

They did. Stygius gave her a blunt account of what we'd found, and Junio added, 'It rather looks as if the face was damaged *post mortem*, after the corpse was dressed in a peasant woman's clothes. Then it was hidden in a ditch, with bits of branches and dead leaves piled roughly over it.'

'But that is terrible.' She was clearly shaken now, but she was a Roman matron and courtesy to guests was paramount. 'Refill the citizen's wine cup, Niveus,' she said, and I realised with a start that I had emptied it. I am not generally a great enthusiast for wine, preferring a bowl of hot mead now and then, but I was glad enough of its reviving qualities today.

Julia looked at the wine jug almost longingly, as if she would have liked to have a glass herself, but contented herself with taking another nibble at her fig. 'Unfortunate enough when we thought it was a girl . . .' She made that hopeless gesture. 'To lose a daughter is a frightful thing, especially if she is of marriageable age, and any father would clearly be distraught. But to lose a son . . .'

'Is even worse?' I nodded. Had I not just acquired a son myself? 'It would be to lose an heir! And if it is an only son . . .'

I did not need to add the obvious – that the death of an only son entails the loss of the family name itself and, incidentally, of the whole paternal fortune too. If there are daughters, their share will go as dowry to their husbands when they wed. Worse still if there are no surviving children left at all, because then there will almost certainly be an expensive lawsuit when the father dies, with the estate dispersed not only to the beneficiaries mentioned in the will, but to anyone who can mount an effective counter-claim, including – quite often – the imperial purse. Even the money a man leaves to his wife – though nowadays she may use it while she lives alone – will finally revert back to her father's family, often to some quite distant relative, unless she bestows it on another spouse. It ends up in the hands of other men's offspring, either way.

'The loss of an only son is a catastrophe. If it were Marcellinus . . .' Julia shuddered. 'I can't bear to think of it. Humiliated by being dressed up like a peasant in that way.'

'It seems it was a wealthy peasant, though,' I said. 'Look what I found hidden in the dress's hem.' I showed her the gold coins I was carrying. 'More than enough to keep a peasant woman and her family for years. Perhaps you would be good enough to look after them for me? I should hate to think that someone might come to claim the corpse, and suppose I'd stolen them.'

'I'll put them safely in my perfume chest,' she said, taking them almost without a second glance and slipping them softly inside her *stola*-top. Gold coins clearly did not have as much significance for her as for us lowlier folk. 'I wonder if the young man gave them to the owner of the dress?' She shook her head. 'It must have been a very young man. Someone would surely have realised, otherwise.'

That was aimed at Stygius, and he looked abashed, but in his mistress's presence he scarcely dared to speak, far less attempt to exculpate himself.

'I should have realised earlier myself,' I said. 'The size of the hands and feet was quite a clue. I actually thought about the body's boyish form, never supposing that it really was a male. But you are right – he must be fairly young. Not fully come to manhood, anyway. His arms and legs were smooth as any girl's.'

Stygius flashed me a grateful look and I was about to speak again when, rather to my astonishment, Junio broke in. The unaccustomed wine had given him the courage to speak up like the citizen he now was, instead of waiting to be spoken to.

'But though the legs were muscular enough, the victim was no athlete,' he observed. 'His chest and back were soft and white – not tanned and hardened by the sun, as they would be if he had been wrestling half naked at the baths, or even running races and playing ball-sports as young men often do.' He picked up his wine cup and took another sip, looking hopefully towards the servant with the jug who was by this time hovering at my side again.

I waved the slave away. Junio was not accustomed to drinking watered wine, especially in the middle of the day. I did not generally serve it in my house and although – like any other slave – he would have been given refreshment in the servants' quarters when we went visiting, that would have been a thin, inferior vintage, vastly watered down. This was a good wine, kept for guests and only diluted to an appropriate degree: I did not think this was the moment for him to experiment with it, especially since there was Marcus's banquet to look forward to tonight.

Junio looked reproachfully at me, but I ignored the glance. A *paterfamilias* has a right to decide things for his son. 'That was well reasoned, Junio,' I said, knowing that the praise would please him – as it clearly did. 'I had not thought that out myself. But you are right, of course.'

Junio was keen to earn another compliment. 'And he wasn't in the army either – that would have hardened him.'

'Perhaps he wasn't even of military age.' Julia was still toying with her fig. 'Poor lad. That would have made him, what – fourteen or so?'

'Always supposing that he intended to join up,' I said. 'It isn't compulsory to do so nowadays.' Service in the army was no longer universal, but it was still the custom for most well-born young men to have a short spell as an officer, since that was the surest route to preference and power. Most citizens had at least one family member in the legions still, and there was no shortage of recruits among those of lower status, who were content to serve among the humble rank and file, as long as the army offered them a secure career with the prospect of citizenship at the end of it.

'He was about that age, Father, wouldn't you have thought?' That was Junio again. 'Just a little younger than I am, probably. Though without his face and features I suppose it's hard to tell. We cannot see, for instance, if he had a beard at all.' He stroked his own cheek, a bit self-consciously. There was the very faintest hint of down upon his upper lip. I knew that he was very proud of it.

Julia put her fig down and pushed the plate aside. 'The thing is, Libertus, what are we to do? We've got the body of what looks like a well-to-do young man lying in our servants' quarters with his face smashed in. We don't know who he was, or who his family is – or even if he came from hereabouts. Meantime, we have a very important visitor in the house. Not only a patrician, with influence at court, but a relative of Marcus's as well. You know that Lucius Julianus is a cousin, I presume?'

I hadn't known, but on reflection I was not surprised. I was aware that Marcus had been born and raised in Rome and that his family was an ancient one – not only very wealthy but patrician too. Marcus joked that his mother, in particular, was inclined to look down on everyone, with the possible exception of the Emperor; his own wedding to Julia had been hurried through to prevent his parents from finding out and choosing him a bride more in keeping with what they thought suitable. Julia had been married twice before, and although she brought a handsome dowry she was from provincial stock. The alliance had met with huge disapproval from Marcus's mamma, and there had been a flurry of reproving letters by every messenger. It occurred to me that this was a potential problem, even now, with their Roman trip in prospect. 'On his mother's side?' I asked.

Julia gave me a glance that would have melted steel. 'You understand, Libertus? Lucius Julianus will go back to Rome and tell the family what has happened here. Honoria – Marcus's mother – will blame me, of course, because I had the servants bring the body here. I believe she blames me for every problem Marcus has – you know she has never forgiven him for marrying me at all. It won't be the easiest of visits, anyway.' She sighed. 'I was hoping Marcellinus would help to win her round, but now I fear that that's impossible.'

I was about to make some flattering remark about anyone who set eyes on her loving her instantly, but she waved the platitude impatiently aside.

'You don't know what Honoria Aurelia is like. She was always superstitious, and she's getting worse, it seems, now that Marcus's father isn't very well. Sees everything as a deliberate sign that people are conspiring with the fates to engineer the family's downfall all the time. According to Lucius she dismissed a slave last month – sold him for almost nothing in the marketplace – because he dropped a plate of food and did not make the proper sacrifice. Said he was deliberately defying all the gods and trying to bring ill-fortune to the house.' She shook her head. 'It was funny when he told us, but it isn't funny now. Think what she will make of this – at the Lemuria, too!'

It was Stygius who shuffled forward, and muttered, with a bow, 'Then – forgive me, lady – but does Lucius have to know? He and the master have been in court all day. The news will not have reached them . . .'

He was interrupted by a dry, patrician voice. 'And what news, pray, is that?'

We whirled round as one. Perhaps we had been too intent upon our figs and wine. Standing in the main entrance of the atrium, accompanied by his attendant bodyguard but somehow, till this moment, unobserved, was Lucius Julianus Catilius himself.

Chapter Five

He strode across the atrium and – ignoring the rest of us as if we were not there – addressed a sketchy bow to Julia, who had risen in confusion to greet him. Junio and I had started to our feet.

'Forgive me, lady, if I startled you.' His cultured Latin was deliberately formal and precise. 'Your husband will be here in just a little while. He went round with the horses – said he was going directly to the new wing of the villa to get changed – and suggested that I came in here to wait. I could not find anyone to announce that we'd arrived' – here he allowed his eyes to dwell a fraction on the pageboy Niveus, as if to suggest that this should have been his job – 'so I brought my bodyguard and came directly in. I hope you do not mind. I am a member of the family, after all.' He gave her a small, condescending smile. 'I did not expect to find anybody here.'

This was not entirely honest, I was sure. It must have taken considerable care to have entered the atrium quite so silently. I wondered how long he had been standing there, listening.

The same thought had clearly occurred to Julia. 'Well, cousin, since you have clearly overheard us, there is no point in trying to disguise the truth from you. The fact is that there has been an unfortunate event.' She had turned a charming crimson with embarrassment. 'Something unpleasant has been discovered in the grounds – the worst kind of omen. My land slave was suggesting that you should be spared the worry of it, at least until we had contrived to make propitiation to the gods.'

Lucius gave a thin, tight smile. 'I see. So Honoria Aurelia was right! She told me before I set off to visit you that she'd had a premonition that something ill-fated was likely to occur.'

Julia inclined her head. The colour had not faded from her cheeks. 'I believe you mentioned it.' Then – rather daringly for a married woman of her rank – she met his eyes, saying with a pretence at levity, 'I imagine, cousin, that if one has premonitions of ill-fortune for long enough, sooner or later one will be fulfilled.'

Lucius had the grace to look discomfited at this sally. He gave a little laugh. 'I see you have the measure of your mother-in-law, my dear. But you can rely on my help. What is the nature of this "unfortunate event"? Not a dead body, surely, at this time of year?'

It was apparently intended as a kind of mocking jest but the guess was so accurate it took us all aback. Julia said nothing. She did not need to speak. Her face had already told him the unhappy truth.

He was evidently more afraid of the Lemures than I would have guessed. He looked quite pale and shaken as he turned to Stygius. 'This is the news that you were speaking of? The information that I didn't have to share?'

The sudden question caught the land slave unaware. The tone had been intimidating, too – Lucius might have been talking to a dog – and Stygius was slow-thinking at the best of times. It took a little while before he faltered into speech. 'Excellence, I meant no disrespect. The situation is an embarrassment for my master, that is all. And the mistress too, of course. We found a body dressed in peasant's clothes, when we were clearing land. We brought it here for funeral. We don't know who it is.'

Once again, I found I was impressed by Stygius. He thought slowly, but he thought to some effect. He had managed to give an outline which was accurate enough, but minimised drama as far as possible.

Lucius was looking much relieved. 'A peasant? Well, that's not too serious, I suppose.' He turned to Julia. 'What will you do with it? Put it on a funeral pyre at once? That would be wise, I think – dispose of it before the Lemuria begins. You can find out afterwards who the family was – if any information comes to light – and show them where you put the ashes, so they can tend the urn. Nobody could ask any more of you than to give the corpse a proper funeral – even the spirits should be satisfied.'

Julia nodded. She looked quite relieved. She would have been glad, I think, to take her lead from Lucius in this and solve the problem by cremating it – though of course the matter was more complicated than Lucius could guess. 'You are a comfort, cousin,' she began. 'No doubt you are right. Stygius, go and—' But she got no further. Marcus and his entourage were entering the room.

He had changed his toga for a coloured *synthesis* – that combination of tunic and draped material which had become his dress of choice at home. The drapes provided the dignity that a toga gives, without the inconvenience of managing those heavy, awkward folds. In fact Marcus had set a little fashion locally: these days every citizen who could afford it wore a *synthesis* at home, not only when they dined, but increasingly at other times as well. This one was pale orange. It gave him the appearance of a temple augurer, I thought, especially as he was attended by a pair of matching slaves.

When he spoke, he sounded like an augur-reader too. 'I have just seen what is outside, in the stable block. One of the servants showed me. You are aware of it, Julia, I suppose?'

'A peasant,' Lucius began. 'We were just discussing the cremation pyre.'

Marcus snorted. 'Peasant? He's no more a peasant than I am – though I understand that he was dressed as one. You found him, Stygius?'

Stygius, who had come to Julia's side, waiting for his instructions, slowly turned. 'I did, master. On that land we were clearing for this young citizen.' He gestured towards Junio.

Lucius was looking quite astonished now. He turned to Marcus. 'The piece of land you pointed out to me the other day? But what was the body doing over there? Surely it was a patch of forest where nobody would go?'

Marcus shrugged. 'Somebody saw we'd cut some standing timber down, concluded that we'd finished harvesting the wood, and decided it would make a good hiding place, perhaps – not realising that we were about to clear the area completely for a building plot.' He spoke as though he had been actively involved in felling trees himself, instead of merely giving orders that it should be done.

That would make a kind of sense, I thought, remembering the sledge of chopped wood near the stable block. Yet it was an explanation which had not occurred to me – for reasons which I hastened to express. 'But even if there weren't land slaves over at the site – and once you'd cut the timber there weren't until today – we could see the area from the roundhouse all the time. During the hours of daylight, anyway.'

Junio looked mournfully at me. 'There was one day, Father, when that was not the case. You took the whole household into town, as I recall, and we did not return to the roundhouse until dark.'

I nodded slowly. 'Two days ago.' The day of my painful visit to the barber, while Gwellia and the slaves went hurrying round the town, visiting the fuller to collect the laundered clothes, and making all the other last-minute preparations for today. 'Then almost certainly that was when the deed was done.'

Junio looked thoughtful. 'I suppose it must have been. It wouldn't be at night. Lighted torches would be too much of a risk – anyone might see them from the roundhouse, or even from the road – and one couldn't do without them. Anyway, what with wolves and bears and darkness, the forest is always very dangerous after dark. So I think you're right. It must have been that day.'

I nodded. 'And we can guess that the man who hid the body there must be a stranger in these parts.'

Lucius had been listening with a disdainful face, as if such grisly matters were beneath contempt, but he pounced like an arena lion on these words. 'What makes you say that, citizen?' he asked. It was the first time since he had arrived in the atrium that he had addressed a word to me, despite our collusion in the courtroom earlier. Obviously the offering in my purse had not impressed him overmuch. Now, however, his blue eyes were fixed piercingly on me, though his expression still suggested that my opinions – like myself – were unlikely to be of any great account.

'Anybody hereabouts would know the site was being cleared, and that the body was likely to be found. If he'd visited the villa, he would certainly have heard.' I summoned up a smile. 'News travels like lightning in any household full of slaves.'

Lucius managed to convey, without a word, that he was unimpressed. I was tempted to point out that I had first-hand experience, but I sensed that Lucius would be even less impressed if he realised that I'd once been a slave myself. I noticed that he was studiously ignoring Junio, who had been fictitiously his servant for an hour.

'Indeed,' I went on, 'look what happened in the villa here today. His Excellence had scarcely got back to the house before one of the servants had told him all about the corpse. When I arrived it was clearly common knowledge among the slaves – I believe they were laying bets about how soon we'd solve the crime – yet I don't imagine that Julia had mentioned it to many of the staff.'

'I was careful to say as little to them as possible.' Julia was looking horrified.

Marcus glanced around, as if observing for the first time that the room was full of slaves. I have warned him before about his tendency to forget that they are there, silent listeners to everything that's said and not mere items of household furniture. 'But they have ears, I suppose.' He waved a hand at them. 'Be off, the lot of you. You can wait outside the door. Except you, Niveus. You can bring me another cup and a chair – and one for my cousin Lucius as well. And Stygius, you can go back and guard the corpse.'

There was a startled moment as the servants filed away.

When she was sure that only we five citizens remained Julia looked ruefully at me. 'You mean that the whole villa will know of it by now?'

'More than the villa, by this time, I should think. Unless you have instructed your slaves to be discreet, I imagine they will be abuzz with it and chattering to any tradesman who might call.'

She was looking stricken. 'We had some olive oil delivered just before you came. And I sent a slave to Glevum to hire dancers for tonight.'

'Then almost certainly the news has reached the town,' I said. I could see that she was shaken, and I went on soothingly, 'But anyway, as I understand it, you have sent your land slaves out to make enquiries in the area about a missing girl. You can hardly expect the matter to be secret very long – and you want the family to claim the corpse if possible.'

'Girl?' That was Lucius again. 'I thought it was a youth?'

'The land slaves supposed it was a girl at first,' Marcus said shortly. 'Because of the peasant dress, I suppose. However, it appears that in fact it is a male. Libertus can tell you – he discovered that.'

'Really?' Lucius turned to me suspiciously. 'How did you come to be involved?'

Marcus laughed. 'I assume that Julia asked him. I would have done the same myself. I always call on him, if there's a mystery to solve. He has a mosaic-maker's brain and sees the patterns that other men might miss.'

Lucius looked more disapproving than ever. 'Of course! I'd forgotten that you were a tradesman, citizen.'

'An artist,' Julia said, and would have earned my gratitude and love on the spot if she had not already had them both. 'And very clever too. He has helped to solve a number of unpleasant crimes, and has even uncovered several plots against the state. He once received a personal reward from Pertinax himself.' She saw the expression of surprise, and pressed the point. 'That's right – the Pertinax who was the Governor of Britannia once – the same Prefect of Rome that you're so proud to know.'

'I see. Then I salute the citizen.' Lucius's expression did not change a whit. 'Obviously, Marcus, he is the proper person to advise on how you should deal with this unwelcome corpse. Myself, I should have counselled that you put it on the pyre – as I was saying to your charming lady here – before the Festival of the Dead begins. But obviously you don't need my advice. I leave it to Libertus, who's accustomed to such things.' His condescending little smile did nothing to mask the harsh, sarcastic tone.

My patron, however, did not rise to the bait. He pretended to accept what Lucius had said as a genuine compliment to my aptitude. 'Then, since there is to be a banquet later on, perhaps you would care to pay that visit to my new bath-house first? I instructed the slaves to light the furnaces last night, and the steam bath and the hot room should be warm by now. I will have a robe and oil and a strigil sent across to you, and Niveus can come and scrape you down and rub you dry – unless you would prefer to use your own attendant for the task?'

Clever. Marcus had acquired this country residence only

a year or two ago and he had been making improvements ever since – including a new sleeping wing for himself and Julia – and this new bath-house was his latest toy: proper little hot and cold rooms and a plunge pool at the end, for which I'd been invited to design the floor. An invitation to enjoy the private facilities in this way could only be interpreted as a compliment – a piece of conspicuous hospitality extended only to the most honoured guests – and since Lucius had obviously been angling for the chance to sample it, he found himself entirely outflanked. He could do nothing dignified except capitulate, muttering his less than heartfelt thanks, and accept the offer with as good a grace as he could muster in the circumstances.

'Ah, here is Niveus now,' my patron said, as the page came struggling in, with a tray in one hand and a pair of folding chairs in the other. 'Stay and take a cup of Falernian with us, and then he can escort you to the bath-house straight away.'

Lucius was too much of a Roman to decline a glass of wine, and he permitted Niveus to pour a measure out. He sipped it thoughtfully – I am no connoisseur of wine, but even I could tell that it was excellent – and pointedly talked of other things, murmuring to Marcus about the coming trip to Rome.

'There are so many splendid new constructions since you saw it last, you'll hardly recognise the place. Triumphal arches, fountains, temples – everything. There are whole new suburbs springing up these days . . .' I thought he was choosing the subject to exclude me from the talk, until I realised that Julia was feeling left out too.

At last, he pushed his cup aside, and rose to take his leave.

'Time for the promised bath, I think.' He clapped his hands, and his bull-headed bodyguard instantly appeared, with an alacrity which suggested that he'd been listening at the door. Niveus was sent trotting off with them, first to lead the way and then to fetch the cleansing olive oil and the strigil with which to scrape it off again.

'Odious man!' Julia remarked, as soon as they had gone. She sank back on to her seat. 'Are all your cousins so self-consciously superior?'

Marcus leaned over and helped himself to figs, and – in the absence of the servants – poured himself some wine. 'Lucius is the only cousin I have left,' he said. 'All the relations on my father's side are dead. My mother had one brother, and he's the only son. I did not see a great deal of him when I was young, or of his parents either.' He rolled the wine pensively around his cup, as if he were reading fortunes in it. 'It was not, I think, a very happy match – a matter of consolidating family estates – and once the heir was born my uncle put his wife aside, though he kept her in some style until she died, I understand. He never actually divorced her, in case she wed again. Wanted to keep her fortune, I suppose. She used to come and see us now and then.'

Julia shuddered. 'What a dreadful life for her.'

'Not at all. She rather liked it, it seemed to me, though of course I haven't seen her since I was very young. She had more freedom than most Roman wives – went to the baths and the circuses, and visited her friends, and spent a fortune on her clothes and jewels. I remember she always smelled of spice, and wore a lot of kohl on her eyes. As a child you notice things like that. I was sorry when I heard she'd died. I looked forward to her visits. She used to laugh a lot. My mother thought she was disgraceful – I remember that, as well.' He popped a sugared fig into his mouth.

Julia gave a sigh. It said, 'Your mother disapproves of everything,' as clearly as if she'd said the words aloud.

Marcus looked at her. 'You mustn't worry, Julia. It will be all right. My mother is patrician, whatever else she is, and she would never be less than totally polite to any visitor. And you will charm her, as you do everyone. Things are a little different in Rome, that's all. Here in the provinces, people take their cue from us. If you and I decide to set a trend, half of the populace will follow suit. In Rome it's more . . . traditional, perhaps. Fashion does follow the Emperor, of course, but since the Emperor is . . . well . . .'

He did not finish, but we all knew what he meant. Commodus's extravagance and outlandish ways were the subject of rumour throughout the Empire. Doubtless Marcus's mother thought him disgraceful too, though of course it would be suicide to voice the thought in Rome. Even here in Britannia it was dangerous: Commodus was as famous for his spies as for his opulent lifestyle – he was almost assassinated by a palace plot quite early in his reign, and now he is said to have paid eyes and ears in practically every corner of the Empire.

Julia looked at Marcus with liquid eyes. 'Do we really have to go, husband? It was bad enough knowing that your mother disapproved of me – and don't pretend she doesn't, because she makes it clear in every letter that she thinks I schemed to trap her darling son, and I know I'm ignorant of proper Roman ways, and all the ancient customs she thinks so highly of. But now there is this dreadful omen hanging over us as well! Would it not be possible to defer the trip, at least? Think of Marcellinus, if you won't change your mind for me. What would you do if anything should happen to your son?'

It was surprising to hear her talking freely in this way in front of me, though it was clear that she had done it on purpose in the hope of my support. Julia is a lively woman of high intelligence, and her husband has been known to seek her views even on financial matters and affairs of state. But to question his judgement – and in public too – was quite another thing. Marcus was affronted, and he made that evident by the way he tapped his fingers on his thigh and set his lips in an unsmiling line.

'Then we shall have to hope that Libertus solves the problem very soon, and disposes of the "omen", as you call it, well before we leave. Because – understand this, Julia – we are going to Rome. Not only has Prefect Pertinax invited us to go, sending a personal message that it would be insulting to decline, but Lucius also brings news, as you know, that my father is unwell and my mother wants me there as soon as possible.' He drained his goblet in a single gulp and got abruptly to his feet. 'I am sorry if it displeases you, but I intend that we shall go. Now, if you will excuse me, I will follow Lucius to the bath.' He turned to Junio and me, with rather a fixed smile. 'If you citizens would like to join us, that could be arranged. Junio, in particular, might enjoy the treat?'

I had been about to decline on behalf of both of us, but one glance at Junio's shining eyes was enough to change my mind. As my slave he had often attended me when I went to the bath-house in the town, but his duties had been confined to helping me to change and watching my belongings in the stone-locker room. I don't think he'd ever been in the baths himself, though there was sometimes a period set aside on occasional special feast days when even slaves could go.

'My son would like it very much, I think,' I said. 'Though I must personally decline this time. My wife will be expecting me at home by now, I'm sure, wanting to make preparations for tonight. I expect she will be needing help, as well.' It was even possible that she would want a big jug of water brought into the house so she could strip off all her clothes and wash. A banquet at my patron's was a big event for her. And our young slave Kurso was here with me, of course – no doubt kicking his heels in the servants' waiting-room. 'But I will look in again on your mysterious corpse before I go, since the lady Julia is relying on my help in this matter.'

Marcus nodded and held out his hand, so that I could deferentially press the seal ring to my lips. Then he turned and left. I saw them as they walked across the court, Marcus surrounded by his attendants, with Junio walking gleefully behind.

I turned to Julia. 'I'll go back to the stables. Can you have Kurso sent out there to me? The land slaves who were sent out to make enquiries should be returning very soon.'

She nodded. 'They may be back already – they wouldn't come in here. I told them to report to Stygius. You can ask him while you're there. And if the cart is back from Glevum with the dancers for tonight, I will have the driver take you and Kurso home. Junio can walk over when he has finished in the baths – or even stay here, if he would prefer. I imagine he will be wearing the same toga later on?'

'He will indeed.' Since it was the only toga that my son possessed, I spoke with confidence.

Chapter Six

There were no slaves waiting outside the door, except for Julia's two maids – the others were all assigned to attend the bath party by now – so I found myself escorted back to Stygius by one of the girls, while the other accompanied her mistress to her room. It was one of Julia's little vanities to purchase homely female slaves, so that she would look more beautiful by contrast, I suppose, and these were no exception. Both of them were plain.

My guide was the taller and the skinnier of the pair, a rather gangling nervous-looking girl whose straight dark hair and pointed nose and chin made her look even thinner than she was. I looked appraisingly at her as she led the way, wondering if I could tactfully raise the question of the corpse. I wanted to discover what the servants' gossip was, in case there was anything to be gleaned from that source – it is surprising how often slaves know more than their masters ever dream of – but I was not sure if she would talk to me.

I need not have worried. She was as anxious as I to discuss the day's events.

'This business has upset the mistress terribly,' she confided, pausing in the peristyle garden where there was no one else to hear, and favouring me with a smile which showed her rabbit's teeth.

I recognised an opening, and I prompted more. 'I've never known her go in for private prayer like that before. She must be really worried.'

A nod. 'I realised that, as soon as Stygius came in to give us the news about the hands – she told us off for giggling at him behind his back, whereas usually she's the one who makes fun of him because he is so slow.' She gulped. 'Citizen . . .' she glanced around to make certain that we were alone, 'do you really think the Lemures will put a curse on us?'

It was clearly a question that was troubling her. She was plucking at a herb bush and crushing the leaves between her fingers as she spoke – the sort of behaviour that would earn her a punishment, if either of her owners had caught her doing it. She saw me watching her, and blushed, hastily putting the offending sprig behind her back.

I saw an opportunity to make an ally here. I answered the question as if I had not seen. 'Not if we find out who this person was, and give the corpse a proper funeral,' I said. 'Something befitting his rank and condition. So if you hear anything whatever about a missing youth, make sure you report it straight away. To me, if possible.'

Rather to my surprise she shook her head. 'It isn't very easy for me to come to you. I hardly leave the house unless I am accompanying the mistress somewhere. We handmaidens don't get a chance to go out very much, and besides, we hardly ever talk to anyone who's not a fellow slave, so it isn't very likely that I'd learn anything of use. I haven't spoken to anyone outside the house for days – unless you count an entertainer who stayed here overnight, but even he was walking back to Glevum through the grounds and could talk of nothing but his performance at the feast and the weight of the bag of costumes he was carrying. One of the mistress's friends might mention something, I suppose, or one of the tradesmen calling from the town, but we don't hear much gossip, in the general way.'

'I see.' I could tell that she was fidgeting with the sprig again. It gave off a faint smell of rosemary.

She realised this herself, and quickly stuffed the aromatic evidence into the bush behind her back. 'If you want real information, you ought to ask the page. He's the one who goes everywhere with the master, so he sees much more than we do of the outside world. He will have heard if there is anything to know.'

'He also comes and goes with messages, I suppose?' I said, suddenly wondering if Niveus's inexperience had played a part in this affair. I knew that Marcus had used his former pages as constant couriers, sometimes with important documents under seal. A letter which had fallen into the wrong hands, perhaps? Some disappointed contact, desperate for news, attempting to reach Marcus in disguise? A dozen possibilities were coursing through my brain.

The maidservant dispelled them. 'Not really, any more. Niveus can ride, of course. For his age, he's quite impressive on a horse – it's one of the things which recommended him – but even the master has reluctantly agreed that the boy is far too immature to send on the roads alone, with any message of importance, anyway.'

I could see the force of that. With his pale, blond looks and that red uniform, any forest bandit would see him coming half a mile away, and Niveus was built for decoration rather than self-defence. Even giving him a weapon would not have helped a lot – he was too small to wield a dagger to very much effect. I unwillingly abandoned my little theory.

The girl was still anxious to be helpful, though. 'You could speak to Aulus, the front gatekeeper, perhaps. He's a fairly horrid person, brutal as a bear, but he does see everything that's passing in the lane, and he speaks to all the visitors, of course.'

'Thank you. That's a very good idea.' I did not mention that I knew the gatekeeper of old. He had been a spy for Marcus once, before my patron bought this villa for himself, and I had already determined that I would speak to him. He still had the informer's habit of noting everything, so I was prepared to brave the stinking breath, though it would cost me something if he had news to tell. Aulus also had an informer's instinct for reward.

The slave girl smiled. 'I'm glad to be of use. My name is Atalanta, by the way. If I do hear anything, I'll try to let you know.' She led the way towards the further gate, ready to usher me into the stable yard.

I paused before going through it. 'And there isn't any gossip in the house at all? None of the slaves has anything to say? No rumours about unusual incidents? No guesses about who the victim is?' Usually, when there is a homicide like this, there are a hundred different theories in the servants' hall – most of them completely impossible, of course, but occasionally there is something which can give a lead.

Atalanta shook her head. 'Not as far as I know. It's quite a mystery. Of course we took it for a peasant, till Stygius saw the hands – and even then we thought it was a girl. But now . . .' She shrugged. 'Everyone seems completely baffled, even the senior slaves, who usually pretend that they know everything.'

I had to smile at this. I have spent long enough as a slave to recognise the type. I would have given her a coin, but I still didn't have a purse – I had given mine to Lucius earlier – so she had to be content with a smile. 'You have been very helpful. I shall remember that,' I said, dismissing her, and went into the outer courtyard on my own.

Stygius had stationed himself in front of the building where the body lay, and I saw that he had armed himself with an ancient wooden hoe – though whether this was to ward off curious eyes, or to protect himself from phantoms, it was difficult to say. The door to the room had been left ajar again, and I could faintly see the flickering candles and the shrouded form.

When he saw me Stygius came lumbering across. 'Ah, there you are, citizen. I thought you would come back.' He looked at me with curiosity. 'Have they decided what they're going to do with that?' He jerked a thumb towards the dead man as he spoke. 'I thought yon Lucius would have persuaded them to light the pyre at once.'

'I think they were waiting to see if there was any news.' I left an opening for a comment, but he offered none. I prompted him again. 'From those land slaves of yours who were sent out earlier, asking questions around the neighbourhood.'

Stygius looked mournful. 'Most of them are back. But they've nothing to report – or nothing of any interest, anyway. They've been, between them, to all the major homesteads locally. Of course, they were asking the wrong questions – they were only enquiring about a missing girl – so perhaps it's not surprising. And being only land slaves, and not proper messengers, they could only ask the servants and the doorkeepers in the main. You couldn't expect rich people to invite them in.'

I nodded. 'Well, they did their best and it was worth a try. Servants will often talk to other slaves much more freely than they'll talk to an official visitor.'

He spat thoughtfully. 'You might be right, at that. In fact, if there was a young man unaccounted for, perhaps my land slaves would have heard. They have come back with all sorts of stories about missing dogs and goats – to say nothing of someone's ancient grandfather who keeps wandering off and has not been seen for days.'

This was delivered in so lugubrious a tone that I found myself smiling. 'But no young people?' I enquired.

Stygius looked surreptitiously towards the corpse, as though it might overhear him. 'No one that could possibly be him. They found a Celtic freeman whose daughter ran away, but it turns out that he's had a message since, saying that she'd met a man, and gone off with a troupe of travelling entertainers in a cart. And there was another household who had lost a kitchen girl. They were the only ones who asked the land slaves in. The owners wanted to make enquiries in case we'd heard of her.

'They think she's run away?' I was surprised. This was a serious matter. The punishment for a captured runaway was death.

'It seems she broke a lamp and was afraid of being flogged – she's very young. Her owners have got the town guard on the watch for her. She's been branded, and she's got the usual slave disc on a chain round her neck saying who she belongs to, so she won't get very far – it would take an ironsmith to strike that off. But the other servants say their mistress is unkind, and often had her beaten till she was black and blue, so she may have gone to throw herself on someone's mercy in the town.'

'Claiming protection?' The law did make exceptions in a case like this, where an owner was unjustifiably cruel, provided that the fugitive put herself under the protection of another master straight away. 'In that case her owner might certainly suspect she had come here – Marcus is famously kind to his slaves.'

He nodded. 'But we hadn't seen her – and it couldn't be our corpse, even when we still thought it was a girl. Those hands did not belong to any kitchen slave, and anyway the missing girl was only eight years old.'

'I see.' I was sympathetic to the girl's predicament, but Stygius was right. This didn't help us with the case in hand. 'But no young men at all?'

He shrugged. 'I'm sorry, citizen,' he murmured, as though it were somehow his fault that the enquiries had failed. 'Though there is still a chance. There are one or two land slaves who haven't yet come back – some of the neighbouring properties are miles away and of course they had to walk.'

I nodded. 'Well, send for me if you hear anything at all. In the meantime, I'll go and have a word with Aulus at the gate. It occurs to me that if anyone passed this way in a cart, Aulus would have seen them from his vantage point.' Aulus had a cheerless little cell beside the gate, where he could sit and shelter, but still have a view of any traffic in the lane. 'I imagine that whoever hid our victim in the ditch must have used some kind of transport to move the body – unless they somehow killed him on the spot. And there has been no sign of bloodstains there, as far as I'm aware.'

Stygius gave his slow, considered nod. 'That's true, when you come to think it out. It wouldn't be easy to disguise a thing like that on the back of a donkey or a mule, and if it had been wrapped in something they'd have buried it like that. Or you would have thought so, anyway. And if it was a stranger, as you seem to think, he'd have had to take it steady down an unfamiliar lane. Aulus would have had a chance to get a look at him.'

I frowned. 'I wonder what a stranger in a cart was doing in the lane. The only reason to come down this way is if you have business here. Most people would take the military road – it's a great deal easier than these steep and winding lanes, even if you have to clear it when a messenger goes by, or there's military traffic of some other kind. Wagons take a dreadful jolting where the roads are bad.' I was remembering my own exacting journey here today, and others of a similarly bruising kind I'd made before.

Stygius was following my train of thought. 'Perhaps that was the idea.' He spat judiciously. 'There aren't so many people on the forest lanes. Maybe they started from the military road, and just drove down here to find a hiding place.'

'In that case they won't have come this far, so they won't have passed Aulus and we won't learn anything at all,' I said briskly. 'But it is the only enquiry I can think of to pursue. Unless another quick glance at the corpse gives me any fresh ideas at all.'

It didn't. It seemed, if anything, more horrible this time, and I was very conscious of the stench of death. I was glad when Kurso trotted into sight and gave me the excuse to pull the covers up and turn away again.

'Come then, Kurso.' I strode out of the building, and leaving Stygius to stand guard over his grisly charge, we went round to the front to find the gatekeeper. We took the long way, round the side grounds of the house, passing the bath-house on the way.

I wondered if Junio was enjoying it.

Chapter Seven

Aulus was sitting glumly in his cell, gazing through the window-opening at the lane, the very picture of bored disgruntlement. At our approach, however, he lumbered to his feet.

'Ah, citizen pavement-maker, I've been expecting you. One of the maidservants said that you were on your way.' He did not look particularly enchanted to see me. His sweaty, swarthy face was creased into a frown and he was fondling his favourite cudgel as he spoke. Not that he intended any harm to us – Aulus would not dare to threaten Marcus's guests – but he was put there to intimidate, and he was good at it.

Kurso looked terrified and sidled close to me.

Aulus ignored him. 'What was it you wanted this time, citizen? You don't expect me to help you in that business of the corpse? They didn't bring it near this gate. It came in through the farm.'

So that was the reason for his unhappy scowl! The gatekeeper had nothing to report, for once, and was disappointed by the lack of opportunity to earn a coin or two. I tried a little flattery – it had paid off with him before.

'It may be that you can give us some information all the same,' I said. 'I know your sharp eyes, Aulus. There isn't very much that happens in the lane that escapes your notice. I'm interested in what went on before today. There may be something you saw which didn't seem important at the time.'

It worked. Something that might have been a smile half spread across his face. It gave him the appearance of a crafty bear. Aulus had cunning, if not intelligence. 'Well, tell me what you want to know. I'll do my best.' He leaned towards me, as if to listen hard, and the smell of stale onions took my breath away.

I took a step backwards to retreat from it, almost flattening Kurso, who had done the same. 'I want to know how the body got to where it was. So, did you notice any unusual carts or other transport in the lane?' I said, in my best official tone. 'Two days ago in particular.'

Aulus thought a moment, screwing up his face. 'As long ago as that? Don't know if I can help you, citizen. There's been a lot of extra traffic coming to and fro, especially with this important visitor from Rome. My memory isn't always what it was.' His tongue came out and flicked around his lips.

I knew that little nervous trick. It meant he scented money. I sighed. 'I'm sure your master would agree to a reward,' I said, 'if there is anything really useful you can call to mind.'

'Well, citizen, I'll see what I can do.' Aulus made a pretence at struggling to recall, which would not have fooled a baby. 'Unusual vehicles?' he said at last. 'Depends what you mean by unusual, I suppose. That was the day the master had a banquet for his guest – no end of councillors and important people from the town, most in hired litters, but two of them had private carriages. Then there were the entertainers – they came in a cart – and there was the slave-trader who called and sold the master another page. He had a little cart with Niveus aboard. Is this the sort of thing you want to know?'

'Exactly what I wanted!' I summoned up a smile. The promise of money had revived his memory quite remarkably. I only prayed that Marcus would agree to pay the bribe. 'Kurso, I hope you're listening to this. I'll have to remember all the details later on, so I can talk to the people who own the vehicles.'

Kurso flashed a frightened look at me. I could see that it was hopeless. Junio would have taken in the facts and helped me reconstruct the list when I got home, but poor little Kurso was so terrified, I doubted he would remember much more than his name.

But Aulus hadn't finished. 'And then there were the extra deliveries, of course – Marcus had ordered in some special wine from town, and all sorts of delicacies from the marketplace. There was a man with oysters and another with larks. Then there was a wagon of extra olive oil – not that the tradesmen came to the front gate, but I can see from here to where the back road branches off, so unless they come across the foot-tracks, the way they brought your corpse, I get to see almost everyone who ever comes and goes.' With that wily expression in his close-set eyes, Aulus looked more than ever like a bear – if a bear could ever be said to look self-satisfied.

I nodded. 'Very good,' I said, although it wasn't good at all. It could take weeks to check on all of this, and I didn't have the time. It would be the Lemuria in less than three days. If I was to solve the problem of the dead boy's identity, and soothe the vengeful spirits, I must do it very soon. I turned to the gatekeeper. 'You're sure that's all the carts there were?'

I meant to be ironic, but it was lost on Aulus. 'Well – there was the hired baggage wagon and another cart that Lucius had engaged. He is going to travel with Marcus and Julia when they go, but he has sent a lot of his luggage on ahead, with his chief slave riding with it to make sure it arrives – though Lucius kept fussing round it, giving different orders right up to the end. Marcus and Julia decided to take advantage of the cart and send off some of their belongings too – things the family will need when they're in Rome. It'll speed up the journey when they leave, I suppose, not having to slow the carriage to let the heavy goods catch up – though I expect they'll take a wagonful of slaves with them anyway.'

'But the baggage wagons came from the villa, surely?' I put in pointedly. 'They weren't just passing by?'

He shook his shaggy locks. 'Well, neither were the others, if it comes to that. They were all coming to the villa or taking things away. "Unusual carts or other transport in the lane" was what you said. You didn't say anything about passing by.' He was affronted now, jutting his chin forward and glowering at me.

I hastened to placate him. 'Perhaps I should have done. Though anything you've told me may be useful in the end. But – was there anything?'

He humphed. 'There was that trapper from the forest with a wagonload of skins – I think that was the day – heading for the tanner's by the look and smell of it. And a farmer from the hills who seems to go past every day, with a cart full of something for the market in the town. I think that's all there was. All that I can remember, anyway, that could possibly have been carrying a corpse.'

I looked at Aulus, and caught him glancing maliciously at me. I was by no means certain that a silver coin would not have wrung a little more from him, but I had none to offer. 'So nothing really unusual at all?' I said. 'Nothing that mightn't have gone past on any day? Nobody you didn't recognise by sight?'

'I'm afraid not, citizen. I only wish I did have something more helpful to report. I'd be glad to have a little extra in my purse.' He bestowed another whiff of onions on me, as he shoved his big face close to mine and gave me a gigantic, knowing wink. 'You won't forget to mention that I did my best?'

'I shall tell my patron exactly what you said when I see him at the banquet later on. In the meantime, keep on the alert. If you see anything suspicious, or if you remember something that might have slipped your mind, make sure you let me know. Now, where's that little slave of mine? It's time for us to go.'

'Here, m-m-master.' Kurso was at the doorway, where he'd retreated, cowering. He looked at the brutish gatekeeper with uncertain eyes. I could understand his feelings, to a point. Aulus was so much bigger, he could have eaten him for lunch.

However, one cannot encourage timidity in a slave. 'Come, Kurso,' I said briskly. 'Attend me down the lane.' I gestured to Aulus, who was standing motionless. 'And you, doorkeeper, may escort us through the gate. I have already taken leave of my patron and his wife.'

Aulus looked surly, but he undid the gate and ushered us outside.

I turned to him. 'I suppose you haven't seen the villa cart come back? Your mistress was promising us a lift if it was here. Though I suppose it would have gone round to the rear – it was bringing the entertainers for tonight.'

He shook his head. 'I would have noticed it. I told you, I can see everything from my guardroom.'

'Even if you were talking to someone at the time?' Aulus had not had his eye to the spyhole while I was in the room.

He didn't answer for a moment. Even Aulus could see the implication of my last remark. He wiped a fat hand across his massive face. 'I would have heard it,' he said defiantly. 'Just as I would have heard anyone who drove past the other day, whatever you might think. Horses and wheels make a clatter in the lane, and that wagon, in particular, is a noisy one. I'll bet a *quadrans*, citizen, that cart has not come back.'

In this, at least, he was demonstrably right, for even as he spoke the cart in question turned the corner of the lane and lumbered into view, with such a squeaking and clattering, such a thudding of hooves and juddering of wheels, that only a deaf man would not have noticed it.

Aulus flung me a triumphant glance. He didn't say, 'You see?' but his smirk conveyed the message with perfect clarity. 'You wish me to stop it, citizen, before it goes round to the back? So you and your slave can ride back to your house?' He didn't wait for an answer, but set off down the lane, gesticulating at the driver as he went.

The wagon stopped, and there was a whispered consultation in the lane, with Aulus motioning towards me with his thumb, and the driver countering by gesturing at his human cargo with his whip. However, a decision was obviously reached, and in my favour too, because presently the passengers began to climb down from the cart.

They were a striking collection. Two handsome, muscular young men in leather skirts, who moved and looked like acrobats, and an ageing one who certainly did not; a pair of stunted men with exaggerated beards and straggling haircuts, who might have been a form of comic turn; and lastly a group of chattering young women – most genuinely Iberian from the look of them, with the typical striking red-blond colouring of Celts from that part of the Empire, though there were one or two with darker skin and hair. All of them were comely. Aulus was ogling them as they got down from the cart, and I found that I was staring at them too.

They invited stares. Their skin was powdered almost white, and they were wearing so much lamp-black round their eyes and wine lees rubbed into their lips and cheeks that I could see it even where I stood. They wore their hair luxuriously long, hanging free around their shoulders in a way no self-respecting Roman maiden would consider (although the effect was very pleasing, in an erotic sort of way). Their costume, too, was not of a modest nature, not only because of the boldness of the dyes – I noted reds and orange, yellow, pinks and greens – but because it was of a daring cut as well, with little tunic-skirts that barely reached their thighs and necklines that almost reached their waists. The floating scarves of different colours suspended from their belts gave only the illusion of covering their legs: at the slightest movement it did nothing of the sort.

They were moving a great deal as they climbed down

from the cart, and Aulus was almost salivating at the sight. However, as each one reached the ground, an older woman, who seemed to be in charge, handed her an ankle-length brown cloak, and when all had descended she hustled them off towards the back gate of the house. Even then they walked with a kind of conscious, swaying gait that made the long, drab cloaks look sensual.

Aulus watched them go, lust and disappointment written on his face, and it was a long moment before he walked back to me. 'The driver will turn the cart round and then he'll take you home. And your little kitchen slave as well – supposing that he ever shuts his mouth again, that is.'

I turned to Kurso. I had forgotten him. He too was staring after the departing girls. He caught my eye and closed his jaw, which had dropped in what I thought was admiration for their looks.

I was wrong. 'All those p-p-proper dancing girls?' He sounded awed. He saw my face, and hastened to explain. 'My former m-m-master had a s-s-single dancer at a b-b-banquet once, and said she c-c-cost too much to use again. And your p-p-patron . . .' He coloured and tailed off.

It was surprising, when you thought of it. Marcus was famously careful with his wealth. The entertainment at his feasts was more likely to be a local poet, or a group of tumbling dwarves, than any sophisticated group like this. These were expensive dancers, you could tell that at a glance: their dyer's bill alone would have kept our household for a year.

I laughed. 'Attempting to impress his cousin Lucius, I expect. I hear that they have entertainments between every course at court, and presumably the rest of Rome follows suit. In the best households, anyway. Obviously Marcus wants to prove that he can do the same, and for once he doesn't care about the cost.'

Aulus gave me a sideways look. 'It's more than that. It's rumoured that Lucius is on the lookout for unusual acts that he can take back to amuse the Emperor. He has already sent one act on its way to Rome with his chief slave and baggage. Apparently there is a lack of novelty at court. Commodus is tired of his freaks and naked dancing girls, and bored with people fighting to the death for him, so providing something different is a route to quick reward. They've had entertainments here every night since Lucius arrived.'

I frowned. 'There's nothing very different about tonight's performers, though. High-class and expensive, but not unusual. If the Emperor's been used to nude extravaganzas, this will seem very tame. There must be dozens of Iberian dancing girls in Rome.'

'I don't know about that.' Aulus spat noisily into the dust. 'I just know there were some performers here the other night, and Lucius offered them a chance to go to Rome. And after that, of course, every entertainer in Britannia wants to come, in case they catch his eye. The master could have had his pick of the best acts in the province and paid them only an *as* or two apiece. He knows a bargain when he sees one – I expect that's what he's done.' He glanced towards the back lane to the villa, where the dancing girls had disappeared from view, and bared his teeth in an unpleasant grin. 'Not that I shall see them. You will be the one to benefit, at the feast tonight.' He leaned forward and the smell of bad teeth came wafting over me. 'You'll tell me afterwards if they were any good?'

I nodded nervously and edged away. Aulus's cudgel was not the only thing about him that could knock a man sideways. 'Of course,' I promised weakly, hoping that he would not want too many salacious details. 'But now I see the driver has turned the cart round, and it is time I went home, or I shan't be ready in time to come back later on. Come, Kurso!'

'And you won't forget to tell the master . . . ?' the gatekeeper began, but I left him to it, and drove home to Gwellia.

Chapter Eight

We got back to the roundhouse to find signs that someone had been very busy while we were away. The earth path from the front gate had been swept clear of weeds and stones, all the way through the enclosure to the door, and fresh new piles of brushwood kindling were stacked neatly on each side. Even as I sat wondering at this proof of industry, Maximus and Minimus came running out and I was handed down from the cart with as much care as if I had been the Emperor himself, while Kurso scrambled down beside me and looked doubtfully around.

'You see what we've been doing, master?' Maximus began, and Minimus went on.

'It was the mistress who suggested it. We brought some water from the stream for her . . .'

'. . . and we were to brush the path and fetch some kindling while she went off to wash . . .'

'. . . and then stand by to help you to get ready when you came.'

They were so enthusiastic that they made me smile. I had almost forgotten that I had this extra pair of slaves (at least until Marcus came back from Rome) and I had expected that they would find my household difficult at first. Their duties at the villa had been decorative ones, largely confined to fetching trays and announcing visitors (rather as Niveus was doing now). They were used to Roman comforts and convenience, not a smoky Celtic roundhouse with a central hearth. No fine mosaics and Roman plumbing here – every drop of water had to be brought up from the stream and all the cooking took place on the fire. Of course a slave must expect to do anything he's asked, but these two were not accustomed to hard and heavy work.

'Well' – I turned to Kurso – 'it appears the mistress has two pairs of willing hands, so she won't need your help for the time being. You can go back to the garden and leave these boys to do the other work – obviously they're very good at it.'

I had intended this as praise for them, but Kurso was as pleased as anyone. He flashed me a delighted smile, and set off for his beloved plants and animals. I saw him disappearing into the enclosure at the back, where immediately a cluster of hungry chickens started pecking at his heels. As I watched he picked up the waiting bowl of kitchen scraps and scattered that, while the goat came over to butt him in the back and claim a share. He looked back and grinned at me, the very embodiment of a happy man.

I turned to the redheads. 'You two have settled in?'

For answer they led me to the servants' sleeping room – an extra building which we'd added recently, between the dye-hut and the front door of the house. It was small and snug, with walls of woven osiers daubed with mud and clay, and a neat thatched roof to keep the weather out – a sort of miniature roundhouse in itself – but I wondered how a pair of Marcus's slaves would take to it.

However, when I peered inside, I saw that they had made themselves at home. Taking their cue from what the other slaves had done, they had selected a vacant piece of floor, piled it with fresh reeds to make a sort of bed, and spread their woollen cloaks on top of it to create a covering. On the floor was a set of 'finger-stones' – five knucklebones which must have come from the villa kitchen at some time and were probably their only possessions, apart from what they wore – with which they clearly had been playing when the cart arrived.

They saw the direction of my glance, and flushed.

'We had a minute, master . . .' Maximus began.

'. . . just before you came.' Minimus darted forward to put the bones away. 'This is not a sign of idleness.'

I shook my head. 'I'll go and see your mistress. You finish off your game, but be sure you're listening to hear me when I call. I shall need you in a little while.'

I left them to their knucklebones and went into the roundhouse proper on my own, blinking against the smoky darkness of the room. As my eyes grew accustomed to the gloom, I looked around, revelling in the dear, familiar attributes of home: Gwellia's weaving loom set up against the wall, its stone weights pulling the fabric into shape; the stools set cosily round the fire, and the sides of meat that I had hung last autumn on the beams above, so that the swirling smoke would cure and preserve them for our winter food.

Gwellia was standing with Cilla on the far side of the room, facing away from me. She was clearly unaware that I had arrived, largely because her face and shoulders were muffled in a dress which the maidservant was in the act of pulling over them. Her bare legs were visible right up to the thighs – still very shapely for a woman of her age.

My guess about her preparations for the banquet had

been right: there was evidence that she had stripped herself and washed from head to toe. A shallow basin of water was still set beside the hearth, and the robe which Cilla was now tugging down into place was a fine new *stola* from the marketplace. Normally Gwellia wore clothes made from the Celtic plaid she wove herself, but today was a special occasion and she was dressing for the banquet like the Roman citizen that she had become.

The new robe suited her. It was of a pale rose-madder pink, which showed off the natural darkness of her hair and eyes. She looked magnificent.

'Gwellia?'

She looked round. I had half expected a rebuke for being at the villa for so long, but she was smiling as she turned about, and twirled to show her *stola* to best effect.

'You like it? You don't think the colour is too strong?'

I thought of the painted dancing girls and smiled. 'It is beautiful. And so are you.'

She looked away and picked up a silver pendant that I had given her, and made as if to fasten it round her neck. 'There was trouble at the villa? You were away such a time. I was beginning to get concerned for you. It is not so long since you were very ill.' It was her way of offering a mild reproof.

I sat down on the three-legged stool beside the fire, and began to unlace my sandal straps. 'It's quite a story,' I said. I told her briefly what had happened at the house.

She listened, the pendant still dangling from her hands. 'A murdered man? Just where the new house was going to be? Poor Junio! And . . .' She stopped, shaking her head and looking seriously at me.

I put my feet into the bowl. The water was cold and not

especially clean but it was very soothing. 'Poor Julia, as well. She is convinced it is an omen for their journey overseas.' I wriggled my toes to rinse the dust from them. 'She even asked Marcus if they really had to go.'

Gwellia made no direct response to this. She motioned towards Cilla with a warning frown. It was meant for me, but the girl took it as a signal to do the pendant up: she stood on tiptoe and reached to fasten it, but it took her several tries to fix the clasp, even though my wife leaned forward to make it easier. I saw that the poor girl's hands were trembling.

I realised then what Gwellia had been signalling to me. 'I'm sorry, Cilla. Of course the new roundhouse is to be your home as well.'

She glanced at me and I saw that her eyes were wet with tears. 'Oh, master,' she burst out. 'This corpse. They'll be sure and bury it before Lamuria, won't they? Even if they don't know who it is?'

Gwellia raised her eyebrows and looked across at me. 'I expect they're hoping that they'll discover very soon. I'm sure they want your master to find that out for them and that is what has kept him all this while?' It was only half a question.

I nodded and she sighed.

'I wish they would not go on making these demands on you,' she said. 'It is not good for your health. But, I suppose, since it is Marcus who is asking you . . .'

Refusal would be even more injurious to my health, is what she meant.

'I would want to do it in any case, for Junio's sake,' I said. 'And Cilla's too, of course.'

The slave girl did not meet my eyes. She looked down at

the floor, where she was drawing circles on the earth-dust with her toe. At last she said, 'I don't want to push myself forward, master, but you've used my help before. If I can do anything to assist you this time, let me know. Slave or not, I'll do whatever I can.'

I was about to ask her gently what she thought she could do, but she was too quick for me. 'You are always saying that there are things that servants can find out that aren't so easy for a citizen. I could ask questions in the villa, while I'm there.' She sounded eager. 'There's one of the kitchen slaves in particular I used to know well . . .'

'Cilla,' I said gently, 'tonight you will be freed. You are invited to the banquet to signify the fact. After that you won't be a servant any more. You'll be a free woman, betrothed to a free man – to a citizen, indeed.'

'You mean my friend isn't likely to confide in me again?' Cilla sounded shocked, as if this aspect of her new existence had not previously occurred to her. 'She'll think that I've joined the owner class and treat me differently?'

It was almost exactly what I'd meant, but I said, 'You can hardly go wandering into the villa kitchens unaccompanied, in any case. It isn't the sort of thing an invited visitor can do. And you will be a guest tonight and not a slave – a special guest, in fact.' I scooped some water up into my hands and rinsed my lower legs.

Cilla's usually cheerful, plump young face creased in an unhappy frown. Then all at once it cleared. 'But I'm not invited till the final course,' she said. 'I'm still a slave till then, so I could talk to her. I could even go and show my tunic off. It's a nice one that my former mistress Julia sent for me – a lady's tunic, all the way down to the ground instead of stopping at the knees the way servants' tunics do. My friend would like to see it. When I was working at the villa we always talked about the things we would wear and the colours we would choose, if we could buy our freedom and have any clothes we liked. "Anything but this old greeny-brown," she used to say . . .'

'Very well, Cilla,' my wife interrupted. Cilla had a tendency to enliven her reports by imitating the voices of the people she described – she'd captured the adenoidal tones of her friend the kitchen maid quite comically, I thought, but Gwellia, for once, did not seem inclined to smile. 'You obviously have an interest in the matter,' she said seriously, 'and if you can help your master to clear it up, I should be very pleased, for his sake as well as yours. What do you say, husband?'

It was clearly not a moment for levity. I turned to Cilla and tried to look properly severe. 'You may question the servants at the villa, if you have the chance. But you are not to go anywhere unaccompanied, or make yourself a nuisance in any way at all.'

She looked chastened. 'Very well, master. I won't let you down,' she said, and Gwellia rewarded me with an approving nod.

Great gods, I was in danger of being ruled by women here! I felt the need to assert authority. I clapped my hands and raised my voice a notch. 'Maximus! Minimus! I need a drying cloth!'

The result was very soothing. I had hardly got the words out before the boys were at the door, though Cilla had to point out where the clean rags were kept, hanging in a bag beside the wall. Each boy selected a likely piece of cloth, and then came across to kneel beside me, one on either side.

'You should have called us earlier, master . . .' Minimus began

'. . . we would have washed your feet.' And as if to prove it they each seized one of my legs, and attempted to outdo each other as they rubbed them dry. I feared they would upset me from my stool, such was their eagerness to prove themselves of use.

I held up a staying hand. 'You first, Maximus!' Deliberately, I presented my right leg to him, and indicated that he should pat that very gently dry, before I permitted his companion to do the other one. Minimus added a light massage to his ministrations. I have never felt so foolish, or so cosseted.

'Will you be changing for the banquet, master?' Maximus enquired.

I was just about to shake my head – I was wearing my best toga already – but Gwellia was far too quick for me.

'He will change his under-tunic. I have had his white one cleaned. So you can help him strip and wash from head to toe. Empty the bowl, and he can stand in it. There is a jug of fresh water by the door that you can pour over him.' She saw my look of slight unwillingness – Junio had washed me just the day before – and as they hastened outside with the bowl she turned smilingly to me. 'Marcus is bestowing a compliment on this house – on Junio and Cilla in particular, of course, but on us as well. Any Roman would have bathed and changed and you must do the same. And, Cilla, your master has said that you may ask the servants questions if you like, but even if you learn something of interest, you'll wait till afterwards to tell him what it is, and not interrupt the banquet. Ah, husband, here's your wash.'

I stood up and rather reluctantly took my tunic off and stepped into the empty bowl the boys placed at my feet. I mustered what dignity I could – a naked man is always at a disadvantage in a situation of this kind.

'Remember, Cilla, it is vital that this evening goes off without a hitch,' I said, addressing the girl over Minimus's head, as he clambered on the stool with the big jug in his hand and formed a sort of human screen between us. 'Any breaking of the rules and the ritual will be spoiled. You might not get your freedom after all. It might be regarded as another bad omen, too. So don't get so interested in your quest that you fail to join us at the proper – aargh! – time.' The water was extremely cold.

Cilla nodded. 'I'll be very careful.' She turned her attention to her mistress's hair.

'In any case there probably isn't very much to learn,' I said, the words coming in little jerks as Maximus rubbed my back with energy. 'If there were rumours at the villa I'd have heard when I was there, but there were none at all, not even when they thought the body was a simple peasant girl. One of Julia's servants said as much to me.' I seized the cloth that Maximus held out and wrapped it round my vitals as I spoke, waiting for lanky Minimus to climb down from his perch and rub the rest of me.

However, the expected pleasant friction did not come. I looked round. Both the boys were gazing at me in astonishment.

Minimus, as usual, was the first to speak. 'You're talking of rumours at *our* villa, master?' He clambered off his stool.

The older boy added, incredulously, 'A *body*, did you say?'

Chapter Nine

It was only then I realised that the two boys didn't know about the corpse.

It had not occurred to me – but of course they were in Glevum when the discovery was made, and they had not spoken to anyone from the villa since. Kurso and I had not said anything to them when we arrived, and they had obviously been too busy with their knucklebones to listen at the door while I was telling the story to Gwellia and her maid. Even now they had only caught the very end of it and they were goggling with curiosity.

'You want Cilla to question the villa servants?' Maximus enquired, and Maximus added doubtfully, 'Does that mean you want her to question us as well?'

I was about to say it didn't, when it occurred to me it should. Of course these two might have some information of their own – perhaps without knowing that it was relevant. I looked at them sternly. 'You don't know anything about a body, I suppose? No rumours of a missing young man or peasant girl who might have been murdered a day or two ago?'

They glanced at each other in what looked like pure surprise, then – both together – raised their shoulders in a helpless shrug, spread their empty hands and pulled down the corners of their mouths like a pair of tragic masks. The effect, however, was quite comical. Marcus's expensive dancers could not have moved in more perfect unison.

As usual the younger boy was the first to find his tongue. 'I don't believe so, master. The only bodies we saw today were the ones that they were taking to the paupers' pit . . .'

'. . . His Excellence sent us to move them off the road, when he and Lucius wanted to drive through with the gig, on their way to the basilica this morning,' Maximus added.

'You probably saw them for yourself,' Minimus put in.

I nodded. I had indeed encountered the soldier with the mule and its grisly cargo – a pair of dead, broken bodies hanging upside down, their red hair dangling in the dust. Roman law did not permit the disposal of bodies within the city walls – not even those of beggars and common criminals – and these corpses were obviously on their way to be taken out and tipped without ceremony into the common pit.

'A pair of Silurians, by the look of it,' I said, then wished I hadn't. The red hair and a smattering of Celtic now and then suggested that these two boys had Silurian blood themselves.

Minimus, however, seemed eager to assist. 'I spoke to the mule-driver when I moved him on. A couple of brigands who'd been punished by the courts for robbery with violence on the Isca road.'

I nodded. The road which led from Glevum to the west was still dangerous – not only did the forests harbour wolves and bears, but the route was famous for the brigands who frequented it – some of them disaffected tribesmen from the borderlands, who had never quite accepted Roman rule and harried the supply trains and hapless travellers.

'Six people robbed and murdered this last moon alone. Marcus was telling Lucius, just the other day. Then these two yesterday . . .' the young slave went on.

'. . . an old man and his daughter, from the sound of it . . .'

'. . . stripped and robbed and cruelly stabbed to death . . .'

'. . . some soldiers caught the robbers almost in the act, with gold and silver in their saddlebags, and the man's possessions bundled in their packs.'

'Even then they pleaded innocence, at first . . .'

'. . . but the authorities beat a half-confession out of them . . .'

They were so keen to tell me all this that I had to smile. 'I heard there'd been a bit of trouble that way recently. But I don't think Silurian rebels are much help to us. Our body was discovered a great deal nearer home.' Then the implication struck me and I frowned. 'Though that makes it more surprising, when you think of it. If our killer had simply left the body on the road, instead of carefully concealing it in a ditch on Marcus's land, it would have been treated as a pauper, probably – somebody would have picked it up and thrown it in the pit, just like the bodies of the couple who were robbed – and there would have been no questions asked at all.'

'The body was concealed on His Excellence's land?' Minimus sounded shocked.

Gwellia interrupted with a kind of mock reproof. 'If you will finish helping your master to get dressed, and prevent him from shivering to death, perhaps he'll tell you all about it from the beginning – with less damage to his health.'

The boys looked chagrined, and set to at once. I found myself telling the story as they worked.

They listened, horrified. Although they were very much Celts by birth, they were raised in Roman households and the whole idea of an unburied body at the Lemuria alarmed them terribly.

When I had finished Maximus turned to his fellow slave and said, 'This happened about two days ago, so the master says. We were at the villa then – we didn't leave all day. I didn't notice anything unusual, did you?' Concern had interrupted the usual duologue. Gwellia's rebuke was not forgotten, though – he was making himself busy fetching garments as he spoke.

Minimus was already standing on the stool, slipping my clean tunic over my head and round my ears, so he sounded rather muffled as he replied. 'We attended Marcus in the morning, didn't we? Because Pulchrus had gone off to Londinium with the carts. And then there was that slave-trader who called in later on – the same one that Marcus always uses – bringing that useless, fair-headed little boy. Snowy, or whatever his name is.' He smoothed the tunic round my neck and got down to tie the belt.

Maximus watched him critically, then gave the garment-hem a little tug so it hung evenly. 'That's right. I don't know why the master ever bothered with the boy. We'd have done the job much better, if we'd had a chance. Not that I am sorry – I am happy to be here.' He was waiting with my toga, and as he spoke he began to loop it deftly round me and fold it into place.

'Why didn't he ask you to attend him, then?' I put in. Given the choice between Niveus and these two lively boys, I know which option I would have preferred.

Minimus pulled a face. 'We aren't sufficiently pretty for the purpose, I suppose. Marcus likes his pages to be glamorous. And didn't Pulchrus know it? I often wondered if he chose his name himself.'

I nodded, with a grin. 'Pulchrus' means 'the beautiful'. 'I would not be surprised.' I raised my arms to let the boys tuck in my toga-ends, which they did with practised skill.

Minimus gave me his cheerful, cheeky grin. ' "Handsome as Adoneus", Marcus used to say. You should have seen Pulchrus when he set off the other day . . .'

'That new scarlet tunic . . .'

'And that new fancy hat . . .'

'Just to impress them in Londinium!'

'More to impress Lucius, if you ask me,' Minimus observed. 'Marcus had the sewing girls make new tunics for all the household staff, before his cousin came. And a whole new wardrobe for himself and Julia . . .'

Maximus gave him a warning nudge. It was one thing to gossip about a page, quite another to discuss their former master in this way.

However, it was interesting to know. It explained my patron's unusual generosity in providing Junio's tunic and Cilla's clothes tonight. As Gwellia had commented when we were in the town, Marcus was happy to be benevolent if the gift did not involve him in actual expense. Not that I was guilty of ingratitude. The tunics in question may have been passed on, but they were of a quality I could not afford and had been worn so little that they looked like new; while

Junio's toga must have been purpose-bought, since even Marcus's discards bore that impressive purple stripe.

Cilla was chuckling. 'Well, Pulchrus managed to impress them in Glevum anyway. I overheard one of the guards at the basilica today remarking that they saw him riding past the gate with Lucius's hired driver and the wagon train. "Done up like a peacock, and twice as proud," they said.' She did her imitation of the Rhineland voice. ' "Too busy preening for the girls to even look at us." Mind you, he was speaking to one of Lucius's attendants at the time, and they are pretty vain themselves, it seems to me. Comes of being reared in the imperial city, I suppose.'

'It's the same up at the villa,' Minimus agreed. 'Won't mix with any of the household staff – insist on having a special sleeping room. Especially that awful chief slave, Hirsius, with his swanky olive tunic and his sneering ways. Thank Mars he's gone to Londinium with the luggage now. Pity that stupid bodyguard didn't go as well. Great stuck-up bully – I don't know why his master thinks so much of him . . .' He trailed off and looked anxiously at me, obviously fearing that he'd spoken out of turn.

'Well, he'll have to be questioned, if I do the job myself,' I said. 'No one who attended Lucius and Marcus in the basilica today could have heard the story of the corpse until they got back home. It is possible that one of them has something he could tell.'

Gwellia had been listening to all this with interest. 'I think it's more than possible. They are strangers to the district – and it seems the dead man is too, since there's no one missing in the area. Perhaps he was coming to visit one of them.'

It was a good point. I turned to the boys. 'Which reminds me of my question a little earlier. Apart from the slave-trader who brought Niveus – whom Marcus asked to come – there were no unexpected strangers at the villa on that day? No peasant women, or young men who might have walked across the farm, and evaded the attentions of the gatekeeper, perhaps?'

I sat down to allow Minimus to strap my sandals on. 'Nothing like that, master,' Maximus replied, and Minimus looked up to shake his head as well.

'Nobody came in, except the banquet guests. And none of them went missing, or we would have heard.'

'And no one at all for Lucius. He had a messenger soon after he arrived, bringing him a letter from his wife in Rome, but apart from that there has been no one wanting him at all.'

'What happened to that messenger?' I said without much hope. 'You saw him leave again? It isn't possible that he might be the corpse?'

Minimus grinned and shook his head. 'Certainly not the one you describe. He was a big, strong fellow – you definitely wouldn't take him for a girl – and armed with the biggest dagger that you ever saw. I suppose he had to be. Riding for miles and miles like that on unfrequented roads.'

'And he didn't have soft hands as a local page might have – they were like shovels and blistered with the reins,' Maximus added.

'Anyway, it couldn't possibly be him.' Minimus, as usual, had the most to say. 'You said the corpse is fresh, but he's been gone for days.'

Gwellia signalled to Cilla to stop working on her hair. She was looking thoughtful. 'That poor girl. I wonder who she was, in any case?'

Cilla put down the bone comb she was using. 'The girl who was killed by the Silures, do you mean?'

Gwellia shook her head. 'I mean the poor creature whose dress was on the corpse.'

The maidservant looked baffled. 'The peasant girl? But there wasn't one. The clothes were only there as a disguise. Probably purchased by the killer, purposely.'

'But don't you see?' I jumped up to my feet, suddenly understanding what had been obvious. 'Your mistress is quite right. That dress belonged to someone, and it's likely she is dead. No peasant would have parted with that garment willingly. Not with all that money hidden in the hem.'

There was a silence, and then Gwellia said, 'I wonder if we're wrong in assuming that the woman was young? Now I come to think of it, from the amount of money that you found in her skirts it seems more likely that she was of middle age. It takes a long time to accrue a fortune of that kind.'

Even as she spoke, I saw the force of what she was saying. My wife can surprise me with her perceptiveness. 'Unless she was particularly young and beautiful and had a rich admirer who paid for her services?'

She shook her head. 'In which case you'd expect her to have demanded finer clothes, not a greasy garment with worn sleeves and fraying hems.' She smiled. 'I don't think you know much about young women of that kind.'

I didn't. However, I did not wish to have my ignorance discussed before the slaves. 'You are quite right, wife,' I went on hastily. 'There is really no proof of the woman's age at all. All we know is that she was of middle height and slim.'

Gwellia nodded. 'You think she was well nurtured then?' It was a valid point. Many women, especially on the land, were skinny to the point of boniness: in a poor harvest peasants always starved, and the women often seemed to suffer most – perhaps because they gave what little food there was to their children or their husbands first.

I nodded. I thought about the dress, remembering the stitching at the waist, which had shown signs of tightness and of wear, as if it had been straining at the seams. 'I think she had enough to eat,' I said. 'Whatever age she turns out to have been, it was not starvation which caused her death, I think.'

'But you agree we are looking for another body?' my wife said thoughtfully.

'It rather looks like it.'

She came across the room, magnificent in her *stola*, and raked her fingers gently through my still-damp hair. 'My husband, I could wish that you weren't caught up in this. It is one thing to be asking questions at present, when your patron's here – quite another when he's gone to Rome. Who will there be to protect you then, if anything goes wrong?'

I shrugged, unwilling to admit that I had the same fears myself. 'Then, wife, I shall have to make sure that nothing goes amiss. In any case, my patron wants this solved before they go away – before the Lemuria begins, in fact.' Actually it was Julia who had said that to me, but it came to the same thing.

Gwellia was still looking doubtful. 'That only makes it worse. You won't have time to take things carefully. And from your description of what happened to the corpse, this killer will do anything to disguise his tracks. He must be merciless.'

I took her by the shoulders. 'I'm sorry, Gwellia. But if my patrons ask me, what else can I do?'

She shook herself away. 'I know you're right, of course. But I have a premonition. I don't like this at all.'

'You are just like Julia's mother-in-law, in Rome.' I tried to lighten the moment with a jest. 'She's famous for her premonitions.' I told her about what Lucius had said.

She gave a rueful smile. 'I'm not surprised that Julia doesn't want to go to Rome, if Marcus's family is all like Lucius. He looked so supercilious in the court today, I was relieved that Junio's manumission went off without a hitch – I would not have put it past the man to decide the business was beneath him and spoil it in some way. Though perhaps I misjudge him. We have never really met.'

'Well, it is time to go and meet him now,' I said. 'It will soon be getting dark, and they will be expecting us at the villa for the feast. It will take some time to get there – especially in new shoes. I can't walk quickly in a toga at the best of times.'

Maximus and Minimus were by my side at once. 'With your permission, master . . .'

'. . . our former mistress, Julia, instructed us that when you were ready to come . . .'

'. . . we were to run down to the villa and request the cart for you.'

'Did she?' I was very much surprised. 'Marcus has never sent a cart for me before, unless I was ill, at any rate.'

Minimus gave that toothy grin of his. 'She told him it would not impress his cousin if you came with dusty hems.'

I laughed aloud. 'Very well then, go and fetch the cart.'

And half an hour later the three of us were on our way – not in a cart but in Marcus's own gig, with Maximus and Minimus trotting at our side. We rode like patricians to the villa gates, where Aulus was waiting to scowl at me again and Niveus came out to show us shyly in.

Chapter Ten

My patron was given to extravagant feasts but that evening's banquet was the most elaborate I have ever seen. So for Gwellia, who had only rarely attended formal meals – let alone for Junio who had never dined in Roman style before – it must have been an amazing experience from the very start. Of course, we knew that all this conspicuous expense was entirely in Lucius's honour – Marcus was clearly determined to impress his visitor and would not have bothered with such luxuries for us – but we were the incidental beneficiaries all the same.

There were scented bowls of water in which to bathe our feet (though we had washed them just before we came) and there were slaves to kneel and do it and pat us dry again with spotless linen cloths. Then came more slaves with floral wreaths, napkins, and knives for us all – as though a man never carried his own cutlery to feasts.

Lucius, as the principal guest, reclined on Marcus's right while Julia occupied the position on his left, where – as the second-ranking guest – I'd half expected to be placed myself. Another couch and table had been arranged for us nearby, at right angles to the first, where I was similarly flanked by my wife and my new son, so that Junio – although a male – was in the most inferior place and the two women were close enough to talk. Apart from the dining couches, an empty stool stood by – obviously for Cilla when the moment came.

I suspected that Julia had had a hand in these seating arrangements, which were unusual – since women did not usually sit at the top table in this way – but actually very cleverly designed. Making me the centre of a table of my own was a kind of compliment and compensated for the fact that I was not at Marcus's side. Besides, it kept Junio (who was in any case a little ill at ease) as far as possible from Lucius, who had probably never before sat down to dinner with a man who at breakfast time was legally his slave. Above all, I think, our hostess wanted to have the higher seat herself, so that she could hear what was being said between her husband and his guest and if necessary steer the conversation carefully away from any possible allusion to the dead man in the yard.

Whatever her reasons for the table-placing, I was glad of it. I was able to whisper instructions to my former slave when – as happened more than once – he was not sure of proper etiquette or had some difficulty in eating lying down, with only one elbow to support himself. In his former short life as a Roman slave, he had never served at table, and we followed Celtic customs in our house.

Once the company was settled Marcus clapped his hands. A player came in with a lute and sang a poem in praise of Lucius; after that a cymbal clashed, and then the meal began. It was a full-scale three-part dinner, no expense spared. The 'tasting course' alone was meal enough for me – eggs, oysters, radishes, and sardines. The serving boys who came in with the platters – silver ones, no pewterware tonight! – were struggling beneath the weight of them. Square loaves of wheat and rye bread were brought in, sweet and spiced, new-baked on the premises from flour grown and milled – as Marcus loftily observed – 'within a thousand paces of this spot'.

Lucius looked pained and commented that Rome was not given to such rustic practices and that he, personally, patronised a baker who made special loaves for him. However, I noticed that he seemed to like the bread, and even more the *mulsum*, or sweet wine, that followed it.

When we had eaten far more than we should, the finger-bowls were passed around and, as I showed Junio how to rinse his hands, first the acrobats and then the dwarves whom we'd seen on the cart came in and entertained us for a time, to give our digestion a little space to work. They were energetic and amusing, and working to impress, until Marcus decided that his guest was getting bored and dismissed them in favour of a singer with a lyre.

After a trio of short songs, he too was sent away, and the main portion of the evening began. There were a full seven courses ('one for each of us, and one for luck', as Junio said later, in astonishment): fish, goose with lovage, lamb with pears and wine, and a main central course of roasted venison (with the choicest portion going to Lucius, of course) followed by the lighter dishes: stuffed sow's udders – a Roman favourite, this – a dish of honeyed dormice, and, last of all, the larks. It was of course unthinkable to refuse a dish outright, though Marcus was sufficiently aware of my tastes to ensure that that dreadful fish sauce the Romans like so much was offered as a condiment and not put on the food before it came to table.

I had experienced Roman feasts before, though not generally on this scale, and remembered to save myself some space, and Gwellia only ever took a taste of every dish; but despite my best instructions that he should do the same, Junio soon began to look a little green. I reminded him that it was possible to slip outside to tickle his throat and bring a little up, and so make room for what was yet to come, but he was too embarrassed to do it. Lucius, however, had no such provincial qualms and he soon strode out to vomit before returning to eat some more.

'Now is your chance,' I said to Junio. 'You can be assured it's quite acceptable, now he has led the way. I will come with you if you like.' He flashed me a queasy, thankful smile, and we went out into the little room which Marcus ordered his servants to prepare when he held feasts, where Junio made use of the large brass bowl and one of the goose feathers from the nearby pot, provided for the purpose by our thoughtful host.

When he stood up, gasping, he looked more himself. 'If these are the privileges of citizenship,' he said unsteadily, 'perhaps it is safer to remain a slave. Though I enjoyed the bath!' He gave a wobbly grin. 'Even the mighty Lucius deigned to speak to me, once he was stripped of his fancy toga-stripes – though only about that wretched corpse, of course. He seemed to think I might know who it was.'

I waited for him to rinse his face in the jug of water, and for the slave who brought it to retire again, before I took him gently by the arm. 'You told him what we had discovered, I suppose? The mark round the neck, and everything?'

'Yes, of course.' He frowned. 'Perhaps I shouldn't have, but I thought if you'd told Marcus . . .'

I waved his fears aside. 'Lucius had no theories about the body, then?'

He made a face. 'I don't imagine that he would have told me if he did. I'm not much better than a slave to him – he would not have spoken to me at all, if he'd not been so keen to know what I had seen.'

I nodded. 'It would be bad form to show his host that he was curious about anything so vulgar as a corpse.'

'And he did not really converse with me at all. He just asked questions – at least till Marcus came, and then he talked exclusively to him – mostly about things in Rome I didn't understand.'

'Which is what I imagine we shall find him doing now,' I said. 'If you feel well enough to go back to the feast? We've been out here long enough.'

I was right. When we returned it was to find Lucius – lubricated perhaps by all the *mulsum* he had drunk – holding forth about politics and literature in Rome. He was gesturing with a choice portion of lark's leg as he spoke, while Marcus chipped in with witty epigrams, which clearly were quotations from some famous poet – though of course I couldn't tell you who it was. My son caught my eye as he regained his seat, and winked.

I frowned a warning at him. A banquet is always seen as an opportunity for this sort of clever talk, which is regarded as a kind of social art. However, I am not particularly interested in such debates myself, and would have much preferred to watch the entertainment now on offer – a hapless conjuror who had just appeared, and was performing to no one in particular. He was a skinny old man in a tattered silver robe, who was making little coloured balls appear and disappear, though nobody was watching except me. Julia and Gwellia, who were reclining very close, were deep in some female conversation of their own, while Junio was doing what I ought to be doing myself – pretending to follow what Lucius had to say, with an expression of rapt attention on his face.

I composed myself into a similar position, and tried to assume an interested look while Marcus's cousin boasted of his senatorial friends and the lavish banquets that he'd attended at the court.

'Of course the Emperor is famous for the brilliance of his feasts,' Lucius observed. 'You know he had a pair of hunchback dwarves smeared with mustard and served up on a plate?'

'Not to eat them, surely?' Marcus asked, appalled.

His cousin smiled – contriving to look pitying and disdainful both at once. 'Of course not. Simply to display them as an amusement for his guests. At court it is often the spectacle that counts – something unusual to catch the eye.' His scathing glance and lofty tone of voice suggested his contempt for conjurors. 'Caesar is always hungry for variety.'

'That is why you were so interested in those people who were here the other day?' Julia enquired, with the sweetest of smiles but clearly stung by Lucius's none-too-veiled disparagement. 'The ones that you engaged? I admit the mimic was a clever turn and very funny, but I should have thought there were a thousand snake-charmers in Rome? Or perhaps you don't have vipers of that kind over there?' It was not usual for women to join in men's talk at a feast, unless by invitation – especially when the subject is at all political – and Marcus looked rather disapprovingly at her. She covered the moment by adding instantly, with every show of a hostess's concern, 'But I see your glass is empty, cousin.'

She gestured to the little serving boy who was carrying the wine – in a silver *crater* half as big as he was – to go round and offer more refreshments to the guests (beginning with Lucius, of course) then turned back to her murmured conversation with my wife.

The wine was delicately watered, best Falernian. No doubt it had been carefully selected, warmed and mixed, but all Roman wine tastes much the same to me. I can only judge the quality by the speed with which it dulls my wits, and this one was doing that quite rapidly. I knew that at any moment the repartee would cease, and we should be obliged to rise while Marcus went over to the altar niche and made oblations to the household gods. He had chosen the old-fashioned Roman timing of the ritual in deference to his guest (these days people tended to make their sacrifices before the feast began), and I did not want to create a spectacle by tripping over my toga in the course of it. I was a little wary, therefore, when the serving boy approached and offered to fill my goblet to the brim again.

'More wine, citizen?'

I nodded. I almost wished that I could drink the weaker, more watered version that the ladies were served. However, it might be considered rude if I refused. 'A very little, then.'

I was so concerned with preventing him from pouring more than a thumb's-width or two that I was paying little attention to the table talk, which was now about the acts which Lucius had singled out to send to Rome. I did, however, realise that Marcus was amused.

'I hope for your sake, cousin, that they divert the Emperor, and you are properly rewarded. Though your choice would not have been mine. That snake-charmer had clearly painted the viper markings on his snakes. I suspect that really they were harmless ones, though what he did with them was quite amusing, in its way.'

A red flush suffused Lucius's thin, patrician cheeks. 'I think he will serve the purpose,' he observed, in a tone of voice so prim that it made me wonder what lewdness the act contained. 'Of course, if the fellow fails to please, he will be taken out and flogged.' He picked the last morsels from his lark, and tossed the bones away. 'Now, if we are ready? I have finished here, I think.'

It was a kind of signal. Everybody stood. The conjuror, who had moved on to doing something with a piece of cloth – miraculously changing it from red to blue somehow – was unceremoniously hustled off, still without having at any point enjoyed the attention of his so-called audience. An uncomfortable silence fell across the room.

Marcus pulled his toga up to form a hood and clapped his hands three times, whereupon a senior slave appeared, bearing a salver laid with salt and wheat, and a little jug of what I knew was wine. There was a hush while the offering was made. Marcus muttered the necessary words and then resumed his place, and after a little embarrassed shuffling we all lay down again.

It was time for the grand finale of the meal – the 'second tables' as the saying goes. With the religious business over, the mood was lighter now. The cymbal clashed, the singer with the lyre came in again, and so did Cilla, looking flushed and proud. Marcus stretched out a hand in welcome, and even Lucius gave a frosty smile, but in the circumstances it was up to me to speak. I rose to greet her.

'Come, slave, I invite you to join us while we dine,' I said. 'In public and in the presence of these Roman citizens, I call upon this company to witness what I do.'

It was a version of the required formula, and everybody understood what it implied. Cilla shyly took the stool – sitting upright rather than reclining, certainly, but officially a member of the dining party now, though she was not yet fully freed. One servant brought her a napkin and a wreath, while another brought a platter on which reposed a single piece of bread and a cup containing a very little wine. He knelt before her and presented it.

Cilla took the symbolic food and drink, and took a tiny mouthful from each of them in turn. She was trembling so much that I could see her fingers shake, but once the token helpings had duly passed her lips it was Marcus's turn to stand up and declaim. 'We have witnessed Cilla eating and drinking at a feast at the invitation of her master. I therefore declare that, by legal custom, she is considered freed and is henceforward no longer held in servitude.'

I applauded loudly and so did most of us – although Lucius contented himself with a brief and silent tapping of three fingers on his palm – and Cilla was overcome with so much self-consciousness that she swallowed the crumb of bread too fast and almost choked herself.

That broke the tension. Everybody laughed, and presently the *secundae mensae* were brought in, tray after tray of delicious honeyed things. Marcus's kitchens had excelled themselves. There were sweet cakes, spiced cakes and peppered strawberries followed by apple and blackberry stew, fresh fruit, dried fruit, stuffed dates, figs, and – my personal favourite – a sort of sweetened pie made of raisins, bread and spices sprinkled with honeyed milk and butter till it formed a crusty cake.

All the gentlemen left the table more than once to make use of the goose feathers and the bowl next door, though the ladies merely nibbled at the tempting treats and showed the refinement expected of their sex – it would have been ill-mannered on their part to go out and follow suit.

There was more wine and more music, although – since Lucius was 'King of the Feast' if anybody was, and there were females in the company – there was none of the elaborate 'drinking on command' that sometimes accompanies such events elsewhere. After a little time, the females withdrew – it is not considered proper for wives to drink too much – and then at last the dancing girls came on.

The performance might have lasted perhaps half an hour, although it seemed at the time to be over in a flash. Looking back I find it hard to imagine how girls can bend like that. They must have bones like anybody else, but the way they swayed and rippled and wiggled different portions of themselves was enough to make a blind man sit and stare. The costumes, too, were seen to full effect, the bright, floating fabrics parting now and then to reveal a tantalising glimpse of thigh or breast. They were accompanied by the middle-aged dragon-lady on a flute and the skinny fellow in the silver coat, who had appeared again, thumping out a rhythm on a hollow, empty cask.

There was no question of the apathy that had faced his conjuring: every eye was fixed on this performance from the start, though not all of the eyes were equally approving. I found that I was a little scandalised myself – especially when one of the more lissom of the girls began performing very close to me, affording a close view of her considerable assets and clicking a pair of wooden clappers in time to every bounce. I tore my glance away from the gyrating flesh and saw that every male in the room had a personal dancer doing much the same for him.

I wondered how Lucius was enjoying this. Presumably he was accustomed to such things at court, but only a faint pinkness round his patrician nose gave any indication that he was other than quite dispassionately bored – and even that hint of colour might have been caused by the quantity of watered wine that he'd imbibed.

I could not look with any decency at what was wiggling suggestively right before my face. I glanced round the room. Junio was revelling in this first experience (it was likely to be the last for a long time, too, I thought – I could not afford this kind of luxury, even if I had wanted to). He was watching every movement with eager eyes, leaning forward on his seat to get a better view, with a smile of youthful disbelief at what he saw.

Marcus, however, seemed preoccupied. I wondered if the dead body in the stable block was on his mind, or whether he was simply dismayed by Lucius. He watched the performance with less interest than he usually displayed – even when the dancers were not half as good as these – and I actually saw him glance towards the water-candle twice, as if he were impatient for the night to end.

I went back to watching my gyrating nymph, who had now retreated by a foot or two, and found I was quite sorry when the music stopped and the performance came to a memorable end with a tableau that was stunning in its suggestiveness. Marcus was the first to lead the clapping and my son and I joined in – though Junio was too breathless even to shout '*Macte!*'

Lucius, too, was sufficiently condescending to applaud and he watched the dancers all the way as they shimmered and shimmied through the door. Perhaps he had enjoyed it more than he allowed. Marcus seemed to think so.

'There, cousin,' he said, with a triumphant smile. 'Hispanic dancing girls, Britannia style. Not naked, as you will observe, but sometimes what's half hidden is more exciting than a nude. And these are the best available, is that not so, madam?'

The flautist manager, who was collecting up the scarves her troupe had strewn about, gave him a mirthless smile. 'I hope so, Excellence. We set our standards high. Turn down twenty girls for every one we take. They aren't all genuinely from Iberia, of course, but the best ones are, because they teach them young. You can't learn to dance like that when all your bones are set.' She waited, politely, to see if Marcus spoke, and when he didn't she went on, 'And now, if you've finished with me, Excellence, I must round up the girls.'

She disappeared, like an outsize female sheepdog, and we heard her yapping in the courtyard as she herded up her flock.

It was late now, and time for us male diners to retire as well. Our wives would be sleepily awaiting us, huddling over braziers in a room nearby, and my little party had a longish walk before we found our beds. We got to our feet – some of us a little more unsteadily than others – and slaves emerged smoothly from the shadows by the wall to remove our lopsided banquet wreaths and escort us from the room.

Marcus and Lucius led the way, of course. I was the last

to leave, and already slaves were brushing the floor and scraping the portions of uneaten food all together on to one big dish, to set on the altar of the household gods. I grinned. They must be hoping that the divinities had no appetite tonight, so that in the morning they could have a feast themselves.

I turned and followed Junio out to look for Cilla and my waiting wife.

Chapter Eleven

When I got out into the atrium, it was to find Marcus and his cousin alone – apart from the usual attendant slaves, of course. The ladies were nowhere to be seen. Lucius was loudly complaining of the cold, despite the glow of a cheerful brazier which had been lit while we were lying down to dine.

'The climate in this province is so unpleasant, cousin, that I don't know how you have survived it for so long.' He looked disparagingly round the handsome room, with its fine mosaic of aquatic scenes. 'No wonder that your atrium is roofed, and you have opted for a pavement picture instead of a real pool. If the room was on the Roman pattern you would die of chill.' He blew theatrically on hands. 'Indeed, with your permission, citizens, I think I shall retire to my sleeping room.'

Marcus wore a smile which did not reach his eyes. 'I believe you will find it a little warmer there. You seem to have been comfortable in it up to now. Of course, you have the bedchamber which used to be my own, and like the dining room it has a hypercaust.'

'Of course,' Lucius acknowledged, although he contrived to sound as if such luxuries as underfloor heating were commonplace. 'My own slave will attend me; I need not trouble yours. If you will simply send me another jug of wine, and perhaps some oil for my lamp? I like to keep one burning – the mornings in this province are so overcast, and the nights so damnably dreary. So, I will say goodnight. My apologies to the ladies, naturally.' He bowed distantly, and turned to where his slave was waiting with a taper to light him to his room.

Marcus watched him go. He said nothing, but from the way he tapped his hand against his thigh I knew that my patron was seething inwardly. I heard him mutter, 'Insufferable man! They should have named him Odius, not Lucius, at his *bulla* ceremony.'

'Excellence?' I gave him an uncomfortable glance. There were servants in the room, and though Marcus's household was commendably faithful on the whole, it was always possible that Lucius's purse had bought a pair of spying eyes and ears.

Marcus seemed to realise what I was hinting at. He frowned. 'I'm worried about him. I'm sure he has already written to my mother about this wretched corpse – he sent a messenger post-haste this afternoon, so half of Rome will know about it by the time we arrive. If we are not careful we shall be thought *nefastus*' – he meant unlucky, if not downright out of favour with the gods – 'and certainly inauspicious to do business with. That would work against me in all my dealings there, and it's just the sort of thing that would please Lucius very much: I'd have to throw myself upon his patronage and make him look important by comparison. Cost me a fortune in propitiatory sacrifice as well. I might have to do that in any case, I fear. You haven't made any progress with the mystery, Libertus, I suppose?'

It was the first time he had mentioned the matter since

we'd arrived to feast, and he said it casually enough, but I could see by his face that he had thought of little else.

I shook my head. 'Unfortunately not. I have made a few enquiries but I've not got very far. I promised Aulus I would tell you that he tried to help.'

Marcus raised his eyebrows. 'Let me know if he tells you anything of use. You can try again tomorrow. I am counting on your help.' He sighed. 'And, for Pluto's sake, don't mention to Julia what I told you about Rome. She is unwilling enough to go there as it is.'

'Where are the ladies, anyway?' I said, attempting to lighten the moment with a smile.

Marcus looked towards Niveus who was standing by the wall.

'They have gone with my mistress to the other wing. I believe they were going to look in at Marcellinus while he slept,' the page said earnestly. 'Should I go and fetch them?'

Marcus looked a little disapproving. He and Julia were unfashionably besotted with their son, but cooing over children was not the Roman way.

'Doubtless Gwellia suggested it,' I said. 'And Cilla of course was an attendant in this house when the child was very young.' I turned to Niveus. 'But it is long past dark and the night is getting cold – outside this warm villa at any rate – and we should make our preparations to depart at once.'

'When you have spoken to the ladies,' Marcus murmured to his page, 'you can go and fetch Minimus and Maximus as well.'

I smiled as Niveus scuttled from the room. I had almost forgotten that the boys were lent to me, and would be waiting in the servants' room to escort us home. I was just wondering whether I should ask for torches – bundles of small branches dipped in pitch and set alight – so that the slaves could light us on our way, when Marcus said, 'The cart is standing by to take the dancing girls back to Glevum. Why don't you ride with them? They will almost pass your door.'

'Tonight?' I muttered stupidly. Of course, with Marcus's warrant the cart could use the military road, which was so well made that it was possible to travel quickly, even in the dark. In fact, with the prohibition on wheeled traffic in the town by day, there was often quite a queue of carts and wagons lining up at dusk – a mass of groaning wheels and shouted oaths, as red-faced men with torches jostled to get in through the gates.

Marcus was amused. 'I did offer them accommodation here tonight, but the chaperon refused. Said it would be too crowded in our extra sleeping room, and they are moving on to Isca tomorrow anyway – the commander there has heard of them and wants them for a feast. Supposing Lucius hasn't commandeered them for the Emperor, that is. But of course he pretends that he's not interested in them, because they have much more exciting dancing girls in Rome. Though—' He broke off as the door opened and our wives came in.

They were attended by Atalanta, the plain maidservant I'd spoken to earlier. She gave me a special, knowing smile, as if there was some understanding between the two of us, and then stood back against the wall where Niveus had been. Cilla shuffled in behind them, a little nervously.

'I am sorry that we delayed you, citizens.' Julia was as charming as always as she addressed me with a smile. 'We have been talking about children, now that Gwellia officially has a son as well. The gods go with you on your journey home, especially Junio and Cilla on their first night not as slaves. Has Marcus suggested that you use the cart?'

I hesitated. 'You are thoughtful, lady, but it would be a squeeze – I saw the number of people who got out of it before, and my wife and family are in their finest clothes.'

Gwellia had no such qualms. 'A ride home in the cart? That would be wonderful. I don't like walking along the lane at night, even attended by servants. There are too many robbers and brigands on the roads. And after they found that poor creature in the ditch, not thirty paces from the roundhouse door . . .' She shuddered. 'What does a little crumpling matter, in comparison to that?'

Julia smiled. 'Then it is quite agreed. Maximus and Minimus can carry extra torches to light the way. It will help the driver on the unpaved road. Ah, here they come, I think.'

But it was not my servants who burst in as she spoke. It was Niveus – and he was looking a little pink-faced and dismayed. 'Your pardon, Excellence. The lady who leads the dancing troupe . . .' He paused, and glanced at me. 'She seemed to think that she had not been paid enough.'

'Tell her that she is to put her people on the cart, but make sure that they leave a decent space for this citizen and his family – for the first part of the journey, anyway. As for the other matter, I will see to that, as soon as the cart has come round to the front.'

'As you command.' Niveus looked unwilling to face the dancing mistress with this news but he disappeared into the court again. Gwellia and our little party made our last farewells, and when the red-haired slaves appeared – with torches at the ready – we said goodnight and Atalanta took us to the gate.

The smell of onions and bad breath told me that Aulus was on duty still. He came out, all solicitousness, to usher Cilla and my wife into the shelter of his cell 'while they are waiting for the cart', he told me with a smile.

Aulus's smile was even less attractive than his scowl, and I noticed that while ushering Cilla into his nasty little niche he found it necessary to touch her several times, although she was smart enough to move away from him. However, it was not very long before we heard the cart, and saw the flaring torches which the driver had set in the metal holders on either side of him. There would be a bucket of glowing embers somewhere in the cart, with a pierced lid, from which he could light another pitch-dipped torch when and if the present ones went out. I only hoped I wasn't going to have to sit too close to that bucket on my journey home. Warmth is a pleasure, but – even set inside a larger pot – an unstable brazier on a moving cart is not particularly comforting.

I need not have worried. There was room for us – the dwarves and the acrobats had presumably accepted the offer of a servant's mattress for the night – and the girls were huddled together, giggling, at the far end of the cart, under the stern eye of their chaperon and the skinny musician-conjuror who seemed to be her husband. They had somehow managed to herd the girls so that we had room enough to stand, and by holding on to the framework of the cart we could keep our balance as it lurched away, though I found myself jammed uncomfortably face to face with the dancing woman.

She glared at me, her face ghastly in the light of the torches. Maximus and Minimus were trotting at the wheels, so I was able to make out her expression.

I countered with a smile. 'You must be very proud of your performers,' I remarked, though the words came out in little jerks in rhythm with the cart. She made no reply, but we were forced into uneasy intimacy by our position, and I tried again. 'It is quite an honour to be chosen by His Excellence.'

That stung her into speech. 'Honour! I suppose so. Just as well. Two rotten *denarii* – that's all he's paid tonight. And I was fool enough to fall for it – all on the promise that we might get invited to serve the Emperor. But one look at that patrician and you could tell it was no use, and of course by then it was too late to ask a higher fee. So our clever magistrate gets a bargain at his feast. I wouldn't have been much worse off if I'd agreed to pay the bribe! Two *denarii* – I ask you! For girls who dance like that.' She spat contemptuously. 'It doesn't even pay me for recruiting them.'

'They do dance very . . . well,' I said. I had been about to say something else, but I remembered that my wife could overhear. 'Girls who move like that must be difficult to find.'

'You would not believe the trouble I have.' Her tongue was loosened now. 'Not in finding candidates – there are always willing girls. We've had three people want to join us since we've been staying here. But they're so rarely suitable. One looked very likely, a nice-looking girl. Nicely spoken, too: it was obvious she'd been properly brought up. I asked her to pick up her *stola* so I could see her legs, and she was horrified. I could have asked a hefty fee for her, but the next day her father came and found her and took her home again. Turned out she didn't like his second wife and simply wanted to get away from home. Just as well we didn't try to use her in the show. Caused enough trouble as it was – he behaved as if we'd taken on a slave that ran away.'

'Does that happen often? Fugitives, I mean?'

She shook her head. 'More often girls who think it's glamorous – simply want to do something different with their lives. Of course, it isn't glamorous at all. The training's very arduous, and they get too old for it and there's little chance of marrying afterwards.' She smiled. 'We do get one or two who get an offer, though, when we put on a show for someone rich – not as wives, of course, but as concubines and slaves – and I usually won't stand in their way, although of course I expect a recompense. What I can't put up with are the ones who get themselves with child, spoil the troupe, waste all those training hours, and not even a financial reward to show for it. Unfortunately there's always someone who is fool enough to fall for that.'

'And what becomes of them?' Junio had been listening. I knew that, like me, he was wondering if this might be relevant – to our mystery.

She looked surprised. 'Occasionally, if they are good-looking, I can sell them on as slaves, and then at least they have a roof above their heads. But the rest of them . . .' She shrugged her shoulders. 'I have to turn them out. I suppose they beg, or work as prostitutes – and I have to find a substitute, sometimes jolly quickly too.'

'And you have plenty of suitable candidates?' I said.

'Suitable candidates?' She laughed. 'And unsuitable as well. We had a smelly peasant turn up the other day – grimy and graceless as it's possible to be.'

'A peasant?' I was paying close attention now. Gwellia,

behind me, clutched my hand, and I realised that she, too, was listening to every word.

'Pudgy face, thick ankles, rawhide boots and a plaid robe she obviously hadn't changed for years,' the chaperon said. 'About as flexible as a chest-plough and as erotic too – her hair was bleached with that awful lime you people use, and it hung in stinking braids right to her waist.'

'Really?' I was genuinely surprised. Celtic warriors at one time used to lime their hair, and wear it in thick spikes to scare the enemy, but it was hardly a thing that females often did – any more than they wore earrings or moustaches. Anyway, the lime paste smelt disgusting, as the woman said.

She nodded. 'I think she must have been dimwitted, but she'd heard about the troupe – swore she had been promised that I would take her on, and she had dreams of going to Rome with us. Of course, I told her in no uncertain . . .' She faltered to a stop. I realised that the cart had halted too. I had been so interested in her story that I hadn't noticed it.

'Well, citizen, are you getting down or not?' the cart-driver shouted, and Junio and I scrambled off and assisted the two women to get down after us.

Gwellia leaned towards me as I helped her down and held her close. 'So, husband, your peasant was probably a young girl after all.' She gave me a quick squeeze. 'Now I must go inside. It is getting late and there are household tasks to do.' And with that she disengaged herself and went into the house, together with Cilla and the slaves, while I stood thoughtfully watching the wagon lumber off. Suddenly, it seemed, there was a lot to think about.

The dancing woman, however, saw me lingering and was

determined to complete her tale. She leaned over the rear plank of the cart, and shouted after me, 'You know she even offered me a bribe to take her on? If people want to join us, they are prepared to pay.'

Bribe? I was thinking about the coins we'd discovered in the skirt, but the cart was already disappearing down the lane. I did, however, have the wit to call, 'What did she try to bribe you with?'

Her voice came floating back to me as the cart lurched on. 'Looked like a gold *aureus*, but I don't suppose it was. More likely a forgery – where would a peasant get a coin . . . like . . . that?'

They turned a corner and the cart was gone.

'Master . . . I mean, Father?' Junio had been standing at my elbow all this time. He peered at me in the darkness. 'It must be, don't you think . . . ? The person who owned the dress?'

I nodded. 'It gives us a description to go on, anyway. In the morning, perhaps we can find out who she was. In the meantime, I should talk to Cilla, briefly, in case she found out anything of use. No doubt she will be bursting to tell us if she did.' I led the way into the roundhouse as I spoke.

But Cilla had disappointingly little to report. None of the villa staff had anything to say about the corpse, except that they wished it buried before the coming festival, and no one had seen a stranger calling at the house.

Of course, Cilla being Cilla, she was anxious to expand and would have given me a word for word account, but by this time it was very late indeed. Gwellia was making signs to me that it was time to go to bed and the boys were doing the last chore of the day, raking some of the ashes round the baking pot so that the yeast cakes could cook in the embers overnight.

'We'll talk again tomorrow, Cilla,' I said with a yawn. 'It's been a long, exciting day and an exhausting one.'

She nodded and went out to the servants' hut where she still had a bed.

Gwellia had already lain down and gone to sleep. I took my sandals and my toga off, snuffed out the taper and did the same myself.

Chapter Twelve

When I awoke next morning it was long past dawn – perhaps Marcus's rich food and wine had had some effect on me. Gwellia was obviously already up, and so was the rest of the household by the look of it – the roundhouse was empty, and two rapidly cooling yeast cakes were standing on a plate, all that remained in a platter full of crumbs. Yet the fire was burning brightly – someone had blown the embers into life again and brought in fresh kindling to make a cheerful blaze. Somehow I seemed to have slept through all of this.

I felt a little twinge of discontent. Why hadn't Junio awakened me? And then I remembered – that was over now. He was not my slave. I could no longer count on him to do that sort of thing.

I crawled out from my cover, pulled an extra tunic over the one I had been sleeping in, and sat down on the stool to eat my solitary meal. For some reason I wasn't hungry, though the cakes were excellent. I decided I must have had too much to eat the night before.

Gwellia would be concerned if I did not eat at all – she had been anxious lately to build my strength again – and the yeast cakes had been made on my account, I knew. I took a listless bite at one of them, but I had scarcely done so before a face peered round the door, and Minimus was grinning in at me.

'Ah, master, I see you are awake!' He was carrying a pitcher of fresh water from the stream, and he came over to my side to pick up a beaker and pour some into it. 'I was told not to rouse you until you'd had your sleep.' He passed me the drinking vessel with a smile. 'The mistress has gone out gathering lichens to boil up for a dye, and taken Cilla with her – to show her how, she says. And the young master has taken Maximus and gone out down the lane.'

'The young master?' I was about to say, when I realised that he was talking about Junio, of course, so I changed the question to 'Did he say where he was going?'

Enthusiastic nods. 'I was to tell you that he was going back to the villa straight away. He knew you wanted to talk to the land slaves Stygius sent out to ask questions yesterday. He thought it would be helpful if he made a start, by finding out which of them it was who spoke to the father of the Celtic girl who ran away with a man to join an entertainment troupe. To see if she matched the description that you had.' He looked enquiringly at me. 'I think that's what he said. Does it make sense to you?'

My spirits had risen, but I tried to sound judicious. 'I think so. We heard about this girl yesterday from one of Stygius's slaves.' I took another bite of breakfast. 'It didn't seem very important at the time, because the slaves had been asking about missing girls, and we knew by the time they returned that we were dealing with a man. But we still have to find the owner of the dress, so if Junio can find out where her parents live we can check with them and see if her appearance tallies with what we heard from the dancing woman last night. It may not turn out to be good news for the family, though, if it does.'

Minimus refilled my beaker before I'd even asked. 'Do you want me to escort you to the villa later on? Your son presumed you'd want to join him when you'd breakfasted.'

I'd finished my first yeast cake now, and I'd found my appetite. I picked up the second and bit into it. It was even more delicious than the first. 'We can't be certain that this is the girl we want,' I said, through a mouthful of warm crumbs. 'But it is at least a possibility. And with hair like that she should not be too difficult to trace.'

Minimus looked enquiring. 'Why, master? What was so unusual about her hair?'

Of course, he had been carrying the torch beside the cart last night and hadn't heard what our informant said, so I outlined the description for his benefit. 'Long, limed, yellow braids,' I finished. 'There can't be many girls of that description in the locality.' I had finished my second yeast cake by this time and I held my beaker out expecting him to fill it, but he did not do so, although he had the pitcher in his hand.

I looked at him in surprise. He was frowning vaguely into the water jug as if he might find inspiration there. 'I think I might possibly have seen that girl myself,' he said at last. 'I noticed someone talking to Aulus one day in the lane – the morning before the civic feast, it must have been – and she had yellow hair. Not ordinary yellow, like Julia's hair slaves have – it was that strange greenish tinge that comes from using lime. I've seen Celtic noblemen whose hair looked just the same. She had it in a great long plait that hung down to her knees. It sounds rather like the same person, doesn't it?'

I pushed my plate away and spoke quite sternly. 'Why did you not mention this before? I asked you yesterday if you had seen any peasant women.'

I expected a spirited defence, such as Junio would have given. Minimus, however, simply said, 'I'm truly sorry, master,' and looked abjectly at me. 'I didn't realise . . .' He stiffened his shoulders as if he expected to receive a blow.

I said, as gently as I could, 'Realise what? That this might be important? After what I'd said?'

He looked at me apologetically. 'That she might be a peasant, master. She didn't look like one. I thought she was a servant on her way to market in the town. She was carrying something in a sack, and she was wearing a colourful sort of tunic thing. I noticed it because it was particularly short.'

'A tunic?' I was disappointed now. Perhaps this was a false trail after all.

He nodded. 'The flimsy sort that slave girls sometimes wear when they are expected to entertain their masters – you know the sort of thing. So short that her hair hung longer than her hems. Probably quite low round the arms and neckline too, but she had a shawl about her shoulders, to cover up the top.' He frowned. 'She certainly wasn't wearing a plaid dress of the kind you talked about – although it might have been in the parcel, I suppose. And she was wearing the sort of heavy boots the woman described. Horrible clumpy shapeless ones – you know, the home-made kind!'

He spoke with the disgust of someone who had always worn custom-made shoes and sandals, cut and sewn to fit, and had never tied pieces of fresh cowskin round his feet – raw side inward, as many peasants do – and been obliged to squelch about until the leather self-cured in place.

I frowned. 'Rough boots? You are sure of that? Not the sort of footwear you'd expect a household slave to wear.'

He looked at me a moment, and then said in surprise, 'Of course not, master. I should have thought of that. What owner would supply his maidservant with such awful ugly boots? They made her legs look even thicker and stumpier than they were.' He grinned. 'You couldn't help but notice, because the tunic was so short. I even wondered if she was a . . . well . . . if she wasn't exactly a servant in the normal sense.'

I nodded. There were several brothels in the *colonia*, just as there are in every Roman town, and the girls in some of them wear tunics, too – at least to start with – if one can believe the advertising paintings on the wall. And some customers have strange fetishes about footwear, I believe. 'So when you saw her with Aulus, what did you suppose . . . ?' It was my turn to grin.

He did not smile in answer, but said earnestly, 'I thought that she was lost. She was on foot and she seemed to be asking directions, or something of the kind – I remember Aulus pointing down the lane as if he was showing her the old route into town. The gatekeepers often have strangers asking them the way, if they have tried to take a short cut down the ancient tracks and missed their road. I simply thought that she had lost her bearings in the woods. In fact, I had forgotten all about her till you described the lime-bleached plaits.' He frowned. 'But why is she important, master?'

'She might well be the owner of the clothes the body was dressed in when it was found. The robe could have been in the parcel she was carrying, as you say, and we now know that she, or someone very like her, offered the dancing troupe a bribe to join the troupe. And that someone was wearing a plaid garment at the time.'

'So isn't it likely she simply sold it on – especially if she hoped to join the dancing girls?' That bashful grin again. 'Woollen plaid is not exactly the most erotic kind of dress, but it's still worth money in the marketplace. Lots of stall-holders would gladly pay to take it off her hands, even if it was a little frayed.'

'Sell it? With all that money in the hem?' I shook my head. 'I wonder if Junio's been able to find out who she was. The gods alone know where she is by now – alive or dead – but it might yet be possible at least to find out where she went to when she left the villa gates.' I did a little calculation in my head. 'That can't have been the same day she disappeared from home.'

Suddenly I was anxious to be at the villa too, making enquiries about what the land slaves knew. There was no time to be lost. I seized the jug and rinsed my face in it, and picked up my warm cloak from the hook beside the door. 'Let's go and see what Aulus has to say. Go and tell Kurso where we have gone, and he can pass a message to the mistress when she returns.'

Minimus hurried off to do as I had asked. He was quick and eager and we were shortly on our way. As we walked along I coaxed a fuller story from the lad about what he remembered of the day he saw the girl.

The facts were clear enough. 'I was sent out by the master with a message for the gate – about where the consignment of larks was to be directed when it came. I was on my own for once, because Maximus was acting as the master's page

– Pulchrus had gone to Londinium by that time, and Marcus wanted someone by his side.'

'What about Niveus?' I enquired. 'I thought he was purchased with that idea in mind?'

'He didn't join the household until that afternoon,' Minimus said dismissively. 'This was still quite early in the day – only a little while after the luggage cart had gone. Anyway, the master sent me out, but when I reached the gatehouse Aulus wasn't there. I looked out through his spyhole and saw him talking to this young woman in the lane.' He gave me a sideways glance. 'Not just talking either. He was standing close to her, one hand pointing down the road, and the other on her rump. She didn't seem to mind it, surprisingly. She was smiling up at him as though he were some kind of Greek god. That's why I wondered if she was a . . .' He shrugged. 'Aulus was quite disappointed when I called out to him, and he had to come and pay attention to my message.'

I grinned, amused by the picture which this conjured up. 'Well, we'll get there very soon and then we'll see what this unlikely Adonis has to say about the girl.'

But Aulus wasn't there when we arrived. The gate was open, but there was no one in his cell, and a quick search up and down the lane revealed no trace of him. I suspected that he had sneaked off to relieve himself in the undergrowth, instead of waiting for his official break and then trailing all the way round the villa grounds to the slaves' latrine, but though we called and waited he did not appear.

I frowned. This was unusual. Marcus was a stickler for guarding all the gates – especially since Julia and Marcellinus were abducted a little while ago, held to ransom and only narrowly escaped alive. Marcus had been doubly careful about security ever since. Aulus would be severely flogged if his owner discovered he'd left his post like this.

However, in the absence of a gatekeeper we went in on our own. Still no Aulus, or anybody else. No servants in the front courtyard, or at the entrance to the house. For the first time ever, I walked into the villa completely unannounced.

I let myself into the atrium with the idea of waiting there, while Minimus went off to find a slave and let his erstwhile master know that I had come Some serious crisis in the family possibly? I could think of no other reason why there should be no one about – usually in Marcus's villa one could scarcely move without inviting the attention of a pair of matching slaves. I was just wishing I had gone round to the back door of the house and thus been able to speak to Stygius without delay, when I was startled to find that I was not alone.

Lucius was already in the room and, unaccompanied by attendants, was pouring a libation on to the household shrine.

I seemed to be making a habit of disturbing private devotions, I thought, and those of the most unlikely people too! I coughed discreetly to let him know that I was there.

His astonishment was every bit as great as mine had been. He started so violently that he dropped the jug, and it smashed into a hundred fragments on the floor. Little drops of liquid splashed among the shards. He whirled round to face me, his face a mask of marble white. 'What in Jove's name . . .'

'A thousand pardons, citizen!' I was mortified. I did not want to anger my patron's relative, and the jug that he had broken was a substantial one. Besides, to find him worshipping at the household shrine was even more surprising than finding Julia, and more embarrassing for both of us.

Lucius was not the *genius* of this house so it was not properly his place to make such sacrifice – and he was just the sort of man who cared about such social niceties. Yet he had clearly intended a substantial sacrifice. There was a scrap of kindling on the altar-top and even a lighted taper standing by, as if he hoped to waft his prayers to heaven in the flame, the way that Christians and other outlandish sects are said to do.

At the moment, though, Lucius did not look especially devout. I heard him mutter, 'Dis take it!' in a furious undertone. He pressed his thin lips together very hard, and I noticed that pinched redness around the nose again. However, a moment later, he forced a condescending smile.

'I did not know that you had graced us with your presence, citizen.'

I began to stammer that there had been no one to announce me at the gate, but he waved my words aside.

'If you are looking for my cousin and his wife, I fear they are not here. They have already left for Glevum. Marcus has taken my advice, and intends to consult the high priest of Jupiter about the best way of affording this corpse a funeral – today, if possible, and certainly before the Lemuria begins. His wife, of course, decided to go too, to order some new sandals to be made for her before she goes away, and your adopted son has gone with them as well. He was anxious to make enquiries about some girl he wants to find for you – in case she had been noticed passing through the gate.'

I nodded. 'Splendid. So he traced her family?'

He was not amused. 'I am not aware of any more details than I've told you, citizen. You will have to talk to Stygius – or whatever that oaf of a chief land slave calls himself. All I know is they have gone to town, and Marcus was going to speak to the garrison as well. I made it clear I did not think that that was very wise – involving half the populace in our affairs and starting rumours in the town, instead of discreetly consulting the high priest and quietly disposing of the corpse as soon as possible – but he thought that you would wish him to pursue the matter, and naturally your views took precedence over mine.' The eyebrows rose a fraction, and the lips compressed. 'It isn't altogether how we manage things in Rome. And, of course, it turned out that I was right. It is most unfortunate that my cousin wasn't here.'

'Something has come up since he went away?'

The thin face pinched still further. 'A messenger. A reply to Marcus's letter to the authorities, with details of the accommodation and the passage he required. But the rider brought another letter for my cousin too – a disturbing message which was already on its way from Rome, and which arrived in this province just in time to catch the courier. You know that Marcus's father has been very ill?'

So I was right about a crisis in the family, I thought. 'Taken worse?' I said.

It was a stupid question. The answer was obvious before Lucius replied. He adopted his most pompous manner. 'I fear that the *paterfamilias* is dead. I have instructed the household slaves to dress accordingly and make arrangements to purify the house.'

Of course! Suddenly it all made sense – the household chaos and the missing slaves. The servants had obviously been dispatched to change their tunic uniforms to such mourning colours as they might possess, and to fetch appropriate candles, food and herbs to plunge the house into memorial. This hasty sacrifice, with Lucius taking Marcus's place, was equally explicable, in fact. As the senior male in the family, in such a case as this, Lucius was entitled to represent my patron in his absence.

'So – you were making an offering on Marcus's behalf?' I said.

'I was. I felt a gesture should be made at once, especially in view of the unfortunate events which have already occurred at this most inauspicious time of the year. I am beginning to fear that my aunt Honoria was right – this family is ill-omened if not actually accursed. I thought I might appease the household gods, at least.' He looked at the scattered fragments on the floor. 'Though I fear that now my efforts may have had the opposite effect.'

It was a sly rebuke. He was suggesting that the failure was my fault for interrupting him and causing him to drop the jug and wine like that. It was a matter of concern. Roman ritual is much like ours, in that regard. One false move – particularly a spillage or a broken dish – not only negates the ceremony but is ill-omened in itself, and needs additional sacrifice in propitiation.

I was anxious to do anything I could to put it right. I was as keen as anyone to see my patron's father's ghost achieve repose – especially if any problems could be attributed to me. 'I can fetch fresh offerings from the kitchen, if you wish, since there seem to be no slaves in evidence. I realise that you will have to start the sacrifice again.'

'Unfortunately so,' he said severely. 'But I must provide

the offering, if I am to atone. I have appropriate items in my travelling pack, along with the icons of my household gods. You, citizen, can help me best by witnessing the act.' He clapped his hands. 'When that fool of a bodyguard of mine comes in answer to my call. Colaphus!'

In fact it was only a moment before the man came clattering in – a big man, built like a battering ram, with a square, shaved head to match, his huge hands already forming into fists. I could see why they called him Colaphus. The very name means 'thump'.

'You wanted something, master? I'm sorry that I kept you waiting for so long.' He was as fast of speech as Stygius was slow. He bowed, exhibiting his close-cropped head, and I was reminded of the battering ram again. That thick, flat skull would have splintered any gate. 'I have given your instructions to the household staff. The funeral pyre is being constructed as we speak, and slaves are gathering wild herbs and grinding ointments for the corpse, and nailing the planks to make a bier to put in on.'

'Pyre?' I was astonished. 'Bier? But surely the funeral will be in Rome?'

Lucius looked disdainful. He was very good at that. 'This is for the body in the stable block, of course. Something must be done with it – it has begun to stink and it must be burned as soon as possible. We cannot have an unknown and decaying stranger's corpse contaminating a house which is engaged in formal grief for a senior member of the owner's family. Now, I must try again to appease the household Lars, lest this time of mourning be more inauspicious still.' His livid colour had faded to an outraged, dullish pink around the gills. He turned to his attendant. 'Colaphus, I need some sacrificial bread and a little perfumed oil and wine. You will find some in my room. Not the big jug on the table that I was drinking from – the containers in my portable *lararium*. In fact, on second thoughts, you can bring the whole thing here.'

'Certainly, master.' He thundered off, returning shortly afterwards with a wooden box which, when opened, proved to contain a tiny shrine, the flasks in question and the miniatures of Lucius's household gods. In Colaphus's great hands they looked especially delicate.

Lucius set up the tiny altar and placed it reverently on top of Marcus's own. 'These are a tribute to my aunt Honoria,' he explained, setting up the pair of little silver figurines behind the shrine, 'since they are the Lares and Penates of her ancestral home – and mine. These icons were her father's – my grandfather's, in fact – and their protection should embrace us all.' He took out a tiny flagon and a little silver box, and placed them reverently beside him as he spoke.

He stood before the altar and from the containers placed minute amounts of bread and wine on it, sprinkled the whole offering with olive oil from the lamp, then solemnly used the taper to set the sacrifice alight. It flickered for a moment, then filled the air with smoke, while Lucius muttered what I supposed were prayers. They were evidently family incantations, and in ancient Latin, too – I could scarcely comprehend a single word.

I hoped that the divinities had understood him, anyway, as he stepped back from the shrine and turned to face me with a smile.

'There, citizen . . . I have done my best. We shall have to make a proper sacrifice in the temple later on, and when I get home I'll ask the Vestal Virgins to say a prayer for us. But in the meantime . . .'

He was interrupted by a dishevelled figure at the door. 'Master?' It was Minimus and he was out of breath. He didn't stop to look about, but burst immediately into speech. 'I apologise for having left you waiting here so long, but I couldn't find Marcus Septimus anywhere. There seems to be a . . . oh!' He tailed off in confusion at the sight of Lucius. 'I'm sorry, Excellence, I didn't realise you were in the room.'

Lucius looked loftily superior, and waved a gracious hand. 'Don't let me prevent you from passing on your news. If you have anything truly new to say?'

Minimus looked doubtfully from Lucius to me.

'Lucius has told me much of it,' I said. 'I know that my patron's father died recently in Rome.'

Minimus nodded. 'Marcus has gone to Glevum with his wife, and doesn't know it yet.'

'He may do so by now. Naturally, I sent the messenger to Glevum after him,' Lucius corrected, in his most condescending tone.

'Well then, master.' Minimus turned to me. 'Your new son Junio has gone as well – but he found the slave who interviewed the father of that girl. All the other land slaves are busy with the pyre, but Stygius has got him waiting for you in the outer court.'

I nodded. 'Splendid. So, if you will excuse me, Excellence . . . ?' I was not sure if that mode of address was appropriate, but it seemed wise to err on the side of flattery.

Lucius graciously half inclined his head. 'By all means, citizen. Doubtless your slave can take you there. I understand he knows the house quite well.'

Minimus turned eagerly to him. 'And I have a message for you, citizen, as well. Aulus the gatekeeper has disappeared – there was no one at the entrance when we arrived, and no one in the villa has set eyes on him.'

I was surprised. 'That's very curious. I thought that he had simply gone to change his uniform.'

Lucius looked at Minimus with narrowed eyes. 'Was he due for a relief?'

The slave boy shook his head. 'He had one just a little while ago. The kitchen sent some cheese and bread for him into the servants' room, and he came in and ate it. Peeled a raw onion with it the way he always does.'

The Roman was dismissive. 'I saw him at it, come to think of it, but surely he went back on duty after that?'

'After he had visited the slaves' latrine. He was seen to leave there and go out towards the gate. And he should still be there. Only he isn't. I've told the chief steward and he's placed a man on guard, but asks if you can spare your Colaphus – at least until they can find the regular relief. Everyone's out helping with the funeral pyre and he can't find a replacement of sufficient size.'

Lucius had that pinkness around his nose again. 'Well, that is irregular, but I suppose it's possible. I have no particular requirement for Colaphus just now.'

The battering ram looked as if he didn't want to go. I could not altogether blame him. A gatekeeper's job is a lonely, draughty one, and if Aulus had met trouble he might do the same. But a slave must do his master's bidding, whatever it might be.

'As you command, master,' he said reluctantly. 'But you will relieve me when the gatekeeper gets back? After all,

Aulus can't be very far away. After all, we spoke to him not half an hour ago.'

And with a last, reproachful look at me, as if this was all entirely my fault, the battering ram went stomping off to take up his unwelcome duties at the gate.

Chapter Thirteen

Lucius stared after the slave's retreating back. There was a moment's silence.

'You went out to the lane, then?' I ventured finally, wondering what errand would take him from the house, especially while Marcus and Julia were in town.

When Lucius answered it was with disdain. 'Of course. I believe I mentioned that there was a messenger?'

My turn to stare at him. A messenger? Why should that take Lucius to the gate? No citizen of his rank would go out to the road to receive an errand boy. More likely the messenger would be required to come in and wait for him – sometimes for a considerable time. However, I could hardly challenge Marcus's cousin outright.

'A messenger from your aunt Honoria, I think? And you received him, since your cousin was not here?' I prompted shamelessly.

Lucius gave a thin smile. 'Indeed. In this very atrium, in fact. But in view of the seriousness of the news from Rome, naturally I did not encourage him to linger here. I saw that he was given food and drink – he had ridden from Londinium without a stop, except to change his horses at the military inns – and sent him on to Glevum, to try to catch up with Marcus at the garrison if he could. Of course, the messenger doesn't know the roads, so I escorted him to the gatehouse and personally asked Aulus to point out the shortest route.'

Without even giving the poor lad a chance to rest, I thought, after his long and dusty journey on the roads. However, it was logical enough. The rider would have a travel warrant to speed his way as regards the horses and assistance at the inns, but he would not know the short cut through the lane that passed my house, which – for a single rider – would cut off several miles.

'And Aulus was at his station then?' I asked. It was a meaningless enquiry, in the circumstances – obviously he must have been, or Lucius could not have asked him anything – and Lucius treated it with the raised eyebrow it deserved. I hastened to add a more judicious thought. 'He did not seem peculiar in any way at all? Not ill, or anything?'

Lucius stiffened. 'What do you mean by that?' His voice was sharp. Still contemptuous of my idiotic questions, it appeared.

'I thought – since he went missing shortly afterwards – there might have been some sign of the reason. Did he seem to be his normal self to you?'

Lucius gave me his thin smile. 'His normal self? I'm not sure what his normal self might be. After all, I hardly knew the man.'

'Shrewd and grasping and malodorous, and willing to sell information at a price,' I said. Lucius looked properly scandalised at this – it is not polite to criticise the servants of one's host. I hastened to explain. 'You must have realised that the fellow was a spy? Marcus has relied on him for years.'

'I heard rumours yesterday of something of the kind. Not that I would have used him in such a way, of course.' He had turned that disapproving fish-gill pink again.

I laughed. 'Don't worry, citizen. It would not have been surprising if you had. Most of us have slipped Aulus a little something now and then. Though, naturally, your rank and purse would get more out of him than I am able to. He has been the ears and eyes of Marcus for so long, he is accustomed to being paid more handsomely than I can generally afford.'

Lucius seemed genuinely interested in this. He lost that stuffed and starchy look. 'You used him, then, yourself?' He glanced at Minimus, and then went on as if the slave boy was not possessed of ears and eyes. 'Aulus did not strike me as having the qualities of mind to . . .' he paused, 'to pass on intelligence with much intelligence.' The pale eyes glinted at this attempt at wit.

'All the same,' I said, 'he is reliable. He does not see the point of everything you ask, but what he does tell you is generally accurate enough. For instance, I wanted to know what vehicles were passing in the lane the other day – the day I think the murder of our corpse took place. He gave me a sort of list. I'm not convinced that it was quite complete – if I'd had money in my purse, I might have learned some more – but I'm certain that what he told me is nothing but the truth.'

'I see.' The thin lips smiled. 'Perhaps I should have questioned Aulus when I had the chance. Or we should have questioned him together, you and I.'

Another jest? He was talking to me as though I were his equal, all at once. I knew I should be flattered by the compliment, but something was niggling in the corner of my brain – a vague feeling that something important had been said, some significant detail which had passed me by. I racked my brains but for the moment I could not work out what it was. Meanwhile Lucius was still smiling in that impassive way of his, waiting for me to answer his remark.

Well, two could play the game of flattery. 'I'm sure your rank and status would ensure success,' I said. I didn't have to add 'your bribe' – that was implicit, as we were both aware. 'Perhaps we could both talk to him when he turns up again.'

'Willingly. Supposing that he does.' Lucius arched his eyebrows. 'Marcus was telling us, just the other day, about the trouble you are having with those rebels in the west, and how it's feared they might now have a hideout in these woods.'

'You think he might have been abducted or attacked?' This was a possibility which had not occurred to me – though perhaps it should have done. What else would have persuaded him to leave his post like that? He would hardly have done so willingly, and risked a flogging for his pains. I thought a moment and then shook my head. 'Aulus is not the kind of man that brigands set upon – not unless there was a well-armed band of them, at least, and even then he would have laid about him with his club, and bloodied one or two of them for their pains. And the way he roars, it couldn't go unnoticed in the house. Besides, there's no sign of a struggle – I can vouch for that.'

'You don't suppose that he simply took the chance to run away? He was always complaining about something, when I spoke to him.'

I had to smile at this. 'And make himself a fugitive, with a price upon his head? Not Aulus. He must have earned his freedom price half a dozen times in bribes, but he's never shown the slightest inclination to buy his freedom and depart. I think he quite enjoys his position as a spy.'

Lucius seemed unwilling to abandon his idea. 'In normal times, perhaps. But no doubt, like the rest of us, he was alarmed by knowing that we had an unburied body in the house, just when the Festival of the Dead is coming up. Perhaps he feared the spirits and made a bolt for it?'

I could not see Aulus as a superstitious man – one whiff of his onions would frighten off any ghost! I shook my head again. 'More likely there was some crisis in the lane and – not finding another servant when he called for one, since there were none about – he left his post to deal with it himself.'

'Unless you are right and he was suddenly unwell.' Minimus had been standing by and listening to all this. 'I remember that did happen to him once before – we found him in the forest, being very sick. He'd gnawed some sort of flower bulbs instead of onions.'

'Your attendant interrupts us, citizen!' Lucius was outraged by this affront to his dignity. 'If he were my servant I should have him flogged.' Shutters had come down across his face, like a shop-front at the market closing up, and his previous thawing manner had frozen hard again.

'Nevertheless, we must investigate all possibilities,' I urged.

But he was not to be wooed into friendliness again. 'Then you can leave me to arrange a search for the missing gatekeeper. You, I believe, have other things to do. I think there is someone awaiting you outside?'

It was a dismissal, and a timely one, in fact. So much had

happened that I had almost forgotten Stygius and his land slave. 'Of course,' I murmured. 'I must go at once. But . . .'

Lucius gave me that tight smile again and raised a warning hand. 'That is your priority, citizen, I fear. Your patron requested you to solve this crime, and it is important that you make a start if you are to put that corpse to rest before the Lemuria begins.' He swallowed self-importantly, so that the cartilage in his throat bobbed up and down. 'I only hope that the disappearance of this Aulus fellow is not another manifestation of a curse upon this household. But, as I say, you can leave that in my hands. I will go and talk to the chief steward now, and arrange a search party.' And without another word he turned away, and strode from the atrium.

'I'm sorry, master.' Minimus was beside me in a trice. 'I did not mean to interrupt you and provoke the citizen.'

I grinned at him in mock severity. 'Then ensure you mind your manners another time,' I said. 'Now, take me to the stable block at once. I'll see Stygius and this land slave, if they're still here.'

They were. Stygius was doggedly standing vigil beside the shrouded corpse – from which, as Lucius had said, a distinctive odour was now beginning to emerge – while his companion loitered uncomfortably nearby. The older man came across to greet me as soon as I appeared.

'Ah, Citizen Libertus, there you are. This here is Caper – the slave I told you of. The one who interviewed the father of that girl. You'll have to speak slowly. He's fairly new to us.'

I nodded at Caper. The word means 'he-goat' and presumably some recent slavemaster had given him the name. I could see why. He was a tall, rangy-looking youth with curly, thick black hair, which sprouted not only from his long and bony head, but from his sinewy hands, legs and forearms too. A straggling beard and whiskers formed a sort of frame around his face so that he did look like a kind of half-tamed animal – a mountain goat perhaps – standing on its hind legs for a trick. He was dressed in a grimy tunic, with a leather apron and rough rags tied about his feet for boots. He raised a pair of wary eyes to me as I approached, and Stygius prodded him forward with one brawny arm.

'Now then.' Stygius poked the unfortunate Caper fiercely in the ribs. 'This citizen is your master's special protégé, so you make sure you answer when you're spoken to.'

It didn't altogether look as if the goat could manage that. He was gazing at my toga with a doubtful air, as if it overawed him.

'You spoke to the family of this girl?' I said.

He nodded, but said nothing. Before Stygius could offer a rebuke, I spoke again. 'You could take me to the place?'

Another nod. 'Nicely place,' he said at last. His voice was what I had expected, gruff and low, with the strong accent of the local tribe. Brought up in some poor family, I would judge, and sold to slavery to help the funds when he was old enough. As Stygius said, his Latin was not good, though obviously he could understand my words. I wondered how he had coped with asking questions in some of the Roman households round about.

'Nice place?' I said, in Celtic, and earned a wondering smile. My dialect was not the same as his, but it was close enough to give him confidence.

'Good pigs, they've got. And hens. And cabbages,' he told me eagerly. 'All sorts of things. It's quite a little farm.'

'How long will it take us to get there?' I asked.

He looked at me, taking in the toga and the greying beard. 'Took me half an hour,' he said. 'Take you a good bit longer, I expect.'

It took me twice that time, in fact. Several times Caper had to wait for me (though sometimes for Minimus as well, I was amused to note) and once again he lived up to his name. He led the way so quickly there was no time for speech. After a mile or two I was panting after him, far too breathless for conversation anyway.

Our destination lay in the opposite direction from my house, and we were soon in an area that I did not know at all. We hurried past the trappers' hut and a scattered farm or two, but Caper did not pause. Away from the main lane he led us at a trot, till we were toiling up hilly forest tracks. We seemed to be leaving civilisation far behind when, stumbling along a little stony path, we suddenly came to a clearing in the woods. Caper stopped, and spread out one arm to indicate the crest of a small hill with a roundhouse enclosure on the top of it. 'There it is,' he said triumphantly.

It was a sizeable homestead, for a peasant farm, and I could see why Caper thought it a 'nicely place'. I could make out four roundhouses at least, a large expanse of cultivated spelt, and half a dozen sheep and horses corralled into a field. But there was evidence of Roman ways as well. There were watch-geese roaming inside the inner yard; plump ducks and chickens pecked among long rows of cabbages, and we had already passed the portable woven fences which were moved around the woods to give swine new feeding grounds while keeping them enclosed. A stack of firewood was cut and standing at the gate, with a sprig of holly hanging over it for luck, and another pile of something (it looked like bundled leaves) was drying in a rick as winter fodder for the animals. Woodsmoke curled up from the roof-holes and from somewhere inside the enclosure a dog began to bark.

Clearly the place was mildly prosperous, but I was rather surprised to find that this was the household we'd been looking for. Stygius had told me yesterday that his land slaves were looking for news of a missing girl with soft, unblistered hands. The inhabitants of such a farm as this would work their land themselves – just as they would have built the roundhouses, dug the surrounding ditches and woven the triple fence. No troops of slaves to do the work for them – the women of the household would labour with the men. I said as much to Caper, when I found the breath to speak. 'You were looking for a girl with tender hands,' I said. 'What made you come and ask your questions here?'

He looked at me, furrowing his eyebrows closer across his narrow eyes. 'They told me at the big Roman house down there' – he waved a vague hand in the direction we had come – 'that there was someone missing from this farm. Apparently the father went down there a little while ago, saying that his eldest girl had run away, and asking if their land slaves had seen any sign of her. Of course they couldn't help him, but they told me what he'd said. So up I came. I didn't think there was much chance of its being any use, considering the hands and everything, but I thought I'd be in trouble if I didn't try. I didn't know then that the body was a man, or I might not have bothered coming here at all.'

'You did the right thing, all the same,' I said. 'It turns out that we may be looking for a peasant girl.'

He grinned – a malicious little smile that showed his long and yellow teeth and reminded me more than ever what his nickname meant. 'Course, that enquiry from her father was a little while ago, before her family got word that she was safe. She has joined a travelling entertainment troupe and sent a message home, saying she was well and happy and not to look for her. You knew that, didn't you?' He seemed to take a gleeful pleasure in the notion that my breathless exertions might have been in vain. 'But there's the father – you can ask him for yourself.'

I looked in the direction where he was gesturing. There was indeed a man – a burly man in Celtic trousers, tunic and plaid cloak. Borrowing from Roman ways clearly did not extend to personal appearance. His hair was pulled back into a long tail at his neck, which emphasised his jutting chin and long traditional moustache. He was leaning on the enclosure fence and staring hard at us. There was a none-too-friendly expression on his face, and I was alarmed to see a huge staff in his hand, while the dog – which was now squatting at his heels – bared his teeth in a ferocious snarl. Hardly the welcoming reception I had hoped.

I was contemplating whether I should go over and speak to him myself, or whether I should send either of the slaves, when the fellow solved the problem by shouting out to us.

'You again, goat-face? What do you want this time? And who is your fancy toga-wearing friend?' He was bellowing in Celtic, probably in the belief that I would not understand.

Caper looked uncomfortable. 'This is the Citizen Libertus,' he called back in the same tongue. 'The favoured client of my master, Marcus Septimus – you know, the magistrate. Libertus is here on his particular account, to ask the same questions that I asked you yesterday and probably some others of his own as well.' Then, seeing that the farmer was about to speak again, he added hastily, 'He's a Roman citizen, but he speaks Celtic too.'

I could see that it was time for me to intervene. 'Indeed I do. And I have a roundhouse, though not as grand as yours. Nor is my family quite as sizeable,' I added, realising that there were several female heads watching us from the shelter of the roundhouse doors. The same heads heard me and instantly withdrew. 'But it's your eldest daughter that I want to talk about.'

The farmer threw me a furious glance. 'And what is she to you? Come to tell me that she is found, have you, and want me to take her back? Well, I shall have to disappoint you, citizen. She ran away, and she can stay away, as far as I'm concerned. She has made a mockery of me and of my family's good name!'

I took a pace towards him but was dissuaded by the dog, which snarled and barked and rushed fiercely at the fence. I stopped and shouted from the safety of the path. 'A mockery?' I echoed, trying to sound as sympathetic as I could.

He spat into the furze pile with ferocity. 'How dare she run away when I have promised her, especially when I found her a decent widower like that. Cost me a pair of cows in dowry, and a lot of money too – and naturally he won't agree to give them back.' Another spit. 'Course he was old and ugly, and inclined to smell of pigs, but a girl like that should be grateful to get any man at all. You tell her, citizen, if I lay hands on her, I'll give her a leathering that she won't forget.'

I was beginning to feel some sympathy for the young

runaway. 'You'd promised her in marriage?' I took another step. The dog contented itself this time with an unpleasant growl.

The farmer hawked, and ran a hand and arm across his mouth. 'Aren't I just telling you I did?' he said. He paused, then went on in an altered tone of voice. 'But surely you must know that, if you've caught up with her. Morella is a bit simple, I grant you, but she wouldn't tell a lie. Hasn't got the wit to make things up at all. Too trusting, in a lot of ways, that's been the trouble all her life.' He cocked an eye at me. 'I expect that's what happened with this travelling act of hers. She found out what the fellow wanted, and didn't care for it? Well, tell him I won't take her – and that's an end of that. I'm not obliged to, when she left here of her own accord. You tell her that as well.'

'I can't tell her anything,' I said. 'I don't know where she is. I've come to ask you what she looked like, so I can search for her.'

'Don't bother. I don't want her, and she sends word she's happy where she is.' Something seemed to strike him, and he glared at me. 'Don't tell me she's already got herself in debt, and her creditors are searching for her? No doubt they'll hold me liable, if they don't find her soon, since she is my daughter, and a simple one at that. Oh, now it all makes sense! That's why the magistrate has sent you, I suppose.'

I tried to deny it, but he paid no heed to me. He was still spitting at the ground and grumbling to himself. 'Oh, dear gods of stone and tree, is there no end to this? I've done my best for her for years, and what's the thanks I get? I've got other children to think about as well. Four more girls to make provision for. How am I to manage?'

I was still wondering what to say to that when he seized a piece of rope which was tied up to the fence, and used the looped end to secure the dog. 'Well, I suppose in that case I'd better let you in.' He came out to the gate and pushed it open, still grumbling. 'What has she done this time? Taken things without permission from a shop?'

Caper was looking doubtful and so was Minimus, but I led the way into the enclosure and they had no option but to follow me – taking care to keep well out of range of the snarling canine which was straining at its leash. The farmer turned without another word and led the way into the largest building on the site – a communal roundhouse, complete with central fire, and tools and bedding ranged around the walls on the far side. The nearer section, however, was expensively furnished in the Roman style with a proper couch and tables, a handsome woven mat, and an ornate brass oil lamp burning on a stand. Morella's father was clearly a successful man, as peasant farmers go.

He gestured to the couch, and I sat down on it while he took up a position on a wooden stool nearby. 'Well?' he demanded. 'What is that she's done?'

'I am not sure that she's done anything,' I said. 'And if Morella is the girl I am looking for, it seems unlikely that she was in debt. She had some money with her, quite a lot of it.'

He did not react to this with anger, as I'd expected he would do. He looked a little puzzled, if anything. 'Well, I don't know where it came from, then. I didn't give it to her.' He folded his arms aggressively across his chest. 'So if isn't money, what is it that you want?'

I glanced at Caper for support – after all he had interviewed the man before – but he evaded my eyes and stood staring at the floor. I took a deep breath. 'We know of a peasant girl who may have come to harm. I hope it's not Morella, but it is possible.'

I expected some response from him at this – even some expression of concern – but all that happened was a lengthy pause during which we could hear the dog still barking noisily outside.

Eventually I said, 'I need to trace her movements for the last few days, to be completely sure. In order to do that there are obviously some questions I must ask.'

Another pause. The farmer still said nothing, so I pressed on anyway. 'Did your Morella have long lime-bleached hair? And what was she wearing when she left the house?'

Chapter Fourteen

I was still expecting the farmer to exhibit some concern, or at least to ask some pretty pointed questions of his own – after all I had told him bluntly that I feared his eldest daughter might have come to harm – but he did nothing of the kind. Instead, he pursed his lips and scowled as though I had insulted him.

'I blame her mother for all that,' he burst out angrily. 'Showed her the way her grandfather mixed lime to bleach his hair, like all the other elders of the tribe.' He ran a proud hand down each end of his magnificent moustache, which had itself been lightly bleached. 'You do hear of women who have limed hair these days – no respect for masculine tradition and the way things should be done. Of course, she wanted to try it for herself. Someone had told her that blonde girls are prettier and how they sometimes shave their heads and sell their hair for wigs, and after that there was no stopping her. As if she could ever be a beauty! Girl looked like a pig.' He spat again, this time into the fire.

'So she did bleach her hair?' I said, returning to the point.

'Bleached it! She nearly turned it green, and damaged it so much that half of it broke off the first time she put a bone comb into it. Her mother had a struggle to plait it afterwards – but the stupid girl was thrilled to bits with the effect. Just before her husband-to-be was going to visit, too! I was tempted to hack it all off with the shears and leave her like a sheep, but her mother persuaded me against that in the end. Said Morella would look even worse if she was bald – said it didn't look too bad when it was braided up, and perhaps the colour would grow out again in time!' He aimed another gob into the centre of the fire. 'I should have given both of them a thrashing there and then. I'm too soft with my womenfolk, that's the truth of it.'

I had to look away as he said this, and I caught Minimus's eye – he was standing at my elbow all this time. His expression was carefully impassive, as Junio's would not have been, and he did not return my glance, but I was convinced that he had understood our Celtic speech – with that red hair he was probably Silerian by birth. I was about to ask him to repeat what he had told me about the tunic and the boots when the farmer abruptly got to his feet.

'About the clothes – I'll have her mother in and you can talk to her yourself. She'll know what the girl was wearing – I couldn't tell you that. I never take an interest in such female details.' He strode over to the doorway and clapped his hands three times. 'Wife! I want you! Come to us at once.'

The wife in question must have been waiting close outside, because almost at once she came hurrying in. She was a little wizened woman, with an anxious stoop and a lined and worried weather-beaten face. She could never have been pretty – her nose was far too long – and age had not been very kind to her. Her neck was scrawny and wrinkled and her hair was thin and grey, though she still wore it in a long, brave braid; and her hands – though strong and brown – had ugly livid spots. I noticed that she had expensive sandals and toe-rings on her feet and, remembering the boots that my slave boy had described, I wondered if I'd come here on a fool's errand after all. If the wife wore proper shoes, I told myself, wasn't it likely that her daughter did so too?

But then my mosaic-maker's eye fell on the pattern of the homespun plaid robe she wore, and I knew at once that it was one I'd seen before. Most Celtic families weave a special pattern of their own, and this was identical to the one the corpse had worn. That dress had belonged to a member of this tribe – if not the woman's daughter, then another relative – and since that person, almost certainly, was dead, I felt a sudden surge of sympathy. But I could not spare her the grief that was in store. I looked at her sadly.

She was smiling a little nervously, showing a row of broken teeth. 'You called me, husband? I was waiting for your summons. I am sorry that I took so long to answer it.' Her voice was soft and squeaky, with an apologetic tone, although it seemed to me that she had come the moment she was called. 'You want me to bring refreshments for your guest?' she added, gesturing to me, since obviously the slave boys didn't count. 'Your' guest, not 'our', I noticed. Clearly, in this household, the farmer's word was law. Another thing he'd borrowed from the Roman way of life – in many Celtic households the woman has a say, and often is as educated as the menfolk are. 'A drop of fresh milk and an oatcake, perhaps?'

It sounded quite delicious but the farmer shook his head. 'No need for that. The citizen will not be staying long. He has a question for you, then he'll be on his way. Tell him what he wants to know, and get back to your work.'

She turned towards me, her grey eyes wary. 'Well, citizen, what is it that you want to know? Something about bees or dyeing wool, perhaps? I am not well informed on many things.'

'Something about your eldest daughter,' I said quietly.

I saw the flame of hope spring up in her. 'You have some news of her? Oh, thank all the gods. I thought that I should never hear of her again.'

'Be silent, woman,' her husband said, much as he would have quieted the dog. 'Listen to what the citizen has to say.'

I broke the news to her as gently as I could. We had found a plaid garment in suspicious circumstances, I explained, and we feared that it might once have been Morella's – though I didn't say anything about the money in the hem. Then I outlined the description which the dancing woman gave. 'So, knowing that your daughter had run away, and gone to join an entertainment group,' I finished, 'I wanted to check if this dress could possibly be hers. It sounds as if it might. I understand from your husband that she'd lime-bleached her hair in a way that made her stand out from the general crowd.'

The woman shot an anxious look towards her man. 'Morella didn't mean any disrespect by that,' she said. 'She's a bit slow of understanding, that's the only thing. She thought that it looked pretty when she saw my father's hair, and when I showed her how he did it, she tried it for herself.' She ignored the furious scowl that her words produced and seemed to stand a little taller as she added, 'My father is an elder of the tribe, you see, and he still keeps up the ancient warrior traditions in that way. Spikes his hair and wears a long moustache – and insists that members of his family do the same.' The faintest ghost of a tired smile flitted on her lips. 'Even sons-in-law,' she added.

Suddenly I understood why the farmer, who clearly favoured Roman ways, stuck to the old traditions in his style of dress. 'Yours is an ancient family?' I hazarded.

She nodded, and was about to speak again when her husband interrupted with a sneer. 'Ancient and feeble-minded, half of them, and all as proud as gods, though they don't have much land or money since the occupation. Still, folks still look up to them. Why do you think I married her? It sure as Pluto wasn't for her wealth and you can see it wasn't for her looks.'

So I was right about the nature of this uneasy partnership – it was a marriage between a common man with money and a woman of good rank. He brought his wealth and she brought her tribal lineage. Perhaps it was her bloodline that still protected her – though she was cowed, she showed no signs of actual violence and I had no doubt that he was capable of it. Probably she still had powerful relatives.

At this moment she was looking at the floor, two red spots of humiliation on her withered cheeks. Poor woman! And I was the bearer of such unhappy news! I felt so sorry for her, I could hardly frame the words.

'And Morella was wearing a dress like yours the day that she disappeared from home?' I said, as gently as I could. 'I think I recognise the pattern of the plaid – though it is different from the one your husband wears.'

She raised her eyes to look full into mine, and I could see the anxiety in them. 'I weave the pattern that my mother used,' she said, 'though sometimes I use his family's colour patterns too. But certainly Morella had a dress like this. I did not weave the cloth for it; my mother originally made it for herself, just a little while before she died. She passed it on to Morella one Beltane feast, when she was too ill to leave her bed any more, and Morella had finished her quick-growing phase. Morella was so pleased with it she rarely took it off, though recently it had been getting tight on her. I know she would have been wearing it on the day she left, although I didn't see her go.'

'And on her feet?' I asked, although I was certain of the answer by this time. 'Would she have sandals?'

She shook her head. 'A pair of home-made boots.' She glanced towards her husband, as if half afraid of how he would respond to what she said. 'I don't know why my husband didn't tell you all this himself. She only had a single pair of boots, and only the one dress that fitted her these days. Her father thought . . .'

He interrupted her again. 'I am not made of money, woman, to have your looms kept busy with needless articles, when woven cloth commands a good price in the market-place in town. Of course she would have had a proper dowry when she wed: two robes if she'd wanted them, from bought material, pink or blue or any hue she chose, with cobbler's sandals and toe-rings and gold balls for her hair. Everything a modern bride could ask for, as well as her own cooking pots and pans. I'd put aside the cash to pay for it. But until that happened, what would have been the point? Her dress still fitted, and there was some wear in it yet, while the younger children are growing up like trees. There's always one of them needs new clothes every year, even if the rest have hand-me-downs.' He glared at her triumphantly. 'And you see that I was right! What would she have done with them if I had given her new things? Run off with them, that's what, and we would have spent all that money in vain.'

The woman looked beseechingly at me. 'So it is certain that she's gone for good? I wasn't sure . . .' She glanced towards her husband, and then added timidly, 'She's quite a simple sort of girl, you see, and I thought she might get tired of it and come back home again.'

'Caper here tells me that you got a message after she had gone. To say that she'd gone away to join the dancing girls?'

'Dancing girls?' The voice was full of hope. The woman was pressing her thin hands together so hard that the knuckles had turned white. 'I knew she dreamed of being one of them, but I never supposed she had the slightest chance.'

I shook my head. I only wished that I had more hopeful news for her. 'If she is the person that we heard about, she didn't join the troupe, in fact.'

A little sigh of what might have been relief. 'Then she did go with the animals, as the message said!'

'That was the message?' I was honestly surprised. 'I'd heard that you were told she'd gone away with a troupe of travelling entertainers, and I assumed she meant the dancing girls. We know she tried to join them, but they turned her down. Then my servant thinks he saw her at the villa gates, a day or two ago, judging by the description of her hair. She'd got herself a tunic – to look more like a dancer, I supposed – and she seemed to be asking for directions to the town.'

I glanced at Minimus for confirmation, and he nodded eagerly.

The woman could not disguise the disappointment that

she obviously felt. 'Then it can't have been Morella. She knew the way to Glevum – she's walked to the market there with me a hundred times to sell our cloth. Besides, didn't you say this happened a day or two ago? It's more than that since Morella went away and we'd had the message from her by that time, hadn't we?' She turned to her husband.

He spat into the fire. 'How am I supposed to know exactly when it came? I was out working all hours in the fields – not like that carter who brought the news to me, who has the time to drive his goods to Glevum every day. Mind you, he's got sons to help him, not like some I know, whose wives are only good for bearing girls.'

She ignored this outburst and shook her head at me. 'I'm sure my husband had had the message before then. Anyway, where would Morella get a tunic from? She didn't have the money to buy one for herself. It must have been someone like her that your servant saw.'

I frowned. This was getting more perplexing all the time. It was true that the girl that Minimus had seen was not wearing the robe of telltale plaid. Was it possible that this was simply a strange coincidence? If Morella was so simple-minded she might have sold the dress – perhaps without knowing that the coins were there – before she went away to join the animals. Or perhaps she had swapped her garments for a tunic in the town, and come back to the villa afterwards? Certainly the rest of the description seemed to match. In that case, did some other person put the money in the hem? And, if so, who and when and why? And what was Morella doing at the gate?

I shook my head. None of this seemed to be making any sense at all. I wished it had occurred to me to bring the dress with me, and to have asked the woman with the dancing girls last night exactly when her unlikely candidate had come to talk to her. Looking back she had not been specific on the point. 'The other day' was all that she had said. Was it feasible that Morella had gone to Glevum, made her approach, been turned away and somehow turned up at the villa later on? And if so, what was Aulus telling her in that confidential way?

I turned back to her mother. 'What exactly did the message from her say? Do you still have the note?'

'Note, citizen? How would we read a note? And how would my daughter send one? She cannot read or write.' She shook her head. 'It was just a verbal message. It was my husband who heard it, anyway, not me.'

He spat into the fire and growled reluctantly. 'Morella had found some travelling entertainment act with animals, and the man had asked her to go away with them – I imagine to clean out the cages or something of that kind.'

'Would she do that? Work behind the scenes? When she really wanted to be a dancing girl?' Cleaning smelly cages did not seem a very appealing lifestyle to me. There would be little pay, if any, and the girl would be hardly better than a slave.

Her mother smiled wryly. 'I believe she would. Of course the dancing had been a dream with her, ever since she met a dancing girl in town, but she was always good with animals, and she would have been content, if the people who kept them were fairly kind to her. Anything to avoid marrying the man her father chose!'

'Be silent, woman!' the farmer shouted, leaping to his feet. If we had not been there to witness it, I believe he would have knocked her to the ground. 'You have answered the questions. Get back to your work.'

All her animation drained from her instantly. 'Yes, husband,' she said meekly, and slunk away again. I heard her moving in the dye-house opposite the door. I wondered how many of the children she had in there with her, trembling in case their father summoned them.

One thing I had learned this morning, anyway. I understood why poor Morella might have run away. Her father held her in less affection than the dog, her mother clearly could not protect her, and she was to be forced into a marriage that she did not want. Even cleaning cages might seem a preferable life, if the animals were affectionate at all. I was beginning to feel real sympathy for the girl.

However, it was clear her father did not share that view. 'So, citizen, I think we've told you everything.' He stood up as if to indicate that I should take my leave. 'You tell your patron that I did my best for you. And if you do find Morella, don't you dare to bring her back. I'll sell her into slavery, if she ever comes. She made her choices – she can stick with them. After I'd arranged a husband for her, too. And now of course he won't have any of my other daughters in her place. Refuses even to come and talk to me.'

'It was a good match?' I enquired, rising from my couch, but lingering nearby. I wanted to hear more about this intended groom – supposing that the farmer would tell me anything at all.

I need not have worried. He was only too anxious to rehearse his grievances. 'A good deal better than the wretched girl deserved,' he grumbled. He walked across the roundhouse to the other side and, from a shelf beside the wall, helped himself to a pottery goblet and a jug, both decorated with combed patterns in the Celtic style. He poured himself a measure of what might have been cold mead, and then – remembering himself – he waved the jug at me. 'Made from my own honey. Want some, citizen?'

I was reluctant to offend him but I shook my head. 'I would prefer water, if you have any. We have walked miles to get here, and it's a long way back. Besides, you've given me a lot to think about. I need to clear my brain.'

It seemed that I had said the right thing, by accident. A surly smile spread slowly across his face, and after he had poured himself a portion from the jug he took another beaker – a Roman one this time – and plunged it into the pottery water-holder standing by the fire. He came across and handed it to me. I sat down again and sipped it cautiously: it was a little brackish, but it seemed clear enough.

He stood above me, swallowing his mead. 'A wealthy widower, with land and cattle of his own. No other living heirs, so it would all have come to us – especially if he'd managed to get a child by her, though I don't suppose there was much chance of that. The man is fifty if he is a day.' (I bridled slightly, being more than that myself, but the farmer seemed oblivious of any possible offence.) He waved his beaker at me. 'All right, she didn't like him – I don't care for him myself, but he only wanted someone to warm his bed and cook and clean for him. He wasn't particular, he said – it's cheaper than a slave. If she'd done as she was told she'd have inherited the lot. And he won't survive much longer – he's already getting frail. Stupid creature. All she had to do was wait. But would she? Not Morella. She hasn't got the sense!' He emptied his beaker, wiped his mouth and glared at me again.

He sounded more belligerent than ever now he'd drunk the mead, and I decided that it was time for us to go. I had learned all that I was likely to in any case, I thought. I finished the water – it wasn't very nice – and put the cup down on the floor beside my feet.

'Thank you for your help,' I said politely as I rose. 'It has given us something to go on, anyway. If we find your daughter, I will see that you're informed.'

He made a noise that might have been a 'Huh!' but he led the way outside the house again and I followed him, accompanied by Caper and my slave. As we passed the dye-house I saw the woman there, with two young children tugging at her skirts. I gave them a little smile and she returned it timidly, but she saw her husband looking and she turned away again, frantically stirring something in a metal pot above the fire. I thought of my own dear Gwellia, and I could easily have wept.

The dog had stopped barking and was whining now, though it aimed a snapping yowl at me as I passed. The farmer let us through the gate, and without a word closed it after us and turned away again, striding towards the dye-house with a determined air.

We had not gone twenty steps, however, before we heard a cry. Not a child's sob of protest, as I had vaguely feared, but a roaring bellow. 'Citizen?'

I whirled round. The farmer was leaning on the gate. 'I've been thinking about what you told us. I suppose the girl is dead?' He was speaking Latin and I realised that he could have done so all along, though it was likely that his wife was not so fluent. From the way he glanced behind him, I guessed that she was not meant to understand this interchange.

I replied in the same language. 'We don't know for certain. We haven't found the corpse.' It wasn't tactful, but it wasn't meant to be. I hoped that I was right in my surmise about his wife, and that my bluntness would shock some reaction out of him.

It did. 'You said that she had some money – quite a lot of it, in fact. In her clothing, was it? So you've found it, haven't you? How else would you have known?'

So that was it. I nodded.

'Well, if Morella's dead, that money's mine now, isn't it? As the father of her family, it ought to come to me.'

Legally, I suppose that he was right, but I could not bring myself to say so. I looked him in the eye. 'Someone else was wearing that dress when it was found. Someone who had been murdered and horribly butchered. So it may not have been Morella's money at all. And if there is any doubt, it will be forfeit anyway – the state will claim it, if no owner can be proved.'

I am no expert in the law, but it sounded plausible and clearly the farmer was convinced. I saw the sullen look come down again. 'You mind you bring it here if it was hers,' he said. 'Farathetos my name is. See you remember it. Or by the gods . . .' He said no more, but let the dog loose from its leash again. It was the other side of the enclosure but it barked and growled, and almost looked as if it was about to jump the fence.

'Home!' I said to Caper, and he led the way.

Chapter Fifteen

Colaphus was still on duty at the gate when we returned. He looked bored and unwilling but he came out to open up.

I went in, taking Minimus, while Caper set off down the track round the side to report back to Stygius and join the land slaves on the farm.

'No sign of Aulus?' I enquired in surprise, as Colaphus shut the gate behind us, and went to retire into his cell again.

He shook his battering-ram head in mock despair. 'They've searched the house and grounds for him, and looked up and down the lane. But nobody has found him, or any trace of him.' He gave an evil grin. 'I hope he has a good excuse when he turns up again. His master isn't very pleased with him, I can tell you, citizen.'

'This is not like Aulus. I begin to wonder if Lucius is right,' I began, and then I saw the implication of what Colaphus had said. 'My patron has returned from Glevum, then?'

He looked up to judge the position of the sun. 'Came back about an hour ago, I'd calculate,' he said. 'Brought the high priest of Jupiter with him. And your son and Mistress Julia. They are all talking in the atrium; I'm told to send you in. But I'm to remind you to perform the special cleansing ritual, since you have been in the presence of a corpse today.

You'll find a bowl of water and a special pot of altar ashes in the servants' ante-room. You are to rinse your hands and face and mark your forehead before you join the family. This is formally a house of mourning now. Do you require a slave to show you in?' He made towards the metal gong that hung beside the wall, and would have struck it if I'd not prevented him.

'I have got Minimus,' I said, and we went into the house, calling in to the ante-room beside the entranceway to make the required ablutions in honour of the dead. A young slave in a dark black-edged tunic hurried in to us, and handed me a linen towel with which to wipe my hands.

'Citizen, I put some bread and cheese aside for you a little earlier. I thought you would be glad of it when you came home again. But they're waiting for you in the atrium. You'd better go there first,' piped a familiar voice, and I looked again and realised the page was Niveus. I had not recognised him without his scarlet finery, and with dust and ashes rubbed into his hair.

Food would have been welcome since it was well past noon and I had eaten nothing since my oatcakes earlier, but obviously I would have to wait a little longer. Minimus might be luckier. He was formally directed to the servants' room to wait, like the slave of any other visitor to the house, just as if he had never worked here in his life. He stumped off disconsolately – his pale blue tunic looking strangely gaudy and inappropriate – but at least, I thought, he would given some refreshment there. I sighed, dipped my finger in the ashes and smeared them on my brow, and – duly purified – followed Niveus into the atrium.

The room was heavy with sacrificial smoke, and it was

clear that more offerings had recently been made – this time by the high priest of Jupiter, I guessed, since there was a smell of burning feathers which suggested doves. A pair of oil lamps had been lit on each side of the room – obviously a gesture, since it was broad daylight still – while rose petals and sweet basil were scattered on the ground and a great bowl of sweet-smelling herbs was standing by the door. Servants, all silent and in dark tunics now, were moving furniture, and seemed to be bringing a large stone plinth into the room, while Marcus and Julia, also in dark clothes, were sitting with Lucius on folding stools nearby.

'Ah, Libertus!' Marcus offered me his ring. 'You find us all in mourning – much sooner than I thought. However, my cousin warned me as soon as he arrived that my father was desperately ill, so I had the servant's tunics dyed in readiness.' It occurred to me to wonder why Lucius had not made arrangements too. His sparkling white toga, even with its wide aristocratic purple bands, managed to look disrespectful and rather out of place.

Julia had undone the bindings in her hair and allowed it to fall dishevelled – or it least in an artful semblance of traditional disarray – around her shoulders. Over her head she wore a veil of net which did not so much conceal her tresses as contrive to frame her face. She looked quite ravishing. She turned to extend a greeting hand to me.

'And here is the very person to design the cenotaph. Citizen Libertus, I am glad to see you here. Marcus is planning a memorial to his father here – you know the sort of thing.'

I nodded. Politicians and other important men often have an *honorarium sepulchrum* like this, when they are honoured in one place and buried somewhere else. My patron was obviously proposing a private version of the same.

'We could have something suitable in a mosaic niche, perhaps. Marcus already has a portrait bust of him that you could copy from,' Julia went on, gesturing towards the servants, who were positioning the plinth. One of them was carrying the marble image of a head.

Obviously it had come from the large cupboard by the shrine, because the doors were open and there was a space on the shelf where traditionally the *imago* masks of ancestors would stand. Most well-born Roman families had a collection of these wax likenesses, each representing a dead male member of the line, which were brought out and paraded – sometimes even worn – at the funeral of the current *paterfamilias*, at which time the new *imago* would be modelled and added to the store. Presumably Marcus's family masks were held in Rome, but clearly he intended to use the bust as a sort of substitute, since obviously some memorial ritual was in train.

I wondered if he had commissioned it since his father had been ill, or whether he'd brought it with him when he first came from Rome. Certainly I did not remember seeing it before.

However, this was no time for considerations of that kind. Marcus was signalling for an extra stool for me. Lucius said loftily, with his patrician sneer, 'I dare say a mosaic niche is quite acceptable, here in the provinces. In Rome the fashion is for marble tombs these days.'

'A memorial niche is not the same thing as a tomb.' Marcus was emphatic, though he sounded sad and tired. 'My father will be cremated and his ashes cold by now. They are going to raise a tombstone to him on the roadside out of Rome, doubtless of the finest marble my mother can obtain. And I see in her letter that she has decreed a feast, and that there will be public games in honour of his name.'

'Exactly!' Lucius looked disdainful. 'And naturally the funerary expenses will fall on you, as heir. So you have done your part. Why then the necessity for another monument? Particularly one that nobody in Rome will ever see.'

'This is a separate tribute, from my family and me. News takes such a time to reach us here. It is too late for me to close his eyes or call his name, or even to attend the funeral, let alone take part in the lament. Not even you were present, cousin, so some servant must have performed the rituals in my place.' My patron sounded stricken and I realised how much it would have meant to him to carry out these simple filial acts. 'I must do something to honour my father's memory. And quickly too, before the Lemuria begins.' He sighed. 'And we must deal with that unfortunate business of the corpse outside.' He turned to me. 'No news there, I suppose?'

'I have made a little progress, Excellence, I am glad to say,' I murmured. 'I am fairly sure I know now to whom the dress belonged, although—'

He cut me off with an impatient smile. 'It's far too late to worry about all that, Libertus, my old friend. There's no time to trace the family now. I am sorry that your efforts on that score have been in vain, but for once I have to recognise that Lucius is right. In the present circumstances we must simply go ahead and deal with the matter right away. Fortunately the high priest of Jupiter has found a strategy for us – sprinkling a little earth on to the corpse. It gives it a notional burial at least, he says – it is an expedient that has been used before and should be enough to appease the spirits. Junio is out there with him, even now – it requires a citizen or somebody of rank. As soon as that is done, I've ordered the land slaves to take the body out and put it on the pyre, so that it is no longer within the confines of the villa walls. Then we can cleanse the stable block and begin the proper rituals here.'

'The high priest is with the body?' I was most surprised. Many priests take part in funeral rituals, of course – there's one acolyte of Diana, the goddess of the moon, who makes a living doing little else – but there are special regulations for the priests of Jupiter. Of course, the current one was not a *flamen* – the most sacred sacerdotal post in all the Empire – nor a prospective one, as his predecessor had been, so some of the stricter rules did not apply to him. But it was unusual to find him deliberately in the same room as a corpse. It was once explained to me that, since the Roman army has a special reverence for the Father of the Gods – every legion sets up a special altar to him, reconsecrated every year with great solemnity – it was ill-luck for his priests to cast their eyes on human death, lest the evil influence be extended to the troops.

But I need not have worried. Marcus shook his head. 'It isn't necessary for him to take an active part. He won't be in the room, just outside instructing Junio what to do. He and Stygius are conducting the actual ritual. Of course, there will be the physical cremation later on, but we can leave that to the slaves – the land slaves for preference, since they don't come to the house. Lucius has suggested that the peasant garments the corpse was wearing ought to be offered as grave-goods on the bier, and then the whole matter will be disposed of with a certain dignity, just as though the dead man were a household slave of mine. Except that none of us will be there to witness it.'

'But, Excellence,' I murmured, 'we don't know who he is. It is still possible that he was a man of wealth.'

'Then perhaps you would consent to perform the rites for him – or Junio could do it, as a citizen?'

'But, Excellence . . .' I protested. I'd brought this on myself. 'I am not familiar with Roman ritual . . .'

Marcus overrode me. 'Libertus, as your patron I am begging you. Just do this task for me. In case the dead lad was a Roman citizen, as you say, there should be someone of that status present at the pyre. You will do as well as anyone. You are not officially in mourning as this family is – it would be quite improper for any of my household to attend. I understand that you're not certain of the proper ritual, but you need have no fear that you'll offend the nether world by that. The priest will give you instructions what to do, and anyway he says the sprinkling of the earth is enough to keep the ghost at bay. This is an additional formality, that is all.'

I sighed. It was not a task I relished, but there was no escape. Marcus had formally requested it, and when Marcus requested something it was prudent to comply, however often he called me 'friend'. I bowed my head.

'I should be honoured, Excellence,' I said untruthfully. 'But I should be glad of an opportunity first to go and see my wife. She will be concerned already that I've been away so long, and I'd like to reassure her about what's happening.'

I meant it, too. Gwellia would certainly be reassured, not only to learn that I was safe and well, but more particularly to hear that I was now required merely to incinerate the corpse, rather than keep trying to discover who it was. In fact, I was looking forward to going home to talk to her. I wanted to hear her views on Morella's history. Gwellia often has a useful line of reasoning, seeing things from a woman's point of view; and besides, she can be relied upon to give a man a meal, and I was seriously hungry by this time.

Julia smiled warmly at my request and would clearly have agreed. She turned to Marcus, obviously to urge that he should let me go, but Lucius was already shaking his patrician head.

'No need. It is already seen to. I have sent word to her. Your freedwoman Cilla was here earlier, wondering where you were, and I explained the situation and sent a message back – only a few moments before your patron came home, in fact.'

My heart sank, wondering what kind of lofty message Lucius would have sent and what my poor Gwellia would have made of it. But once again there was nothing I could do, except say reluctantly, 'In that case, patron . . .'

My words were interrupted by the arrival at the door, from the direction of the inner courtyard, of the high priest of Jupiter. He was a short, round person with a florid face and thinning hair under the folds of toga he had draped to form a hood. He strode towards us, looking smug.

'Well, that should take care of the spirits, anyway. You can cremate the body when you are ready to. As soon as possible, is my advice – though the ceremony need not be elaborate. Our rituals have only been token ones, of course – we didn't have a name to call him by, for instance, so we just called three times on "whoever you may be" – but I am satisfied that the minimum requirements have been met. Officially he is symbolically buried as he is, so no need to cut off any other bits and bury them before you put him on the pyre. I've left Stygius to sweep and purify the stable block for you. Fire and herbs and water, that's the trick of it. And, if your little slave will bring that bowl of consecrated water from next door, I'll do the same thing for myself.'

He crossed to the bowl of herbs and took a pinch of them, placed it on the altar, where the ashes were still smouldering, and held his fingers above it in the smoke, turning them this way and that and rubbing them together as if cleansing them. Then, seizing a lamp, he walked three times round the room, turning right-handed to avoid bad luck. Niveus had by this time brought in the water bowl, and the priest pushed back his hood and plunged his face in it. All this to purify himself, when he had not even set eyes upon the corpse! I wondered how long a process would have been required if he'd happened to come upon the dead man by accident!

However, the little ritual seemed to sober him, and he spoke less briskly when he said, 'I have told them to let me know as soon as the cleansing of the stables is complete and the influence of death is lifted from the premises. Then we can move on to our ceremony here. I presume that you would like me to officiate? There is no problem for me in doing so, of course, since there is no corpse, but we should still think of sacrificing a young ram to the Lars, as one would normally do to close a family death. An animal without any kind of spot or flaw, of course. I could arrange one for you, from the temple, at a price, but of course it would take a little time to get it here.'

Lucius looked enquiringly at Marcus, who said wearily, 'I

think we can manage to provide our own. I had a word with Stygius on the subject earlier. He has been keeping a spotless ram apart ever since I first feared for my father's health. And I have already ordered him to kill a calf and a pig and told the kitchens to prepare a feast tonight.' He looked at me. 'Libertus, you and Gwellia may join us for that, if you wish. Oh, and your son, of course. I had forgotten him.'

Lucius glanced up contemptuously. 'A freedman pavement-maker and his wife, and his ex-slave of a son? That is your choice of honourable guests for your memorial feast?'

Marcus was clearly nettled, but he said evenly, 'These are my loyal *clientes*, cousin: it is fitting they should be present. However, naturally I took the opportunity, when I got the news in town, of inviting a few senior councillors as well. Some of the people whom you met the other day. Though it is short notice, they have promised they will come. It is not respectful to my father that we should honour his memory alone – although of course no one in Britannia knew him.'

Lucius had turned pink again, but he said nothing more – just gestured to Niveus to take the bowl away. The little slave boy looked terrified and slunk away with it.

The other servants had set the bust upon its plinth by now, and were weaving garlands to set around its brow. Julia had arranged her net veil across her face, and Marcus pulled his toga up to form a hood again. At any moment the family eulogy and lamentations would begin, and the unknown body was waiting at the pyre. It was time for me to go.

I held a hasty consultation with the priest of Jupiter, sent one of the servants out to get my slave, and with a growling stomach – set off to find my son and do my gruesome duty at the cremation site.

Chapter Sixteen

Standing on a windy hilltop in incipient rain, with the draught sneaking under your toga-hems and whistling round your knees while Stygius and half a dozen bored land slaves try to set fire to a corpse, is not a pleasant way to spend an afternoon – especially when your stomach is grumbling all the while. Add to this that Britannia is a gentle backwater, where most funerals continue to be held at night, with lighted torches and processions of hired mourners wailing through the dark – old traditions that have long ago been swept away in Rome – and you will understand why this hurried cremation, in broad daylight with no other witnesses but the slaves and Junio, and the identity of the corpse still a mystery, seemed very peculiar and discomfiting.

Of the actual ceremony, such as it was, the less said the better. Sufficient to report that I more or less remembered what I had to say and that – with the addition of quite a lot of oil – the pyre was finally induced to burn. I even recalled before it was too late that the eyes should be opened before the fire was lit. It was in the course of pulling back the sheet to see to this that I realised that the body was now clothed again, in what looked like a scarlet tunic such as Niveus wore.

I completed my ceremonial task and stepped back to

Juno. 'Somebody has dressed the body, then?' I murmured, keeping my voice deliberately low. We were at a funeral, after all.

'Stygius and I. And we put a *quadrans* in his mouth as well.' He too was talking from the corner of his mouth. 'All done at the suggestion of the priest of Jupiter. He said it was disrespectful to burn the body naked, when it is usual to deck a person in their best, so the steward brought out two or three old slave's tunics from the house and we selected this. Marcus supplied new ones for all the household staff when Lucius came.'

I frowned. 'But not for Niveus, surely? He wasn't there by then. And this is a page's uniform.'

Junio glanced warningly at Stygius and his men who were standing respectfully a little distance off, but all of them had their eyes fixed firmly on the ground, and facial expressions of careful piety. They seemed to suppose that all this muttering was some kind of muted prayer.

'It must have belonged to Pulchrus, I suppose,' he murmured. 'It was by far the smartest tunic, though it was stained across the hem, and they'd taken all the trimming off. It seemed to fit all right. They were going to cut it up to use for cleaning rags, but it's found a higher use. I don't suppose that in the afterworld a stain will matter much.' He gestured towards the pyre which by now was well alight. 'Time to put the grave-goods on the flames, I think.'

I picked up the plaid shawl that had accompanied the corpse, and carefully tossed it into the centre of the fire, where it caught light and began to smoulder instantly. I stepped ceremonially back to Junio again. Even as I did so, an idea occurred to me.

'Great Mithras! Pulchrus!' I whispered. 'I'd forgotten him. With those soft hands and everything, it might have been a page. You don't suppose . . . ?' I nodded at the pyre. 'If he was supposed to be carrying a message to Londinium, no one would know he was missing anyway.'

Junio shook his head. 'I suppose that's possible – I should have thought of that myself. But I don't see how it can be Pulchrus, Father. He was carrying that letter about arrangements for the trip and Marcus received an answer from Londinium this very afternoon, by the same messenger who brought the news of Marcus's father's death. And that was under the seal of the commander of the fleet – the *classis Britannica*. I saw him open it.'

'So Marcus's letter obviously reached Londinium, you mean? But that does not prove that it was Pulchrus who delivered it.'

Junio grinned. 'But it seems as though it was. There was a hasty message from him attached to the reply, scratched on a piece of bark, saying that he and Hirsius – that's Lucius's chief slave – had left the wagons now and were riding on ahead, to make arrangements for the next stage of the trip. It's a long way to Rome from where they'll land in Gaul. And there's no doubt that he sent it. He personally asked the messenger to bring it here, it seems – and from the description the fellow gave, it must have been Pulchrus – dashing, smart and vain. And anyway Marcus recognises the way he wrote the words.'

I nodded, grudgingly. If Marcus knew the writing, then that settled it. Pulchrus had been taught the rudiments, of course – most pages have to have a smattering of script – but I'd seen a rare note that he'd written once, myself, full of idiosyncratic spelling and peculiar letter-shapes. Quite unmistakable.

I sprinkled a little more wine and oil on the fire to help it burn. 'So we are sure that Pulchrus reached Londinium all right?' I was reluctant to abandon my neat theory here, but I was forced to admit that it was too convenient. Why would anyone kill a page if the message was going to be delivered anyway? I put the point to Junio. 'No one had tampered with the letter on the way?'

'It seems not, since the reply answered the request for information point by point. Apparently Marcus's party is now going to stay with the fleet commander overnight – he has a fine villa just outside the town – because the governor's palace is undergoing repair, new frescos and all that sort of thing, in preparation for the incoming governor. Anyway, the commander is a kind of relative – he is married to Lucius's other cousin, it appears.'

'A cousin of Marcus's?' I almost squeaked in my surprise.

He shook his head to warn me to speak more quietly. 'Only by marriage, on Lucius's mother's side. Marcus lost touch with his aunt and her relations after Lucius's father put his wife aside, and it seems he never met this half-cousin in his life – though of course he'd heard of her. He didn't realise she'd been stationed with her husband in Londinium. But it turns out to be convenient, as these things often are. The husband will take them to Dubris in one of the finest ships in his command, and accompany them in another, larger one to Gaul. It was all in the letter – I heard Marcus reading it to Julia. She was quite relieved to hear that they were going to family.'

'So that's not the answer to the mystery,' I said

reluctantly. Indeed, when I considered all the facts, this corpse could hardly have been Pulchrus anyway. He'd left the villa accompanied by slaves with a whole cartload full of luggage – to say nothing of the entertainers who were travelling with them – and we had witnesses in Glevum who saw him pass the gates. He could hardly have been murdered without someone's seeing it. However, it had given me an interesting idea. This was not the only household that used mounted messengers. If there was any other rumour of a missing page, or the answer to someone's message had failed to arrive . . . ?

Junio nudged my arm. 'Sandals?'

They were a pair of old ones, belonging to some slave. They had broken straps and mended soles and would not have fitted anyone bigger than a child, but I put them solemnly on the fire. A spirit should not reach the underworld without a pair of shoes, and presumably a ghost can modify its shape. Junio added some token wine and victuals to the blaze – to sustain the soul on its journey to the Styx – and that completed the ceremonial.

I raised my head and said in ringing tones – for the benefit of the audience as well as the gods – 'With these grave-gifts we commend this unknown spirit to the underworld.'

'Unknown indeed,' my son said in my ear. 'And now we may never find out who it was.'

I looked at the pyre. It was burning fiercely now and the body would soon be little more than ash. Whoever he was it would be hard to prove his identity now. Perhaps it did not matter. Marcus didn't care, and at this stage it could make no difference to the murdered man. The mystery would have to remain a mystery. If the corpse had been a household page, he'd had a decent funeral; if a citizen we'd given him the minimum at least.

I called for a final blessing from the gods, pulled down the folds of toga which I'd been using as a hood, and took a step or two away from the cremation pyre. Stygius came bustling over with a large container full of wine.

'You've finished, then?' He did not wait for a reply. 'We'll let the fire burn down a bit, and then we'll pour this over him. That will cool the ashes and we can get them put into the ground. The mistress has provided a pretty jug for them.' He gestured to Caper, who was standing at his side. 'One of the ones the servants use to drink their watered wine.'

Caper said nothing, but gave a goatish grin and held the jug aloft in hairy hands for me to see. When the conversation was in Latin, he wasn't talkative.

I nodded. 'Very good. So I can leave you to it?' I would be glad to go inside. It was beginning to drizzle in earnest now. If it were not for the fire, which gave off a lot of heat, it would have been very chilly and miserable indeed. 'I'll tell my patron the cremation is complete. He wanted it finished as soon as possible. You need not worry about accompanying us back. Junio and I can find our way all right.'

Stygius shook his head. 'The master wouldn't like it. I'll go with you myself. Caper can take over here till I get back again. It will take a little while for the fire to burn down, anyway.'

'Won't take too long to quench it, if this rain persists,' I said, but Stygius appeared not to have heard. Instead he was already striding down across the field, and waiting for me and Junio to join him at the farm gate to the lane. He swung it wide ajar, and looked at me intently as I walked through it down the hill. 'You won't be wanting answers to your questions now?'

I shook my head. 'Marcus has lost interest and wants the matter dropped.'

'This young gentleman seemed to think you wouldn't give up so easily. He said as much when we were doing that so-called burial. If I can help you, citizen, in any way . . .'

'I told you, Marcus wishes the matter laid to rest. In deference to his dead father, I believe.'

Junio gave me a sideways grin. 'But I notice that you didn't put the plaid dress on the pyre, although I know that Lucius proposed it. That suggests to me that you have not entirely lost interest in the case.'

I tried to look affronted. 'The high priest agreed that it was not appropriate. It was almost certainly Morella's garment, as I pointed out, and it should have died with her.'

Junio glanced at me. 'You've discovered that the peasant girl was called Morella, then?'

I had forgotten that he did not know. I briefly outlined the happenings of the day. 'So you see,' I finished, 'I couldn't burn her garment with some unnamed man who'd been dressed up in it. That's disrespectful to the souls of both of them. Assuming she is dead. I was only too happy to follow the high priest's advice.'

'Besides, you were reluctant to destroy a piece of evidence? And neither did you offer up the coins – although they are unlikely to have been a peasant girl's. Because you still want to find out where she got them from?'

There was some truth in this, of course. Whatever Marcus's instructions about the corpse might be, the question of Morella's fate was still a mystery, and, whether she was alive or dead, I could not help feeling that it should be solved – although Gwellia would not like it if I went on with the investigation, especially when Marcus had told me I could stop. So, having no answer for Junio, I simply frowned at him.

We were walking side by side along a stony track by now, and neither of the others said anything at all. They were avoiding looking at me as they picked their way, although I noticed that they were exchanging glances now and then.

'The body is destroyed, in any case,' I said. 'It would be impossible for anyone to identify it now.'

'So the murderer has had his way about that after all – since you're still convinced that's why he battered in the face.' Junio's voice was sad.

'And what about the shoulders?' Stygius put in.

It was an invitation, and I fell into the trap. 'I have been thinking about that, ever since I saw the body on the pyre. When I saw him in that slave's tunic, it gave me an idea.' I outlined my thoughts about the softness of the hands and the fact that a messenger might not be quickly missed, if he was carrying a missive between two distant points. 'All right, it isn't Pulchrus,' I went on, 'but it could still have been a servant from another house like this. If so there might well have been a slave brand on his back – and that wound would remove the identifying mark. And there was that narrow line round his neck as well – exactly as if a slave disc on a chain was used to throttle him. It would have been cut off afterwards, of course.'

Stygius thought a minute, and then said in his slow, stolid way, 'A page? That would explain the well-developed legs: he'd get them from clinging to his horse and running about with messages.' He walked ahead to undo a second gate and lead the way across another field. His stride was slow but it propelled him well on this uneven ground. We had to hurry to keep up with him. 'But I'm surprised that no one has set up a hue and cry. A good pageboy is an expensive thing to lose.'

I was puffing, bouncing across hillocks and a little out of breath.

Even Junio was breathing hard. 'His master might not even realise that he is missing yet. But if it was a messenger, what happened to the horse?'

'We ought to be asking questions about that,' I said, pausing at a rugged tree to lean and catch my breath. 'Not just in local households, but perhaps at Glevum gates, in case the watch has heard of any missing page, or anyone unexpected has tried to sell a horse.' I caught the glance that passed between the other two, and stopped. 'Only, of course, the matter has been closed. So there is no point in our discussing this. Please drop the subject, and we'll talk of something else.'

Junio gave me a knowing look. 'You will not be interested in hearing what I learned in Glevum, then?'

'And what was that?'

I saw my son exchange a glance with Stygius, and grin. 'Not very much you didn't learn yourself, in fact, though the gate guards recognised the description straight away. It was the hair that made her look conspicuous, of course. But they've seen her – Morella, is she called? – come to the market with her mother lots of times.' He hesitated.

'And?'

'Then recently she turned up one day on her own and

asked directions to the inn where the dancing troupe had rooms. The soldiers thought that it was comical, of course, and laughed at her. One of them suggested that she find Lucius's chief slave – he was taking bribes, apparently, to have acts selected for the villa, to come and do their turns in the hope that they would be selected for the Emperor. That bears out what the dancing woman told us, doesn't it? That the girl was willing to bribe someone for the chance of going to Rome. Only, of course, it was a waste of time. This fellow Hirsius didn't have the authority to arrange it anyway. Only Lucius could possibly do that.'

'And Morella?'

'The guards didn't think she had the money – it was just a silly jibe. But they told her where the dancing troupe were lodged, and off she went. Unfortunately no one paid particular attention after that, but someone recalled seeing her later in the marketplace, and another guard thought she might have gone out past him later on, but he wasn't sure.'

'Any use, citizen?' That was Stygius.

I was affronted by this clear conspiracy with my adopted son. 'How can it be useful, since the matter's closed?' I said, and trudged in disgruntled silence till we reached the house. 'Junio and I must go in to take our leave. You have the funeral ashes to dispose of, I believe.'

'As you say, citizen.' And he went plodding off again towards the distant hillside and the still-rising smoke.

Chapter Seventeen

Whatever family ceremony had been taking place in the atrium while we were away was clearly over by the time we returned.

The statue of Marcus's father now had a wreath round its neck, another on its forehead, and a little pile of flower offerings laid in front of it. There was fresh blood on the household altar where the wether had evidently just been sacrificed, and the smell of burning flesh and feathers lingered in the air. An oil lamp still burned on each side of the shrine, and another pair flanked the garlanded patriarchal bust.

Of Marcus and his party there was now no sign, nor was the high priest in evidence. However, the room was not deserted. Atalanta was there. Dressed only in a mourning tunic, barefoot and with her hair spread loose, she was seated on the stool which I had earlier occupied, playing a melancholy air upon a lyre and singing very softly in a keening croon. With her strong plain features smeared with ash and her hair in disarray, she looked like a Fury from some painted frieze, but the music she made would have charmed the gods themselves.

I was not sure whether I should speak to her – if she was officially commencing some sort of lament, she should be permitted to do so undisturbed – but she looked up at us and smiled when she saw who it was.

'If you are looking for the master and mistress, citizens, I am afraid they've finished here. The mistress has gone to oversee arrangements for the feast; the master is drafting a letter to send home. The priest has retired to the bath-house for a little while. Apparently more purification was felt to be required.'

'And Lucius?'

'Having a strip of mourning stitched round his toga-hems, in preparation for tonight. Fortunately there was still a bit of Marcus's left over in the house,' she said, her fingers rippling ceaselessly across the plaintive strings.

'We simply wanted to take leave of them, and let them know that everything was done,' I said.

She smiled. 'I'm afraid I cannot assist you two citizens myself – I have been left here to play a requiem – but Niveus is in the ante-room, if you require a slave.'

I clapped my hands, but there was no response. I waited for a moment, then I made up my mind. 'I suppose that we should go in there and cleanse ourselves in any case,' I said, 'since once again we have been in contact with a corpse. We will go and find Niveus, instead of waiting for him here. I want him to fetch my slave for me, as well, so that I can go home to my wife as soon as possible.'

Junio look startled for an instant. 'Your slave?' Then he grinned. 'Oh, you mean Minimus, of course. In that case, Father, lead the way.'

We went through to the ante-room, though Junio remained dutifully a step or two behind. Niveus was dozing on a stool beside the door, with a pile of linen towels stacked upon his knee. He did not stir as we plunged our hands and faces in the bowl, then all at once he started into wakefulness. When he saw us, he was on his feet at once. Under the dust and ashes his face had turned as scarlet as his usual uniform.

'Citizens! You wanted me? But of course you did. You will be wanting that refreshment you did not have time to eat. If you go back to the atrium, I will bring it there at once. In the meantime, here are towels for you.' And before I could stop him, he had thrust the pile at me and was disappearing in the direction of the kitchens at a trot, as if he was intent on earning some winning garland at a race.

I dabbed my face, and Junio did the same – doubtless as pleased as I was to have rinsed at least some of the pyre-smoke from his skin. There is a lingering smell in charring human flesh which is inclined to stay with one for days.

My son grinned, and took my towel from me – some slave-like habits are hard to break, it seems – while I smeared the altar ashes on my face again.

'You would have no objection to refreshment?' I enquired. 'I know that we are invited to a feast tonight, and really I had hoped to get away, but I have not eaten since I left the roundhouse shortly after dawn – and had only a small beaker of spring water to drink. It might not be polite to eat things in the atrium just now, so soon after the familial sacrifice and with the memorial statue there, but we could always retire to the *triclinium*, I suppose.'

Junio folded the towels and dropped them on the stool. 'I snatched some bread and water at the garrison, and was given refreshment when we got back to the house. But I too would be happy to have something now – burying and burning corpses is very thirsty work.' He patted some ashes on to his own boyish brow, and stood back to escort me to the atrium again.

Atalanta was still expertly plucking music from her lyre when we returned, but to my regret the tune was coming to a close. She concluded with a long, high, throbbing final note.

'That was beautiful,' I told her, to her evident delight. 'Where did you learn to play the lyre like that?'

She gave a rueful smile. 'The slavemaster who reared me up for sale saw that I was taught. "When a girl's as plain as you are," he used to say to me, "she needs some kind of talent, if she's to fetch a decent price. I've spent too much on raising you to have you sold for fifty *asses* as a mere kitchen slave." At first I did not like it – the hag who taught me used to try to beat it into me – but in the end I found I had a certain gift for it. So whenever I was exhibited for sale my master made me take the lyre. But it's impossible to play it when your arms are chained, and he sometimes beat me round the hands because I didn't sell.' She said it without bitterness, as though this were no more than commonplace.

'And that tune?' I said softly. 'Did you devise that yourself?'

She shook her head. 'I learned a lot of dirges – the woman who taught me was an undertaker's slave and my master hoped to sell me to someone similar. But then Julia came along and picked me anyway, though she has never required me to play a single note. It is quite a delight to have the chance again. Besides, you know, citizen, it enables me to sit – which is a pleasure in itself. But, excuse me, I must begin again. There is one final tune of homage I should play.' She closed her eyes and began to strum and croon, a cadence so plaintive that, I felt, it might have brought tears to the statue's eyes.

We were still listening with pleasure when Niveus returned, not with the bread and cheese which I'd been promised earlier, but with a tray of honeyed dates, a folding table and a pair of stools. He must have seen the disappointment on my face, because he turned bright red again, and immediately began to apologise.

'I'm very sorry, citizen – it is all my fault. I forgot to tell the kitchens that the platter was for you, and I am afraid they gave it to your slave. Of course they are very busy now with the memorial feast, but it was suggested that I should bring you these.' He was setting up the little seating arrangements as he spoke. 'I'm to offer the same to any visitor who comes to pay respects. Though I don't know who would, except for the people invited to the feast. There's hardly been time to spread the news. It was only this morning that we heard of it ourselves, though it wasn't unexpected. The master had our tunics ready several days ago, and Lucius had guessed before he even cut the seal. Though there's been so much happening since the messenger arrived that it seems like days ago. Here you are, citizen, this is ready now.' He set the tray down with a flourish and invited me to sit.

Dates are by no means a favourite food of mine – they are too sweet for me, especially in the honeyed form that Marcus seems to like – but I was so hungry that I could have eaten the serving dish by now, and I could see that Junio was grinning in delight. Such delicacies as honeyed dates were still rare treats to him, so I said, 'Thank you, Niveus. You may go and fetch my slave. He should be waiting in the servants' room.'

The slave looked startled. 'But, citizen, the wine! I wasn't able to carry everything at once.'

'Then you may fetch it after you've brought Minimus to me,' I said, and with that I popped a date into my mouth. It was as sweet as I'd remembered, but it was welcome all the same. I took another and another and swallowed those as well, though my son was still relishing his first, letting the sweetness linger on his tongue.

I was just beginning to wish that I had ordered the wine at once – half a dozen honeyed dates do not improve a thirst – when the outer door was opened and Marcus strode in. He was accompanied by Minimus, much to my surprise.

I rose to my feet in some embarrassment. The remnants of my last date were proving hard to swallow. 'Patron,' I murmured, through sticky teeth. Junio, meanwhile, had scrambled to his feet and was bowing respectfully, while Atalanta quickly brought her homage to a close, rose and stood in silence, dangling her lyre.

'Thank you, Atalanta, that will do for now. You can come back and play some more a little later on.' Marcus waved his hand benignly, and she tiptoed from the room. Even funerary music had to wait its turn, it seemed. My patron smiled at us. 'I am glad to see that you have been offered hospitality,' he said, 'though Niveus has failed to bring a drink, I see. I have given him the simplest duties, but it seems he never learns. That is what I want to talk to you about, in fact, Libertus, my old friend.'

'Of course, if I can be of any service, Excellence,' I said cautiously. 'Old friend'? It always made me wary when he called me that. What did he want of me this time? Not another wasted walk into the hills, I hoped.

But I need not have worried. It was not *my* services he was after, it appeared. 'I want to borrow Minimus back from you for a little while. I need someone to go to Glevum to take a letter to the garrison and link up with a messenger from the imperial post. I have been writing home. A difficult message, in the circumstances, but an important one – since I am the heir, there are arrangements I shall need to make. I don't want to entrust the note to Niveus this time. He is too young and vulnerable to ride the roads alone, and anyway there is a good chance that he would contrive to get it wrong. Not insist on seeing the commander personally or something of the kind.'

'Use Minimus, by all means.' I was quite relieved that it was nothing more.

Marcus rewarded me with a grateful smile. 'I won't deprive you of him longer than I need. I'll send him back to you as soon as he gets home.'

'Which will be tomorrow, I suppose?' I said. I have known Marcus make arrangements several times for a servant to be accommodated at the garrison overnight, since it takes some little time to get to town and back on foot.

He laughed. 'He should be back this evening, though perhaps not till after dark. Minimus can ride, you realise? He was trained as a page, and it's one of the reasons why I bought him when I did. I shall put him on a horse. That way the letter will get there as soon as possible, and you are not inconvenienced for so long.' A thought seemed to strike him, and he added with a smile, 'In the meantime you can borrow Niveus, if you like. At the very least, he can escort you home.'

I was about to accept this offer with gratitude – it would give me a chance to question the young page, I thought – when Niveus himself came scuttling in again, carrying a jug of wine and two goblets on a tray. 'I couldn't find Minimus for you, citiz—' he began. Then he saw Marcus. He stopped in the doorway, speechless with dismay.

'It is all right, Niveus, you may bring in the tray,' Marcus said, impatience obvious in his tone. 'And then I have a little task for you. The citizen Libertus—'

'Excellence!' Niveus was so anxious that he actually interrupted the remark. That could have earned him a whipping, but he was too flustered to care. 'You're here! And I have only brought two cups! Give me just a moment and I'll fetch another one!' He hurried over to the table and put down the tray, so eager that he knocked a metal goblet to the floor, and in trying to retrieve it nearly spilt the wine.

'You see, Libertus?' Marcus raised his brows at me, as though seeking recognition that this was an idiot.

Niveus looked very close to tears. He gulped, turned pink and then burst out again, 'I'm sorry, master. And you too, citizen. I know you asked me—'

I intervened before he managed to make matters any worse. 'Niveus, thank you, but I do not think I shall require a drink just now.' It was a lie – my tongue was almost cleaving to my palate as I spoke – but it was obvious that something must be done. 'And Minimus is found, as you can see. Your master needs him for a special task, and has said that Junio and I can borrow you to escort us home. So, if you are ready?'

He glanced at me with gratitude, but said uncertainly, 'Should I go and get a cape, then? And who'll man the ante-room? I'm supposed to greet the visitors and hand out towels . . .'

'I'm sure my steward can find someone to do that onerous task.' Marcus gave me another of his looks. 'Even Colaphus could do it, if only Aulus had returned.'

'The gatekeeper's still missing, then?' I frowned. 'Lucius had a theory that the Silurians might have—'

My patron gave a short impatient laugh. 'Aulus? I see little chance of that. He's stronger than an ox. Though I can't imagine where he's got to – leaving his post at such a time! I'll have him soundly whipped when he returns and reduced to bread and water for a week. None of his precious onions. And you too, Niveus, if you make a mess of this. Now, Libertus, Junio, I'll leave you to make your own arrangements with my page – and have a little wine, if you should change your mind. The sooner I get Minimus safely on his way the better. I want the letter in the hands of a courier today.' He nodded curtly. 'Till this evening, then.'

He left the room. Minimus gave me one last, apologetic look, and followed at his heels.

Chapter Eighteen

Junio had been standing quietly all this while, as befits a junior citizen in the presence of a senior magistrate, but as soon as my patron had safely left the room he became his usual lively self again.

'Father,' he said, with an excited air. 'You were telling me about that slave girl – Morella, was she called? – and the tunic she was wearing when Minimus saw her here, which it seems she didn't have when she left home. So she must have bought it somewhere, mustn't she? It occurs to me, if Minimus is going to Glevum anyway . . . ? That is surely the most likely place? Or are you really not going to enquire into the matter any more?'

I gave him a sideways glance. 'Well . . .' I was forced into the admission with a sheepish grin. 'Exactly the same thought had occurred to me!' I beckoned to the page. 'Niveus, come here. I want you to take a message to Minimus for me. Listen carefully. "There is a woman in the forum who sells old clothes. When you have delivered the letter to the garrison, go and see if she sold that tunic to the girl you saw." Can you repeat those words exactly?'

Niveus did so, looking mystified.

'Very good,' I told him. 'Now go and say the same thing, word for word, to Minimus. Tell him that the message is from me. You should find him at the stables, being provided with a horse. Hurry, before you miss him. And when you have done that, fetch your cloak, and come back here to us.'

'On my way, citizen.' Niveus was almost pink with pride. I heard him muttering as he hurried off, 'There is a woman in the forum . . .'

Junio gave me an approving glance. 'If more people gave him clear instructions of that kind, perhaps he would be more successful as a page.' He gestured to the table. 'Speaking of which, would it be in order for me to pour you out some wine? I know that strictly it is not my place – I am not a slave of Marcus's and never was – but I know that you are thirsty and he did suggest that we could have some if we liked. The trouble is, he didn't actually tell Niveus to pour it out.' He did not wait for my agreement, but began to serve the wine.

'I learned to give instructions to scared slave boys long ago,' I teased, 'and it seems I was successful, because he learned to read my thoughts!' I took the goblet he'd filled for me and sipped it gratefully. Marcus would not have approved of it at all, I thought – Niveus had watered it too much for Roman tastes – but it suited me far better than if it had been strong. I sat down on the stool that the page had brought, and grinned at Junio. 'And not just about the wine.'

My son returned my smile. He had poured another cupful for himself, and was drinking with a certain relish, I observed.

'Reading your thoughts? You mean about your interest in that slave girl, after all?' He laughed. 'That did not require any special skill. It would have been obvious to anyone who knew you, I should think.'

I was quite affronted. 'I don't know what you mean.'

His grin was broader now. 'You do not like to leave a question unresolved, so naturally you would want to make a few enquiries about her if you could. Even Stygius could see as much, and that was before you told us the story of her life. When the chief steward came out with the tunic for the pyre and announced that Marcus now wanted the matter to be dropped, Stygius said—' He stopped. 'Great Minerva! That is something that had not occurred to me!'

'What is?' I enquired.

'The tunic that Morella had! It could not have come from this household, I suppose? You know that Marcus had new ones made for all his slaves, so there must have been a number of discarded ones – including the one that we put on the corpse. They can't all have been intended for use as cleaning cloths. Marcus is far too careful with his cash for that.'

That was perceptive and it made me laugh. 'You are quite right, of course. Most of them were dyed for mourning and are being used again.'

'Yet Pulchrus's uniform was among the most expensive of all. Why consign that for rags?'

I frowned. 'Because the colour was already bright and it would be more difficult to put the new dye over it? Gwellia would tell us – she understands these things. And the elaborate trimmings had all been taken off, so sparing it for the corpse was not wholly profligate. But Morella's tunic . . . ?' I thought about it for a moment and then shook my head. 'I don't think it is likely that it came from here. Most of the tunics of the household slaves are blue – though there are a few exceptions here and there. Minimus worked here, after all, and knows the colours of all the uniforms. I'm sure that he would have told me if it looked like one of theirs. However, I might speak to the steward, just in case. Niveus can fetch him . . . ah, here he comes.'

But it was not Niveus who came bursting in, nor the steward either. It was Colaphus, his bull-face flushed with outrage and affronted dignity. 'I am no longer wanted at the gates.'

'Aulus has come back?' I made the obvious deduction, and was surprised to discover that I was quite relieved.

Colaphus shook his head. 'I would not have minded that so much,' he muttered bitterly. 'After all, it is his job, not mine. But there's still no sign of him. Yet they have relieved me at the gate – put some fellow in my place who's only half my size – and sent me in to do the work of that accursed page instead, greeting visitors and handing namby-pamby towels! I don't know what my master Lucius will say when he finds out. But the steward is insisting. I was put at his disposal in the interim so he maintains he can use me in any way he likes. Oh, and I'm to give you a message too. There's a man and two women asking for you at the gate.'

'A man and two women?' I put down my cup and I looked at Junio, but he clearly was as mystified as I was. 'Who are they?'

'I didn't ask them and I didn't let them in. They don't look the sort of people who should be calling here.' Colaphus looked as prim and self-righteous as a battering ram can be. 'I told them the household was in mourning, which they claimed they knew – though I don't see how they could possibly have heard – but they would not take the hint and go away. They are clearly not people summoned to the feast, and the man, in particular, was not appropriately dressed to come into a household that was honouring its dead. They would've had to go through all that cleansing ritual. Besides, I understood that you were leaving very soon. I told them that they would have to wait for you out there . . .'

I could not let this pass without rebuke. Even in a house of mourning it is not polite to keep a guest's callers waiting outside in the lane. 'One fewer lot of towels and ashes for you to deal with, too?' I said. 'You should thank Jove for these small mercies, I suppose.'

He shrugged his massive shoulders, but had the grace to flush.

I turned to Junio. 'I'd better go and see them, whoever they might be. You stay here and wait for Niveus. And you can talk to the chief steward for me, if you like. About that matter we were speaking of a little while ago. There might be something useful he could tell us, I suppose – and if not we can at least eliminate the possibility you thought of.'

I was being deliberately elliptical, partly because Colaphus was clearly bursting to know what I was talking about and I was still annoyed by his discourtesy, but also because I suspected that anything he learned would get back to Lucius and my patron in a flash, and I did not wish to be forbidden to pursue enquiries. Marcus had told me to let matters rest about the corpse, but he had not mentioned the girl who owned the dress: a technicality I did not wish to have pointed out to him. So I simply gave the bodyguard my warmest smile and said, 'Since you are standing in for Niveus for a while, perhaps you would be good enough to escort me to the gate.'

It did not please him but there was nothing he could do,

and he led the way with ill-disguised bad grace. A little way short of the gatehouse cell he stopped and waved a vague finger in the direction of the road. 'There you are, citizen. Exactly as I said. Not the sort of people I could lightly have let in, when the house is preparing for a memorial. Don't even speak good Latin, most of them. Besides,' he added, in half-apology, 'the man has got a dog with him. I could not have let that in, in any case.'

A dog? A horrible suspicion was forming in my mind. But I could not imagine what Morella's father could be doing at the villa gates, or why he wanted me – I was sure my comments about the murdered corpse had frightened him. Unless he'd found his daughter? I brightened. That was possible. Or, of course, this might not be Farathetos at all. Well, there was only one way to find out.

I dismissed my escort with a nod, and went on to the gates where one of Marcus's larger garden slaves was standing with a spear. He was muscular enough but he looked sadly ill at ease, though he rushed eagerly to open up for me.

No sooner had I set foot out in the lane than I knew I'd been been correct. It was Morella's father – I recognised the face, and even more certainly I recognised the dog. There was no mistaking it, in fact. It started barking and leaping up at me the instant I appeared and though its owner jerked it sharply back it went on snarling and growling in its throat. The creature seemed to have tolerated everybody else – I hadn't heard it from inside the gate – but now it was straining at the rope leash round its neck and making snapping motions in the direction of my knees.

I glanced towards the hooded females who were standing by – just long enough to take in that they were older women, not the missing girl – but as soon as I diverted my full attention from the dog the creature made a sudden lunge at me. It took me by surprise. I am usually very fond of dogs – in my youth I had several hounds myself – but this one seemed to share its master's malice towards the world.

'Down!' I said sharply, and it skulked and bared its teeth.

I kept my eyes fixed firmly on it as I addressed the man. 'Farathetos! I hear you wanted me?'

He answered me in Latin. 'That's right, citizen. I want a word with you. Alone if possible!' He jerked a scornful head towards the women as he spoke. 'This is men's business, not for women's ears.'

Then, to my astonishment, a familiar voice broke in. 'This gentleman came asking for you at the roundhouse, husband. He wouldn't tell me what it was about, but says he is the father of the missing girl. I knew that you were anxious for any news of her, so naturally I brought him here at once.'

I whirled to face her, taking my eyes off the dog again. 'Gwellia!' It was indeed my wife. I almost went towards her, but a growl prevented me.

She gave me an understanding smile. 'I am sorry if we have disturbed you at an awkward time. I told this fellow what Cilla had earlier told me – that the villa was in mourning and that you were required to stand in for Marcus at the cremation of a slave – but he was insistent that he'd discovered something that you'd want to know, and was not content to simply leave a message at the house.'

The farmer scowled. 'Can't even speak in Latin now and not be listened to! But she's quite right, citizen. This is not for anyone else's ears but yours.'

'As he says, husband,' Gwellia went on in her sweetest

tone, 'he wished to speak to you himself. I reasoned that a slave funeral would not take very long. So, seeing that I was known to all the servants here, and I was planning to come anyway, I suggested that I would accompany him and ask the gatekeeper to have you found and brought to us.'

Farathetos spat impatiently. 'And what a waste of time! I would have done better to have come and asked myself.'

I braved the dog this time, and crossed to Gwellia. 'I'm sorry you had such a discourteous greeting here.' I took her hand and pressed it.

She smiled up at me. 'I didn't know the man on duty at the time. And it was mutual!' She nodded towards the gatehouse. 'What has happened to Aulus, anyway?'

I shook my head. 'That's another problem: no one seems to know, though Marcus does not seem to take it very seriously yet. I'll tell you later. You go on inside – Junio is there. We were going to go back to the roundhouse to see you very soon, but there is no need since you have come to us. Perhaps you would let the pageboy know he won't be needed now.'

She nodded. 'But I think we should go back home in any case. You will want to get ready for the feast tonight. I was only anxious to see that you were well. But since I've come, I'll go and pay Julia my respects and offer the household my condolences. I will see you when you have finished here. Meanwhile your toga-hood's in disarray.' She reached up, as if to put it right, and as she did so she whispered in my ear, 'There may be things that I can help you with. I have had an interesting conversation with the wife.' Then she turned and went in through the gate, which opened instantly to let her pass.

Chapter Nineteen

I gazed after Gwellia's retreating form. She had spoken of 'the wife'. I looked across at the other hooded figure in the road, and there was Morella's mother standing patiently by. I had been so busy with the dog, and then with Gwellia, I hadn't realised who she was.

She saw me looking and raised her face to me, gave me a brief, abject, snaggled smile, and dropped her eyes again. Of course, she would not have followed much that had been said – we had been speaking in a tongue she didn't understand. I turned to face the man and the still grumbling dog.

'You have news about Morella?' I spoke in Celtic now.

He recognised the strategy. A brusque, unwilling nod.

'Something that has come to light since we talked earlier? You haven't found her?'

He snorted. 'I only wish I had. I'd give her such a beating she'd wish she'd not been born.' He still spoke in Latin, as he'd done throughout – as if he had deliberately declined to take my lead. 'She's stolen money from me, that's what she's done! No wonder you said that she had quite a lot!'

'Morella didn't mean it,' her mother pleaded. She had clearly derived his meaning from his tone. She turned to me. 'I don't know what he's saying, but she is not a thief. If she took money, she thought it was her share. He must have told them a hundred times that he'd put cash by for them all. I know Morella – she won't have taken it all. It can't have been more than a few *denarii*.'

'Not an *aureus* for example?' And some other golden coins?' I had supposed we were talking about the treasure in the hem.

The worn face looked quite startled. 'Good Jupiter! Where would a farmer get gold pieces from? Why, the only time I've ever seen an *aureus* in my life was when my uncle got a couple amongst the coins they gave him for his farm land, years ago.'

'Silence, woman! What has that to do with it?' Farathetos was speaking Celtic now.

I paid no attention. 'Your uncle's land?' I said. 'That was a payment from the army, I presume?'

She looked apprehensive, but she answered with a nod. 'Six gold pieces they gave him, when they seized his farm. He was quite pleased to start with. More than his forefathers had got, he said – but when he took one to the market they confiscated it. Said it wasn't proper coinage, or something of the kind. The disappointment was what killed him in the end, I think. He had the others buried with him when he died.'

The man had been trying to interrupt her throughout, between attempts to quell the dog. I ignored him. A horrible suspicion was forming in my mind.

'Buried with him? As his funeral goods? I can imagine that. We Celts like to give a man his finest possessions when he dies, so that he has them with him in the afterlife. And there is nothing that a Celt likes more than gold. Even if he cannot spend it in the marketplace.' I glanced at her husband, who was scarlet-faced.

She looked defeated. 'It was still pure gold,' she said. 'Valuable if it was only melted down. I think he always meant to do it, though he never did. He feared they'd confiscate the rest of it as well.' She glanced towards her husband, who was looking thunderous. 'But I don't know why I am telling you all this. The gold was buried with him – nothing to do with what Morella took. It's just that you asked about the *aureus*. Of course there was no question of anything like that. The most she could have taken were some silver coins.'

'How much exactly?'

She looked at him for guidance, but he simply scowled. 'There might have been a double *denarius* or two, and altogether it could have added up to quite a lot – though I never saw it personally, of course. My husband never told me where he'd hidden it, though he was always saying he had a wedding portion for the girls, and threatening to cut them off if they displeased him in any way.'

It was too much for the farmer. 'Silence, wife!' He aimed a kick at her, and in the process almost loosed the dog. 'Here, take this blasted animal and keep an eye on it and leave us men to talk without your whining on. It's half impossible to hold a conversation like this.'

He thrust the rope into her veined and work-worn hands. The creature was too strong for her, you could see that instantly, and I was afraid that in her less restraining grasp the brute would get away and go for me again; but once it sensed its freedom it rushed off the other way, down the lane and into the forest opposite, dragging the unfortunate woman after it. We could hear them in the distance: the dog's persistent bark, and the woman's plaintive cries for him to stop.

'Caught the scent of something,' was all the farmer said. 'Stupid woman hasn't the first idea how to handle that dog. Fortunately it will always come back when I call.' He spat and rubbed his hands. 'Now where were we?'

'You discovered that Morella had taken money from you, I believe,' I said. 'Four golden coins? Is that the truth of it? Money that you stole from your wife's uncle's grave?'

He had turned a shifty red but he held his ground. 'Of course I wouldn't stoop to steal them from the grave. They weren't ever buried – and they were mine in any case. The dying man had told me to keep them for myself, and that is what I did. I took them out before we sealed the grave. Of course I did not say anything to anyone – they'd only have insisted that I put them back. I was going to have them melted down, in time – the gold has got value if the coins have not. And why shouldn't I? He'd given it to me. It was the family's money and it was no use to the dead.'

I stared at him. I did not believe a word of his account and I doubted that his wife and her family would either. I wondered what would happen if they learned he'd robbed a grave. Probably, at best, he would be outcast from the tribe – lose his wife and children and his land as well, and be driven into exile by being wholly shunned. At worst? It made me shudder. Yet, by claiming that Morella had robbed him of the coins, he had put himself in danger of something of the kind. So why had he come to me?

Because he knew I might be able to trace the coins back? They were so unusual that it was more than possible. Some army requisition officer had clearly palmed the uncle off with coinage which was a problem to dispose of otherwise: probably he had taken it as loot himself or as a secret bribe, so he would hardly come forward to acknowledge it, but it would not be difficult to find out who it was: the man who had been in charge of requisitioning the land for expanding the *territorium* – the army farm – would be a matter of record in the garrison.

But if Farathetos had not told me that he'd lost the coins, I would never have known the story of the purchase of the farm, so why should anybody learn that they weren't safely in the grave? I knew he wouldn't tell me what his reasons were, even if I asked. I tried another tack. 'And Morella knew where you'd hidden the coins?'

He spat. 'She wouldn't have gone digging by the hollow tree by chance. She must have known where I hid my money all along. She didn't know I had those particular coins, of course. She'd only seen them when we carried her great-uncle to his grave. But she knew that I had money. As her mother says, it was supposed to be her wedding portion, and her sisters' too.'

'Yet she only took a part of what you had concealed?' I said. 'She might not have realised exactly what she'd found.'

'Not realised?' A derisive snort. 'Of course she realised! Morella's simple-minded but she's not completely daft. She knows gold when she sees it – and she must have guessed where I had got it from.' He glared at me. 'And now look what she's done. She's going to ruin me. I had matches in prospect for my next two girls, you know – far more valuable and pretty than Morella ever was.'

'And you can't afford to pay the dowries now?'

'Worse than that, by Mithras.' He was scowling at me as

if this whole affair had been my fault. 'I'd made a marriage pact for them, though I haven't told them or their mother yet. Two brothers in the jewellery business in Corinium. Not young, but quite successful. I've dealt with them before. They agreed to take the girls, on condition that I would give the coins as dowry when they wed. It seemed a neat solution, with benefits all round – they could melt them down and work the gold, and no questions asked. I didn't tell them where I got the coins from, and they didn't enquire. I didn't have to tell the women what the bargain was.'

'And these jewellers have been known to handle that sort of thing before?' I asked. I have been to Corinium many times myself, and I thought I knew the shady little goldsmiths he meant.

He didn't answer. 'I was fool enough to swear a contract with them half a moon ago. Before seven witnesses – they insisted upon that. Five gold pieces I promised them. I don't think the value in *denarii* would do, even if I had it, which I don't.' He looked at me and I could see the desperation behind the angry eyes. 'When you talked this morning about that cursed girl having a bit of money in her skirts, I never thought of this. I thought she'd got a few *quadrans* the way she did before, letting some farmer fellow have his way with her.'

'Morella did that?' I was so startled I interrupted him. This was a new aspect of her history and not a happy one.

'Promised to marry her, I expect, though of course he never would. Morella would always believe what people said to her. Just as well I got to hear of it, and gave her the thrashing of her life, otherwise we would have had another mouth to feed, and then I'd never have found anyone to take her off my hands. Always a danger with a girl like that. Why do you think I was so delighted to get her married off?' He shook his head. 'Stupid little cow! And now see what's she's done. After you left I went out to the tree to make sure my little hoard was safe – and when I dug it up, I found the coins were gone! Not the silver ones – those I wouldn't mind so much, and in fact I would have paid a few *denarii* to be rid of her – but, may she rot in Hades, she had to take the gold!'

He was almost shouting in frustration by this time, and the gatekeeper on duty came out to have a look. Perhaps it was just as well for me, because the farmer had seized me by my upper arms and would have shaken me, I think, if the guard had not been there. As it was he let me go and took a step away.

I rearranged my toga. 'And what has this to do with me?'

'Citizen,' he almost bellowed, with anguish in his voice, 'you found the coins. I've got to have them back. She stole them, I tell you – they belong to me. I know what will happen if I can't produce them when I'm asked. The prospective grooms are wealthy – they understand the law. They'll claim that I should pay them and the contract stands, or they will take me before the magistrates and lay a charge on me.'

Now I understood why he was so upset, and why he had taken the risk of saying what he had to me. Such a formal bargain is enforceable in court on penalty not merely of a very hefty fine but – since the farmer was not a Roman citizen – probably of scourging and imprisonment as well. And claiming that his daughter was a thief was no defence – her father was her guardian in law, and thus legally responsible for redressing her misdeeds.

So he had taken the risk of coming to find me – and had

not been able to come without his wife! No doubt the tribal elders had insisted that she accompany him. Perhaps he honestly believed that he could keep the facts from her, or prevent her from telling her family what he'd done – or perhaps he simply feared the torturers more than he feared the tribe. If the Corinium goldsmiths were the ones I knew, they would pursue him through the courts for everything he had. Either way, his future did not look very bright.

I did not feel disposed to show him sympathy. There were not, in any case, as many coins as he claimed. 'I have handed the gold pieces to His Excellence,' I began, and saw the look of horror cross the farmer's face. I was about to add 'or rather, to his wife' when we were interrupted by a distant cry.

There was a muttered imprecation to the Celtic gods, a great deal of crashing through the undergrowth, and there was Morella's mother waving through the trees, her hood thrown back and her skirts in disarray, her face a mask of horror and dismay.

'Citizen! And you too, husband! Come at once. The dog has found something I think you ought to see.'

Chapter Twenty

The farmer looked as if he might refuse to move, but I did not wait to argue. I turned without another word and followed the woman as she retraced her steps, crashing almost heedless through the trackless undergrowth, following the broken sticks and bracken which marked her headlong flight through the forest to the villa gates. It was awkward going in a toga, but I stumbled after her, her husband, still grumbling, trailing in the rear.

'Stupid woman! Now where are we going? Couldn't you see that we were occupied?' But there could be no doubt of the direction we were following – each pace brought us closer to the frantic yowling of the dog.

Louder and louder, until at last we reached a clearing in the trees. There was a shallow dip there, screened by low bushes from our vantage point, and on the other side of it I could see the animal, snuffling at something with an excited air. It looked up and howled at its mistress's approach. She flapped a hand towards the hidden hollow place, but kept her head averted, as if she could not bear to look.

'There!' she muttered. I moved forward to look into the dip, and saw what she had seen.

It was Aulus – I knew at once although I could not see the face. That massive bear-like form would have been unmistakable, even if it had not been wearing the distinctive cloak and tunic of the villa guards. He was huddled face downward on the forest floor, pitched forward on his knees as though he had been overcome while kneeling down, and there were fresh bleeding scratches on his legs and thighs all the way from his tunic-hems to his huge sandalled feet. One hairy hand was still clutched to his throat, and there were traces of vomit all round where he lay. Perhaps it was that which had so aroused the dog, which even now was rushing to and fro, its muzzle to the ground, emitting intermittent yelps and growls.

'I'm very sorry, husband.' Morella's mother sounded weak with shock. 'I could not hold the animal. It got away from me.' She held out her hands to show the welts the running rope had made. 'Then, when we got here, it was even worse. It started standing over him and wouldn't let me near.'

'Huh!' The man took a striding step towards the dog, caught the leash and yanked it backwards with considerable force. I felt a momentary sympathy for the unhappy brute as the pull jerked it savagely up on its hind legs, and almost toppled it on to its back. It snarled, snapped at its master, then regained its feet and, deprived of its interesting quarry, sat down on its haunches and gave a whining howl.

However, it was at least now under some control. I ventured past it rather nervously, and picking the cleanest bit of ground I could find I knelt by Aulus and tried to raise his head. His face was never an attractive one, but now – a livid colour, with his eyes rolled back and leaf mould sticking to vomit round his mouth – he was a dreadful sight. It did not need the shocking coldness and the weight to tell me he was dead.

I had never been especially fond of Aulus in his life, but suddenly I found a dreadful sympathy for him. I should miss his grasping avarice and his onion breath, and his massive brutal presence spying at the gate.

'Is it serious?' the woman ventured, as though Aulus might simply have knelt down for a rest. She edged a little closer. 'It looks as though something he ate or drank has disagreed with him.'

'That is an understatement, madam, but essentially the truth. Aulus has been poisoned, by the look of it,' I said, 'though it must have taken quite a dose to topple such a man.'

Even Farathetos was sobered by the sight. He tied the dog's leash to a tree – which did not please the animal at all – and came to squat beside me in the dip.

'This is not the dead body that you were talking of?' He did not wait for me to answer, but did so for himself. 'Can't be. That was "murdered and horribly butchered", you said. And this man could never have been fitted into Morella's dress.' He had lost his belligerence, and sounded merely shocked, and I noticed he was speaking instinctively in Celtic now. 'This is another corpse!'

I sighed. 'It seems so. This is my patron's gatekeeper. The one my wife expected to find on duty when she came. He has been missing since early in the day and now, I think, we know the reason why. Somebody has poisoned him.' I tried to turn the body over as I spoke, but it was difficult. Aulus was in any case a very heavy man, but he seemed to be twice as heavy dead. He was stiff and unresponsive and in the end I gave it up.

I turned to Farathetos, seeking help, but he was already

getting to his feet, his sullen face creased in a doubtful frown. 'Someone poisoned him? I don't see how you can be so sure of that. Strikes me he might have taken the poison for himself. After all, he seems to have come into the forest on his own, rather than going into the villa to seek help.' The idea seemed to cheer him up, if anything. 'Guilt of that other murder, preying on his mind. You mark my words, citizen. Here's the man who put that body in Morella's dress. Afraid of someone finding out what he'd done, and handing him to the torturers to force him to confess.'

'I do not think so,' I said soberly, although I admit I did briefly consider the idea. But a moment's reflection disposed of it at once. The murder had happened a day or two before, when Aulus had been on duty at the gate from dawn to dusk and – even if he had the opportunity to kill – would have had no chance at all of disposing of the corpse. Besides, he would hardly have hidden it in the ditch where it was found – he must have known that the land slaves were going to clear the land.

But Farathetos was unwilling to abandon his idea. 'Perhaps he was the one who robbed and murdered my Morella, too. In that case I shall make a claim against his owner for my loss. Important magistrate or not, I'll take him to the courts – you see if I don't. It's a lot of money for a man like me to lose.'

'Then don't waste any more of it on useless claims,' I said. 'Let's concentrate on finding out what happened, if we can.' I turned to the woman, who was still standing further off. 'Was there any sign of how the gatekeeper came here? Any tracks to show the way he'd come?'

She nodded. 'Along that path beside the thicket over

there, I think,' she said, indicating a faint track which I could just perceive. 'That's where I was walking when the dog picked up the scent. It had been tracking something right along the trail and all at once it veered away and dragged me over here. You can see the bracken, where he pulled me. It's all been trodden down.'

I got up to look more closely, leaving Aulus where he lay. Taking care not to disturb things more than I could help, I traced back along the trail – a zigzag route that led here from the path, getting more random as it came along – right through the bushes, in some places, rather than going round them as I had to do – as if the person walking had lost all sense of place and simply been reeling helplessly around till he fell. And that, I was quite certain, was what had happened here. I'd already noticed the telltale signs on Aulus's legs, and as I looked carefully along the way he had come I found fresh blood visible on several jagged twigs, and broken branches where he had blundered through.

'See, there is vomit in places along the path as well.' I realised that the woman had followed at my heels. She gave me a conspiratorial smile. Out of her husband's hearing, she had more confidence. 'I had an awful time to keep the dog away, and once or twice he pulled so hard I almost trod in it.' She glanced back to the clearing. 'Was it something that the poor man ate that killed him, do you think?'

I smiled. 'It's possible.' I recalled what Minimus had said about the time when Aulus had eaten flower bulbs instead of onions and been very ill. Was it possible he'd made the same mistake again? I shook my head. It would be too much of a coincidence, and anyway his previous misadventure had not laid him low for long. But Aulus had gone into the forest then, and was discovered vomiting. It was obvious why his instinct was to come this way if he was taken urgently unwell – the forest was much closer than the slaves' latrine and much quicker to get to from his gatehouse cell.

The woman was looking at me enquiringly and for some reason I found myself explaining this last idea to her.

'I see,' she said, with that shy smile again. 'I suppose I would not go back into the house of my master, either, if I wanted to be sick. But why keep moving, once he was under the cover of the trees? Or do you think he felt so ill, by then, that he didn't really know what he was doing and just went on stumbling along until he fell?'

'It must have been something of the kind,' I said. 'Someone must have given him a massive dose to be sure of killing an enormous person like him – enough to fell three ordinary men – and once it began to take effect it would very quickly show results. I expect he felt so dreadful that he could hardly stand, let alone decide which way to go.'

'But how could he be poisoned, anyway?' she said. 'Surely his master would provide his food and drink?'

It was the very question that I was asking myself, and I was about to commend her for voicing it aloud when there was a shouting noise behind us, followed by a bark, and we turned to find Farathetos and his dog crashing towards us through the undergrowth.

The farmer was scowling by the time he got to us. 'Going to leave me there all afternoon,' he said, 'while you stand here and chatter to my wife? Well, I'm sorry, citizen, but I've got other things to do – especially if that other matter is now with His Excellence. So if you have quite finished with us, we'll be on our way. And if there is a reward for discovering the corpse, remember that it was my dog which led you to the place.' He gave a tug to the rope leash as he spoke, and the creature bared its teeth.

I came to a decision. 'In fact,' I said, 'I have a task for you. And for your dog as well. I want you to stay here and mount guard over the corpse, while I go back to the villa and fetch some help to carry it. They will want to cremate it as soon as possible, before the Roman Festival of the Dead, which starts in the middle of tomorrow night.' I could see him looking doubtful, and I went on hastily. 'No doubt my patron will be grateful for your services – and gravely displeased to learn that you'd declined to help.'

It was a threat, of course, and an effective one. Farathetos could no more have refused than he could have brought the corpse of Aulus back to life again. The farmer gave me a slow, unwilling glance and forced himself to smile. 'At your command then, citizen – of course.'

'Very well. Be sure you are here when I get back, and don't let anyone go near the corpse. Or that dog either, if you know what's good for you.'

And with that I turned back down the path, in the general direction of the villa and the gates, while Farathetos set off the other way, accompanied by his dog and his unhappy wife. I could hear them both snarling at her, in their different ways, as they went back towards the clearing where the body was.

I came to a decision. I turned and called to them. 'On second thoughts the woman had better come with me. I shall be required in the house and someone will have to show the bier-carriers the way.'

She flashed me a grateful look and came hurrying after

me. 'Do you think this is related to Morella's fate?' she said, as soon as she caught up with me again.

I looked at her sadly. 'I'd been hoping he could help me in my search for her.' That was an understatement. I had been relying on Aulus, as my only lead. 'This is the man she was speaking to the last time she was seen alive. Now we shall never know for sure what she was asking him.'

'You are sure that she is dead then, citizen? Even though the body's not been found?'

'It is what I am afraid of, more than ever now.' I tried to avoid the look of anguish in her eyes, and shook my head. 'But there is no time to linger. We must get back to the house. My patron will be waiting, and so will my wife, and besides there are a great many preparations to be made if Aulus is to be disposed of decently before the Lemuria begins.' I turned and led the way briskly back along the path, not wishing to discuss the matter any more.

Chapter Twenty-one

When I reached the villa, it was to find Junio at the gate with Niveus, both of them peering anxiously up and down the lane. I had forgotten that they would be waiting to escort me home and, further, that with his new status as a citizen my son was likely to come looking for me here, instead of waiting meekly in the servants' room.

He turned to say something to the duty gatekeeper, and as he did so he caught sight of me. 'Father!' He sounded not a little startled to see me emerging from the woods with a woman.

'Stand here,' I muttered to her, and I hurried over to my adopted son. 'That is Morella's mother,' I explained. 'She and her husband came here seeking me.'

Junio's expression was inscrutable. 'Mother told us that you were talking to the girl's parents at the gate, but when you did not return we began to be concerned. More so when we came out here and found you'd disappeared, and the gatekeeper did not seem to know where you had gone. There have been too many mysteries at this villa as it is, what with Aulus vanishing and the corpse and all the rest.' It was as near to a rebuke as he would ever dare to offer me.

'Well, one of those mysteries is solved at any rate, at least in part,' I said. 'We have just found Aulus's body in the woods – or rather it was sniffed out by a dog. He has been poisoned, by the look of it.' I saw the shock reflected on his face, and added, more gently, 'I was going to go round straight away and ask Stygius to send some hefty land slaves out to bring him home. The slaves will need something to carry him back on, I suspect – a wooden shutter or a sledge or something of the kind. The woman will lead them to where the body is.'

Junio was suddenly all brisk efficiency. 'Don't worry about looking for Stygius yourself. Niveus or I can see to that for you. Do you need to ask your patron for permission for the slaves?'

'I don't think so, in the circumstances,' I said. 'It would just cause more delay. There have already been orders to all the villa staff to look for Aulus and use any means to bring him home. The sooner the body is brought back here, the sooner funeral preparations can begin – there is no time to be lost if he is to be decently cremated before the Festival of the Dead begins. That's midnight tomorrow, as I'm sure you know.'

'I will go and talk to Stygius,' Junio said. 'You had better go inside. Your presence has been missed. My mother is concerned for you, and your patron has been demanding to know where you went. Even Lucius has roused himself to send his bodyguard down to your roundhouse to see if you were there.'

This was alarming – it was not wise to be elsewhere when Marcus wanted me. 'Very well. You make the arrangement with the land slaves, and I'll go in and tell Marcus what is happening,' I said. 'I should have to report to him in any case, if only to tell him that Aulus has been found.'

Junio made a face. 'He won't be very pleased. A gatekeeper like Aulus is expensive to replace. And just when the family's about to go abroad and leave the villa without an occupant!' He meant 'no occupant apart from slaves', of course, but the principle was sound. A house where the owner is away for months is obviously a tempting target for opportunist thieves. And there were those rumours of the rebels in the wood. A good guard is a vital deterrent at such times.

Aulus was especially valuable, I thought, because not only was he intimidatingly large, but he was also so useful as a spy. I glanced at the current stand-in, who looked half Aulus's size and was taking no interest in Junio and me. Any owner would be inconvenienced by losing an effective gatekeeper but I suspected that Marcus would feel genuine regret.

'I will go directly to the atrium and break the news,' I said. 'You can give the message to Stygius if you will.' I could see Niveus hovering anxiously nearly, like a puppy dog waiting to be thrown a stick. Clearly he'd hoped that I'd trust him with that task. 'I will have to cleanse myself, yet again, of course! Niveus, you can come into the ante-room and hand the towel for me. I presume that Colaphus is not on duty there, since I understand he's gone down to the roundhouse seeking me.' I turned to Junio. 'Are you coming with us through the house?'

Junio shook his head. 'I will go round the other way. I'm not sure that Stygius will be in the rear court now – he may have gone back to the fields again to supervise the slaves, and if so there's a chance that I shall see him on the way. But I'll make sure I find him, wherever he may be, and see that he gets the message and sends the party out at once. Shall I meet you in the villa afterwards, or will you have gone home?' He grinned. 'I know my mother hopes that you will change your tunic for tonight, and give Maximus a chance to sponge your toga-hems.'

I looked down at my garments, suddenly aware of the disastrous effect that my day's adventures had had on my attire. I sighed. 'Look for me in the villa,' I said. 'I expect I'll be some time. Someone will have to arrange for Aulus's funeral, and with Marcus's bereavement he won't do that himself. You'd better mention it to Stygius as well. The land slaves will have to get busy with the pyre, if they are to get it properly rebuilt. Yet another corpse to dispose of before the spirits walk.'

'I'll be as prompt as possible,' my son replied.

I watched him disappearing down the farm track to the back. Morella's mother was still staring at us from across the lane, so I went over and explained to her what the arrangements were, and then at last I went in through the gate and crossed the courtyard to the house, with little Niveus padding at my heels.

'I gave that message to your servant, citizen,' he announced proudly, as if to reproach me for not trusting him with messages again. 'He's gone to Glevum now. The master put him on the fastest horse. Wanted him to catch those entertainers up and see if they could provide an interlude tonight. Pity that Marcus let them go at all. They only left when he came back from Glevum – I suppose they were waiting to be paid.' He stood back to let me precede him to the door and let me in.

'Entertainers?'

He nodded. 'The ones who were performing at the

banquet yesterday. You remember that some of them stayed here overnight. In the stable with the extra sleeping space – where Colaphus has a bed. If there are entertainers overnight, they're always put in there.'

I hadn't known that, but I nodded anyway. 'The athletes? And the dwarves? For a funeral feast?'

He grinned. 'That's just what Lucius said! But the mistress thought the athletes might be able to devise a stately dance or something, which would be appropriate. And the chief dwarf claims he can write a poem for any circumstance – it's one of the things he sometimes offers as an act, though Marcus did not have him do it yesterday.'

I snorted. 'I doubt that writing tribute eulogies is what he meant.'

'It's not the sort of thing that any of them is usually called upon to do, but, as the mistress pointed out, it's impossible to find anyone else at such short notice, anyway. Of course, there is always Atalanta and her lyre.' He pushed open the door of the little ante-room and stood by while I performed the ritual with the water and the ash. There was a pile of towels still sitting on the stool and he fetched me one and waited while I dried my hands and face.

'Shall I announce you in the atrium?'

I shook my head. 'I'll see myself in. You wait here for me.'

The atmosphere in the room was noticeably tense when I walked in. Gwellia was there, with Marcus and his wife: and there too was Lucius, standing on his own and looking grim and imperious – though his tunic was now trimmed with dark-coloured mourning bands, instead of his patrician purple stripes. I was ready immediately to burst out with my news, but a warning glance from Marcus prevented me.

Of course this was a house of mourning and it was necessary to observe the proper protocol, especially since Lucius was there to disapprove. I made my due obseisance: first to the statue, then to the living men. Marcus accepted my homage with a benevolent, vague nod, while Lucius looked even more disdainful than before. Only Julia had the grace to smile.

'You have news for us, citizen?' she enquired, as soon as I had scrambled to my feet again. 'Your wife informs me that there was an unpleasant man offering to give you information at the gate. In the light of recent happenings we were quite alarmed for you. Weren't we, Gwellia?'

By appealing directly to my dear wife in that way our hostess was inviting her to speak, which might otherwise have been inappropriate for a female visitor of no especial rank, in such circumstances and in such company.

Gwellia was quick to seize the opportunity. 'I do not know that the man was offering to *give* him information, Lady Julia. More likely to demand payment, from what I saw of him.' That was my Gwellia, I thought. A tactful hint to my patron that I might need recompense! 'I have explained to Marcus who the people were – that their daughter was probably the owner of the corpse's dress, and that it seems she had run away,' she said to me, and then she turned back to Julia again. 'But if that was her father, then I am not surprised. Even his wife seemed quite afraid of him. So when he insisted on speaking to Libertus on his own I was a bit worried about what he had to say and whether he was going to set his awful dog on him.' She gave me her special look, as if to remind me that she had more to tell, at some time when we found ourselves alone.

I flashed a smile in acknowledgement and turned back to my host. 'He did give me information of a kind,' I said. 'He claims the girl had robbed him of the coins that we discovered in her dress. I think he was hoping I could arrange to give them back, but until I have more proof I did not promise to do anything at all. But I do bring other news – much more immediate and serious, I fear. I have found Aulus.'

'Aulus! Where is he? What has he to say? Bring him to me instantly. What are we waiting for?' Marcus was annoyed. Almost without seeming to be aware of it, he had pulled a piece of ferny branch from one of the floral offerings round his father's neck, and was tapping it impatiently against his other hand, as though it were his magisterial baton. This was a habit I'd often seen before: it augured no good to those who crossed him in this mood. I felt actually uneasy when he turned to me and scowled. 'Where did you find the wretch?'

'He was in the forest,' I answered the simple question first. 'I have taken the liberty of sending some of your land slaves out to bring him home again. I've sent Junio to make the arrangements for it now.'

'Why in the name of Jupiter do the land slaves—' Marcus began hotly, then seemed to realise that something was amiss. His manner changed. He looked into my face. 'You don't mean that something has befallen him? Not Aulus, surely? He's too big to be attacked.'

I said nothing. It was more than eloquent.

'Are you telling us that the fellow's dead?' Lucius rapped out the question, like an officer giving the order to throw spears. The answer must have been written on my face, because before I could summon a reply he turned his back on me. 'I can't believe it, cousin. There must be some mistake. He was perfectly well when I last spoke to him. What can possibly have happened to him since?' He shook his head. 'If this is true, I have to suspect a supernatural hand. This is another omen, as surely as Jove makes thunderbolts. I don't know what my aunt Honoria will say.'

Marcus held up a hand to silence him. 'My mother is unlikely to find out,' he said, with the kind of resolute finality he did not often show in the company of his visitor from Rome. 'Not until I get there, anyway. Unless, of course, cousin, you propose to write to her? Which, given her bereavement, I suggest you do not do. No need to cause her added anxiety, I think.'

It was as near a prohibition as it could politely be. Lucius looked affronted, and said in strangled tones, 'She is your mother, cousin. You must do as you see fit. She is under your official tutelage and protection now.'

Marcus smiled bleakly. 'Exactly. Just as this household is.'

It was a reminder of who was master of the house, but Lucius was not so easily subdued. 'So you will want to make immediate arrangements to cremate your slave. Fortunately we already have the funeral herbs and the pyre is barely cool. I left the priest of Jupiter in the new wing of the house – he asked to have a rest after his ritual exertions and his visit to the bath-house afterwards – and he will advise us as to how we should proceed. It is fortunate that he has not left the premises – I assume that he has been invited to join us for the feast.'

'Then you assume correctly,' Marcus snapped, 'in that regard at least. But whatever customs may prevail in Rome, in Britannia we do not shuffle a faithful gatekeeper on to a funeral fire without a proper ceremony as tribute to his soul. Nor without attempting to discover how he came to die.' He turned to me. 'Libertus, old friend, you say you found his corpse. Have you any idea what might have brought about his death? Dragged away by brigands or attacked by bears? Or is this another of those unfortunate affairs with mutilated features and a choke-mark round the neck?'

I shook my head. 'None of those things, Excellence. I believe that he was poisoned.'

'Poisoned!' The cousins spoke together, though their tones were quite distinct. Marcus sounded horrified, and Lucius full of scorn.

'How could he possibly be poisoned?' Marcus said. 'He eats the food and drink that all the servants do.'

There was a little silence. Julia had turned pale, and Gwellia was looking at me with a glance that said 'I told you this affair was dangerous' more forcefully than if she'd voiced the words aloud.

'Of course, there was the messenger who came from Rome,' I said. 'I suppose it is possible that something changed hands at the gate.' I was not convinced by this theory, but everyone had been looking expectantly at me and I felt that some intelligent suggestion was required.

Lucius gave a bleak grimace that might have been a smile. 'I suppose that's possible.'

I was encouraged by this unexpected praise. 'But who in Rome would want to poison Aulus? He wasn't known to anybody outside Britannia. Unless there was an effort to bring poison to the house, which Aulus managed to take by accident.'

The smiled had faded, and Lucius looked dour. 'Of

course, you're right. It is preposterous. More likely the gatekeeper strayed into the woods, and was bitten by a snake or something of the kind. I understand you have vipers in the forest hereabouts? I remember it was spoken of the other night.'

'Would that make him stagger and vomit?' I enquired. 'It looked more as if he'd swallowed something poisonous to me, but I have never seen a person bitten by a snake. Certainly there have been vipers in the wood from time to time, but in that case I would have expected to see swelling in his legs.' Yet even as I spoke, I realised that I might not have noticed fang marks among those streaks of blood.

My wife stepped forward. It was brave. She had not been invited to contribute anything. 'Your pardon, Excellences, but I doubt it was a snake. For one thing it is not the time of year. And for another, Aulus is so big. It would have taken quite a lot of venom to have killed him with such speed – our snakes are not like those of other lands which will kill a full-grown man so quickly that he has no time to go for help or suck the venom out. A child, or someone old and frail perhaps, but hardly a strapping brute like Aulus. What do you think, husband? Is it possible?'

'I think that you convince me that it isn't, wife,' I said. I was impressed by her clarity of thought, but it was evident that Lucius was not. His look of pained disdain would have shrivelled the marble statue beside him on the plinth, let alone the shrinking woman he was glaring at.

'You are an expert on these things?' he asked, in icy tones. 'Perhaps you would care to view the corpse and give us the benefit of your experience? Enlighten us as to what the poison was?' He turned to Marcus. 'It seems that in

Britannia, cousin, one must learn to take instruction from the most unlikely sources. Freedmen, slaves and women seem free to interrupt the conversation of patricians and – without being asked – offer their opinions about anything at all. This pavement-maker even has the impudence, it seems, calmly to issue instructions to your slaves and tell you afterwards. I assure you, you will find that manners are quite different in Rome.'

There was a stunned silence. Gwellia looked abashed. Marcus was visibly furious but, like me, he held his tongue. Even the attendant slaves against the wall were exchanging little glances. In the end it was Julia who spoke.

'In Britannia, cousin, when we delegate a task, we do not expect to be constantly consulted as to how it should be done. My husband asked Libertus to investigate a death, and I believe that he is doing that, as usual. I can't think that Aulus's poisoning is coincidence. He has served this household without incident for years, and all at once we find that he is dead. It occurs to me to wonder what is different, suddenly?'

Lucius had turned that ugly pink again. 'Are you suggesting that my presence here . . . ?'

Julia looked at him in obvious amazement. 'Not at all. I meant that Aulus's death was surely related to the other corpse,' she said.

Yet Lucius's reaction was an interesting one. Supposing that Lucius was the connecting link? He did not know anyone in the province except his family, so it seemed unlikely on the face of it. Yet if he had a secret enemy, perhaps, someone who had followed him from Rome? That had to be a possibility – Lucius was just the kind of person who did make enemies.

So suppose that there was someone who had tracked him down? Someone who poisoned the gatekeeper to gain access to the place? Attempted to get in more than once, perhaps – there was still the young man's body to be accounted for, and cremation had not solved the puzzle of its identity. Another person who was party to the plot? Or – I was excited by this piece of reasoning – had our mystery young man stumbled on the would-be murderer somewhere near the house and had to be disposed of and buried hastily? To be a danger he would have had to recognise the man – someone that he'd seen before, perhaps in some quite different place? That would fit my theory that the corpse might have been a page – messengers by nature move from place to place, meeting a lot of people as they go, and – as Junio had pointed out – they may not immediately be missed.

But even supposing there was some truth in this (and the more I thought of it, the more I thought there was), how did Morella enter into it? And – the thought struck me with a sudden chill – what had happened to Lucius's would-be killer now? If he had poisoned the gatekeeper to get into the house, it was possible that he was lurking even as we spoke.

'Forgive me, Excellences, if I am speaking out of turn,' I said with all the humility of a net-man at the games, 'but it occurs to me to wonder if the poisoner has not finished yet. Aulus doesn't seem to be a likely target in himself. There might yet be danger to someone in the house. I think that everyone should be on the alert.'

'More guesswork, citizen? Save your imagination for your pavements, I suggest.' That was Lucius.

I had not mentioned my idea that the threat might be to

him in particular – I knew that he would merely dismiss it if I did – but his scathing rudeness made me regret that I had bothered to say anything at all. After all, I was only trying to protect his wretched life. Well, I'd not do that again. If anyone wanted to murder Lucius, I thought, I could see a certain merit in their point of view.

However, I merely cleared my throat and was about to launch into an explanation of what my thinking was when the rear door was opened and Junio came in.

No need for the homage ritual this time – Junio had presumably done all that before, and, unlike me, he had not since been in contact with a corpse. Marcus, therefore, greeted him at once.

'Ah, Junio? You have sent out a party to bring Aulus in?'

Junio inclined his head in deference. 'Indeed. And Stygius has sent land slaves to rebuild the pyre. He asks if there are other arrangements that you wish him to make.'

A slight frown furrowed Marcus's brow. 'Aulus was a member of the funeral guild,' he said. 'They would see to everything, and ensure that all was done with decency, with anointers and lamenters and a proper bier, if they were notified. But I doubt that even they could do it before tomorrow night – the ceremonies would have to be completed before midnight, when the spirits walk, and it is already very late to take them word today.'

'Surely, cousin, if you made it clear that it was your request?' Lucius sounded scornful. 'A man of your rank and influence? I'm sure it could be done. Even if it is a little rushed, they have the wherewithal to see to it – hired mourners and musicans and all that sort of thing. They could quite easily bring them over here. And even if they couldn't, does it really signify? The fellow was only a household servant, after all.'

Marcus ignored him. 'I suppose I could get the stables to harness up the cart and drive someone to Glevum before the gates are shut, but by the time the cart was ready it would be getting dark. I've already sent Minimus on the fastest horse, and with the feast tonight I don't really have another slave I can spare.'

I wondered if Niveus could overhear this from the anteroom and would suddenly dart in, eager to offer his services as a messenger. But Junio stepped forward. 'Your pardon, Excellence, but perhaps we could send a message with the man who brought the wine. I passed him in the rear courtyard just a little while ago, unstacking amphorae from his cart. If we are quick about it, he won't have finished yet.'

Julia laughed, a laugh of real relief. 'A splendid notion, husband. I had quite forgotten that we had ordered fresh supplies for the memorial feast. I'm sure the driver would deliver a message, if you paid him to. Although he is a freeman, I expect he'll find the guild.'

A wild idea was forming in my brain by now. 'Patron, how long is it before your guests arrive?'

He looked at me, surprised. 'An hour or two at best. Not all town councillors have water-clocks or sundials, you know – many of them simply have to estimate the hour, and if they prefer to travel out here in the light, I expect the first ones will soon be on their way. Though we won't lie down to dinner until all of them arrive. Is it important?'

'It occurs to me that one of us might go to Glevum, Excellence, if your wine merchant will agree to take us there.

And if one of your guests could be persuaded to bring me back again . . . ?'

Marcus almost twinkled. 'From which I deduce that you intend to go yourself? But it seems a good suggestion. You know where to go?'

I nodded. 'I have dealt with a slave funeral before. It won't take long,' I said. I did not add that there were other things I hoped to do as well – like talking to the dancing girls again, if possible.

'Then I will arrange it, if you are sure, old friend.' He clapped his hands, and this time Niveus did come running in. 'Go and tell the wine merchant I need his services. I want him to take a passenger to Glevum when he goes. Perhaps he could take Junio and Gwellia as well as far as the roundhouse, since the lady wants to go.' He turned back to me. 'I'll write to the garrison, asking them to waylay one of the town councillors coming here to dine and get him to wait for you. Or, if necessary, bring you back themselves. There is plenty of military transport they can use. I will go and do that now.'

And with that he might have left the room, but Lucius forestalled him with a smile. 'And, cousin, if I might use your seal to send it by official courier, it occurs to me that I should send a message to my aunt. Offering my condolences on this unhappy day.'

'Of course. My mother would appreciate the gesture, I am sure. Libertus can pick the letters up at the gate, and set off as soon as possible. Meanwhile, Julia my dear,' he added with a smile, 'perhaps you could entertain the high priest for me. I see he's coming through the courtyard garden now. You can take him into the new reception room, perhaps? I'll send a slave with some refreshments by and by.'

Julia looked reluctant, but she went without a word, taking Atalanta with her. I wished my patron had not mentioned food – with the discovery of Aulus I had quite forgotten how hungry I'd become, but now I was reminded. I was ravenous.

'Farewell till later then, my friends,' Marcus said graciously, and he left the room with Lucius and the usual scattering of attendant slaves.

I turned to Gwellia. 'At last we have the chance to talk,' I was saying, when I was aware of a small scuffling at the entranceway.

Niveus was still hovering there. He looked nervously at me. 'Master?'

I realised – eventually – what the trouble was. 'Find the man in the wine cart and say to him, "Come round to the front gate and wait for passengers," ' I explained, speaking the message with careful emphasis. 'And then come to the gatehouse and find me there yourself.'

Niveus nodded gratefully, and disappeared at once.

Chapter Twenty-two

Gwellia was not looking very pleased with me. I was in my patron's villa, and our son was watching us, but I was still tempted to take her in my arms. Fortunately I recollected what is acceptable, and merely raised my eyebrows with a smile.

'What is it, wife?' I murmured.

She looked up at me. 'You are still working on this business, aren't you? And I'm afraid for you. Morella's father is an ugly man. And you propose to present yourself at this memorial feast, it seems, without the opportunity to wash yourself and clean your toga-hems.'

I laughed. 'Thanks to the cleansing rituals which I've had to undergo, I've washed my face so many times today that I'm surprised it hasn't washed away. And as for my toga-hems, don't worry about them – ashes and tatters are a measure of respect.'

She made a tutting noise. 'Only for the mourning family,' she exclaimed. 'And don't change the subject, husband. This matter's dangerous. That poor woman who was here a while ago – you know she thinks her husband may have killed the girl?'

That was a new idea. I turned to stare at her. 'I'm sure that he could do it,' I said thoughtfully, and then remembered what had happened at his farm. I shook my head. 'But

I don't believe he did. He is afraid of being questioned by the torturers – his actions this afternoon have made that clear – but he wasn't frightened when I spoke to him at first. He was concerned lest I had found her and was going to bring her back. And angry that she had left him with a settlement to pay. Money is more important to him than her welfare, I'm afraid.'

'And if he had killed her he would have taken the coins from the dress?' Junio had been listening.

I shook my head again. 'I don't believe he knew this morning that she'd taken them,' I said. 'He would have been more anxious to ask me about them at the time, instead of having to walk miles to look for me.'

'Perhaps she was not wearing the plaid dress when he killed her,' Gwellia said.

Junio exchanged a glance with me. 'Minimus says she wore a tunic later on,' he said. 'Apparently he saw her with Aulus at the gate the morning of the civic feast, not long after the luggage cart had gone.'

I nodded. 'The day we think the murder must have taken place. And she was spoken to by a carter afterwards – he took a message from her to the farm.'

Gwellia looked thoughtful. 'So she was seen as recently as that? Then her mother must be wrong. She said Morella had been talking to a man in the forum market when the snake act was there – by my calculations, that was two days before the feast – and when her father heard about it he beat her savagely. Then, the next morning, she had disappeared. Her poor mother was terrified she'd perished in the night, and her father had done something with the body while they slept.' She raised her eyes to me. 'I think she'll be relieved to know that isn't true. She blamed herself for telling the father what she'd seen.'

I frowned. 'But surely there was a message from the girl, saying that she had run away to join an entertainment troupe?'

'Only the father heard that message, as far as I can see. He simply came and told the family what he claimed the carter said. Morella's mother was convinced he'd made it up. Then when you came and said that she'd approached the dancing girls, you gave her hope again – until she realised that you thought the girl was dead. Now she is torn between despair and hope, and terrified of what her husband might have done. She married him against her parents' wishes, it appears, but he was wealthy and she persuaded them – then learned too late that he was miserly and cruel.'

So miserly he'd stolen money from a family tomb, I thought. But something more pressing had occurred to me. 'That message from the carter – it might be possible to check. Perhaps I should have looked into it before, though he might be hard to trace . . .' I stopped. 'Great Mars! Why am I such a fool!'

'What is it, Father?' Junio enquired.

'That carter! I think I might know who it is – in general terms at least. Something that Aulus said to me. He talked about a farmer from the hills who went past here each day, taking a load of produce to the market in the town!'

'And you think that load might once have concealed a corpse?'

I shook my head. 'Unless he killed her, I doubt it very much. But if we can trace him, we can ask him what he knows, and whether Morella really sent a message home with him.'

Junio looked puzzled. 'But what makes you think that this farmer is the carter that took the message from the girl? There must be many carts that come and go along the lane.'

'But very few from there,' I said. 'You haven't seen the area where these people farm. It's miles along the lane and up a winding track. Who but a farmer would go that way at all, and be well known enough to give a message to? And Morella's father mentioned that one farmer had a cart – and sons – and so had the time to go to market with fresh produce every day.' I paused, to give added emphasis to this. 'He would have to pass the gate here, if he was doing that. There's no other way to reach the market, without taking twice as long.'

Gwellia nodded. 'He would not want to make the journey any longer than he need, especially if he was coming and going there every day. Obviously he'd take the best road he could find.'

I was staring at her. 'Coming and going! Of course! I must be getting old, or I would have thought of it before. Junio, bring your mother to the gatehouse when I send for you – assuming that she still wants to change her clothes.'

Gwellia looked flustered. 'I must wear a darker robe. I'll have to come in my pink *stola*, but I have a deep blue over-tunic I can put on top which will be a bit more suitable. But why the hurry, husband? What do you propose to do?'

'I will wait out in the lane for the wine cart and the letters that Marcus and Lucius want to send to Glevum with me. It occurs to me that I might see this famous farmer in his cart. If he goes in to the market, then he must come home again – it might take all day to sell a load of produce, I suppose, but he wouldn't choose to travel on those roads in the dark.'

Gwellia looked doubtful. 'He may just unload his produce in the morning and go home. Have a friend or relation with a market stall, perhaps?'

'In which case I shall ask around till I hear news of him. If not, there is a chance I'll meet him on the road. He might be passing at this moment, while we are talking here. I'll go outside at once and keep a watch for him.'

It seemed a useful strategy, and I had hopes of it. I went out to the gate where a pair of garden slaves were occupied in fixing a bough of evergreen, under the chief steward's watchful eye.

'A sign that we're in mourning,' the steward said to me, as if I required an explanation for this activity. 'It isn't proper cypress, like they'd have in Rome, but we don't have a lot of cypress in this part of the world. This is the nearest to it, so the mistress says.' He shook his head. 'I don't know what that visitor from Rome will make of it, but that's the mistress's orders. I just do as I'm told.'

I murmured something non-committal in reply, and went to take up my station in the lane. It would have been immensely convenient, of course, if the farmer and his cart had just happened to come by, but the Fates were not spinning in my favour, it appeared.

The road was resolutely empty. Not even a glimpse of Aulus and his makeshift bier.

Finally the wine merchant came lumbering down the farm track in his cart. He was dark and surly and quite belligerent – not at all pleased at having being ordered to carry passengers. However, rank and money are effective arguments and Marcus, as usual, was going to have his way.

The man was even less delighted at being asked to wait, first for Niveus to come running out with Marcus's and Lucius's letters in his hand, then for him to disappear again and fetch my wife and son.

At last we were assembled and ready to begin. My family squashed up on the driver's seat, while Niveus climbed up among the wine amphorae in their racks. I did not demand the letters – there was time enough for that – though I could see him clutching them from where I sat: both scratched on wax tablets and both sealed up with such care that you would think they were concerned with affairs of state, and not merely a request to have me brought back here and a letter of condolence to some relatives in Rome.

We lurched down the lane to the roundhouse, and Gwellia and Junio were duly delivered to the enclosure gate. Maximus and Cilla came out to help them down, and I took the opportunity to send in for some food. So I was munching a welcome piece of bread and cheese when Niveus came to sit beside me and we could talk again.

'Do you know a farm cart that brings produce to the town?' I said, between mouthfuls, as we set off again and made our way towards the military road. It was the long route to the town, but by far the safest one since the cart was piled with racks and racks of fragile pots of wine. 'I know you haven't been working at the villa very long, but you might have noticed, since it goes past every day.'

Niveus nodded. 'I think I know the one. Rather a battered-looking vehicle – and the farmer's old, as well. Tall and withered, with a creaky voice. I've seen it several times. I even spoke to him one afternoon when there was a delay with litters at the gate. The farmer was on his way back from the market and had to wait for us. He wasn't very happy, though I apologised.'

'Well, keep looking out for him as we drive along,' I said. 'I want to have a word with him if I get a chance.' But we'd got to the military road by now, and there was no sign of the cart.

There was a good deal more coming and going on that larger thoroughfare: slow ox-wagons and donkey-carts lumbering along, piled high with goods to be delivered in the town, in no especial hurry. Most were aiming to arrive outside the walls at dusk, because wheeled transport was not permitted in the *colonia* in daylight hours and they would otherwise have to join the queue outside the gate. Foot-travellers and horsemen had the opposite idea – hurrying to get there as soon as possible, since strangers were often turned back after dark and forced to seek accommodation in the seedy inns outside the walls. And there were people coming the other way as well – though no sign of the cart that we were looking for.

I was alarmed in case we came across a group of soldiers on the march – any military traffic had priority. For one thing we would have had to retreat on to the margins till they passed – where there was a good chance that our axles would bog down in the mud – and for another its simple presence would have delayed us very much, and separated us neatly from anything on the far side of the road. A marching unit, though it always keeps up a spanking pace, is often accompanied by carts full of unofficial wives and their supplies (a soldier cannot marry until he leaves the service, of course), to say nothing of the tradesmen and general hangers-on, who follow the peacetime army everywhere it goes. Such a procession can take a long time to go by.

Today, however, there was no such problem and the sun had hardly dipped by half an hour before we found ourselves bowling down the road towards the town.

There was the inevitable gaggle and turmoil at the gate and the road was almost blocked. Wagons which had got there early were waiting for dark, and the unloaded carts of market traders were drawn up at one side pending the reappearance of their owners when the forum shut. Many of them were battered, and I glanced at Niveus, hoping he would point out the one we were looking for, but he made no sign.

Closer to the gate, and closer still. Here there were hiring carriages and litters jostling for trade – and, taking up the very middle of the road, a smart private conveyance with a bored slave at the reins. And foot-travellers always struggling to get through – women with baskets full of eggs, a thin man with an even thinner cow, two slave boys carrying a huge baulk of wood.

The wine merchant stopped the cart and looked resentfully at me. 'Here you are, citizen. This is as far as I can go. I have a storehouse on the east side of the town. I'll have to hurry before the gates are shut – not really made for passengers, these carts. So . . .' He held his hand out, hoping for a tip, but I knew that Marcus had paid him earlier and I had nothing I could give him. I got down hastily, and so did Niveus.

'I'll mention it to His Excellence when I get back,' I said, and saw the man flush sullenly as he drove away, forcing his way back through the throng by flourishing his whip, and loudly cursing at other drivers as he passed.

A fat guard was trying to keep order at the gate, red-faced

and hollering in an effort to be heard above the shouts of drivers and the rumbling of wheels. 'No pushing there, or I'll arrest the lot of you!' he shouted, waving his baton as a sort of threat. Then he saw my toga, and his manner changed. 'Make way for the citizen. You, with the handcart – get it out of there.' He began to wield his weapon against shoulders, backs and legs, and, very suddenly, the crowd obeyed. A sort of pathway opened up to allow me past. I sent Niveus over to deliver the wax tablets to the guard ('tell him they are for the attention of the commander of the garrison') and set off ahead of him through the archway in the gate – just as a horseman came the other way.

I stepped aside to let the rider through – I may be a citizen, but I know my place, and this was an expensive animal. A rich man or his messenger by the look of it – I glimpsed a hooded figure in a handsome cloak. I crammed myself against the woman with the eggs, and flinched as he went flashing past within an inch of me.

There was no time to straighten up again. There was a pursuit in progress – that was clear to see. A pair of sturdy townsmen came charging after him, urged on by a puffing, plumpish woman in a shawl who brought up the rear. 'Stop him! Stop that rider!' But he was out of sight by now. They rushed into the gap the passing horse had made, using their elbows mercilessly to force their own way through, and the shouting and excitement moved off towards the gate.

I extricated myself from the egg-seller for a second time, and was in the act of smoothing my toga down when I heard a shrill voice calling my name.

'Citizen! Libertus! Master!' I spun round to see where the words were coming from. The little pageboy was standing at

Chapter Twenty-three

It was a good deal quieter once inside the gates, so I walked a little way, then stood to one side of the thoroughfare and waited for Niveus to come back.

He didn't appear. I waited longer, wishing – again – I had a purse with me. I had enjoyed my little meal of bread and cheese, but the smells from the hot-pie sellers passing in the street – and even from the hot-soup stall nearby – were reminding me that I hadn't eaten much.

Still Niveus didn't come. I would give him a proper scolding when he did, I thought. Trust him to be caught up in the excitement of a passing chase, and just abandon me! Junio would never have left me on my own like this.

People were beginning to turn and stare at me – the man with the handcart in particular, since he'd been forced to let me through, and here I was standing stock-still in his way. I craned, trying to pick the page out in the crowd beneath the arch. Pity he wasn't wearing his crimson uniform, I thought – and realised suddenly why Marcus always chose that striking colour for his private messengers.

I stepped up on to the pavement to get a better view – good Roman pavements are always a little raised, so that pedestrians can walk dry-shod above the level of rainwater and mud and the inevitable traces of passing animals –

though Glevum was not too bad in that regard. An urchin came round the *colonia* every day, collecting up the sweepings to sell to farmers round about. I could see him busy in the distance now, armed with a home-made handcart and a battered spade. It was a sign that business was nearly over for the day.

There was still no sign of Niveus. I cursed myself for having let him slip away from me like that – though, in truth, I could hardly have prevented him. I was just wondering how I should proceed – whether to go and find the slaves' guild now, or whether to stop and hunt for Niveus – when the question was answered for me in a surprising way.

The fat guard from the gateway came shouldering through the crowd, standing on tiptoe to look up and down the street. When he caught sight of me, his face relaxed and he came over to me self-importantly.

'I am sent to find you, citizen, and take you to the gate-house as soon as possible. You are Libertus the pavement-maker, I believe?'

I indicated – rather nervously – that this was the case. 'My patron is Marcus Aurelius Septimus,' I added, making it clear that I could call on powerful protection and support. I learned long ago that it was always wise to mention this, especially where the military was concerned. 'In fact, I brought a letter from him to the commander of the guard.' I was sincerely wishing that I'd taken charge of it myself, and not left it in the page's custody.

The guard's next words made me wish it even more. 'I don't see any letter in your possession, citizen.'

'My attendant had it – he's delivering it now. I thought

that he had given it to you.' It sounded feeble, and I knew it did.

He grinned, a little grimly. 'That's interesting, citizen. I'm glad you told me that. We've got someone in custody who's known to be His Excellence's slave – and did deliver a letter with his seal on it – but is now claiming your protection and saying you'll pay the costs.'

I groaned. What expense had Niveus got me into now? Broken eggs or something, probably, and no means to pay. Well, I hadn't either. I had come without a purse – I was not expecting to be in the town today. Perhaps I could borrow something from the councillor who was asked to take me back – if I could get that request delivered before it was too late.

'Niveus was bringing you that note on my behalf,' I said. 'Perhaps you could make sure . . .' I tailed off in surprise. The fat guard was shaking his grizzled head at me.

'Not as I understand it, citizen,' he said, 'and Niveus is not the name he gave, as I recall. You wouldn't call him snowy anyway, from what I've seen of him – though there was another boy who answered that description, I suppose. He was the one who told us that we could find you here.' He was tapping his baton on his palm now, in a gesture which reminded me of Marcus very much. 'I don't know who our prisoner is, but you come along with me and you will soon find out.'

I was still pondering. It wasn't Pulchrus – he'd gone overseas. Could it be the messenger who'd come from Rome that day? He'd brought a letter to Glevum under seal, and it was just possible he hadn't left the town. But I'd never met him – why should he ask for me? I didn't like the sound of this at all. 'I'm waiting for my attendant,' I began. 'And I have pressing business in the town . . .'

He tucked his baton in his belt and drew his dagger out instead. 'I don't want to have to threaten, citizen, but the commander wants you now.' He puffed out his cheeks like a self-important frog. 'He doesn't like to be kept waiting, and nor do I, with all respect. I'm supposed to be off duty – they've relieved me at the gate – but they sent me because I recognised the description the boy gave, and was daft enough to say I'd seen you when they asked. So, if you would be so good as to come along with me at once? I think that would be best – for both of us, don't you?' He ran his finger down the edge of the blade, as if to let me know that it was very sharp.

I know a veiled threat when I see one, and this wasn't very veiled. I swallowed and then nodded. 'Lead the way then, guard.'

He did not permit me to follow him, of course – he took up his place behind me and walked me towards the gate, keeping his drawn dagger in the region of my back. He didn't touch me, but I knew that it was there. I was effectively a prisoner, and people knew it too. I was aware of pointing fingers and furtive whispering. 'Under arrest! I wonder what he's done.' I heard a burst of laughter. 'And him a citizen!'

It was humiliating, but it did have one effect: people melted back at once to let us pass. Fortunate perhaps – if we'd been jostled, I'd have run into the blade – but it is a phenomenon that I have seen before. When someone is being marched to the garrison under Roman guard, everyone gives him as much space as possible – as though his fate might be contagious, like the plague, or leprosy. It wasn't long before we got back to the gate.

It was dark and cool inside the guardhouse, as it always is, though there were candles burning in sconces on the walls. We did not pause in the guardroom as I'd expected to; instead my escort gestured with his dagger up the stairs to where the garrison commander had his room. I was to see the most important officer in town.

He rose to meet me as I came in: a tall, rangy, athletic-looking man with a lined and weathered face, and the general appearance of a shrewd intelligence. His armour shone so you could see your face in it.

I glanced around. A bare room, furnished with a table and a stool, with the shadowy statue of a deity on the far wall. A pile of scrolls and scraps of folded bark showed that he had been working on letters when we arrived. No comforts except an oil lamp and a flask of wine. The commander of the garrison had always been austere.

The fat guard snapped to a salute. 'In the name of His Imperial Divinity . . .' he began, but his superior brushed all that aside.

'Citizen Libertus? I think we've met before.' His voice was cool but courteous and his eyes were sharp.

I nodded. 'In the service of my patron, Marcus Septimus,' I said, getting that important name in as early as I could. 'I was privileged to help him with a problem he had.'

The commander smiled. 'So I recollect. In fact he was here a little earlier – with your adopted son – asking some questions on your behalf, he said. So perhaps you can resolve another little problem we have here.' He nodded to the fat guard. 'Bring the young man in.'

I heard the hobnailed sandals go clattering down the stairs, and a little afterwards come clattering up again accompanied by softer footfalls, which proved to belong to . . .

'Minimus!' I exclaimed.

The commander of the garrison looked stonily at him. 'You admit that you know this boy then, citizen? There seems to be some doubt about whose slave he really is. One moment he claims to be in Marcus's employ, bringing letters which are fastened with His Excellence's seal, and the next he is causing a rumpus in the streets, and insisting that he belongs to you.' He came round the table as he spoke, and, pushing back the styluses and seal-wax and pots of octopus ink, squatted on the edge and looked very hard at me.

'It's really very simple.' I was burbling. I thought I understood what had occurred, by now. 'He is in the service of my patron, but he's been loaned to me – there's another one as well, a snowy-headed one, who came into town with me. The one who gave you my description, I believe. I'd just sent him on an errand when the horse went past. I think that Niveus saw that it was Minimus and tried to make him stop . . .'

The commander raised a laconic eyebrow. 'Not because he had been robbing the market stall, you mean?'

'Stealing?' I was horrified. Only a few years ago, theft by a slave was a capital offence, and even now it often meant a sentence to the mines. I could not believe that Minimus would be so foolish as to take the risk, and I was about to protest on his behalf, but when I glanced towards him the words died on my lips. He was pink and guiltily staring at the floor, the very personification of discomfiture.

'He can hardly deny it. They found him with the goods.

We brought you here to see if you would intervene on his behalf.' The officer was clearly doing his very best for me – and for my patron at the same time, of course. The usual treatment for a thief was very different.

Minimus gave me a shamefaced, sideways look. 'I'm very sorry, master, but I didn't mean to steal. I thought I had a contract for borrowing the things. I even left my leather belt behind, as surety for her.'

'A belt which by your own admission is not even yours. It's simply part of your villa uniform, and therefore belongs to your owner – not to you!' The officer was sharp.

Minimus had no reply to this. He went back to examining his sandal straps again.

I looked at the commander. He raised his brows at me. 'He does claim he made a promise to bring the asking price, if his master found the goods were satisfactory.'

I nodded in relief. Such an arrangement is not unusual, when a slave is sent to negotiate a purchase on his owner's behalf – the more so if the owner is a well-known wealthy man, and has not actually seen the goods himself. 'But surely, if he was acting on His Excellence's behalf, any stall-holder would be happy to agree to such a thing?' I assumed it was Marcus the boy was acting for – I hadn't asked him to buy me anything.

The shrewd eyes were boring into me. 'Exactly so, my friend. So it comes as rather a surprise that the moment that he mentioned it, the woman changed her mind.'

'We had an agreement . . .' Minimus began, but a jerk from the fat guard silenced him at once.

I raised my eyebrows. 'But they did have a legal arrangement, didn't they?' And then I realised. 'Oh, I see.

She claims that the verbal contract has no force in law, because he is a slave?'

'I see you understand. She suddenly declared that it was null and void. But he had the goods by then, and . . .' He waved a languid hand. 'She tried to stop him, but he rode away.'

'I saw a group of people giving chase,' I said. 'Of course I didn't realise then it was Minimus on the horse.'

'She called on some other stall-holders to help. She obviously couldn't run fast enough herself. They didn't catch up with him until he'd gone through the gates – I don't think that they would have stopped him even then, if that child hadn't darted out and clutched the horse's tail.'

The boy looked ruefully at me. 'I slowed down because I heard someone call my name. It was Niveus, of course, and once he'd taken hold I couldn't gallop off and drag him down the lanes.' He shook his head. 'I'm sorry, citizen. I didn't mean to bring this trouble on us all.'

The commander quelled him with a single look. I was to be treated with a certain courtesy, but the favour did not extend to slaves.

'So he was arrested?' I said, finally.

'That's the funny thing. At first the woman didn't seem to want to make a charge – until we threatened to flog her for falsely claiming to be robbed. As I said, she now accuses him of theft. And you know what the punishment for that is apt to be?' He gave me a half-smile which reminded me that he was on my side – thanks to Marcus, as I had no doubt. 'Unless you are prepared to act on his behalf, confirm that he was acting as your agent in all this, and that any penalty should be referred to you?'

My spirits sank. I knew what this would mean. A fine was the standard penalty for petty theft, when it applied freemen and citizens. Fourfold restitution was the standard rate – and no doubt the woman would quote the highest asking price. Of course, I'd not mandated Minimus to purchase anything, but I could not see him sentenced to the mines on my account.

I sighed. Whatever this famous item was, it would cost me very dear. I only hoped that it was worth the price.

'He was acting on my mandate,' I said reluctantly. 'I agree to formal liability for any debt or fine. Though I too will have to ask for a delay. I have come to Glevum without my purse.'

The commander nodded. 'Then we shall have the woman in, and see if she consents – all three parties must agree, of course – and if she does, we'll let this fellow go.' He got to his feet. 'Soldier, go and fetch her.'

The fat guard was looking rather sourly at me, as if this outcome had disappointed him. He clearly felt aggrieved that he was still on duty, and not in the barracks enjoying his weak wine and army stew. But he said, 'At once, sir,' and set off down the stairs.

The commander had turned his back on us to return to his stool, so I took the opportunity to mouth at Minimus, 'What was it?'

He just had time to answer silently, 'Tunic!' before the guard came in again, with the plump puffing woman I'd seen before.

Chapter Twenty-four

When she saw Minimus she waved a fist at him. 'That's him – the one who robbed me. And me a widow, too. Thinks he can come and trick me, because he has a fancy horse. Then telling me he was His Excellence's slave! Well, I knew that it was nonsense, so of course I changed my mind. I've seen His Excellence's messengers in town – all scarlet tunics and fancy capes and things. Give a good price for one of those, I would.' The woman folded her plump arms across her chest. 'And that's another thing. What would His Excellence want old tunics for?'

'I think he will be glad to see it,' I observed. 'If it's the tunic that I think it is. Did you sell one like it to a passing peasant girl?'

I had confirmed that my patron had an interest in the case, and I saw that the officer had taken note of that, but the woman rattled on without pausing for a breath.

'Sell it to the peasant girl? That's what the slave boy asked and I told him then I've never sold her anything at all. Of course, I've seen her in the forum market with her mother many times – the girl with the peculiar greeny plaits, if that's the one you mean. In fact, she used to come sometimes and look at what I had. If anyone needed my stuff it was her – that dress she wore had got to be at least a size too small. But

I used to shoo her off because she never bought. Where would she get the money from?'

'She did have money, before she died,' I said.

'Not when she came to me she didn't, citizen. The last time I saw her, she even said as much. She was bemoaning the fact that she didn't have the means to bribe that fellow in the town who was offering all the street acts a chance to show their skills and possibly be chosen to be sent to Rome. Not that she would have had the slightest chance – she couldn't sing or anything as far as I'm aware, and anyway he disappeared and most of the acts were disappointed in the end. But she was desperate to try and he was taking anything people offered him, even a few *quadrans* if it came to it. But she didn't even have that. So she certainly couldn't have afforded that tunic – even if I'd had it at the time, which I didn't anyway. It's not a cheap item, as I told the lad.'

The commander was clearly impatient with all this gossiping. 'So, what is the value you claim that you are owed? It was a second-hand tunic, is that what I understand?'

'But an expensive item, mightiness, all the same. Almost entirely unused, and lovely soft material – flimsy, cut low round the arms and neck, and dyed in the most expensive yellow dye. Granted there is a nasty tear across the back, but it could be mended with a little care. The nicest thing that I have had all year – and he just thinks he can walk off with it.' She nodded towards Minimus with a spiteful look. 'Or are you going to pay me what he owes me, citizen?' She named a price that would have made a statue blink.

The slave boy shot me an apologetic glance. 'That's what I promised her. I'm sorry, citizen. But I was certain you'd want the tunic when I saw it on the stall.'

'Silence, slave!' The commanding officer was brisk.

'Speak when you are spoken to and not before. You hear?' The fat guard gave the boy a shake to underline his point.

Minimus looked appealingly at me. 'But master! It's the one I saw Morella wearing that day. I'm sure I'm not mistaken – it's not a colour or material that you see every day. I thought it would help you and His Excellence with your enquiries—'

'Silence, prisoner! I am making the enquiry here!' The commandant gestured briskly to the guard. 'Take him outside until I call for him,' he ordered, and without further ceremony the boy was marched away.

'So there might be more enquiries?' I saw the woman blanch, and tug at the leather apron she wore. Something had made her nervous, and it gave me an idea.

'Where did you get the tunic from, anyway?' I risked a little enquiry of my own. 'Since the servant says he saw the girl in it, and you agree that it was on your stall today?'

The change in her manner was quite remarkable. 'I'm just a poor old widow, citizen. I bought it in good faith. If it was stolen, how was I to know? I don't ask too many questions – in my trade, you don't. A young man brought it to me, and I gave him a good price. That's all I can tell you.'

I glanced towards the officer for permission to go on. He had been listening intently, and he signalled his agreement with his brows.

'This young man you speak of. Would you know him again?'

She shook her head. 'Not really. It was not a face I knew. Funny sort of accent, that's what I noticed most – I guessed he'd come from Venta, or somewhere west like that. He clearly was a trader: he had pots and things to sell.' A reluctant shrug. 'They were good items – I didn't haggle.'

'Items?' That was the commander.

She nodded. 'Offered me some sandals – very nearly new. I didn't put those on the stall, because they fitted me. A little bit small across the top, but good enough to wear.' She lifted her brown tunic to exhibit them. 'And *those* were not Morella's, I can tell you that! She was still wearing those awful boots of hers when I last caught sight of her.'

'What do you mean, "still wearing"?' I pounced on this at once. 'You saw her in that tunic, didn't you? And don't attempt to lie. Remember, we can make enquiries in the marketplace. If you saw her, other people will have seen her too.'

The market woman had turned an unhappy scarlet by this time. 'All right – I might have seen the girl in something similar, I suppose – if you ask round the market they will tell you that – but how was I supposed to know that this was hers? Anyway, it seems that the previous owner had discarded all the things. The fellow said he'd found them stuffed into a hedge, wrapped in a bit of sack – well, who'd do that if they still wanted them? Stands to reason they'd been thrown away.'

'You said yourself the tunic was most unusual,' I said. 'You must have been suspicious when it turned up for sale. Didn't you even wonder what had happened to the girl? Especially since you knew her well enough to know her name.'

'I thought she'd gone off with that fellow she was looking for – and if he took advantage, it was no concern of mine.' The tone was grudging now. 'She came to the forum in that tunic late one afternoon, asking everybody where he had gone, and trying to leave messages for him if he came back. That's when I heard her name. "Tell him Morella wants him and she's got the money now," those were her very words. Well, I know the girl was simple, but boasting of money in the marketplace? That was almost asking to be set upon and robbed.'

'And you thought that's what had happened?'

She was about to answer when she saw the trap. Knowingly selling stolen goods is treated as theft – and though she was presumably a freewoman at least, and therefore only subject to a fine, there was a case to answer. No magistrate was likely to accept that she believed the goods had really been accidentally discovered in a hedge!

'I told you, I thought she'd gone off,' she said defiantly. 'If she had money, she might have paid the fellow to let her tag along – and he might have let her do it, for a little while at least. He'd do anything for silver, from what I saw of him.'

'I thought you said she had no money when she last spoke to you,' the officer put in. He had sat down at his table now, and was looking searchingly at her. The focus of this enquiry had changed dramatically.

But she had an answer. She gave a crafty smile. 'But that day she didn't speak to me at all. She'd turned up in that tunic – far too short for her – and a great big bundle of other things as well. She didn't need to come and look at my poor stall that day. She went and stood by the basilica – where that young man used to stand – and when it was clear he wasn't going to come, I heard her asking people to pass the message on. Of course I would have done it for her,' she added virtuously, 'only I never saw him in the market any more.'

'Nor Morella either? You didn't think that odd?'

'Well, I knew he'd gone to Londinium, with those acts and everything. The ones that did get chosen to go to Rome. Naturally I thought that she'd caught up with him.'

'Can you describe this young man she tried to bribe?' The commander was scribbling something on a piece of bark. 'In case we need to seek confirmation of all this?'

'Well, of course I can. Big, sandy fellow, with enormous hands. Wears an olive-coloured tunic – wonderful material, you can tell it cost the earth. Ask anyone in the forum, they'll all say the same. The slave of that visitor from Rome with all the stripes, he was, and supposed to have a lot of influence with him. Not the sort of person you'd want to argue with. So if he'd made her sell the tunic, to pay a little more, it wouldn't have surprised me. She had her other clothes. I told you, citizen, I bought it in good faith.' She seemed to feel that she had given a plausible excuse.

It seemed that the garrison commander agreed with her. He had no especial interest in the fate of a peasant girl and he was clearly anxious to be rid of all of us. 'Well, citizen, are you satisfied with that? Or shall I arrest this woman for selling stolen goods?' He looked at me with a calculating twinkle in his eye. 'Perhaps some sort of accommodation might be reached? It would be a valid reason for the slave to seize the article, of course, if he had reason to think that it was dishonestly obtained.'

He was offering a graceful end to this affair. I took his cue before his patience frayed. 'If she will drop the charges she made against my slave, I will not insist on her arrest.' I could see her looking hopeful, and I said hastily, 'Provided that I can take the tunic with me now, that is. It may help us trace the girl. Her father is anxious and – as I think you know, Commander – my patron has an interest in the case.'

The stall-woman had looked as if she might resist my request, but the mention of my patron was enough to change her mind. She licked her lower lip. 'You'll pay the promised price?'

'I think that might be an infringement of the law, until we ascertain that it was not stolen from the girl. Otherwise it is not yours to sell.'

I looked at the commander of the garrison with surprise. I had not expected him to take a moral stand over a second-hand tunic with a tear in it, however unusual it might prove to be, but his next words made it clear that he was seeking to find a compromise that would cost me nothing. 'I think I will confiscate it temporarily, and have it sent to show His Excellence – you may not realise, woman, that he called here himself today? Concerning a body which was discovered near his house and a young woman who has disappeared.'

The woman let out a fearful shriek at this. 'A body! So that trader did kill and rob her. I was afraid of that. But I didn't know it, citizens, I swear by all the gods. I thought she'd gone to Londinium with the other acts.'

The commander was sharpening his pen again by now. He dipped it in the ink. 'What other acts are these?'

'He's got a cart of reptiles with him – or did when he left here. And some sort of comic actor – that's what the rumours say. They weren't even local. His master must have seen them somewhere else and chosen them – they only came here to catch up with him. Some of the better acts round here were furious when they knew – but no doubt the chosen ones had offered bigger bribes.'

He made a note of this. 'So if we want to find this fellow it should not be difficult . . . "accompanied by a cartload of snakes" . . .' He sounded sceptical. 'You haven't any other information about him, I suppose?'

I frowned. 'I think his name is Hirsius,' I said. 'I've heard of him before. A servant of that cousin of Marcus's who is visiting. And it is true about the entertainment acts. Apparently the Emperor rewards variety and Lucius has been seeking out a few to take back with him to Rome. I believe they may already have reached Londinium – according to a message my patron got today.' I frowned. 'Though they have must have made good progress – with the baggage cart as well.'

'Baggage?'

'There was a wagonload of luggage too, I understand, some of it belonging to His Excellence himself. He's hoping to catch up with it before he sails, I think – most likely at the house of the commander of the fleet, where my patron and his wife expect to stay a day or two.'

The garrison commander put down his pen and sprinkled ash on to the document to dry the ink. He smiled. 'Of course. I have just forwarded a letter to that very house. Well, that explains it. I could send a message there to see if the girl is with the carts, but otherwise there seems little I can do, unless her father wants to bring some kind of charge?'

I thought about the coins. 'I doubt that very much.'

He pushed away the memo that he'd been scribbling. 'In that case, citizen, I will restore to you your slave – and you, woman, can go back to your stall. It's almost closing time. And you will return that belt that you were given as surety. I'll keep the tunic here until I see His Excellence. Guard!'

The fat soldier put his head round the door. 'Show this woman and this citizen downstairs, and you can release that servant boy as well. There will be no charges.'

It was a dismissal. The woman puffed off down the stairs to close her stall up for the night, but I stood, considering. I would scarcely have time to reach the funeral guild now, and certainly I could not visit the dancing girls as well.

I turned to the commander. 'I had another slave – I think I mentioned it? – the one who stopped the horse. He was delivering some letters to you when all this began. Do I understand that he is in the gatehouse too?'

The officer picked up an official scroll and opened it. 'He did give me the letters, certainly, and the instructions as to where to send them to. They are already on their way. But I think he said he had another errand to perform. Something about the slaves' guild and a funeral? He said that he would come back here when he'd accomplished it.'

So Niveus had shown some initiative at last! I was still smiling as I went back down the stairs.

Chapter Twenty-five

Minimus was looking chagrined as they marched him out to me – as well he might. If it were not for the connection with Marcus, I was sure, both of us would have been lucky not to spend a wretched night in jail, since I was not carrying the wherewithal to pay any kind of fine – and though my toga would have saved me from the worst, I could not have bribed the warder to take special care of us.

'I am truly sorry, master,' he ventured finally, when we were clear of the gatehouse and standing on the road. 'You asked me to make enquiries about whether she had sold that tunic to the girl, and when I saw she actually had it on the stall, I thought that you would want it. She did agree to sell it – till I mentioned Marcus's name, and suddenly she changed her mind and wouldn't let it go.'

I nodded. 'Afraid that it would get her into trouble, I suppose, knowing that Marcus is a senior magistrate. She clearly guessed that it was stolen – she almost said as much. Do you want to go after her and pick up your belt?' I motioned through the arch where the woman could even now be seen, waddling in dudgeon back towards her stall. 'Before you find she's sold it to another customer?'

I meant it as a jest, but Minimus looked alarmed. 'I suppose I'd better go and claim it. And the horse, as well. I don't know what the guards have done with that. They took it from me when they arrested me. I suppose they took it to the stables at the garrison.' He looked at me ruefully, his reddish eyebrows raised. 'But you will need an attendant, since Niveus isn't here.'

I was amused at his assumption – derived from serving in patrician Roman households – that I must have a servant with me at all times. As a tradesman I have often walked these streets without a slave – while I was laying pavements, Junio was usually left behind to mind the shop for me. 'I have a little business on my own account,' I said. 'I want to go and find the leader of those dancing girls – if I can discover which inn they're staying at. You don't know by any chance, I suppose – since Marcus sent you to engage their services?'

He shook his head. 'He did not send me to find them. I don't know where they are.' He brightened. 'But I'm sure that one of the soldiers could tell you, citizen – the army always know all about pretty girls like that.'

'Then find out, when you go and ask about the horse. Do that quickly, and I can go there now.'

He frowned at me. 'But do you still want to do that, citizen? I thought you knew all about Morella and tunic by this time.'

'I still don't know the most important things. Where did she get it from – since it appears she didn't buy it from the stall – and what has happened to her since.' I tried not to sound impatient. Junio would have worked this out at once.

Minimus said 'Oh!' and closed his mouth again.

'I think it's possible she got it from the girls – perhaps without their leader's even knowing it. Who else would have such tunics, after all? If not, I'll try the brothel – the girls in there might know.'

'Do you need me to find out where the . . . ?' Minimus began, and trailed off, scarlet. 'I'll go and see about the horse at once. And I'll ask that new soldier on duty on the gate about the dancers. He's quite a friendly chap. He was the one taking those bodies to the paupers' pit yesterday – I've talked to him before.'

'That might have been a little different,' I said. 'You were escorting His Excellence and Lucius at the time.' But it did not deter him, and I watched him hurry off and speak to the soldier at the gate. He must have been successful, because first a gesturing arm directed Minimus round behind the gatehouse to the stable yard, and then the guard looked up and signalled me to come forward.

I was making my way towards him – the throng was lighter now – when a sudden thought struck me, like a hammer blow.

If the plaid dress was at the villa, and the tunic on the stall, what was Morella wearing? A naked body was surely the most conspicuous kind. I closed my eyes. Of course. Why hadn't the possibility occurred to me before? Two corpses found out on the Isca road, one of them a girl who had been 'stripped and robbed'. And rebels who had only confessed to half of the crime, even under torture?

And this guard had been involved! I wondered what he knew. I hurried over to ask him about it, but he held up his hand as I approached.

'Not so fast, citizen. No need to rush like that.' He looked at me, his tanned face wrinkled in a knowing smile. 'I hear you want to find those dancing girls? I hope you've got some money, then, that's all I can say. Cost you a fortune to have just one of them.'

I smiled weakly. I was a little impatient of his teasing, but I dared not let him see – I did want the information, after all, and I needed his cooperation with the other matter too. Better to grin and bear it. 'It isn't for myself,' I said. 'It's for . . .' I was going to say 'His Excellence' but the soldier winked.

'For a friend?' he said. 'Of course, it always is. Well, I'll tell you where they're staying, but I don't know if they're there. Half a mile or so along the military Aqua Sulis road you'll find an inn. Used to be a hiring stables at one time, but now it just operates as a lodging house. Bit more extensive than a lot of them – they've turned the old carthouse into extra rooms. That's where the girls are staying, I believe.' He chuckled. 'I wish you luck. Always supposing you can get past the dragon in charge.'

I wished, not for the first time that day, that I was carrying a purse. A little tip would not have gone amiss. 'Thank you, soldier. And there's another thing . . .' I was all at once so nervous that I had to clear my throat. 'Those rebels that you executed a day or two ago, for robbing travellers on the Isca road . . .'

This was a different matter. The friendliness had vanished all at once. 'What about it?' he said suspiciously, and then a look of recognition spread across his face. 'Of course! I knew I'd seen that red-haired slave of yours before. He spoke to me that day. Only – he wasn't accompanying you. What are you doing with His Excellence's slave?'

I nodded. 'It's a long story,' I murmured. 'But he's now been lent to me. He told me that he'd seen you with the rebel corpses on the road. The thing is, I believe there was a girl they were accused of having killed?'

'So I understand. They found her with lying with her father in a ditch – both stabbed and stripped and left there by the road. There's been a lot of trouble in those parts in this last moon or two.'

'You're sure it was her father?'

'Well – we could hardly ask! But he was too old to be her husband. Who else would it have been?'

'And the rebels denied killing her?'

'Well, of course they did – according to them they didn't even know that she was there. But we had the evidence; there couldn't be much doubt. One of the Silurians actually had the old man's bloodstained clothes with him, bundled underneath him like a saddle on the horse. And the other had a leather pocket purse – cut off at the drawstring but still full of silver coins. Seemed the ancient was a hermit and lived more or less alone – apart from this daughter whom no one'd seen before – so no doubt the rebels reasoned that he would not be missed. But as luck would have it he had been to town that day, and there were people to say that they'd seen him with the purse and wearing the very garments which the rebels had in their possession. You didn't have to be a rune-reader to see what had occurred. Anyway, the torturers obtained a confession in the end.'

'For both the murders? Or only for the man's?'

He shrugged. He was becoming the impatient one now. 'I don't know, citizen. Does it matter? The rebels would have been executed just the same however many people they had killed and robbed!'

'The girl's fate may be of some interest to His Excellence,'

I said, choosing my explanation with some care. 'I believe that her garments were discovered at his house. If it's the young woman I think it is, that is. Can you describe the girl?'

He looked at me suspiciously. 'I don't know, citizen,' he said again. 'I didn't see the victims. I was only detailed to take the rebels under guard, and take them off for burial when they were finished with.'

That was a blow, when I felt I'd been so close. 'So you wouldn't know, for instance, if she had greenish-yellow braids?'

He shook his head. 'Couldn't tell you, citizen.' He paused, and frowned. 'Though, come to think of it, the hair was hacked off anyway – chopped off a thumb's-width from the scalp, I heard.' He raised his armoured shoulders in an apologetic shrug. 'Some of these rapists have strange propensities and do that kind of thing. A sort of humiliation for the victim, I suppose. Like leaving her wearing nothing but those awful clumsy boots.'

'She still had her boots on?' This was more than I had hoped. The clouds seemed to stand still for a moment in the sky.

He nodded. 'So I understand. Not that they had any value, I suppose. They wouldn't have fitted anybody else. No point in casting lots for them, or bringing them back to the market stalls to sell.'

'So what would have happened to them?'

'They would just have been thrown into the public pit with her, I suppose. You could have gone and had a look, if you'd thought of it earlier, but those corpses were put in there several days ago. By now there will be others thrown in on top of them – and very likely they'll have been covered up with soil to stop the stink. I doubt you'd get authority to dig them up again.'

Poor Morella. By this time I was quite certain it was her. 'Cruelly stabbed' and left beside the road with an old man who had already been set upon and robbed so that she looked like another victim of the Silurians, then tossed into a ditch with all the paupers in the town. And rape? That was most likely guesswork – there was no way to tell unless there'd been clear violence, and he hadn't mentioned that. Perhaps the soldiers had assumed it, because the body was naked and the head was shaved – and it was the sort of thing they might have done themselves. But I was sure that the missing hair was no sexual deviance, but a cold desire to disguise the identity of the victim. Those plaits were so distinctive, they might be recognised and, if my deductions were correct, the murderer had intended that the body by the roundhouse (if it were ever found) should be supposed to be Morella from the fragments of the cloth. So the corpse on the Isca road must not be recognised as hers.

Of course, there may have been a sexual interlude – from what I had heard of Morella earlier, it was more than possible. Possible, even, that she'd agreed to it. The poor girl might have willingly undressed herself, in fact, and made her killer's job a little easier.

I turned back to the soldier. 'You think it was a rape?'

He gave me that knowing look again, clearly suspecting me of an unhealthy interest. 'I remember hearing that she was badly bruised – as if she had been beaten, or savagely attacked.'

I sighed, remembering what her mother had told me earlier. 'That was her father, not her murderer, I think. He beat her for talking to a stranger in the town.' Merely for talking! No wonder the poor child had tried to run away.

The soldier was looking at me suspiciously by now. 'And what exactly is your interest in all this? She's not your daughter, from what you have just said. And no one has suggested that she was a slave – no slave brands on her shoulders or head, or anything. So why are you asking these questions, citizen?'

'I told you, it may be of interest to His Excellence,' I said. 'I will make a point of telling him how helpful you have been. And now, if you will excuse me, I think I see my slave. It seems that he has now been reunited with his horse.'

I gestured towards the barracks as I spoke the words, and there indeed was Minimus, leading his splendid mount towards the gate. While the guard was looking at them I quickly slipped away. It is embarrassing to be in Glevum without a purse, sometimes.

Chapter Twenty-six

Minimus was surprised to find me standing there – almost exactly where he'd seen me last.

'Did you not get your directions, citizen? To find the dancing girls? The man seemed quite certain he could tell you where they were.' He glanced towards the gatehouse where the tanned guard was glaring rather mutinously at me.

'Oh, he gave me good directions,' I replied, 'and rather more than that.' I outlined Morella's story as I understood it now.

Minimus gaped. 'So you think that someone took her out and simply left her there? Heard about the other victim – and put her next to him?'

'Or simply found him there, and made the most of it. Perhaps that's why her murderer chose to go that way. It's quite clever really. I understand that there have been a number of attacks on that road recently – even without the old man's corpse, it's likely that the Silurians would have been held to blame.'

He nodded. 'I can vouch for that. Marcus was talking about it in the villa, just the other day. Half a dozen rebels have been caught and brought to trial for robbing travellers.' He gave a troubled grin. 'He hoped the sentences he meted out would stop it happening again.'

Instead of which, if anything, they'd made it worse, I thought. When the penalty for murder is no worse than that for theft, thieves are more likely to kill their victims – because dead men cannot talk. However, I did not say that to Minimus. Instead I gestured back into the town. 'You will have to hurry if you want your belt tonight. I will walk the half-mile to this famous inn and see if I can find the dancing girls. If you see Niveus get him to wait for me at the arch – there's supposed to be a councillor who is going to take us home.'

He was about to ask another question, I could see, but I shook my head and started down the road. 'I'll see you at the villa,' I called back to him. 'Or at the roundhouse, if you get there first.' I quickened my pace and hurried down the lane.

It was beginning to get distinctly late by now – not dusk exactly, but getting close to it. Dark clouds were already banking in the west and soon they would blot out what little light was left. I would have to hurry if I wanted to pay my visit to the inn and get back to Glevum in time to catch my lift, without infuriating some important councillor by compelling him to wait. Even the paved roads were difficult to negotiate at this time of the day, but I was almost trotting by the time I reached the inn.

It was a good deal smarter than the last time I had called – the stable yard was swept and scrubbed, the walls were freshly limed, and the old carthouse had been turned into a sort of dormitory. A stout woman in a woollen robe came bustling towards me through the yard as I arrived, carrying a bucket of water from the well. She stopped to fix me with an icy stare.

'There's no rooms available this evening, citizen. I don't take passing trade so much these days in any case.'

I explained that I was not looking for a room. 'I hoped to speak to the dancing girls,' I said.

Her expression didn't alter, but she raised her voice. 'Rufus!' A swarthy little fellow, no more than half her size, poked an enquiring head round the door.

'What is it, wife?'

'We've got another of them, Rufus – looking for the girls! You get rid of him! I must put this in the soup.' She disappeared inside the building, giving him a shove in my direction as she went.

He stood on the doorstep looking at me with pale, hunted, rheumy eyes. 'Well, citizen,' he rubbed his fingers on the sacking apron that he wore, 'you can see how it is. We have a lot of visitors asking for the girls, but I'm not allowed to let them in. I don't have any personal objection, you understand, but my wife doesn't like it – and nor does the woman who manages the troupe.'

'That's the one I want to speak to,' I explained. I could see now why I had been greeted as I had – no doubt a lot of hopeful men came visiting the girls, hoping for a private demonstration of their charms. 'She would agree to see me, I believe. I was speaking to her after a feast the other night . . .'

I was right. His manner altered. 'I see, citizen. That's different.' But he made no move. I had expected him to usher me inside. 'A business matter, is it?'

'I want some information. I want to trace a girl.' He was still immobile, and I took the plunge. 'If I am successful, there may be a reward.'

It worked – up to a point at least. Aulus had taught me something. 'I would like to help you, citizen, by all the gods I would!' The rheumy eyes were almost watering with regret. 'But you can't see her. You see, the girls aren't here. They're away in Isca, doing a performance for the garrison.'

I cursed beneath my breath. Isca! Of course! I knew that, if only I had thought! Marcus had actually told me that they were going to go. So all my breathless trotting down the road had been in vain. And some important councillor would be chafing at the gates while I kept his carriage waiting – all for nothing, it appeared.

My mortification must have been written on my face. The innkeeper's husband (I could not think of him as running the establishment himself) came sidling up to me. 'If you would like to come back tomorrow, or the next day, citizen? They should be back by then.' He saw me shake my head, and added sorrowfully, 'I can't help you otherwise, I very much regret. There's no one here except their sewing slave.'

I found myself staring at him in surprise. It had not occurred to me that the troupe of dancing girls would keep a slave, but of course it was likely, when one thought of it – somebody to make those costumes and keep them in repair, and perhaps to grind the perfumes and the paints and help the girls to do their hair before performances? It was exactly the sort of thing you'd use a slave girl for.

'You want to speak to her?' the man enquired. 'She might be able to tell you when they will be back. They pay my wife for lodgings, if they're here or not – that way we always keep a room for them, and it doesn't signify what time they return.'

I nodded. 'If you could take me to her?' He led the way,

into the building which had once housed the carts, and up a staircase to the upper floor. It had once been a sort of storage loft for grain but it was transformed now into a single sleeping room, with two long rows of palliasses on the floor, each with a cupboard at the side of it – some draped with discarded costumes of various vivid hues, others neatly stacked with perfume phials and mirrors and white whalebone combs. There was a curtained area at one end of the room where obviously the dragon woman and her wizened husband slept, and a largish table at the other end. There was a pile of fresh reeds under that, as though it sometimes formed a bed, but at the moment a thin girl was sitting on a stool, stitching at a piece of brilliant orange silk by the light of a single candle mounted on a spike.

As soon as she saw us she started to her feet. 'Gentlemen! I am sorry – my mistress isn't here!'

The man made a lugubrious face at her. 'I am aware of that. This citizen wants to have a word with you.'

'With me?'

'In private!' I added, since he showed no signs of going.

'Very well. In private.' He nodded to the girl. 'But remember, if you need me, I shall be right outside.' He turned, and I heard him clumping down the stairs. I wondered what he thought I might do to her and how he imagined he could stop me if I tried – he was so furtive and ineffectual I could have felled him with a blow.

The slave girl was still standing and I motioned her to sit. 'It concerns a girl who came here, a little while ago, wanting to join the dancing troupe,' I said. 'A girl in a plaid dress with yellow-greenish plaits. I think she may have somehow obtained a tunic from someone when she came. It occurs to me that, since you are concerned with costumes, you might know if that's true.'

I had come to the right person, that was evident. Her face had turned the colour of her handiwork, and she refused to meet my eyes. 'There has been trouble, has there? Someone has complained?' She picked up her bone needle and began to stitch again. 'I only meant it kindly – I was sorry for the girl. The lady who manages the dancers was so unkind to her.'

'You heard the conversation?'

'I could hardly fail to hear. The girls were downstairs, most of them, rehearsing in the barn. Grandad – that's what they call him – was down there with the drum: he takes them through their stretches and their movements every day otherwise they stiffen up and lose the knack of it.'

I laughed. 'So Grandmother was up here, with just you and the girl?'

There was the faint hint of what might have been a smile. 'They don't call her Grandma – they call her the Wardress. But otherwise you're right. The girl came asking, and they showed her up, and the Wardress took her behind the curtain at the end – she does that sometimes to look at applicants. Wants to see their legs and figures, so she makes them strip.'

'And that is what she did?'

'I imagine so – though it was obvious there wasn't any point. Certainly the girl took off her dress. I could hear her babbling. Full of hope she was – she'd heard some fellow talking in the town, about how anyone could get a place to entertain the court if they only had the money to bribe him for the chance. She thought perhaps the Wardress would agree to do the same, and let her join the dancers if she paid us well enough. Well, of course, the Wardress simply laughed at her. Said that she had legs like tree trunks, a bottom like a tub, and a face to frighten horses. It was horribly unkind. And when she'd done it she just went downstairs to see her precious dancers, and left the girl alone. In floods and floods of tears she was when I went in to her. I let her have the tunic to cheer her up a bit.'

'You gave her a tunic? You had authority for that?'

She fiddled with her needle. 'Well . . . not exactly gave it. I have to keep accounts. She had all this money . . .' The flame of her cheeks was now much brighter than the silk. 'She could afford it – and it helped us both. It gave her a bit of hope – the man had told her to come back when she'd found a proper outfit and a substantial bribe, which was probably sarcastic, but she took him at his word – and it helped me to put a bit aside towards my freedom price, though obviously I had to put a little in the kitty for the cloth. And the tunic wasn't wanted – it was torn across the back. The Wardress had already said it was no use to us, and was talking about unpicking it and using it for trim.'

'So you sold a torn tunic for an *aureus*?' I said. 'And you want me to believe that was a kindly act? Not taking advantage of a rather simple girl?'

She looked at me helplessly. 'You know about the gold? Well, in that case you'll realise that I did look after her. She was carrying it just tied up in her shawl-end – did you know? Five gold pieces and she carries it like that – simply asking to lose it or be set upon and robbed.'

'So you showed her how to hide the money in her hem?'

She nodded, with a sigh. 'Then she wouldn't put the plaid dress on again, of course! Insisted on wearing the tunic right away, and going straight to the forum to try to find the man. I had to help her make a proper bundle out of it – gave her a piece of old sack from the pile.' She raised her eyes to look sorrowfully at me. 'But the coins were stolen, that's what you're telling me? So I'll have to give it back? I suppose I'm not surprised – she said they were her uncle's legacy, but I should have known they weren't.'

'There is more truth in her story than you might suppose. If the coins were stolen it was not by her. Though her family might have a case against you, I suppose, for charging her so highly for what were damaged goods. A bargain made by someone who can be proved to be a simpleton has no validity in law.'

She looked abashed. 'It wasn't only the tunic that I gave her. I felt a bit guilty about it afterwards, and when she came back, a little later on, I found her somewhere she could sleep and gave her food as well.'

'She came back here again?' This was important news. I had been wondering what had happened to the girl after she left here with her tunic, and before she was seen in the morning talking to Aulus at the gate. 'Back here?' I said again.

'That's right, citizen. She hadn't found the man. He'd left when she got there and he wasn't coming back – at least that's what was being rumoured in the town. She was awfully disappointed. She'd even been trying to find out where he lived. I was here alone by that time – the troupe had gone out to perform at the vinters' guild that night – so I looked after her. They'd left some bread and meat for me, and I gave her some of that. And I found a warm spot in the rehearsal barn for her – I knew that no one would go in there again that night.'

'So she didn't find him?' An awful possibility had occurred to me – that Hirsius might have been the murderer. After all, the rumour was that she had gone away with an entertainment troupe – the sort of thing that Hirsius was signing up in town – and she had been actively looking for him earlier that day. But now it seemed that she had not caught up with him. 'Not at all?'

'Not that night anyway. She was quite upset, but very grateful that I didn't let her down. She was terrified that somebody was going to send her home. She was black and blue with bruises – I saw them before she put on the tunic. She said her father beat her, and it looked as though he had – that's why she was so keen to find the man she was looking for. He was staying at some villa, I don't know where it was – somewhere on the western side of town, I think. Anyway, the girl had found out where it was. She was going to go and find him first thing the next day – and I suppose she did, because when I came down after dawn I found that she had gone.'

'Wait a minute!' There was one detail of this story which I found startling. 'Did you say the western side of town? Out across the river? You are sure of that?' Marcus's villa was firmly to the south, and a little east of here, if anything.

She made a face. 'I don't know for myself. I met a street musician the next day who told me that – I asked him if he had heard about the fellow taking bribes, because I was concerned about the girl. I knew that lots of street performers had been paying him, so I thought there was a fair chance that he'd know.'

'And did he?'

A rueful smile. 'It seems that he had given the man a hefty

bribe himself, but it had got him nowhere. All the local acts were up in arms, he said, and were thinking of going out to the villa to confront him face to face, but by that time the fellow had moved on in any case. He'd been seen at the west gate, riding into town, to catch up with the party that had already gone – the acts that *were* selected, and a sort of luggage cart. They'd gone round the outside of the town, of course, being wheeled transport, but he'd ridden through, and several people had shouted after him.'

The west gate, I was thinking. The gate that led in from the Isca road. The very place where Morella's body had been found. So Hirsius would have had the opportunity to put it there! Indeed, he was the only one who might have had the chance, it seemed. But why should he kill Morella? It made no sense at all. Not for the money – she would have given it willingly for the chance to go with him. And he'd hardly spoken to her, by all accounts – Morella had been beaten savagely for 'talking to a man' without consent, so it was hardly something which had happened every day. 'I don't understand it,' I said aloud.

The slave girl misunderstood me. 'They were angry, I suppose, that he hadn't taken a single entertainer from this area. But of course there was nothing that anyone could do. It was the master's decision, after all, what acts he chose to take and it was someone else's villa that he was staying in, so even then he might not have had the final say on who performed. But people hope, don't they, even though the slave had only promised to put in a word for them. I know the Wardress wondered about bribing him herself – and we're considered the finest dancers in all Britannia.'

I was still considering the force of what she'd said. 'Wait a minute!' I spoke aloud again. 'Hirsius left the morning of the civic feast. And took the snake man with him! That makes sense – Aulus told me that Lucius had sent one act ahead. But there should have been another one as well – a comic actor – Julia talked about him, at the feast, and you have just talked about the "acts" that were on the cart that day! So where was the other performer when the transport left? Walking across the farm paths with his parcels to the lane – the way that Aulus told me he could not see? Atalanta even told me that she had seen him there, carrying a bag of costumes in his hand! Great Jupiter! I wonder if that woman from the stall was telling us the truth!' I turned to the sewing girl, who was looking mystified. I realised that I had been talking to myself. 'It's time I got back to the villa – as soon as possible! Thank you for your assistance. You've been a lot of help.'

'You're not arresting me? For taking the gold piece?'

'Not at the moment. Thank the Fates for that. But I may require you to repeat what you have said before the senior magistrate. You understand?'

She nodded, terrified.

'Very well. Go down and find the . . . innkeeper and ask him to fetch a lighted torch for me. I must get back to town as quickly as I can, and it is getting dark. Well?' I added, as she scuttled to the stairs and hesitated for a moment at the top. 'What are you waiting for?'

'The woman will want money, citizen. As payment for the torch.'

Dis take it! And I didn't have a purse. 'I think it has been paid already? Wouldn't you agree? Or do you wish me to explain that you have got the necessary gold?'

Chapter Twenty-seven

'Here you are, citizen. This where you want to be?' The innkeeper had slowed up a short way from the gates. 'There is the lad I am looking for.'

He waved towards a tattered figure waiting on the roadside with a handcart piled high. I recognised the urchin that I'd noticed earlier. 'It's the boy who collects the manure and ordure from the streets!'

'Not very pleasant cargo, I agree, but I have to make a living, citizen. Now that we don't keep many horses any more – on account of those dancing girls filling all the space – I have to come for extra now and then to fertilise the field, or I couldn't grow the turnips to keep the inn supplied.' He had reined his bony animal to a stop, and was already preparing to jump down from the cart.

I followed, more discreetly. It is difficult to dismount with dignity when carrying a burning torch, but I did my best. I was likely to be under scrutiny, I told myself, as I looked round for the promised carriage and the councillor.

There was no sign of either. The night traffic had disappeared into the town by now, and the crowds long since dispersed. The area outside the gates was shadowy and dark, almost deserted except for the two carts and the figures who were shovelling the stinking load between the two. Almost deserted – there was someone in the gloom, cloaked and hooded and skulking near the arch. There were unlikely to be brigands this close to the guard, but I felt an uncomfortable stirring of alarm.

I had held up my torch to get a better look – I was grateful for its light, though it was burning down – when there was a noise behind me and a hand fell on my arm.

'Citizen Libertus?' I whirled round at once. The fat guard was grinning at my discomfiture. 'I have to ask you to accompany me again – the commander is waiting to have another word with you.'

He had done it on purpose, I was sure of that. And he had succeeded. I was trembling. So much so that I couldn't find the voice to form a word, and I followed him in silence through the gate to the guardhouse, leaving the innkeeper and the dung-boy staring after me.

It was the same man that I had seen before and he'd been courteous then, but he seemed a good deal mellower in his manner now. Perhaps it was the effect of watered army wine, or the cheerful brazier that now burned beside his desk, but he was almost fulsome as he greeted me – and from the warmth with which he invited me to sit, I might have been my patron His Excellence himself.

'My dear citizen, it's most unfortunate!' Despite the smile, the words were not encouraging. 'The guard has told you what the problem is?'

I managed to murmur that I'd heard nothing yet.

The officer looked uneasy, but he forced another smile. 'A clear misunderstanding. I must apologise.'

So whatever the trouble, it was their mistake, not mine! That was a relief. 'In that case . . .' I tried to sound as gracious as I could. 'Perhaps we could discuss this at another time. I am expected at my patron's and I'm already late. I believe a senior councillor is waiting for me.'

The garrison commander ran a hand across his brow. 'That is just the problem, citizen. The message wasn't passed on. It was not until your pageboy came and asked if you were here, and whether I had found a councillor to take you home again, that I realised the mistake. Not the boy we spoke to earlier – the other little chap.'

Niveus! I might have guessed. I gave an inward groan. 'He did not deliver Marcus's note to you, requesting transport for my journey home?'

'Well, he brought it – but together with another note, you see, and a direction which asked me to forward the accompanying correspondence, under seal, to the home of the commander of the British fleet, by the first available imperial courier. It was very urgent, the covering letter said – and since it was under your patron's private seal, naturally I complied at once. I saw that the other message – the one that you tell me was about your transport home – was addressed to "The Commanding Officer", but I did not realise it meant me. I thought it related to the naval man, of course, so naturally I forwarded that to Londinium as well.'

I was holding my head between both hands by now. I raised it long enough to say despondently, 'And Niveus didn't tell you? The little page, that is?'

The officer was looking quite embarrassed now. 'He did say there were instructions, but he seemed hesitant. I told him everything was written down, and I knew what to do. And both the letters were so magnificently sealed – it did not occur to me to question it. And he did not insist.'

'He wouldn't!' I was thoroughly dejected by this time. I would be extremely late, and Marcus would take it as the gravest disrespect, not just to him but to his dead father too. Why had I not delivered those messages here myself? I had noticed the extensive nature of the seals – but I hadn't guessed at the misleading instructions Lucius had sent.

'Just a minute!' I was sitting upright now. 'Where did you say you were told to forward them?'

He was looking startled. 'To the home of the commander of the British fleet. I told you that just now. I think I even mentioned it when you were here before.'

I stared at him. 'You did. Of course you did. But I didn't realise the implication then. Lucius claimed that he was sending a message of condolence to his aunt in Rome – not writing to his relations in Londinium! Yet you tell me that his letter was addressed to the commander of the fleet.'

'Perhaps he was hoping that they would forward it? Obviously he was very anxious that it should arrive as fast as possible.'

I shook my head. 'Then why did he not write the letter earlier? A messenger came from Rome today with news of his uncle's death – it would have been simplicity itself to send a note back with him. But Lucius didn't do it – so why was it suddenly so important later on that he had to borrow Marcus's seal – and even arrange to use the military mail? What had happened to make him feel so differently?'

'Too overcome with grief, perhaps, at first?' the officer suggested sympathetically. 'It was a member of his family, after all.'

I thought of Lucius as I'd found him at the sacrifice. He had been startled, certainly, when I'd walked in on him. So startled that he'd broken that jug of sacrificial wine. But overcome with grief? 'I don't think so.'

He misinterpreted. 'Your patron's father, is that not correct? And this Lucius is closely related to the wife? His Excellence explained it to me earlier. He was with me here when that messenger arrived. I saw him break the seals and open all three notes.'

'All three notes?' I echoed.

'There was the one from Rome, and one from Londinium as well – with an enclosure from His Excellence's page, I believe, Pulchrus is he called? – confirming the arrangements for the journey. It was given to the messenger to bring at the same time, since he was riding down. So that makes three. That adopted son of yours was here as well when the messenger arrived – I should have thought he would have told you that the notes had come.'

He had – of course he had. He'd told me in detail what the letters from Londinium had said. Yet . . . surely? I shook my head. Something disquieting had occurred to me. If Marcus had unsealed the letters – and two people now had told me that he had – how did Lucius know what they said? It was possible the messenger had simply told him verbally – but Niveus had said he saw Lucius cut a seal. So was there yet another note from Londinium, to Lucius himself? A note which he had afterwards destroyed? It would not be difficult to get rid of it – there were braziers enough. Indeed – I started up at this – I had actually seen him with a fire!

I was a fool, I told myself. A blind and ageing fool! I did not see what was in front of me. A jug of sacrificial wine, indeed! Where had he got that from? I had heard him tell Colaphus not to bring the wine jug that was in his sleeping room. That was the one that Marcus had supplied. So where had this second one come from, and what had it contained, that Lucius had been intending to pour on to the flames?

And then another terrible idea occurred to me. I suddenly realised what was different 'later on' when Lucius wrote that letter. Aulus had been found. And Aulus had somehow taken poison, hadn't he? Though Lucius had tried to put us off the scent by pretending that a viper might have stung him in the woods. Vipers! It was only the glimmering of a theory, but if I was even partly right there was no time to lose. I got sharply to my feet.

'Citizen?' I realised the officer was looking mystified.

'That messenger you sent. The one who took the letters to the fleet commander's house? Would it be possible to catch up with him?'

The officer looked startled. 'It would be difficult. He is a courier for the imperial mail. He will stop only to change horses at the military inns and perhaps to have a meal and rest at one or two of them. Of course he was not instructed to make the highest speed – the official mail that he was carrying was generally routine, no special orders or other matters of high priority. I suppose it might be feasible to overtake him on the road, if it was a matter of imperial concern. We could set up a pursuit using fresh riders at each stop. But that would be exceptional, requiring official sanction and huge expense, and even if we did catch up with him, it is a capital offence to interrupt the mail.'

'Even if one is the sender of the document?'

He looked perplexed. 'In that case, I suppose . . .'

'Both of those letters you sent were under Marcus's seal – one was to you, asking you to arrange transport for me later on, the other, as he thought, from Lucius to Rome. But they're on their way to the commander of the fleet. Marcus did not intend that either of them should be sent to that address. But that is what you authorised, if I understand aright. I do not imagine that His Excellence will be very pleased.'

It shook him. 'I suppose there is a rider I could send tonight. And I could give him a warrant for the top priority. But what about the cost? And if someone denounced me to the Emperor?'

I heard myself saying, 'I will answer for the cost. On behalf of His Excellence, my patron, that is.' I sought for a tactful way of putting it. 'This affects his family – and is of great concern.'

The commander seemed to hesitate, and then he said, 'I see. I know you enjoy his greatest confidence. Well, on your assurance I will send a messenger to intercept those notes. But, understand this, citizen, this is on your head and I will not take responsibility for opening the mail. I will have it returned to His Excellence – that is all that I can do. And Jove protect you if you're misleading me.'

'My patron's letter was addressed to you, in fact,' I said, as much to reassure myself as anything. 'He cannot object if you send off after it.'

He acknowledged this with the faintest raising of his brows. 'He will not be happy that I did not do as he asked.'

'He was asking you to arrange a lift for me – in military transport, if it came to it. If you care to do that now, you could send word to him and ensure that he agrees that you should recall those messages.'

'So I'll delay the messenger until I hear from him?'

I shook my head. 'There is no time to lose. The courier must be sent as soon as possible if we are to intercept the letters on the road. You'll have to take my word for it, and if I am wrong, you will have me in your transport, won't you, and can lock me in the cells?'

He looked at me, and nodded. 'Very well. I'll do as you suggest. But rather than send word to Marcus, I will come with you myself. It's most irregular, but so is all of it.' He went to the doorway. 'Guard!'

The fat guard came puffing up the stairs.

'Have my gig made ready, and find a courier. The best man available and the fastest steed. And a warrant paper, and some sealing wax. I will write instructions. In the meantime, take this citizen downstairs. He will want to see his page.'

'At once, sir!' With obvious distaste, he led me to the guardroom, where he motioned to a bench. 'Sit there, citizen!'

And there I sat for what seemed like half an hour, with soldiers passing by and peering in at me, until the fat guard bustled in again with Niveus in his wake. A chastened Niveus, cold and shivering, despite the cloak and hood that covered him, which Minimus had been wearing a little while before. When he saw me his blue eyes opened wide.

'Citizen! Master! There you are at last. I have been waiting at the arch for you, as you commanded me. Minimus gave up and rode ahead. He said you told him to.' His small face brightened into a hopeful grin. 'I managed to arrange the funeral with the guild. They are coming tomorrow to anoint the corpse, and get it ready for the pyre. They'll provide the mourners and musicians too, and a priest of Diana to perform the rites.'

I thought about the poor creature we'd cremated earlier that day – already it seemed like several lives ago – and of poor Morella in the paupers' pit. Aulus would have a better funeral than that.

I sighed. I couldn't help it.

Niveus looked anxiously at me. 'Did I do well?' he said.

Chapter Twenty-eight

It seemed to take a long time, even then, before the soldier came and told us that the gig was ready and awaiting us. But once we were all three crammed into it – there was seating room for me beside the officer, but poor little Niveus had to crouch on the floor – we bowled along the road at a surprising pace. A military gig is built for speed, of course, and the driver was skilful, even in the dark – the torches which were mounted on either side of him gave off a cheerful glow and helped to keep him warm, but were not much help in illuminating the road.

Moreover, we had the advantage of military rank, and such other travellers as we passed moved smartly from our way. So, though we were jolted far too much for speech, we found ourselves turning off on to the lane which led to Marcus's country house in not much longer than we might have done by day.

I would have liked to ask the gig to stop and let me go into my roundhouse and rinse my hands and face – Gwellia would be proud of my instincts there, I thought – but I feared to annoy my patron by any more delay, and I'd resigned myself to driving directly to the feast. I was just wondering what Marcus would have to say to me, and whether they'd begun without me several hours ago, when a figure with a lantern rushed out of my gate into the road.

'M-m-m-master? Is that you?' It could only be Kurso, stammering like that.

'What is it, Kurso?' The gig had stopped by now.

'The m-mistress s-says that you're to c-c-come inside.' The lantern was bobbing in agitation now. 'There's s-s-someone here that you were l-l-looking for.'

I glanced at the commander. 'You'd better go,' he said. 'It may be the girl in question. I'll wait here for you. Don't be very long. I don't have to remind you that you're already late.'

And Gwellia knew that as well as anyone, I thought, as I climbed down from the gig. I was getting skilled at managing on carts. I went through the enclosure and through the roundhouse door, and was startled by the domestic sight that met my eyes. There was a man – a stranger – sitting on my stool, beside my fire, drinking from my bowl and laughing with my wife. I felt a surge of helpless jealousy, even as I noticed that Junio was there.

He looked up and saw me, and jumped to his feet. He had been crouching by the stranger, near the hearth. He came across and seized me warmly by the arm. 'Father, at last. We've found that man for you!'

'Man?' I was bewildered.

'The farmer in the cart. You went to the villa gate to keep a watch for him, and said that you'd be looking for him on the way to town. Well – we saw him passing, or rather Mother did, and she persuaded him to come and wait for you in here. It wasn't easy – he wanted to get home – but you know what Mother's like. She charmed him into it.'

I did know what Gwellia was like, indeed, and I was

ashamed of my reaction when I first walked in. I might have known my family would find some way to help. I nodded and went over to stand beside the fire. My wife, who had been stirring something in a pot, looked up and saw me and greeted me at once.

'Husband! This is the farmer from the uplands that you were looking for. He knows Morella – he was just telling us.' She gave him an understanding smile. 'I have explained that her parents have been to see us here, and that you were trying to find news of her.'

'That's right.' His mouth was full of something, but he gestured with his hands. He was just as Niveus had painted him, thin and ancient and not altogether clean. He spoke reasonable Latin, with a heavy burr. 'Knew her well, I did – poor little lass. Your wife assures me that you only want to help, and you are worried for her safety, so I'll tell you what I know. I don't want to get her into trouble with her father, though – if he lays hands on her he'll beat her black and blue.'

I closed my eyes, thinking of a wretched naked body in the common pit. 'He won't hurt her any further. I can promise that.'

'Well then.' He took another bite of something in his hand. 'What can I tell you? Last time I saw her she was looking happier – better than I've ever seen her in my life. Turned out nicely, too – new clothes and everything. Little bit skimpy round the top, perhaps, but she looked quite good in it.'

'And she had a bundle with her, of her other clothes?'

He spluttered crumbs at me. 'That she didn't, mister. Nothing of the kind. Just a pair of sandals hanging round her neck – tied up by their laces, though they looked too big for her.' He gave a barking laugh. 'Had her hands full, just holding on to that dratted animal – couldn't even let him go to wave goodbye to me. She wasn't holding bundles! I'm quite sure of that.'

'She had the dog with her?' Suddenly I wasn't making any sense of this.

'Dog? Course she didn't. I'm talking about the horse. Lovely animal. Must have cost a fortune, if I am any judge, and good-tempered too, judging by the way she was clinging to the mane. And she didn't really have to; the chap was holding her.'

'The chap?' I remembered the descriptions that I'd heard of Hirsius. 'Big fellow, was he, with sandy-coloured hair? Wore an olive-coloured tunic and a cloak to match?'

He nodded sagely. 'That's the very one. Didn't look too pleased when she called out to me – I suppose he was afraid he'd have her father after him. But if he makes her happy, who am I to grudge? Time that poor creature had a bit of happiness.'

'What did she say, exactly? Can you recall her words?'

'Said to tell her parents that she had run away. Gone to join the entertainment troupe and work with animals. I said I saw she had got some pretty clothes, and she said that she was going to have some others by and by, and another pair of sandals that would be a better fit. "The other fellow's got them in his bag," she said, "but he couldn't stop to sort them out just now. He's got to ride the hard way as it is, along the lane, to catch up with the carts before they reach the town. He's got all the costumes and the wigs with him. You better not go down that way along the lane," she said, "because he's still there changing his costume for the act and he hasn't even got his tunic on. I would have walked right into him and seen his you know what, if my friend hadn't stopped me in time! And wouldn't that have been embarrassing." And then she giggled – you know what she was like. Or, pardon, citizen, probably you don't.'

I thought about that dreadful mutilated corpse. That, surely, was what she had been prevented from looking at? 'And what did her companion have to say to that?'

'He got quite cross with her and told her not to talk. Said they had to hurry, because the cart was up ahead and they had a lot of things to do before they caught it up. That made her giggle – I wondered what he meant.' He cocked an eye at me. 'She was a bit given to that sort of thing, if you know what I mean. Didn't have much affection from her father, I suppose, and wanted to find it any way she could. I didn't mind her, though she wasn't very bright – though I wouldn't have liked my sons to want to marry her.'

'And you are sure she wasn't carrying a bundle at the time?'

'Positive! The fellow had a sack behind him on the horse, an enormous one all tied up with a string – but there was nothing in it. I asked where they were heading, but he didn't answer me, just turned and galloped off. Morella was clinging on for dear life all the time, and laughing like an idiot – that's the last I saw of her.'

'You'd be prepared to swear this, if I asked it? You can't hurt Morella – I'm afraid she's dead. I'm just anxious to bring the murderer to account for her death.'

His face had fallen. 'Dead? You're sure of that? But she seemed so jubilant . . .'

'Then remember her like that. It may have been the

happiest moment of her life. But your story – I can rely on you for that?'

He nodded glumly. 'If you have to, I suppose. I'll have her father setting that wretched dog on me and claiming that I ought to have said something earlier. I did give him the message, but he didn't seem to care. More worried that he'd lose a wealthy son-in-law than interested in his daughter, it appeared. So I didn't say too much – I didn't want him catching up with her.' He got up abruptly. 'Now, you know where to find me. I've told you what I know. With your permission, I'll be heading home.'

'Of course!' Gwellia was already bringing him his cloak. 'Your wife will be half frantic about you as it is. And you have been very helpful – my husband won't forget.'

He turned to her, his withered face alight. 'It's been a pleasure, lady. He is a lucky man. Now, if I could have a servant to help me with my cart? I've left it at the corner, at the junction with the lane – the very spot where I saw Morella and the horseman, that day. But I've unhitched the horse, and I will have to harness it up again.'

'I'll take you to the slave hut and find a boy for you,' Gwellia said grandly, as if we kept a horde of servants in the room next door. She took a candle and led the way for him.

Junio was squatting beside me in a trice. 'You've discovered something, master. I know that tone of voice. And Minimus told us you'd found the tunic on the stall, and had gone off to see the dancing girls. What have you been doing since he saw you last?'

I told him, as briefly as I could. After a moment, Gwellia came in, and stood behind us, listening carefully as well. When I had finished she sat down by the fire.

'So Hirsius killed Morella and left her by the road, hoping the Silurians would get the blame for it? Do you think he really hid the tunic in the hedge?'

'It rather looks like it. After all, it was conspicuous. Even that farmer commented on it. Together with the sandals that Morella had? Now where on earth had they acquired those?' She stopped and stared at me. 'Oh, of course – there must have been that other body, lying in the lane.'

'Exactly, Father. Is that why Hirsius killed Morella, do you think? Because she came across the body, and she might have talked? The farmer has just told us that they were riding from that direction – and isn't that a little bit peculiar in itself? If anyone was going to ride to town, that is the quickest route – and yet she was going the other way, by all accounts.'

'And it isn't suitable for heavy carts,' I said. 'Don't forget that Hirsius said the carts had gone ahead.'

'So why was Hirsius in the lane at all? He was supposed to have been accompanying the luggage and the entertainment cart. And where was Pulchrus? He set off with them . . .' He stopped, and looked at me, his face appalled. 'You don't think . . . after all?'

I nodded. 'I'm afraid so, Junio. We thought the other day that the body we cremated might have been a page.'

'Because of the soft hands and pampered feet?' my wife enquired. 'Poor Pulchrus! I am glad that you were there and able to give him a proper funeral.'

'So it was Pulchrus all the time.' Junio sounded saddened. 'We kept on asking who had visited the villa on that day. We never asked who'd gone away from it.'

There was a moment's silence before Gwellia remarked,

'But I still don't understand. Why was he discovered in Morella's clothes? Doesn't that suggest that she was present when he died?'

'I've been thinking about that. I think it's more likely that she turned up afterwards. Remember she was asking for Hirsius at the gate, and Minimus saw Aulus pointing down the lane – which suggests that Hirsius had already gone that way. So he and Pulchrus took the short-cut into town instead of accompanying the baggage-cart on the road. Suppose Morella turns up on the scene when Pulchrus is just dead? I don't think it's likely she saw the corpse – she wasn't a girl to hide her feelings, and she'd have told the farmer if she'd seen a body in the lane – but it's almost certain that she stumbled on the murderers.'

'The murderers?' Gwellia sounded shocked. 'You think that there was more than one of them?'

'I think there had to be. I'm sure Hirsius did the actual killing – throttled Pulchrus with the slave disc round his neck, I'd guess, then pulled it off for the false page to wear – but he did have help. Someone who came through Marcus' land, of course. Consider what we know. Hirsius and Pulchrus were on horses when they left. Cilla told us that Pulchrus had been seen accompanying the cart – very distinctive in his new uniform. But he doesn't deign to speak to anyone – that was not like Puchrus, I thought so at the time. But it wasn't Pulchrus, it was someone in his clothes – which means that someone had to be working with Hirsius. It wasn't Hirsius himself; he was on the Isca road, disposing of the witness who had seen too much. You remember what Morella told the farmer at the time – that the other fellow was just trying his costume on? Obviously she came across them just as he was putting on the uniform. He would have had a wig, of course – in that bag of costumes Atalanta saw him with. Hirsius told Morella it was some sort of preparation for the show, and she was such a trusting soul, she didn't question it.'

'But why put her dress on Pulchrus? Why not make a straight exchange? The murderer must have been wearing something at the time.'

'I think that might have been their original idea. But Morella's arrival must have startled them. We can't know what happened, we can only guess, but it seems as if this other man was putting on the page's clothes – presumably the naked corpse was on the ground nearby – when Morella came walking innocently down the road towards them. She was on foot, remember, with a bundle in her hand. What does she see but Hirsius, whom she's been looking for? No doubt he went to meet her, to keep her well away, and she would have told him that she had the money now – and even offered him the bundle, so he could have the coins. But for once, he isn't interested in that. His only thought is to get her away from there as soon as possible, and stop her from noticing the presence of the corpse. Perhaps she sees the sandals, so he gives her those and promises more garments later on. He tells her that the other man is putting his acting costume on – which is probably enough to stop her coming close, and gives a sort of reason for him changing in the lane. Hirsius offers to take her with him, and puts her on the horse, where she needs both her hands, so he leaves behind the bundle with the dress in it, saying it will be taken to catch up with the cart.'

'But why put it on the body?' Gwellia was looking strained and horrified.

'I was about to come to that. The dress itself is just a nuisance – they don't know about the coins, so it seems as if the mock-Pulchrus had a good idea. Instead of merely swapping garments with the corpse, he dresses the body in the woman's clothes and hides it in the ditch and puts his own tunic in the costume sack. If the body is discovered, in a year or two, it will seem to be the girl's – supposing that by that time there will be nothing left but bones and a few fragments of material.'

'And some hair, perhaps. Of course!' Junio sounded almost jubilant. 'The hair might be a problem, so he hacks it off – together with the slave brand – just in case. And he smashes in the face so it can't be recognised.'

Gwellia was doubtful. 'You don't think that was the original intent?'

'I doubt it very much. More likely they intended to take the body out and leave it on the margins where Morella's corpse was found. They even had a sack with them they could have put it in. But Hirsius would have had to take it out there on his horse – he would have had to be careful to disguise the shape – while the imitation Pulchrus was being seen near town. But Hirsius couldn't do that, since he had Morella now, so his partner was forced to improvise and find a hiding place. He might have succeeded, too, if work for the new roundhouse had not disturbed the corpse so soon.'

'And Lucius's servants didn't mix with the villa staff, so obviously they hadn't heard about the plans.' Junio was still following my train of thought. 'But who was this second servant? He would surely have been missed?'

'There was no second servant. You must have realised that. It had to be an actor to get away with it – and we heard from Julia that the mimic had been really excellent. That's why Lucius had engaged him to go to Rome, of course – that and the fact that he was much the same size as Pulchrus was. Lucius and Hirsius would have met Pulchrus in Corinium, when he went to meet them and escort them here, so they knew what he looked like and how big he was.'

'But they could not have guaranteed that they would find a man like that. And anyway, this murder happened on the morning before the civic feast. How could the acts have been at the villa then?'

I nodded. 'I know. That confused me, at first, but of course the acts that Lucius ostensibly chose to take to court weren't at that feast at all. They can't have been – they were already on their way to Rome. They must have given their performances in front of him and Marcus at a different dinner on some other day. I believe that Hirsius had seen the acts before, and arranged for the most suitable to meet him here, so he could "select" them to perform at Marcus's feasts and thence go on to Rome. I have learned that not a single local act – however excellent – was chosen to be sent to entertain the court, and there is a rumour in the town that it was all prearranged. Hirsius took bribes from all the other acts in town. It made it look convincing – and he profited, of course.'

Gwellia was looking more stricken all the time. 'But why kill Pulchrus in the first place?' she said helplessly. 'Why try to take his place? It could only be to stop him doing what he was ordered to, but the message that Marcus sent to Londinium with him was delivered perfectly! Junio was telling me about it earlier.'

'It was delivered, certainly,' I said. 'To the commander of

the British fleet – who happens to be a relation of Lucius, in fact. We hear that Marcus is to be entertained there for a day or two, since the governor's palace is not fit for guests. I wonder if the new governor is aware of that? And what will Marcus and Julia have to say when they discover that the arrangements for their trip are those that Lucius wanted them to make?'

'I don't know what His Excellence will say to that!' I realised that the commander of the garrison had come in with Minimus, and was standing listening to all this at the door. 'But I'm prepared to guess what he will say to you, if you dare to keep him waiting for a moment more.'

Chapter Twenty-nine

I have never moved so quickly as in getting to that feast. I travelled with the garrison commander in his gig, and – since we had blocked the farmer from passing in his cart, even after Maximus had helped him put the horse between the shafts – Junio and Gwellia followed us in that, with Niveus, while Minimus galloped on ahead to say that we were on our way. He had been sent to find me, it transpired, and from his agitated state I could imagine how irritated my host was going to be.

The new gatekeeper looked scandalised when I arrived so late. 'They have already started, citizen – at least an hour ago. It's a solemn memorial, as I told your slave. I'm not sure I should permit you to interrupt them now.' He held up his torch to have a better look, and took in the presence of the military commander by my side. 'But if it's army business, I suppose you may go in.'

Minimus was waiting just inside the gate. 'You'd better hurry, master,' the redhead said as he hustled us towards the area where the feast was being held – a large space created by pushing back the screens between the *triclinium* and the adjacent rooms. It made a splendid banquet hall for formal feasts like this and tonight, with the funeral wreaths and flowers everywhere, it was an impressive sight.

The feast, when we entered, was clearly in full swing. The room was full of sober citizens, impressive in their togas or their *syntheses*. There were no women present – either they had left, or Julia was entertaining them in some other room – but the most important men in Glevum were all assembled here. Each wore a garland of dark petals and leaves round his head – a version of the dining wreath appropriate to tonight – and the tables were strewn with empty platters and hundreds of fresh flowers, which had been arranged in ribbons to decorate the board. The villa servants must have been working on the preparations for hours.

Lucius was holding forth as we came through the door – on his favourite subject of the Emperor – and the attention of the room was fixed on him. 'He claims to have killed a thousand net-fighters in combat,' he declaimed. 'Ignore the traitorous rumours that he uses poison on his sword, and that some opponents are given imitation tridents which aren't sharp enough to stab.' He swallowed another gulp of Marcus's wine. 'No doubt such infamous gossip has reached you, even here?'

Marcus looked uncomfortable. It was hard to know if Lucius's question was the result of drink, or an attempt to trap someone into indiscreet remarks for the benefit of a pair of listening ears – in which case the penalty might very well be death.

'Caesar's prowess in the ring is well known everywhere,' my patron said, evading the moment skilfully. 'I hear that he once transfixed an elephant?' He signalled for the *crater*-bearer to fill the cups again, and as he looked up he saw me standing there. His face grew furious, but he raised his cup to me. 'Libertus! So you have deigned to honour us? I was concerned lest some accident had befallen you. I could not believe that you would choose to come so late, when it is a question of honouring the dead.'

There was a deathly hush and all eyes were turned on me. I bowed my head. 'Your pardon, Excellence. I meant no disrespect. Your orders for the provision of a carriage went astray. I have brought the commander of the garrison – he will vouch for me.'

Lucius looked scornful. 'So not only is this man insolently late, he brings an uninvited guest with him! Such behaviour would never be tolerated in Rome.'

His intervention was quite fortunate. Marcus looked furious at this public slight, and forced a smile at me. 'I'm sure the citizen has reason, as he says. Libertus, I think that you'll find there is space for you somewhere on the couches in the corner of the room. There are only seven diners on the table over there. We were rather expecting your son to come as well. The servants will find some bread and meat for you – we were about to be entertained by Atalanta on the lyre, before we moved on to the sweeter course.' He waved a hand towards the vacant places as he spoke. 'Lucius was telling us about events in Rome.'

Once Marcus had accepted me the awkwardness passed. People were beginning to chatter among themselves again, and slaves were already appearing with a dining wreath, and a bowl of water to wash my hands and feet. The only sane thing was to take my place. But I looked at Lucius and said, in the clearest tones I possessed, 'I would be more interested to hear him talk about what happened here.'

There was a gasp around the tables at this impertinence.

'Libertus!' Marcus was white with anger. 'You forget yourself!'

'But I remember Aulus. He was your gatekeeper. Poisoned in this very household while you were out today.' I had fixed my eyes on Lucius and I stood my ground.

There was an awful silence. The diners held their breath. Even the *crater*-carrier was standing statue-still. Marcus was looking shaken.

'Libertus,' he said, with careful gentleness, 'I know you are concerned. But all the wine this evening has been tasted by a slave. If the poisoner is waiting he cannot strike tonight. There is nothing in the house that I did not provide.'

'Ask Lucius, patron. That isn't quite the case.'

Lucius was frowning. He got slowly to his feet. 'Cousin! I protest! This is preposterous! You know that I brought no provisions to the house – and certainly I haven't ordered any since I have been here. You would have heard of it – the servants would have known.'

'Just as they knew that you had been out to the gate and given fresh instructions to Pulchrus and your slave, the day that your luggage and the snake act went away? Because you must have done. Pulchrus would never have abandoned escorting the cart, and gone the steeper way to town, unless he had explicit orders to do so, and then he would have wanted to alert his master to the change of plan. And I think that is exactly what he did. I thought that you'd killed Aulus because he'd spoken to the girl, but I realise there were other reasons why he had to die. He saw you give fresh orders – he mentioned it to me. Said you were fussing around the luggage cart, changing your orders until the moment they left. You must have had a dreadful fright when you found out

Aulus was a spy – and that I'd been asking questions about what he might have seen.'

I could feel the eyes of the whole room fixed on us, but Lucius managed to look simply pained. 'Kill Aulus? This is monstrous, cousin. Have the man locked up. Something has obviously afflicted his brain. How could I kill Aulus? Especially poison him? All the provisions in the house are yours. You know I have brought nothing of that kind of my own.'

'Not even the little flasks in your *lararium*?' I said – and knew from the way he paled that I was right. 'I should have thought of it when I first saw you pouring liquid on the altar fire. You said yourself the offering would have no force unless you provided the wherewithal for it. And yet you were using a jug of Marcus's when I arrived at first – though you contrived to break it, so no one could discover what it had contained, and what you were trying to dispose of on the flames.'

He had recovered now. 'Cousin, you provided me with a jug of Rhenish when I went to bed. So it was my wine I offered, for all practical purposes.' He looked around the assembled diners for support, like an advocate in court. He knew he'd scored a point.

'But this was not that jug,' I muttered doggedly. 'You expressly told Colaphus not to bring you that – so I imagine we will still find it in your sleeping room if we look. This was a big, coarse drinking jug of the kind the servants use, just like the one they sent me with the funeral wine today. I say that the one you broke was used for Aulus's lunch. No doubt the kitchens can confirm it – the pieces will be lying in the rubbish pile somewhere. Nor do I believe that there was only wine in it.'

'This is quite scandalous. You have no proof of that.' But he was breathing hard and that telltale pink was round his nose again – a sign that he felt guilty, as I now realised, or was about to be discovered in a lie.

I pressed my advantage. 'And you knew that he was dead. I was half aware that something was peculiar at the time. There was a little niggle worrying at my brain, and now I realise what it was. The whole time he was missing you spoke of him in the past, as though you were certain that he wasn't coming back. And when I told you that I'd found him, you guessed that he was dead before I'd had the chance to tell you that he was.'

Lucius was clearly shaken but he kept his calm. 'Cousin, are you going to listen to this burbling all night? The man is a menace – I have told you that before.'

I saw Marcus hesitate and glance towards the burly slaves beside the wall. I burst out to Lucius – before he quite convinced his cousin to have me hustled off – 'So you deny that you killed Aulus? And that you had Marcus's messenger waylaid and killed, so that the clever mimic you hired could take his place for you?'

Lucius sat down again, the picture of contempt. 'And why should I do that?'

'So that you could arrange for your cousin to stay with your relative, instead of visiting the governor's palace as he planned? I'm still not certain why you wanted that. I think it must be so that you could poison him as well – and possibly his little family too.'

The Roman had turned as white as linen by this time, but he still contrived to sneer. 'And no one would have noticed? Come, be rational!'

'I think you'd planned to blame it on the snakes – no one could ask questions if vipers had got loose, especially in the narrow confines of a ship. Why else were you so anxious to employ the snake-charmer? Everyone said the act was very poor. But of course that didn't matter – that was not the point. You had already made arrangements with him for an "accident" – no doubt offered to pay him very well. But then you discovered that our vipers here don't have the venom to finish off a man – thanks to the intervention of my wife. Is that why you wrote a letter to that house tonight?'

I paused. It was the officer who made the point for me. 'Be careful how you answer – we have stopped the messenger. The letter will be returned tomorrow to your cousin here – quite properly, since it was travelling under his private seal.'

Marcus was looking at his cousin in dismay. 'But why? For money? It would come to you, I suppose, once my poor father died, if my heir and I were conveniently disposed of in this way. My mother would inherit, and you'd be her guardian, since you would be the nearest agnate male. But I can't believe it of you.'

There was a shrug of the patrician shoulders as Lucius replied. He had the Roman gift of stoicism, which they so admire. 'Then don't believe it, cousin. Of course it isn't true. Did you ever hear such a confection of lies in all your life? Do you seriously believe that I would go out to the gate and get Pulchrus to write that little note to you just so that I could have it sent back to you later on, to convince you that Puchrus had arrived in Londinium safe and sound?'

Marcus looked sorrowfully at me and shook his head. 'I agree! It is preposterous. For once, Libertus . . .'

But I interrupted. 'What little note was that?'

Marcus frowned, impatient. 'A note to say Pulchrus had ridden on ahead, to arrange accommodation for the party in advance. It was in his handwriting – I knew the script at once. Of course, now you draw my attention to the fact, the words are rather ambiguous, I agree, and could just as easily have been written here. But, Libertus, why on earth should you imagine that? Why would Pulchrus write a letter while still outside the house?'

'Because he'd had new orders – and he would not deviate from your instructions without informing you. I think that Lucius persuaded him to write the note to you by telling him that you were busy at the time. I think it's possible that he dictated it – then sent it on to Londonium to be sent back to you.'

Marcus shook his head. 'The messenger was quite certain who had given it to him.'

'A man in Pulchrus's uniform who behaved like Pulchrus. That mimic was obviously very good indeed,' I said. 'But, patron, think of this. How did Lucius come to know about that note at all – or that it was Pulchrus who had written it? As I understand it, it was delivered to you in the town, and the commander here was with you when you broke the seal. Just as you broke the seal of your mother's letter from Rome, which brought the news about your father's death. Yet Lucius knew about the contents of that, too, by the time you got home.'

'The messenger told me verbally, of course.' Lucius was still defiant even now.

'But Niveus and I saw you opening a seal.' That was Atalanta, waiting with her lyre. Like many wealthy Romans,

I think that Lucius had half forgotten she were there, or that slave girls were endowed with working eyes and ears. 'Craving your indulgence, master, but I thought you ought to know.' She turned back to Lucius. 'And I saw you talking to Aulus afterwards – in the slaves' waiting room where he was eating lunch. You told him he could finish the wine that you'd begun, because you didn't care for Rhenish. I saw you pour it out.'

'Along with a little something from your *lararium* flask, perhaps,' I said. 'Or do you still deny it, citizen?'

Lucius was defeated but he faced me with a smile. 'Of course I still deny it. I will prove it, too. Slave!' He motioned to his bodyguard who was standing close to him, staring as though he'd been turned to stone. 'Go to my sleeping room and fetch the travelling box. I will show you that there is no poison in any of my flasks.'

'Go with him, Atalanta,' Marcus said. 'Make sure he brings it. And the rest of you – please go back to your seats.' Most of the dining guests had risen to their feet and were clustered in a startled group against the farther wall, shocked as statues and very near as pale.

There was a lot of hurried whispering, but one or two obeyed, and others were beginning to follow suit when Atalanta and the bodyguard reappeared. Colaphus held the *lararium*, which he carried to the front and laid before Lucius on the table-top.

'You still doubt me, cousin?' Lucius exclaimed. 'I'll soon prove who is the liar here.' He took the box, produced a key and slowly opened it. I felt the crowd lean forward in their seats, and heard the gasps of admiration at the craftsmanship. Lucius took out the silver flasks – the whole array of them – and poured the contents with a flourish into his drinking cup. Then, rising to his feet, he raised the cup to me, rather as Marcus had done when I came into the room.

There was a titter of amusement around the room at this.

I felt extremely foolish. Was I mistaken after all?

'Your good health, citizen. I drink to you, and to your imaginative tales!' He met my eyes, and in that moment I knew what he had done. I might have stopped him, but I let him drink.

It was several seconds before it took effect.

The death of a dignitary at a memorial feast is not usually the signal for a lightening of mood, but strangely tonight that seemed to be the case. I found I was surrounded by cheering citizens, clapping me on my shoulders and congratulating me. I felt like a victorious net-man being applauded at the games – as if I had entrapped my victim in my web and brought him to his knees, and he'd escaped dishonour by falling on his sword. Perhaps, indeed, that was exactly what I'd done.

Someone was pressing a cup of wine on me – it wasn't Lucius's, I made sure of that – and others were leading me towards a dining couch. I sank down on it and permitted slaves to take my sandals off and bestow the luxury of washing both my feet. Then it was my patron who was bending over me, personally placing the dining wreath upon my balding head.

'Libertus! I applaud you. You must sit at my right hand.' He gestured towards the table where Lucius had sat, and from where his lifeless body was now being hauled away in an ignominious fashion by a pair of slaves. They were treating him as parricides and traitors are traditionally treated –

dragged backwards by his heels so that his head bounced on the mosaics as he went, while his proud toga rucked up round his armpits and exposed his spindly legs and leather loinstrap to public ridicule.

I was reluctant, but he led me to the place, then rose and addressed the assembled company. I noticed that the commander was now reclining at the back and that Junio had come in and joined him there.

'Citizens, councillors, friends.' Marcus was shaken but he was a Roman through and through, and knew how to disguise his shock with dignity. 'You were invited here tonight in honour of my respected father – but one of our number has disgraced his memory by scheming against his family and heirs. He has taken his reward!' There were sporadic cheers and claps at this, but Marcus raised his hand. 'So, now, I bid you truly to keep this memorial in the way that I know my father would have wished. Please, fill your glasses and drink to our safe deliverance, and we will offer a thanksgiving sacrifice later to the household gods. My slaves will serve you the "second tables" now, and I will call on Atalanta to play for us again. Something a little more lively, in honour of our joy.'

It was not what she was trained in, but she did her best, and with the arrival of another *crater* of finest mulsum wine and – a little later – of my wife and Julia, there was a general mood, if not of cheerfulness, at least of shared relief. Julia was even prevailed upon to sing – she did not have a strong voice, but it was very sweet – and the evening was as successful as it could possibly have been, given the extraordinary happenings of the night.

Marcus said so, when the last carriages were gone, and my

little party was preparing to leave too. I had lingered to tell my patron everything I knew about Morella and the tunic.

'I wonder what happened to Morella's hair?' Junio said, as Minimus helped him with his cloak. 'Pulchrus's was short enough to scatter in the woods, but they could hardly have taken those plaits to Londinium with them.'

I shrugged. 'Perhaps we'll never know. Sold in Corinium, perhaps – there was enough to make a wig, and the actor would be familiar with several wigmakers. Or perhaps it was simply buried somewhere by the road. Or dropped in the Sabrina – Hirsius must have taken a river ferry when he took Morella west – they would have been spotted by the Glevum watchmen otherwise. No doubt we will be able to determine that.'

'And the coins? I still have them in my casket. What should we do with them? Return them to her father?' Julia enquired.

I smiled. 'To her mother. I will take them there myself.' I would leave it to the tribe to deal with Farathetos, I thought. 'And I'll return the dress. I'm glad we didn't burn it at poor Pulchrus's funeral.'

'Ironic that we should put him in his own tunic on the bier! I shall have you build a little shrine for him, and see that his grave is tended every year with food and water for the afterlife. In his way, he died in my defence.' Marcus placed a heavy ringed hand upon my arm. 'And I shall have you build that memorial pavement to my father too – with no expense spared. We can never thank you properly, Libertus, my old friend. I never liked Lucius, but I did not think that of him.'

I asked the question which had been on my mind. 'And now what will become of him? Will you have him buried with

Morella in the common pit? At midnight tomorrow it will be Lemuria.'

His face darkened, but it was Julia who spoke. 'I think we should put him on the servants' pyre and burn him after Aulus has been laid to rest,' she said. 'He does not deserve such dignity, but he was a family member, after all.'

Marcus looked rebellious. 'It is more than he merited. But the pyre is ready, and it would not take long. And he is my mother's agnate – so I consent. Perhaps I shall provide some burial herbs for him – and even a coin for the ferryman.'

Epilogue

Late the next evening we were all awake. There was still the problem of the roundhouse site to be resolved. Gwellia and I had talked into the night, and decided that – for Juno and Cilla's sake – we should honour the rituals of the Lemuria ourselves.

It was difficult to estimate when midnight had arrived, but in the event we need not have been concerned, because when it was approaching the appropriate hour Caper and Stygius came knocking at the gate. They had been selected because they found the corpse. Minimus and Maximus went out to let them in, and we could hear them chattering as they came up the path.

'The family are ready. They've counted the black beans . . .'

'And I've fetched clean water specially from the spring . . .'

'And now they are waiting in the roundhouse with the ashes and the bronze . . .'

'All dressed in their best Roman outfits,' Maximus finished, 'as you can see yourselves.' He ushered the two land slaves into the roundhouse as he spoke.

We looked like a typical Roman household, in all sorts of ways. Two men in togas and two women citizens, with Kurso and the red-haired boys attending us as slaves – so it must have been surprising to find a Celtic central fire, and all the trappings of normal roundhouse life. Caper was delighted. 'It's just like home,' he said.

Stygius stumped over, and said in his slow way, 'I was to tell you, citizen, you were right about that note – the one that Lucius had sent to the fleet commander's house. It was brought to the master just an hour or so ago. It said snakes in Britannia were not venomous enough, and they'd have to get a foreign one or wait till overseas. It's enough to have the fleet commander brought in for questioning, and Hirsius and the entertainers – the mimic and the snake-charmer – will be arrested too. Marcus says that he'll preside over their trial himself – he has decided to delay his travel for a little while, and he'll have them all brought back to Glevum to appear before the court.'

I thought about Hirsius – his olive tunic, his large hands and his sandy hair. His lofty manner would be chastened now, the basalt eyes turned dull with fear and pain. As a mere slave his fate would be neither quick nor merciful – though doubtless the fleet commander and his wife would find an advocate, appeal to the Emperor, with sufficient bribes, and suffer nothing more than exile or a fine. It was hard to pity Hirsius, but I almost did.

'So, if you are ready?' Stygius prompted me.

I picked up a taper. 'It's time to go,' I said, and one by one we filed out into the dark. It was cold and frosty, and the night was still, and it was eerie walking through the trees without a light. We came to the cleared site where the new roundhouse was to be, and formed into a circle round the fatal ditch.

Kurso brought the ash bowl and I placed my thumb in it and made a sign on my forehead, as I'd been told to do. Junio did the same, followed by all the women and the slaves – if there was any doubt about the efficacy of this ritual, I thought, I wanted it performed by all of us.

Maximus brought water, and I washed my hands – and this time it was only for the men. I felt a little foolish as I turned round three times, taking care I didn't stumble: it was uneven underfoot, and to miss my footing would have been the worst of omens now. Minimus brought the beans – in the blackness they looked blacker still – and I took a handful and, with averted face, threw them behind me, saying nine times over the all-important words: 'These beans I cast away, with these I redeem myself and mine.'

The words and actions were duly repeated by my son, and without a backward glance we began to walk away. Caper had been carrying a covered bowl of coals till now, and as I touched water, and clashed the bronzes I had brought, he whipped the lid off and there was suddenly a glow of cheerful light.

We fairly strode now, back the way we had come, Junio clashing the bronzes all the while and all of us demanding that the ghosts should take the beans, accept our offering and leave the place in peace. As I reached our own enclosure I heard a distant clang, and knew at the villa the same ceremony was taking place.

It must have been effective. Junio's roundhouse has been built in almost record time and he and Cilla are moving into it. Marcus and Julia are so pleased with me they have gifted us the boys and given me the commission for the memorial pavement, too, for which they are promising to pay me handsomely. Little Niveus has been sold on again – slightly more confident than he was before – to a kindly master who is good to him. Even Morella's mother has found a kind of peace: her husband was so frightened of reprisals that he has run away, and she and her daughters are farming in his place.

The trials were duly held. Hirsius was sentenced to death – as he well deserved – but found a way of talking poison in his cell. Perhaps the fleet commander had provided it, although – as I had predicted – he and his wife appealed to the Emperor and (no doubt at the cost of some exotic gift) managed to escape the justice of the courts. The snake-charmer and the mimic were not so fortunate.

Marcus's mother, when she had recovered from the shock, declared that the whole thing was exactly what she had always feared, and might have been predicted if he'd listened to her dreams. She foresaw more evil auguries – and wrote to say so almost every day, right up to the time that Marcus and his family left for Rome. However, the honours that were piled upon him there must have made her wonder if the auguries were right.

My little household is as happy as it has ever been – without the slightest visitation of phantoms or bad luck. We must have pacified the Lemures that night.